MOUNTAINS
OF THE
BLUE
STONE

MOUNTAINS OF THE BLUE STONE

Dorothy Cave

Many trails wind up the mountain,
but they all lead to the top.

SUNSTONE
PRESS

SANTA FE
New Mexico

Sunstone books may be purchased for educational, business, or sales promotional use. For information please write: Special Markets Department, Sunstone Press, P.O. Box 2321, Santa Fe, New Mexico 87504-2321.

FIRST EDITION

Library of Congress Cataloging in Publication Data:
Cave, Dorothy.
    Mountains of the Blue Stone / by Dorothy Cave.—1st ed.
        p.cm
        ISBN: 0-86534-272-5 (hardcover) ISBN: 978-1-63293-144-3 (softcover)
        I. Title.
PS3553.A9656M68   1998   98-7915
813' .54—dc21   CIP

Published by   SUNSTONE PRESS
                    Post Office Box 2321
                    Santa Fe, NM 87504-2321 / USA
                    (505) 988-4418 / orders only (800) 243-5644
                    FAX (505) 988-1025

For Jack
with whom I have climbed many backroads
to the little places, hidden, like Descanso,
among the forgotten pockets
of God's overalls.

Preface

Descanso, New Mexico, does not actually exist. But it could be any of a number of small Hispanic villages, ancient remnants of an earlier time that are tucked among the hidden valleys of the great southwestern mountains.

Yet it is none of these. Or, perhaps, it is all of them, its people the Everymen of these sturdy hamlets who cling so stubbornly to the old ways and the old beliefs, resisting the mechanized madness that would seek to devour them.

Should you drive north from Santa Fé you may feel, as I have, the strange pull of the mountain, turn onto a certain byway, and begin the winding ascent into the lofts of history, myth, and legend. Somewhere in these mountains, it is said, the early ones emerged from earth's center into the light of the sun. Who can say it didn't happen that way? Or maybe in ages unremembered they crossed from Siberia and pushed down from the north in waves. In any case, the wanderers settled, in time, to build America's first permanent homes along the few and far-spaced waterways of the southwestern vastness.

This is the New World's wombland.

Here, too, long before the first British foot touched our continental soil, rode the *conquistadores*, those incredible Spaniards of the cross who were first to pierce the interior and they, too, began to settle along the life-suckling Río Grande.

Pulled by the mountain, they spread up the few small streams that feed the river, searched out the valleys, and in the peak-girt eyries they planted the villages where their descendants still live peacefully isolated while time hangs back to smell the piñons. Here man and mountain met and merged.

They seem unreal, these tiny clusters of humankind in mud-brick houses, the hills around them dotted with low, windowless *moradas* where the *penitente* brothers enact their strange and secret rites. So far in mode and mold they are from the world that I inhabit. In these hamlets I return to a past four centuries old.

Somewhere along the graveled way I come upon one of these ancient villages cupped in a hilly lap and the world of time and substance falls away. I never know just when it happens—when the ruts of history merge with the airy paths of legend. One can stand on that divide as on that of the continent itself, unaware that the waters of land or life now flow another way and seek another sea.

Life itself is such a journey toward the transcendental.

Once in one of those villages I rented briefly a small house where I could work in splendid, phoneless isolation. In it lived a witch—a *bruja*—or rather the ghost of one. Her name was Ermalinda.

I didn't believe in ghosts or *brujas*. I could still shrug off a witch's distant fireball as a vagary of weather or the wails of La Llorona as a fitful night wind—not that anyone in the village cared. Nor did Ermalinda. With or without my acceptance she was, quite simply, there. I have not encountered these mysteries in my world; I have in theirs. The waters on our two sides of the divide flow their separate ways to find their separate destinies and one is as valid as the other.

The mountain, material or mystic, calls to some *anima* inside us all; and you, if you hear and answer, may ascend to such a place as Descanso. A resting place. A village painted in the deep wine tones of history, dark with age like the paintings of old masters. But you will not find Descanso.

Or perhaps you will. Perhaps across the unseen divide you may sense that Descanso and those who live there are very real—as tangible as the life of the spirit. Along such air-drawn paths may lie the greater truths of life.

. . . Corruption
never has been compulsory, when the cities lie at the
monster's feet there are left the mountains.
—Robinson Jeffers

1

*N*ovember wind snarled down his neck and snapped at his pants legs and Drake Cavanaugh remembered how the air blew cleaner up on the mountain without the trash of civilization to hurl about; and he thought, too, that coming back to life was going to be more complicated than leaving it had been.

Traffic rushed past and several taxis with it until one pulled to the curb and then Drake was inside. The driver cracked his door, reached around to loosen a paper hamburger wrapper from the windshield, and applied a toothpick to a molar. "Where to?"

"Rancho Ribera."

"Gonna cost you." He eyed the sheepskin jacket and the dirty canvas bag and the weedy beard and Drake didn't blame him because he knew he looked like a wind-dumped wetback.

"I've got it." A grin pulled up one side of his mouth. He flashed a Ben Franklin and the driver shifted and lurched into the current. The meter ticked, a clock in front of a loan company showed a quarter to twelve, and Drake was back where time counted—or was counted—coolly riding back from infinity in a Yellow Cab to tell a story nobody wanted to hear. Or believe.

Albuquerque jerked past, a glutted gray reptile that gorged on the valley and it hadn't changed, except for a few more porno shops and seedy lounges. Mainly Drake looked at the cabby's head which wore a new haircut and the skull looked raw. The cab smelled of stale cigars and the ashtray held a wet stub. Drake lit a cigarette and held out the pack.

The driver shook his head. "Trying to die early?"

"Die?" Drake leaned back and took a deep puff. "I already did. Nine years ago this month. . . ."

Nine years had passed since Charles Drake Cavanaugh cashed a check for half a million dollars and quietly departed this life, leaving Leona twice that in the bank, quadruple in securities, and power of attorney; nine years since he dumped the trash of suburban existence, opted for paradise, took off on the annual elk hunt, and simply neglected to return.

The cabby shrugged. They crossed the river and cruised toward Rancho Ribera. Drake wondered if Leona still lived in the Spanish colonial they'd built with a fireplace in every room that she wouldn't light fires in because of the mess, and the five-acre lawn she wouldn't allow a dog to run in—or a child.

Noon split the day into pale halves which would never again be joined, but it didn't matter. The trading post out of Descanso had sold round stones to tourists—their choice for fifty cents—to be split in hopes they'd bought a geode. Most were like the day—gray, uncrystallized. It didn't matter. They hadn't paid much.

The meter ticked. The clock outside an electric company pointed both hands up toward infinity. A bell shrilled and the high school disgorged adolescents. Tires squealed and horns shredded the air. Drake fingered the little stone fetishes he'd brought back from the timeless time.

The driver didn't have change so he waited outside the bank while Drake exchanged the Franklin for smaller bills. The teller looked at him with suspicion.

So did the clientele in the cafe where once he'd been a steady, before he died. It thrummed with talk and dishes and people swallowing lunch at polished wooden tables. He looked around. Everyone reminded him of somebody else and no one looked like anyone.

Then he saw Joe Emmons in his banker's gray, not looking any older, really, just a little blurred with no edges, like warm Jell-O. He was alone.

"Hello, Joe." Drake threw his canvas bag in a seat and sat down and half his mouth smiled because Joe didn't recognize him behind the beard and the wind-carving on his brown face and the nine years. "Mind if I join you?"

"Looks like you already have." Joe was unfolding a newspaper behind his coffee cup. A waitress poured some for Drake and Joe ordered the special.

"Make it two," Drake said. Then he headed Joe off before he could duck behind the paper. "Remember a guy named Drake Cavanaugh?"

Joe lowered the paper but kept up his guard. The saggy lines around his eyes tensed. "Cavanaugh? Yeah. Lawyer. Yeah, I knew him. Who are you?"

"They call me Carlos, *señor*."

Joe looked at him hard. "You're no Mexican."

"Okay. But I know Drake Cavanaugh."

"Begging your pardon—*señor*—but you can't. Drake Cavanaugh's been dead for ten years."

"Nine. Are you sure?"

"Hell yes I'm sure. I was there. He went after a mountain lion. . . ."

"Early. You and Manby Fremont were still in the sack. You'd all gotten plastered the night before." Joe's eyes remembered. The waitress brought their corned beef. "He talked about that night later," Drake added.

Joe banged his cup down. "How could he?"

"He remembered it. He wasn't that loaded."

"You gotta be crazy . . ."

"That's purely possible."

". . . because Drake died—Drake Cavanaugh was killed—the next morning."

"Was he?"

"I found the spot. Up there in the rimrock and his thirty-ought-six lay there and you could see the signs of struggle—bits of clothes and blood and where he went over the ledge." Joe was playing with a spoon, remembering. "It snowed the night before and Drake went out early. Hell-bent to get a lion. I don't know why."

"It was a sort of symbol."

"Symbol?"

"Of what man was once. The pioneer. Before he got himself emasculated. Before civilization started chasing its tail. Before God cancelled woman and created Leona."

"That's how Drake talked," Joe said. "Anyhow, he plunged over. River gorge below. They searched. Sent out parties. For days." He seemed to hunt for something misplaced in his mind. "Whenever you knew him—it was some other time he talked about. We always got plastered at the lodge."

Drake grinned. Oh yes, once a year old Joe traded his bank-president gray for hunter's dun and got soused and felt macho. The rest of the year he was a citizen of substance who never entertained a new thought or an old love and led the United Way drive.

"You talked about women that night . . ."

"We always did."

". . . and the mountain lion Drake was going to get . . ."

"He'd been after that lion for years."

". . . and he'd had a row with Leona."

"That was SOP too."

"He was fed up. Threatened to disappear. Walk out."

"Yeah, Drake always did have a loony streak. And he'd just turned forty. We didn't pay much attention. But we remembered it later."

Drake leaned forward. "Remember the note he left? 'Three blind mice. . . .'"

"Yeah—that was it. Three . . . ? My god, man. Are you saying . . . ?"

"I'm saying Drake Cavanaugh didn't die!"

2

Drake pulled onto the ledge, sat with his rifle across his legs, and looked from the rimrock out onto the snow-stippled gray space that opened to the gorge five hundred feet below. On the far rise across the river dark posses of piñons patrolled. A few sullen snowflakes wandered in the icy air like lost soldiers without a regiment. From the valley cold fog rose.

He pulled a Lucky from the pocket of the Air Force parka he'd filched when he mustered out after the Korean insanity, lit it, and let it warm his fingers.

They'd all three been pretty potted the night before. Alcohol released Drake's disgust. "What a macho crew we are," he'd said. "Great white hunters roughing it in a quarter-million-dollar hunting shack, hoping an elk will stumble up and surrender. Three-day beards and three-day smells. Oh, are we macho!" Manby, who was a partner in the firm, had built the lodge a few years back to get away from his wife who was a do-gooder.

"Know what's wrong with us?" he asked.

"Yeah, we're drunk."

"We're eunuchs. Running from our wives. We drink and cuss and stink and play poker. And maybe we stumble on some senile animal and drag its carcass back home to show what big guys we are. Christ!"

Manby splashed more bourbon in their glasses and asked what was bugging him and did he want dancing girls too.

"Hell, it's been three months since I've slept with my wife." Drake grinned. "There's something homosexual about coitus with Leona."

"So screw somebody else's wife," said Manby. "We all get bored. Man is not monogamous. . . ."

"Crap! We're the three blind mice. Three emasculated goddamned rats. See how we run! We've cut off our own balls."

He made the speech about going out next morning to find his mountain lion. "I've heard he restores potency." He made the speech every year; but this time he went.

He drew a crude sketch of three rats gnawing at their balls, propped it against an empty Jim Beam bottle, smiled on one side, and thought he would've made a hell of a cartoonist if he'd ever learned to draw. He picked up his thirty-ought-six and walked out.

Well, he'd never find a lion this way. He ground out the cigarette, clicked off the safety, and pulled on his glove. His head was starting to clear in the early cold and he felt superior to Manby and Joe back there in the sack, superior to the whole damned race of rats turning on themselves in the garbage heap—women who wanted to be men and males who wanted to be men but could only play at it.

He remembered the pustules of the latest anti-Nam protest that erupted on the university campus. He'd tried to volunteer himself out of disgust for the wimps—though he didn't tell Leona who'd have called it quixotic. But they didn't want a forty-year-old pilot.

He remembered Korea when the twitch-assed politicians wouldn't let Mac win the war. Drake had been down on the flight line when the word came they couldn't chase the Chinks across the Yalu. Now, he thought, they're doing the same stinking damn thing to the kids in Nam.

He was sick of law, too. He'd won his latest case, which he shouldn't have because his client was a goddamned swindler, but a high-class swindler with country club clout. He'd known the man for years and their wives were best friends, so he took the case, disgusted with himself, and won on a technicality.

He crawled farther along the rimrock, let himself down to another shelf, and looked down to the black river where white fog was rising. Damned if this country didn't get in your blood. He'd felt it from the first time he'd seen it, when he was first sent to Kirtland air base. This country was still uncreated.

His fingers itched. God, how he'd like to draw it all. Put the great sweep of it on paper. He grinned his lopsided way and remembered a long-distance manifesto, collect, back when he was in Yale, about how he was going to quit law school and go to the art institute. His father was not amused. In the end, he stayed in Yale and drew caricatures of his professors. Then Korea.

"Back in these hills," he had told Manby and Joe, "lie dozens of Mexican villages. Unmapped and unsuspected. Little organisms left over from the seventeenth century. With two sexes, clear and separate. Real women who aren't liberated and don't want to be . . ."

"He wants to screw a Mexican, Joe!"

". . . where you could walk a few miles and disappear forever."

"You're drunk, Cavanaugh."

"But I was perfectly sober when I put my affairs in order last week." He felt the money belt padding his middle with the half a million. "I have concluded . . ." He gazed into the fire.

"For god's sake, stop cracking your damned knuckles!"

"Sorry." He flexed his hands, picked up his glass, and thought that whenever he got to drinking he sounded like a professor. "I have concluded that civilization is doomed."

"Good," said Manby. "Maybe income tax'll go with it."

"Unless we go back to the beginning. Man has progressed toward the civilized state in three stages. Physical, metaphysical, and intellectual. In that order."

"I couldn't say, I wasn't there." Joe yawned.

"How do you know? Maybe there's some gene memory left."

"Hot damn, now we're going to swap cave-man stories!" Manby poked at the fire. "Back in my Neanderthal days. . . ."

Drake started cracking his knuckles again, caught Joe's scowl, and began to doodle on a paper napkin. "For the most part we've forgotten. We've pushed out the gene memories and forgotten how we got here." He threw down his pencil and sat forward. "How many of us could stay alive in these mountains without shelter or cars or a Circle-K? We've lost the art of survival."

"That's why we go hunting." Joe refilled his glass.

"Balls. And we've lost our religion."

"The churches are doing okay," Manby said.

"I'm not talking about the churches. I'm talking about something we once called God."

"Seems like I heard he died." Joe laughed loudly.

"No, he didn't, Joe," said Manby. "He just went hunting to get away from his wife!"

"And the intellectual process suffers permanent atrophy. . . ."

"Come off it, Cavanaugh. Yesterday the moon, tomorrow Mars."

"Sure. We've invaded space and lost contact with our own planet. Our high school graduates can't read, most of their teachers can't either, and our college grads can't add without computers. Nobody ever reads a poem any more. We've got to go back and start over again."

"You want to go live in a cave?"

"I'm serious."

"You always are when you've had a few."

"Physically and intellectually, I'm getting flabby, and impotent. I—and civilization."

"What the hell are you talking about?"

"Emasculation, gentlemen. Emasculation and death!"

He walked to the liquor cabinet and poured three fingers of Jim Beam. "Ever want to just walk out of the whole goddamned world?" He paced to the poker table, picked up the deck, and arced it in his hands Then with a snap he let fly all fifty-two and the joker. One hit the edge of the ashes that spilled onto the stone hearth.

"Now what the hell you do that for?" Joe leaned over the arm of his chair, picked up an ace, and studied it while his brain waddled toward something. "That's the baby I needed on that last hand!"

Drake slouched in his chair and watched the card smolder in the warm ashes. It was the queen of spades.

So much for last night's spiel. He crawled on. The ledge deepened, ran under an overhang, and darkened into a recess partly blocked by a clot of piñons growing from a cleft. He squeezed around it into a shallow cave. A strong sour odor of life or death floated ghostlike from its shadows. He froze listening and breathing the stale smell. He felt a great aloneness but his head was clearing, opening to whatever might share life in this vast hollowness.

He doubted if the cave extended beyond the shadowy corners but he started tentatively to investigate. He cradled the thirty-ought-six and took a step. Nothing stirred. He moved again into the dark recess. It seemed to continue. He hesitated.

Something moved. A deep snarl uncoiled from that secret dark. A shape solidified. Quills of fear erected all over Drake's body. He knew lions lurked in these rimrock caverns but a lion is as elusive as myth and he hadn't really believed it.

He raised his rifle and pressed the trigger. He heard the click.

My God, the chamber's empty! How in hell. . . ?

Eyes emerged from the dark as if from some subterranean passage. Sad chthonic amber eyes bored. For a second they soul-traded, man and beast, and each understood only that they could never understand. For a moment a common life flowed intensely between them. The life and the mystery, the ineffable taunting *otherness.*

Move fast! He pulled back the bolt. Four fast clicks.

The eyes focused and he was frozen.

Another snarl, then two hundred tawny pounds of controlled sinew sprang, hurled at him. Tearing claws, heavy claws raked to disarm not to kill, tore through his heavy clothes, through the soft shoulder flesh. His rifle fell. He leaped backward. The cat crouched on bent heavy legs, her serpentine body tensed. Force spilled through her writhing tail. Her eyes burned fire, and will met will as man and lion faced. Drake felt his warm blood flowing out in uneven throbs, felt it saturate his jacket.

Still she crouched with contained energy, taut, terrible energy, all heart and courage, and he thought, *there are no useless parts in a lion.* A muscle suddenly rippled in her great tawny breast and shoulder and she tensed to spring again. A gut reaction propelled Drake backward on the narrow shelf.

Suddenly, horribly, he teetered, his body in slow-motion counterpoint against his racing mind. One foot lashed desperately in enormous space and sought a solidity, and his arms stretched, jerked toward lifesaving spikes of piñon which only shredded his hands that left carmine streaks on the rocks.

Then he was falling through that great gray hollowness and against a looming kaleidoscope of dark piñon clots on dark cliffs he saw only the bruising image of those tawny sorrowful eyes.

Somewhere in that vast white fall, piñon claws snatched at him, lacerated the torn shoulder and breast, slowed his terrible descent, then gave him up to space again. Still he plunged, hurled from that altar of dark gods.

In some vacuum he emerged from a snow-clouded subconscious into the snow-clouded air and he was hazily aware of the stillness, of his blood oozing onto the snow-crusted rock where it glistened and ran diluted into wet earth. He supposed he was dying and for a vague timeless space he rued the uselessness of it, but faintly.

He'd said he wanted out . . . said he'd disappear . . . planned to . . . the money belt proved it . . . wouldn't need it now . . . could have fired ... but those eyes . . . it didn't matter now.

He felt his *anima* withdraw like something separate and he perceived his body lying cold and dark and alien, an unresisting pulp on the spiny earth.

▲

The river cuts like death through the double sides of life that rear on either side. Young and lusty, it carves dark abyss and darker mesa and like death it replenishes life. Long ago it nourished the ancients in the ruins that stand silent and eloquent in the canyons and *potreros* and it yet sustains life for their descendants who still plant corn in the old way, the sacred way.

To the west the Jemez peaks guard the ancient gods of earth and sky and the Spanish God of the Cross and the newest white god of the unleashed atom. In the east blood-red in the dying sun, the crags of the Sangre de Cristos rise. Peak upon peak they pile against the moving sky.

A highway follows the river and, branching from it, smaller roads snake upward toward the high, hidden places where man still climbs to worship. One of these crawls up from the canyon floor and north of Española takes off in an easterly direction, up past Chimayó of the sacred healing mud, up past the pueblo on the Quemado, up past Colinas, where it peters out except for a forest access road and a rutted trail to Pájaro, brooding gray and somber on the topmost ledge of a sheer plunging cliff and to Descanso below it, halfway up from the river floor on a broad sheltered ledge with a long white *prado* which serves as pastureland.

Somewhere along the ascent the world falls away, and only the cross-gashed peak towering above it is real, the peak that broods and commands, that protects and punishes. Slashed in its rock by ancient gods, the great cross gleams purple, the purple of penitence, and it gleams and glowers and shapes the little lives below, far more than they ever dream.

The villagers found him almost dead, and they bore him—though he didn't know it—from the canyon up to Descanso on its ledge beneath the cross-gashed mountain, to die, or perhaps to live—*¿Quién sabe?*

3

"*D*rake always had a loony streak," Joe said again.

Requiescat in veritas, Drake thought. We don't usually hear our own obituaries.

"But we saw the place," Joe said. "He had to have died."

"He hoped it would look that way. Later when he got resurrected he hoped that."

"Anyway, why in bloody hell would Charles Drake Cavanaugh want to disappear? He had it made. Good law practice—not that he needed it for the money, he'd always had that. Brains. Personality. Good-looking wife and no bitchier than most. Beautiful home."

"Maybe he was looking for manure," said Drake.

"What?"

"Fertilizer," said Drake. "Bedrock. Smoke?"

"No, I'm trying to stop," he said. "Can't afford to with what I'm paying my shrink. He's trying hypnosis."

"Why not just stop?"

"If it's that easy, why don't you?"

"I'm not the one who wants to quit."

"I might try acupuncture."

Several people spoke to Joe and looked sideways at Drake, but none came over.

"I still can't understand. . . ."

"He was just sick of it all. He walked out."

"You trying to tell me he deliberately walked over a precipice?"

"Oh, not deliberately," said Drake. "He walked out deliberately. He didn't plan the cliff. He was closer to the edge than he thought. And she'd just taken a hunk of his shoulder. Hell, it was her cave—he wasn't going to stand there on her porch like a goddamned Avon lady."

"Then the fall killed him," said Joe. "My God, man, it was nearly a thousand feet straight down! It's a matter of. . . ."

"Gravitational imperative?" Drake shrugged and smiled his half-smile and said, "Does it matter? He died and went to Descanso."

"Where the hell is Descanso?"

"Off the map."

"*What* the hell is Descanso?"

"I'll tell you," said Drake. "In the old days," he said, "when the funeral processions wound on foot, the coffin grew heavy with the soul that still clung to the body—this is how the old ones tell it—and often on the way to the cemetery—the *camposanto*—they stopped to rest and pray.

"The people of the villages marked each stopping place with a wooden cross, and they called it a *descanso*: a resting place. A place of transition. To think. To be quiet."

"Don't give me a goddamned history lesson."

"You asked. They say once a procession wound toward the *camposanto* with the body of a young woman whose baby had tried to be born for three days before she died. They stopped to rest and to pray.

"They were about to go on when they heard a feeble cry like a small lost ghost. Nowhere could they find its source. It sounded again. It was very faint and it seemed to come from within the wooden coffin.

"The young husband fought them off and flinging himself on his knees beside the casket, he seized his knife and pried up the lid. Then he cried out at what he saw and said he'd witnessed a miracle. His young wife was smiling in her death. And his son had been delivered!"

"Impossible," said Joe.

"Of course," said Drake. "But they tell it. The family built a chapel there. When the old village shifted to its present site, it came to be called Descanso."

"I don't know what you're talking about."

"That's purely possible," said Drake.

▲

Like a nomad between two lives he seemed to wander through some sand-blown desert, to follow those tawny cat eyes that rose from the deep well of some uncreated worldsoul. The pain pulled him back each time, though the amber eyes still followed.

Darker eyes pierced his awakening perception and someone spooned hot bean juice into his mouth. He moved and the pain blazed and then there was the reality of the woman's dark well-eyes and black hair and beyond her the wall, white except for islands where the plaster had peeled.

Still later he emerged into the larger frame of that gray village nested in piñons but for many days he saw only the eyes and felt the pain. Sometimes the woman eyes became the lion eyes and he would close his own, weak against their intensity.

A time came when he grew aware and a later time when the pain began to dull and light questions swirled like dust devils. He wondered where he was and he must have asked aloud.

"Descanso. Julián found you."

"Julián?"

"Julián Romero."

"How long . . . ?"

"Long enough." She had a wide mouth that smiled easily and a voice like fine sandpaper.

"Who are you?"

"Soledad."

She had learned healing arts from old Teresita and from her own womanness. Her young husband had died of a stab wound before she conceived a child so she tended other life instead—stray cats, hurt dogs, lost goats, men—and when Julián and the rest found the pulpy mass in which the life clung so weakly, they brought him to her.

Neither she nor the other villagers who drifted in and out asked who he was or seemed to care and he felt too distant from himself to bother telling them. They called him Carlos, or just *señor*.

The old life where he had danced the dance, trivial and successful and impotent, defocused into blurred distance and the winter sun lit the days through the dusty little window by his bed; and the stars burned at night and they were distant too, but clear. Soledad clattered about and talked to him in Spanish and soft English. Sometimes in her wine-dark voice she sang husky songs he had never heard.

For a time she dosed his mangled body with hot compresses saturated in herbal concoctions that smelled sharp and camphorous and she gave him strange-tasting liquids to drink.

One tasted of ashes. *Sí*, it was the ashes of corn tassel mixed with well water. "It cures the witch-made hurts."

"It wasn't a witch," he said. "It was a lion."

She shrugged. "Maybe a witch, too. *¿Quién sabe?*" She made him drink and then rubbed the medicine over his body and smiled a womansmile.

Soledad slept close by in her bed on the other side of the faded green curtain that divided the bare room and often she arose in the night to apply her strange remedies. Slowly he grew less feverish, though still detached as if held in some strange suspension.

From time to time Soledad's jut-beaked grandmother who was the ancient *curandera*—some said witch—poked his body with bony claws and probed his soul with strange blue eyes, cold eyes without expression, and the blue so rare in the earth face. He thought her vulture-like but he felt her power. Teresita muttered to herself and to Soledad but she never spoke to him.

Often Julián sang. Julián had a goat face, slash-eyed and beard-pointed, and his ears were sharp triangles and he wore his jeans tight. He would bang his guitar and cut his wicked goat eyes at Soledad and they sang together and laughed.

Sometimes Soledad danced, unstructured and fluid, until the music was spent and she dropped against him and they fell together on the floor and she laughed and he didn't. Once she bit him and he became angry. Drake lay in the next room with no door on the frame.

Sometimes he heard hard breathing and soft laughs and he knew Julián lay behind the curtain with Soledad and he thought, in a detached way, of Leona and his own impotence.

Other times Julián became inturning and his blood brooded. Then he didn't talk but only struck throbbing chords, deep and minor and alien, and Soledad smiled the secret womansmile and went about her business with pots and herbs and ignored him. Often he sat in the dark mood for hours and left without saying anything; and Soledad's dark eyes like wells grew deeper and she kept smiling the womansmile.

Sometimes Julián talked with Drake, man-talk about Soledad. He was her *novio*, he declared, and he would marry her in the church, someday. His papa was disgusted with him for staying so long unmarried, but Soledad would wait. She was a widow, and not so young as she used to be—older than he was. They would marry when he became *un hombre importante* and built a big house with a long *sala* and wooden floors and many windows.

How would he do this? Drake asked once.

With his guitar. "I play for the *bailes*. Here, in Pájaro. In Colinas, Española. The gringos hear me, they love me! When it is summer I will go to Taos. They will pay me much money to play for the *turistas* in the fancy *restaurante*." He would come back with many dollars, and he would start the *casa*.

"For now . . ." He flashed his white smile which was both gentle and arrogant. "For now, I come here. Things are good at Soledad's."

He slept at Soledad's sometimes, but not permanently, because the new priest didn't like it and Julián did anything Padre Andreas told him (like a *bobo*, Soledad said). When he stayed he turned the face of the *santo* to the wall in its *nicho* above the fireplace, even when Soledad mocked him. "*Bruja*," he said, and crossed himself.

"*Cabrón*," she answered, and then they made love.

Once Julián told Drake how he found him. "You lay on a broken piñon branch. *¡Ójala!* It had cut you! But it broke your fall. And now—you mend! *¡Y qué milagroso!* You did not break your neck. Only a lot of piñon trees!"

Slowly the pain dimmed, but his will did not return, and he lay on the lumpy bed and watched the window world. He learned the moods of the dull green tamarisk as they changed in sun and shadow and he heard it scrape the wall in the night winds like a lonely ghost. Sometimes he watched Soledad, wide-hipped and wide-faced, and always with clots of children and dogs around her as she spread her washing over the tamarisk's branches in the dry cold sun.

He saw the cubed houses of the villagers, man-molded squares of earth; and beyond rose the hill, gray and spiny and cruel, and on it, in the corner of his vision, stretched the low building, windowless, secret, guarded by a tall lean cross. He didn't know what it was but it made a dark solidity in his pale mind-fog. Closer stood the parish church, its square bell tower pink-toned in the early sunlight, and the bells rang pink-toned too. He heard them before he saw the church.

He watched the frost crystals mass like stars on the pane as if those distant fires had chilled and moved to earth for the comfort of presence; and sometimes in the night he wasn't sure which were fire-stars and which ice-stars. In those timeless hours when earth and cosmos were one, he felt himself a spirit in both planes and he wondered if they were the same. Stars of ice, crystals of fire, they were all remote and boundless in the giant cold outside.

When the candle shone in the room (Soledad's house had several electric lights, but the bulbs were usually burned out) the panes became mirrors and brighter and warmer than starfrost. Drake watched its shine and saw himself.

Panes become mirrors at night, he thought. *In daylight we reach for the world but the night makes us see ourselves.* He wasn't worth looking at, so he snuffed the candle and returned to the stars. Cats wailed in the wind.

Often in that cloud world between waking and sleeping, he saw the lion. Sometimes he felt eyes on him; sometimes they were Soledad's woman eyes, sometimes the memory of Leona's gray flat eyes looked at him, but more often they were lion eyes and they burned with that uncanny fire.

Drake knew he had almost died and that now he wasn't going to, knew he'd stir one of these days and wonder what the hell he was doing here in a Mexican hut in a place he'd never heard of. From time to time pale thoughts came of Leona, of the firm, of Manby and Joe, and how they must all be searching; and another thought came also, that he didn't want to be found.

Somehow Christmas came and went. He heard snatches of music from Soledad's radio in the kitchen. He was aware of masked youths running past the window chasing smaller children who shrieked, "*¡Los agüelos!*" In the night the pink-toned bells rang and sometime later in the pearl shell of dawn another bell rang, hoarse-toned, and children shrilled "*¡Mis Crismes!*" and thundered at the door. Soledad gave them candies and they ran past the window puffing steam into the air.

He thought of Christmas in Rancho Ribera, of the cocktail parties and the big bash at the country club and the office brawl where the wives wouldn't speak next day, and the present he always bought for Leona—the diamond jewelry or the pink Cadillac or the honey mink, or whatever else she told him to get. Once he tried to surprise her with a puppy, a wriggling apricot poodle. That was when the marriage was still new and possible. She was surprised all right. "We can't have it in the house!" she said, and after a week of pure hell she gave it away. After that she picked her own presents.

▲

The air began to warm. The frost-stars came sporadically and spring winds streaked the sky with sand and often Drake couldn't see the sky-stars either. Sometimes the dust thickened so the *camposanto* disappeared and the houses blurred. Even the church and the figures coming and going seemed insubstantial and the tamarisk scraped. The long dark structure on the hill ceased to be.

One day wails began to ride the wind like Valkyries from its direction, inhuman wails, from human throats and a high reed flute, and Drake knew what the building was. He was in Penitente country and it was the meeting place of the *Hermandad*—the secret brotherhood. He'd read of their Lenten ordeals that climaxed in the Good Friday processions of flagellants who followed the *carreta de la Muerte*—the cart carrying Death, the skeleton with the awful death arrow— and ended with the symbolic crucifixion of the chosen brother.

"That building's the *morada*, isn't it?" he asked.

Soledad smiled and moved his bed from the window.

She boiled the concoction she had used on his torn flesh—he knew that camphorous smell—and carried it out in a pail. He knew she bore it to the *morada* to bathe the flagellants' backs, but he asked no questions.

It was the first curiosity he'd felt, though it was faint. After he lost the window world, he was pulled into the immediate hut world of Soledad and of Julián who never went to the *morada*—and of the children.

Two were Soledad's, though he didn't know it at first. They moved in groups and, though he could hear their shouts outside, they grew mute when they came in to fetch herbs for their mamas or to gaze at Drake with shiny eyes. Their scrutiny made him nervous and sometimes he pretended to sleep, but the stifled giggles unnerved him. Other times he tried to make conversation but they answered in shy monosyllables.

One child, perhaps nine or ten years old, came often, a pond-eyed little boy whose black hair cupped his square head.

"You're Mario, aren't you?"

"*Sí.*"

"They call me Carlos."

"*Sí.* It was in the belt around you. With the money."

The belt! Strange he hadn't thought about it. There were identifying papers. Charles Drake Cavanaugh: Carlos. They'd looked ... the money ... God knew where, now. Little grains of concern appeared like motes in the formless air of his lethargy, but he felt too tired to strain after them now.

"Does your mama send you for herbs?"

"*Mi mama?*" His eyes widened a little and his curly lips smiled. "Soledad is my mama, *señor.*"

Drake asked later if he were displacing the child from his own bed.

Soledad shrugged. "They sleep in the loft. Mario and Alberto. Or with their *primos.*"

Drake assumed they were Julián's. She lost her husband before she conceived, she'd said.

He thought of the money and approached the subject obliquely. "Why do you call me Carlos?"

"You had papers in your belt, *bobo.* And much money."

"The money?"

"You get well now—you think of the money!"

For the first time he noticed how even were her teeth when she smiled.

She brought him the belt and he was ashamed to count the cash. "You must figure what I owe you."

"There is time." She shrugged. "*Mañana.*"

When Drake could sit up she propped him in a straight-backed chair by the corner fireplace in the large center room. A piñon fire crackled. Above, in its *nicho*, the cottonwood *santo* with his down-turning eyes and flat-planed face and gaunt cheeks stared darkly at him.

Francisco had carved him. "He is our village saint—San Juan Nepomuceno. He guards secrets. Padre Andreas doesn't like him." Father Andreas was the new priest and it seemed there was little he did like. Drake contemplated the *santo* and pondered whether the flat lines and austere molding were those of folk-art crudity or the simplicity of mature wisdom.

Soledad had also a Santa Inés. Once the goat got out and Mario went after him to the *prado* to head him off before he got to the loco weed that is the curse of early spring. When it grew dark and Mario was still gone, Soledad loosened a splinter from the base of the little saint and threw it into the flames. The fragment blazed blue for an instant.

"Why did you do that?"

"Santa Inés brings back lost flocks and children," she said. "A piece of her in the fire gets to heaven quicker, *¿no es verdad?*"

In a little while Mario drove the goat back into the *jacal.* Soledad smiled the womansmile. "*¿Cómo no, Carlos?*"

28

Once he tried to draw San Juan on Mario's tablet that he brought from school. His sketch didn't look much like the saint but it fascinated Mario and after that the boy came often and begged him shyly to "make for me a picture, please, *señor*." He made a list and gave Soledad money for drawing materials for Tonito Valdez to buy in Española and amused himself as well as the children with his clumsy attempts. He worked harder to gain skill.

He and Mario became great friends. They had long solemn discussions and once he told the child about the mountain lion.

"Make me a picture," the child said, round-eyed, and Drake drew a lion with sinful saint eyes.

Life at Soledad's rushed like a spring *acequia* from the early hour when she set the milk, still goat-warm, in the sun to clot for cheese, until she took the beans and chile for supper off the wood *estufa* that sat next to the butane stove she seldom used. She kept her patio garden green with water dipped from her well. Always something needed feeding—the dogs or the goat or the stray cats that appeared in the *jacal*, or Drake, or Julián, or the children. When summoned for a birth or an illness, Soledad went, sometimes with Teresita, more often alone, for the *curandera* grew old and slow.

She moved through the hours, chattering with the children as they flowed in and out, or singing her husky songs. Sometimes she glided, quiet and sensuous with languid eyes; other times she moved with contained, in-turning grace, as if her pulse beat in a sort of flamenco rhythm.

Drake made sketches of her.

He grew familiar with the little house and forgot its discomforts. It was one of the best houses in Descanso, she told him. Only two others had wooden floors—the Romeros' and the house where the widowed Doña Rosalía lived with her widowed brother, Enrique Peralta, and his strange daughter Luz. She plastered inside and out every year with *soquete* and kept the walls cleanly whitewashed. Regularly she burned the *barbasco* or hung its branches about to keep away the *chinches*.

It was a good house, built by her father, with a *portal* in front, a patio behind, and a bathroom that her brother who lived in Española and worked for the D and RG Railroad had built on. The loft slept the boys and often their *primos* warmly. It was a good house.

"My papa made much money," said Soledad. "He was a horse thief." She tossed her black mane proudly. "A good one!"

Sometimes she opened the doors and let in floods of yellow sun, though the air was yet chilly. As the days warmed, she sat him in the patio. "The best one in Descanso," she bragged. It was high-walled and tile-floored, though the tiles were old and chipped and it smelled damp.

The well was old, too. Soledad had taps in the kitchen and bathroom from which she filled pots to heat for washing or bathing, but she watered her plants and cooked her beans in the water she drew from the well. She kept well water in the large *olla* to drink and to use in her curative concoctions.

"It tastes funny," he said.

"A ghost lives in it. *La Llorona.* It makes you well again, this water."

"A ghost?"

"*Una sombra.* You are afraid of ghosts?"

"I don't know any. Tell me about yours."

"Sometimes she sobs in the night, very soft. Maybe sometime you will hear her. Maybe not."

"Why does she cry?"

"I don't know. For something lost."

"You've seen her?"

"I've seen her candle glow, very soft but very bright, and it goes into the well."

"Looking for what's hidden?" He smiled.

"You mustn't mock."

"I don't. I'm just not familiar with ghosts."

"The light is not to search with. She sees without it."

"What, then?"

"Maybe she guards a treasure and tells me where it is. Only . . . I can't go in the well to find it."

"What kind of treasure?"

"*¿Quién sabe?* That she does not tell me."

Once he drew the ghost for Mario as the child described her but it didn't look much like a ghost and they laughed.

"You have a little boy somewhere, Carlos?" asked Soledad.

He shook his head.

"You ain't nobody's papa?" asked Mario, round-eyed. "Then you can be my *tío.*"

Drake said he'd like that. They laughed again, and he felt happy. *If Leona had ever had a child.* . . .

She'd wanted to wait a year and then another; and when their friends began to have families she thought it positively revolting how otherwise sane people became so child-oriented. Birthday parties, piano lessons, Cub Scouts—it was all so tedious.

Leona fled from thoughts of tedium.

▲

The days warmed toward summer and primal green stalks of hollyhocks in Soledad's patio pushed up through the dusty herbs toward the sun.

He watched the sparrows peck at crumbs he threw and he learned to marvel at their tiny wings in strong motion. He listened to their talk and to the sound of moving air in the high pines and he smelled its resinous odor. The air was never still in Descanso. A subtle restlessness hinted of spirits and, moved by no breeze, the tamarisk branches scraped the 'dobe walls.

He watched Soledad move like an earth mother about her patio as she drew splashing water from her well and ladled it sparingly in her garden. He watched her beyond the wall where she planted squash and beans and corn and chiles and he thought she'd never been a virgin.

He watched her as she fed her chickens and milked her goat with her strong hands in the little aspen-log corral; and as his life flowed back he learned to milk it for her in the evenings when Mario brought it in.

Julián brought her wood and chopped it , when he thought about it, with powerful strokes and then strutted about in his tight jeans. Once Drake started to help him carry a load inside.

"I am her *novio*," Julián grated and Drake saw dark anger flare in his hooded goat-eyes.

Behind him Soledad smiled.

The Saturday after Lent was over, Soledad and Julián went to the *baile*. In the night Drake was awakened by Julián's reedy voice singing as they walked up the road and he was laughing from too much *aguardiente*. When he sat on the frayed velvet couch in the next room he tried to pull Soledad onto him but he missed, fell to the floor, and promptly went to sleep.

Through the doorway Drake watched Soledad efficiently empty her *novio*'s pockets of coins. She winked at San Juan keeper of secrets, pried a splinter from his backside, tossed it on the fire, and smiled.

"It's time I left," Drake said next morning.

"Where to go?"

"Anywhere." He still had the money except for what he paid Soledad from time to time. He tried to pay more but she was proud. Funny—she'd steal Julián's change, but she never touched his. Funny, too—it didn't seem to matter.

He should go home. *They must think I'm dead by now*, he thought. *Let them. They won't miss me long—Leona or the firm or the people we called friends.* He'd left Leona well fixed and it wasn't as if there'd been children.

I just don't care anymore, he thought. *I've walked out on my responsibilities. I'm a bum. Hiding.*

He was too tired to think about it now but he wanted to go on hiding, for a while at least.

"But I must leave here. Because—oh, many reasons. Mario and Alberto need their bed back." He'd stay in the village, though. There'd be someplace vacant.

Meanwhile he sent the boys downstairs, moved into the loft and insisted on paying more rent.

They must have searched for him, he said one day. Had anyone come asking. . . ?

"*Sí.*"

"What did you tell them?"

"They didn't ask here."

"They talked to someone."

"San Juan keeps secrets." Her smile was a quick white flash. "They ask. But," her strong hands opened helplessly, "nobody knew nothing!"

"We don't know nothing," said Francisco. The old *santero* sat in a square of sunlight and deposited a crushed paper sack on the chipped tile of the patio.

He looked like the *santo* he'd carved, a spare small man with flat long cheeks and weather-pured skin that shone with the sun-washed wind-scoured cleanness of age, like the dried cottonwood roots from which he carved his saints. His eyes were long like the *santo*'s, though merrier when sometimes a small thought flickered. Drake thought maybe a saint peered from their dark windows.

If so, the time for its release to heaven was not yet upon it, for the old man spoke with earth words and smiled like Puck.

"We don't know nothing. The *gringos* come looking for a lost man. So very sad about this man." His voice was like shaggy cedar bark.

"Why didn't you tell them?"

"We hadn't nothing to tell. The man they was looking for was dead. Killed by a *león*. But you. . . ."

"You knew my name."

"Oh, *sí*. Would you like a smoke, Señor Carlos?" He took from his faded blue shirt pocket a pouch of tobacco and measured it into the cupped corn husk.

Drake hadn't had a smoke since the accident. "Thanks."

The old man continued the ceremony. He rolled one for each of them before he spoke again. He nodded to a brown canyon wren perched on the wall. "Ah, there's a little fellow." They watched him balance with his long russet tail and puff his white breast to the sun. "You'll find no bugs up there, *tontino*," said Francisco. "But the sun is warm, *¿no es verdad?*"

He passed a cigarette to Drake. "They did not say the name of the dead man, I believe. How are we to know it might be you?"

"No one in the village said a thing?"

Francisco looked down at his stained knotty hands and his thin lips lowered and caged the saint inside. "San Juan is our *patrón*, Señor Carlos. He guards secrets."

"How do you know it's a secret?"

"All men have secrets, *¿no es verdad?* In Descanso we live the old way. We do not give up our guests to intruders. That is for you to do if you wish."

"What if I'd died?"

"Then I believe it would not have mattered to you." He looked up at Drake and the saint looked out again, innocent, candid, and—laughing? "And the little bird, he didn't tell either. Did you, *pajarito?*" He smoked a minute. "I brought something to you, *señor*."

He had met the hunters as they carried Drake into the village, he said, carried him with his soul just hanging to its body with limp, hopeless hands, and Julián was prancing about like a goat telling everyone what they could plainly see. The old man, helping to remove Drake's blood-crusted clothes while Soledad boiled poultices, had without thought tucked something of their guest's into his pocket.

He picked up the sack. "I'm sorry it got broke when you fell. But here you will not need it anyhow, I think."

Drake began to laugh. Inside lay his gold watch. It was a shattered corpse. It marked no time.

▲

Descanso warmed in the sun and Drake's blood with it. He began to walk to the *placita* and, in time, beyond, even to the trading post down the road toward Colinas.

Sometimes he went to Señor Romero's store to buy gray soap for Soledad, or a bag of *masa*.

Sometimes she sent him with eggs to Padre Lorenzo, especially when Father Andreas was the old priest's guest. The young priest lived in Colinas, served seven villages and the pueblo and visited them all in a Super Cub. He was a serpent-entered man with electric blue eyes and he distrusted Drake's casual presence at Soledad's.

Drake spoke to the villagers as he walked and they gave him friendly courtesy. He would nod to sharp-beaked Teresita with her startling blue eyes, who they said was a witch—a *bruja*—as she swept her bare yard barer and aimed her sharp eyes on him to see if he mended properly.

He would take Doña Rosalía's fat left arm—her right hand clutched a puffy *buñuelo* whose shape she somewhat resembled—to guide her across the road as, trailed by her grumpy dog Perdido (who had come as a stray, now fed and fattened into a replica of her own shapeless self), she walked each morning to the house where she sorted the mail, when there was any. Doña Rosalía had a faint mustache and a couple of extra chins. She was capable of negotiating the road but she was a very important lady—the postmistress—and she accepted the homage.

Sometimes Drake accompanied the children to Marta's house on some errand—Marta was Soledad's sister, and she was married to Doña Rosalía's son Luis—and he would always stick his head into the room Doña Rosalía presided over which served as post office. Sometimes he drank a cup of the strong coffee she brewed on the electric burner that was always hot. He would sit on one of the two chairs (there were three, actually, but one was reserved for Perdido who bit anyone who attempted to use it) and listen to Doña Rosalía's high fat voice as she recounted village gossip or told of the "signs" she frequently received from another world that warned of things to come.

He learned to regard solemnly the wall on which she tacked the pictures of wanted criminals. Doña Rosalía tended her gallery with the same scrupulous purpose with which she tended the pictures of the presidents she hung in honor about the room, though in no order, for she frequently regrouped them as other women regroup furniture.

Sometimes Drake saw Tomás Archuleta in his *cantina* or gossiping at Señor Romero's or the good-for-nothing José Villareál who was a *sinvergüenzo* and chased Archuleta's daughter.

On the bench in front of Romero's store sat Alarico Vicente who had fought in the big war. Alarico had a face like a startled burro and a voice like frayed burlap and he drank *vino* in the sunshine when he could afford it and strawberry soda pop when he couldn't and told tales of his great adventure.

"They called it Bataan," he said. "A place you ain't never heard of."

"Yes, I have," said Drake. "You're in the history books."

"That so?" asked Alarico. He didn't seem to believe it.

Often Drake ambled to the edge of the village to visit with Segundo Sifuentes at his garage where his one pump furnished *gasolina* for the battered pickups that carried the men to work in Colinas or Española. Sometimes he filled ten-gallon drums for the airplane Father Andreas landed in the *prado*. Inside he had butane tanks that Tonito brought up from Española and behind the garage the corpses of dead vehicles lay in rusting heaps to furnish parts for the ailing pickups Segundo ministered to.

Sometimes Drake helped Manuela Baca carry papers home from the school. The older children went in to Colinas when the weather was good and they could get to where the rutty road joined the graded one where the school bus ran, but for the first three grades they attended Manuela's school in Descanso. There'd been quite a row over it, too, Doña Rosalía told Drake. The *gringos* in Santa Fé wanted to send all the children to Colinas because certified instructors wouldn't stay in Descanso. One after the other teachers came fresh-faced up the mountain and, after a month or so, they always retreated clutching their tattered ideals to their bosoms. The parents refused to send their little ones to the alien influences of the *gringo* school; the solution was Manuela, uncertified, but resident.

Sometimes he greeted Luz Peralta, fawn-shy, silent as winter moonlight as she glided across the *placita* toward the church or home again or to Padre Lorenzo's little house which she cleaned for him. Always Luz smiled at him, then turned her dark eyes toward some more distant object and ducked back into some privacy of her own.

"She's Doña Rosalía's *sobrina*," Soledad told him. "Her brother's child. She's going to be a nun."

Sometimes, when Drake walked past Francisco's toward the *camposanto*, he saw the head of old Padre Lorenzo with white hair wispy like a thin cloud. The padre was retired, though he still ministered when the younger priest was not about and he often walked in the *camposanto* among his old friends, and talked to them—some said to himself—and read his missal, when he could find it.

He smiled when he saw Drake and floated like a breeze-prodded cloud to the wooden fence. "*Dios le bendiga, señor.* You walk better each day!"

Sometimes Drake saw him scud through the *placita* with the grin he always wore when he'd just played some small prank on Father Andreas, who was of sterner stuff; and those he greeted grinned back, for the padre like a gentle breeze stirred titters where he gusted.

"I might have been in heaven now," he said once, "but I stopped to laugh along the way."

Sometimes Drake stopped at Francisco's hut, a solid square of earth surrounded by a froth of apricot orchard which was an act of faith amid the tough encroaching growth of shaggy hills. He always stopped his work—whether tending the trees or releasing a *santo* from its cottonwood prison—and he talked, and his old face, planed by the seasons and sorrows of years, glowed like a dusty sunset.

Once he pointed to his orchard. "They have more faith than other trees, the apricots." Already the buds swelled, though the nights were cold. "They are the first to bloom."

"Don't the late frosts kill them?" Leona's apricot tree always bloomed too soon and got frozen back.

"*Ay*, sometimes." Francisco touched a trunk with light fingers and looked up at the buds that swelled with hope. "You know that, don't you *arbolito? Ay*, he's a brave one, he knows his chances. But if life were certain, living would not be an act of faith, *¿no es verdad?*"

Drake began to sketch the village and its people—goat-eyed Julián and well-eyed Soledad and the pond-eyed children. He sketched Teresita, bent and hood-lidded and talon-clawed like an ancient owl, and Padre Lorenzo like a wispy ghost, and square saint-eyed Francisco, and Doña Rosalía with her little eyes tucked behind fat cheeks.

At some time in the passing days, the marks on his sketch pad began to take on some sort of life and what had been idle entertainment began to acquire a hazy significance.

There aren't many of these little places left, he thought one day, and he began seriously to capture its life, to arrest it and to partake of it. *Like a sacrament*, he thought; and lest he take himself seriously, he grinned and thought, *Sacrament: a crazy word.*

It fit, though. Sacraments are outside time and space. So he drew the patient 'dobe walls and the patient people who came and went until they came to rest in the *camposanto* with its patient crosses; and he drew the crosses too. The outward and visible signs—of what?

He only knew it was something worth the drawing. He began seriously to sharpen his skill, that he might become worthy of the subject; and though he mocked his motives and his methods, it was a tentative act of faith.

▲

The *acequia* flowed!

Snowmelt from above rushed in furious freshets into the gullies and creeks and *arroyos*, to be diverted into the *presas* and the *acequia madre*, and Diego Salazar who was *mayordomo*—the ditch boss—ordered the day of cleaning winter's clottage from the channels that opened into the fields. The men of the village assembled early, spades and hoes over their shoulders, and Drake arrived with them. He didn't expect to be of much use but he'd never get stronger lying around like a drugged toad and it was a way of showing appreciation to those who harbored him.

Soledad was more practical. "Everyone who uses the water sends a man to work or they pay two dollars," she said, though she laughed and said he probably wouldn't be worth two dollars. He'd smashed nothing vital, praise to *Dios* and the *piñones* through which he'd fallen, and the fevers had gone, but the shoulder muscles hadn't knitted yet and he limped badly.

He trudged to the field with Soledad's spade and a bit of *oshá* she'd put in his pocket to keep away the snakes. He was still weak and his shoulder throbbed but he was ready for man company. They accepted him a bit deferentially but soon the constraint wore off and they chaffed one another.

"*¿Qué pasa, abuelo?*" someone called to ancient Domingo Pacheco whose fly was open. Domingo was Cipriano's father and was said to have been a Rough Rider. "How many *mujeres* you screw today?"

Domingo grinned widely and showed both of his yellow teeth. "*¡Ójala!*" he cackled.

Drake knew some Spanish from college but it was book Spanish so he didn't understand most of the jokes, though the overtones were universal. He didn't listen too hard anyhow. He concentrated on each spade thrust and set his teeth against each stab of pain, intent on surviving the day.

Julián never seemed to tire. José Villareál dug with the spasmodic stoicism of the mildly hung over and Drake smiled at a fellow sufferer. José flashed back a rueful grin and made lewd banter with the rest.

Somehow time lurched into afternoon. Drake had to rest often but despite his physical struggle he felt as if he were being gradually absorbed into some rhythm, some stream that ran between the dark men and the dark soil, some interchange between the secret earth and the men who made her bear.

Finally he watched the newly diverted water course into the *acequia*, at first confused and muddy; then, finding its direction, it cleared, as he could sense his own mind beginning to clear with some purpose, hidden, but there.

The horseplay stopped and the dark men with the Indian blood strong in their Spanish veins stood in intuitive silence with the awe that primal men have felt at the birth of life in each spring's vigor since man himself emerged from some womb of time and earth; and suddenly and simply it came to Drake that man, who must release the prisoned life, had in him also some of the god.

He watched the *acequia* bear its frothing god-wine to the waiting earth, the water, melted from winter snows and risen from the inner springs, and he felt something in his own veins melt and flow again and fill some emptiness and he throbbed with the old pain and a new longing for some waiting soil to receive his own new fullness.

The women and the solemn pond-eyed children came then and they bore the *santo* on his platform to bless the ditch and the fields it watered. He was San Ysidro in his blue coat and flat red hat, the farmer's saint, and he prayed while an angel drove his oxen.

"Like all men, he would rather pray than plow, *¿no es verdad*, Ysidro?" Padre Lorenzo said and those around him laughed. He often teased his saints. "Shouldn't they laugh too?" he asked.

The people bowed their heads and Padre Lorenzo in his thin vague voice asked San Ysidro to bless the fields and then they walked to the church for a rosary.

Drake looked around the dim, whitewashed church, softly lit in candle glow, where Christ and the Virgin and some saints he couldn't name gave hope to those gathered within and he felt something nodal, a swelling of life like that of the field, that he'd never felt in his well-dressed Anglican respectability where he thought out his briefs during the service. He watched the people, patient people who had learned to endure the seasons, and death, and living, and patronage by those they knew were their inferiors. He saw José, who had made rude gestures and lewd jokes in the fields, pull into some deep well of mysticism and Julián had tears in his long goat-eyes.

Drake felt his own throat tighten with something he didn't want to define; something heavy and wine-red flooded his breast. It wasn't the religious thing the people around him felt but it was a strong emotion and he had to step back from it, had to tell himself not to be carried away so he could observe it closely. There was some inner essence he wanted to understand, to preserve on the sketch pad, something he tingled to catch.

Soledad heated water for him when the long day ended. He sat in the patio, exhausted, and the old pain throbbed but he felt a free thing flow through him like a cleared *acequia*. In the last rays of western light he watched Soledad, saw her pour water on her little walled garden, saw her move between well and wall trailed by a threadbare black dog, once fuzzy, whose hair fell out in great patches. As she moved her breasts swayed freely beneath the gauzy stuff of her blouse and her dark nipples swelled like ripenesses behind the thin curtain.

Drake's veins flowed full and without thought he reached out and softly touched the dark warm globes, felt them grow taut, and he watched her black eyes. *Madonna eyes*, he thought, *harlot eyes*.

She flashed her quick wide grin. "*¡Ay, Dios!* You mend!" and she bent again over her hollyhock shoots, thrusting up like phalli. She moved to her own rhythm and she smiled.

That night Drake fell asleep with the thick ache of tears in his chest as he had done, sometimes, as a boy.

4

"You're crazy," said Joe. "Nobody just disappears. Not in the twentieth century."

"You wouldn't think so," said Drake, "but that's the way it happened."

"And this Descanso. I never heard of it."

Drake said he hadn't either until he went there. "I just told you," he said. "It's not on the map. People come there sometimes but they don't stay. They came looking for Drake, only they didn't know its name."

"You trying to make me believe in some bloody twilight zone?" Joe asked.

Drake said no he wasn't, it just didn't have a sign. "You've heard of wide places in the road? Well, that's Descanso," he said. "Except the road isn't much. More coffee?"

"Might as well," said Joe, "though I've got an appointment at two." They motioned to the waitress who had a button missing and a greasy orange spot on her gray starch. The coffee slopped onto Drake's saucer and he put a paper napkin under it.

"You know so much about Drake Cavanaugh, what happened to the money?"

"Yeah, Drake figured that's what they'd worry about. The money. And that's an interesting story," he said.

"I'll bet it is."

Drake started to draw doodles on the napkin but Joe's eyes had a funny look in them like trying to remember something, so he stopped. "Back in a minute," he said.

The toilet doors were painted with a sombrero and a mantilla. Inside a man fading from a golf-course tan leaned over the lavatory. He held his head under a wide-open faucet and massaged it with square hands and groaned. "Godawmighty."

His friend with the pads of a double chin in early stages sympathized from a urinal stall. "Kinda boozed it up last night, didn't ya?"

Drake stepped into his stall and thought the sufferer seemed in terminal stages.

"Godawmighty," he groaned again. "Christawmighty."

"Don't forget the Holy Ghost," said Drake.

"What?" asked the dying Gaul.

"Nothing," the other said. "My goddamn zipper's stuck."

"You said something."

"No I didn't. Only my zipper's stuck."

They both glared at Drake.

"Hell with your zipper. I've gotta be in Santa Fé at three on the dot and sharp and meet with the head honcho. With the whole goddamn Russian army having target practice inside my skull."

"Price you pay for promotion."

"Godawmighty don't I know it. And another big stink up north. We spend more goddamned money on schools those fucking Mes'can winos won't even send their kids to. Stinking greasers."

They both looked at Drake as he shared the lavatory. He grinned with one side of his mouth. "*Dios le bendiga, pendejos,*" he said pleasantly as he limped out.

"That's the greaser been sitting with Joe Emmons," said the flabby-chinned man. "Wonder what he's trying to panhandle."

Drake didn't hear the answer because just then the newly promoted VIP began to barf.

▲

Everybody agreed later there had never been such an affair as Julián Romero's going-away party. Except for old Teresita who never attended festivities, all Descanso came, with dogs and cats and three uninvited goats that belonged to Cipriano Pacheco.

The trader down the road got them forty-two dollars and sixty-four cents worth of illegal fireworks with which they accidentally set Cipriano's hay shed on fire. They drank the entire stock of beer from Tomás Archuleta's and left a fair-sized dent in the *aguardiente*. The kids finished off four crates of strawberry pop, two of Pepsi, and thirty-one bottles of Dr Pepper. Nobody counted the pots of beans and roast *cabrito*.

It isn't every day a man becomes a celebrity, a star in the great cosmos beyond his own mountain.

No one really thought Julián would. He got big ideas after the trader's wife, who'd been a professional musician from New York or Hollywood or one of those places before she married the trader, told him he had great talent and started teaching him the finer points of Spanish guitar. Actually, as she told the Anglo later, she'd come from Saint Louis; but she recognized talent and a sensitive soul when she met it and she taught Julián all she knew and gave him a push and a blessing when he surpassed her own ability.

Then Mr. Bernie Weinfeld, who also came from the big outside, heard him and offered him a paying job entertaining summer tourists in his fancy restaurant near Taos. "I'll write you," Mr. Weinfeld said in September and all winter Julián began every third sentence with "When my letter comes . . . ," or "When I go to Taos. . . ." He cultivated a mustache. It remained thin and impertinent, but still, it had an aura.

Three days a week Tonito Valdez, who was Doña Rosalía's grandson, drove to Colinas for the mail in the old blue pickup with the smashed tail light. He got paid for this by the government and people in Descanso paid him to pick up other stuff as well—sundries for the women, supplies shipped to the bus station for Romero's store, car or machinery parts for Segundo, or the butane tanks he sold in the *gasolina* store.

Sometimes he drove Doña Rosalía to Española to the Bella Doña Nu-Mod Beauty Shoppe. Doña Rosalía was the only woman in Descanso who indulged in such vanity but it befitted her station. She was a woman of the world and she proved it with the blue felt hat she wore on these occasions, with the yellow rose on it.

Tonito had a fair delivery business in addition to the mail franchise which, except for the one day a month when the government checks came, would hardly have been worth the gas, to say nothing of the tickets he kept getting because he had no brake-and-light sticker and his muffler had fallen off last July. There just wasn't that much Descanso mail. Whenever anyone got a letter—a real one, not the Sears Roebuck catalogue or the church publication—everybody knew it.

Doña Rosalía got tired of Julián hanging around like a lusting *cabrón*.

"*¡Fuera!*" she snapped. "*¡Zape!* Scat!" Then she chided him for being such a *chango*. "That letter won't never come," she told him. "That Bernie Vinefield forgot he ever seen you."

"Weinfeld."

"*¡Ay, qué mala suerte!* Ain't no good goin' to come out of this! You listen to me. I been around, I know those kind." She ran her fingers through her permanent and frizzled it even more than the Española hairdresser had done. "Those kind snort in big stalls in Santa Fé. They talk a lot. They spread around plenty muleshit, Julián. But they never plow it under and plant it with squash and beans! So you forget that letter that ain't goin' to come." Then she snorted and told him to go chase rainbows on the mesa and, frustrated, rearranged the presidents' pictures on the wall again. Because Rosalía didn't like to see any form of life suffer, she gave him *buñuelos*, her unfailing cure for any kind of hurt. "And don't sit on Perdido!"

He wasn't about to. The ill-tempered little beast bit anyone who tried. No one wanted to sit in that chair anyhow because Perdido had methodically pulled most of the stuffing out. No one knew where Perdido came from; and when Doña Rosalía first started feeding him he was plenty happy just to be fed. Then she let him sleep on her feet one cold night and after that he began to demand his rights.

Julián ate the *buñuelos* but it didn't ease the longing and it didn't stop his hanging around. The letter would come *mañana*, in spite of Doña Rosalía's lack of faith.

But Doña Rosalía, for once, was wrong.

"Julián got a letter," Tonito told José Villareál outside Romero's store one day early in May and José passed it along to Cipriano Pacheco who was on his way inside for a bag of flour and any gossip he could pick up.

"Maybe it really did come at last," Cipriano said to Antonio who was picking his teeth behind the counter.

"Or just another *broma*," said Alarico who was extracting a strawberry pop from the cooler just inside the door. "You got change for this quarter?"

Cipriano stopped on his way home to tell Segundo Sifuentes who was making 'dobe bricks in his yard to build another room onto the house his family was outgrowing; and Segundo's wife, Catalina, trailed by several children and swelling like a fast-ripening pear with her sixth Sifuentes, waddled over to Soledad's. Soledad, with Marta and their combined children, was gathering *quelites* along the *acequia* but Catalina relayed the message to the Anglo Carlos who was in the chicken house engaged in an ownership dispute with an irate hen over the contents of a nest.

"So who needs telephones?" he asked, called a truce with the hen, and offered Catalina coffee. She was finishing her second cup when Soledad returned. Soledad had already heard the news.

So the word danced like a bee from hollyhock to hollyhock, circuitously but surely bearing its pollen to the hive and fertilizing Descanso's foliage on its way until it found Julián who, in a rare bout of industry, was helping his mama plaster the Romero living room.

Meanwhile Doña Rosalía, leaving a grandson in charge of the post-office room, trailed by Perdido, charged puffing with the letter to Romero's to leave with Julián's father. Julián had already skittered to the post office; then, finding Doña Rosalía gone, he completed the circle behind her. When he finally pranced into the store in his tight jeans with his shirt open to the waist, a fair-sized delegation loitered, outside and in, to witness the drama.

Julián turned the letter over as if it were a papal encyclical, examined all four edges of the envelope and then carried it outside where he again scrutinized it with love, as a thirsty man who has allowed himself not a single *copita* for all Lent will, when the period of penance ends, inhale the odor of his *aguardiente* and savor it at length before he takes his first satisfying taste.

"Open it, *primo*!"

"See what it says!"

"Matter, can't you read?"

Flashing his goat-eyes and grinning like a satyr, Julián ripped the missive open with a flourish, unfolded it, and let his long eyes follow his finger back and forth across the paper as one plows a field. For a moment no expression lit his face; then, as comprehension pierced his mind, a happy light poured from his eyes and animated his mouth, and a joyous bleat erupted.

"*¡Chihuahua!*" he roared. "*¡Santa María!* Son-of-a-bitch!"

Julián, waiting for the day Tonito would drive him to Española to catch the bus for Taos, agonized through May alternately "getting his show together" in Soledad's patio and making love to her or thinking about it when she was otherwise occupied. His father growled that he grew more useless than ever, especially after he caught him dreaming beside the ditch on their day to irrigate and allowing it to overflow into Cipriano Pacheco's field whose day for water it was not. Not that Cipriano minded—it gained him the water and saved him the trouble.

May contained Descanso's feast day for their patron saint, San Juan Nepomuceno, and because it was only a day separated from that of San Ysidro who blessed crops, Descanso celebrated doubly. For a week before, Julián worked at the church. He plastered the walls, he cleaned the window, he mended the roof. He wasn't the *sacristán*—that was Alarico Vicente—but a dark demon lurked in Julián's soul and threatened him with eternal fire unless he exorcised it repeatedly; and so he regularly and passionately confessed, humbly and diligently performed his penances, and spasmodically worked in the church.

He'd amassed a lot of penances lately because he'd sinned a lot; his transgressions ranged from sloth (which was habitual) to pride (which under the circumstances he felt justified) to an excess of fornicating. Padre Lorenzo had always inclined to a measure of tolerance over the last so that Julián felt God looked the other way for men's more natural functions; but Padre Andreas represented a sterner God, enjoyed his own militant celibacy, and dedicated himself to the proposition that others should do so too.

In Descanso they still called Father Andreas the new priest to distinguish him from wispy Padre Lorenzo who was retired and with whom they were comfortable. The new priest was part German and spoke bad Spanish and his mind, like his language, had an Anglo accent.

The two fathers intermittently waged a gentle but persistent tug-of-war over local traditions. Andreas insisted on strict ritual observance; and Lorenzo, trusting God to understand the idiom, indulged his people in their native forms. God was, he believed, more concerned with the chile than the bowl it was served in. "Why chase a fly when the goats are loose?" he asked in his thin vague voice and Father Andreas looked exasperated and his eyes snapped blue fire.

Father Andreas and Julián shared one emotion. Neither could tolerate the *Hermanos Penitentes*, the one because he was demon-driven and suspected them of forbidden rites, and the other because his childhood worship of his oldest brother had turned to black jealousy of his high and holy attainments in the sacred sect.

Julián was the youngest child. Since he first could walk he had followed

Emilio, twelve years older, who carried him on his shoulders like San Cristóbal carrying the *Santo Niño* so that Julián was taller than anyone. Emilio made excuses for him when he committed some childish sin, stood between him and their father's discipline; and Julián followed Emilio as a *cabrito* follows the belled leader. But a devil leaped like a trout in his veins and lured him into mischief and as he grew older the wildness did not tame.

Like all the children, he learned to work. He drove the goats and chopped weeds in the fields and broke winter ice for the pig in the *jacal*. He developed great physical strength in his wiry little body because he resented being the youngest and small by nature. He grew defensive if he were corrected. He longed for his father's "*Bueno*, Julián! Well done, *hijo*," but he lacked self-discipline and when he could he shunned work entirely and performed feats where there was small competition and high praise. He became Padre Lorenzo's most faithful acolyte and he sang in his childish soprano with truer pitch than anyone in the village until his voice began to crack. Then everyone laughed and the black rage of humiliation washed over him as he flung from the church.

One didn't laugh.

Soledad Quintero, who had newly become Soledad Baca, didn't laugh.

She found him flinging rocks into the *acequia* and she smiled a smile that seemed somehow to admit him to the world of men and asked if he'd help her haul some wood. Her husband, Filemón, was working for the D and RG down in the valley and she needed a man to help.

Soledad was older than he but the Indian in her was strong and she had that always-renewable look about her like the field maiden, the virgin mother, the old-new earth that forever responded to seed and water. He followed the habit of stopping by to help her with heavy jobs as a man follows a plow along the winding furrows in the strong warm earth without thought; and those times he felt himself a man.

But Julián was not a man.

After Emilio joined the *Hermandad* he spent much time at the *morada* like their papa. Julián accepted his father's participation—that had always been—but he resented Emilio's increasing preoccupation which too often removed the shield against his father's anger when he transgressed.

When Julián drove the Romeros' goats through Amadeo Baca's melon patch, Señor Romero's wrath crashed like summer lightning bolts around the tall mountain.

"You grow tall like a man but you act a child. You have destroyed the life God sent to the field," he said and he laid his belt on Julián's hide and left welts like storm marks on trees. These were less painful than humiliating: to be treated like a *niño* when he ached to be a man! By the time they healed he had worked himself into slow hard vindictiveness for Emilio who had been at the *morada* when Julián needed him. He felt wronged for this had been an act of vengeance, an affair of honor: Señora Baca had falsely accused him of stealing watermelons from her husband's field. He hadn't. He and his friends had rifled every other field around but not those: Baca's melons weren't ripe yet!

He blamed the brotherhood for Emilio's disaffection and when, after one Holy Week, Emilio doubled injured arms painfully to his gaunt chest, Julián's revulsion crested and broke into furious foam.

From the *morada* the high sweet notes of the reed flutes wove sensuously toward the mountain above and something dark in him responded. Sperm-memories in his Moorish blood warred with womb-memories from bronze men who had climbed from Earth's center until he felt he would be pulled into many pieces.

He'd heard the reed flutes always but with his new awareness they sliced through the raw nerve-ends of his own sin and his own mortality and his blood spumed like the icy torrents of wild spring streams. Sometimes he heard them when no one else did, not from the keening air but from the moving currents of his own soul until he could scarcely stand them, must assign the sin elsewhere and share the dark mortality.

When Emilio married Consuela Madrid from Pájaro, Julián stood at the wedding with dark eyes and darker heart though at the feast afterward he danced wildly and cut his goat-eyes at all the girls and got very drunk. When Emilio moved to Pájaro to farm the plot for Consuela's dying father, Julián considered his defection complete.

In time he learned to push away the dark thoughts, follow his own demon and laugh at the villagers who talked of his wild ways. Still, those thoughts like vultures returned to circle death-reminding above him so he attended his soul, however sporadically, with many beads and acts of contrition.

When Father Andreas came and inveighed against the *Hermanos*, their mutual abhorrence drew them together. Julián found a safe altar to run to when his demons circled. As Emilio had once shielded him from his father's wrath, the new priest could shield him from the terrors of the soul.

As the saints' days approached, he worked side by side with the *sacristán* to apply fresh calcimine to the walls in the little church and ready it for the celebration and he felt surely he'd be forgiven a flooded field and a few pleasures of the flesh.

On the festive day he offered his music to God at the mass and he felt his own power throb in the plaintive chords that surged thin and rich like communion wine through the candle-lit dimness and moved the people and the saints and surely God Himself. Tears came to Julián's eyes when he heard his own beautiful music.

Later at the feast he infused a fiesta mood as he banged out wild rhythms and sang bawdy songs that made them laugh. He felt his power and dreamed of the larger audiences in the sophisticated world that was Taos.

Still later he walked Soledad home, lay his guitar on the hard little couch, cut his wicked eyes at her, and turned San Juan to the wall.

Julián had become Soledad's lover soon after Filemón was stabbed in Tomás Archuleta's bar in a fair fight over whether to toss the two hippies out of the *cantina*. A bunch of punk Anglos had set up a commune at the end of a trail off the Colinas road and they sometimes went native and slopped over and washed up to the villages. The villagers called them *Las Lucas*—the Crazies. No one had much use for the hippies, especially after they grew a field of marijuana and brought state authorities' attention farther up into the natives' own marijuana fields they'd always grown in privacy. It merely confirmed their earlier impressions—namely, that the hippies meant trouble for everybody in their mountains and valleys where they had lived for centuries in relative peace.

Filemón and Pedro Villareál were for kicking their asses down the mountainside; some of the others didn't want to bother and favored just ignoring them. It was a friendly enough argument in the beginning.

Old Teresita had just that day let drop to Filemón that Pablo Anaya had said the reason Filemón stayed in the valley so much was because he wasn't stud enough to service Soledad. So, inflamed by Teresita's insinuation, Filemón was already laying for Pablo; the argument about the hippies was all Filemón needed and things started to get nasty.

It was Saturday night. A recent blizzard had kept everyone at home too long and the sparks lit on the dry brush of a week's boredom and broke into a very satisfying brawl—except that Filemón ended up on the wrong end of a knife.

The hippies had long since ducked out.

No one was sure who did it; many carried knives. No one intended serious injury, the wound seemed superficial, and the authorities didn't pry too deeply.

But the knife had penetrated farther than anyone realized. For days Filemón grew weaker while Soledad, with Teresita's help, nursed him. Julián came every day to tend the goat and carry the wood.

Padre Andreas offered to fly Filemón to a doctor in Española—when he took the back seat out of the Super Cub there was just enough room for a man to lie down—but Teresita said he couldn't be moved.

Despite the women's ministrations, before the month was gone, Filemón was dead.

The faithful gave him a heartfelt *velorio*. It was terrible for one so young and lately married to go. It was a great tragedy; but it was a natural one.

Julián watched Soledad in the church and later as she followed the coffin through the hard snow to the wind-filled *camposanto*; and through the days that followed he came by each day to tend the chores. This daily habit acquired the importance of ritual.

One evening he appeared with his burro laden with wood which he stacked beside her patio wall. He brought in the goat-warm milk in the early dark and she fed him *frijoles* and fresh-made tortillas and strong coffee.

"You cook good, Soledad."

"A woman needs a man to cook for." Her voice was husky and he felt very much a man. Replete with a meal in his belly he followed her from the kitchen and watched her move with her swinging skirt.

She pulled the white curtains across the deep-silled windows. "To keep out the *brujas*," she said. She crossed to the *fogón* and threw a log of damp piñon on the smoking fire.

He came up behind her, aware of his body, of the strength and energy within his tight jeans, aware of Soledad. "You need a man to keep out the *brujas*!"

He grinned a wide grin as she turned from the fire and he saw the sudden smoke move across her well-eyes. Then he reached up and carefully turned the little *santo* toward the wall.

▲

Early on the morning of Julián's party the smell of roasting *cabrito* spread from the school yard, mated with that of bubbling beans and chile and baking bread and cakes, and ascended to tantalize the gods on the mountain.

By the time the sun sank below the rimrocks, villagers clotted the school yard where the meat had roasted all day and deposited their offerings on the long tables in the shade of the cottonwoods along the *acequia* that bordered the playground. Later those who wanted to could dance in one of the two large rooms inside the schoolhouse built by the bosses in the State Department of Education in Santa Fé, a gray concrete-block monstrosity erected fifteen years before to the god of Ugly.

The clustering women spread blankets and gossiped, the children ran about like shooting stars, and the single men, and some who weren't, passed around a bottle of *aguardiente* from Pedro Villareál's pickup.

"Here comes Julián!"

He skidded to a rock-scattering stop in Tonito's truck, alit with a grin, lifted Soledad's boys and three of Marta's from the back, and waved. Soledad handed him a pot of beans and followed clutching still-warm loaves. She'd had to make bread twice she told Delfina Romero as she deposited it on the table. The first loaves were rising when Segundo Sifuentes had come to fetch her because Catalina's pains had begun and when she returned the dough had over-risen and collapsed and she'd had to throw it to the chickens. "And all for false pains," she half-grumbled. "You'd think Catalina would know by now!"

Catalina, still expanding like ripe dough, was there with Segundo and their brood. "I told her make it wait for the party!" he said, and she said she'd make *him* wait and everybody laughed but before he could answer, a yell went up over by the trees because someone discovered one of Cipriano's goats demolishing a paper plate that still had three *bizcochitos* left on it. They ran the goat off but it soon returned with two others and Cipriano staked all three behind the privies because it was too far to take them home and they'd probably broken the fence anyhow.

One of the children threw up and after that a glass-shattering sound signaled that an errant ball from the game behind the school had found a window and everyone laughed. The party was off to a good start.

Everyone came. Among the battered pickups that lined the road stood several from Colinas, and Val and Fergus White came from the trading post. The trader and his wife didn't go to parties much but Val had nudged Julián to stardom and, being part of his success, she wanted part in the celebration. When Val wanted something Fergus wagged and fetched.

She helped serve the children and the old ones who always ate first thing and Fergus stood about and drank with the men and grinned and drawled an occasional joke in his low voice; and he watched Val with his funny pale eyes like his faded jeans. Fergus was built like a skinny forked cedar pole and his yellow hair hung below the greasy Stetson with the rattlesnake band. He claimed he'd killed it barehanded but no one anted up stakes on anything the trader said because he could tell a lie without a flicker.

Carlos, who'd paid for all the beer and whiskey at the party, came with Francisco. Julián recounted once more how he'd been one breath short of dead when they carried him to Soledad's. Though he still limped heavily, he was nearly well now and had arranged to rent the old house Francisco's papa had lived in until he died as soon as he fixed it up a little. He seemed to have no place to go back to.

Julián pranced from group to group and was just taking his first swig from the bottle in the pickup when someone yelled that he should play them some music—that's what the party was all about, ¿cómo no?—and someone fetched his guitar. He said Val should play with him and that brought a cheer because she was partly responsible for all this too.

"Why not?" She shrugged and borrowed José's guitar. She and Julián looked at each other, struck their chords, and let fly a loud wild rhythm.

It had all started when Julián was riding the school bus down to the Colinas High School where he sat in the back seat and alternated between mute boredom—his teachers said stupidity—and various attention-getting devices successfully designed to distract the girls. Sometimes Julián got off the bus when it stopped at White's trading post and often he managed not to get back on again.

He hung around the post a lot and one day he saw a guitar behind the counter and asked if he could try it out. At the other end of the room, Fergus negotiated with some Indians over a box of jewelry and Val, tending some customers, shrugged and said sure, and handed it across. She was big-boned with yellow hair and freckles and she wore her jeans low on her straight hips like a man. Julián played chords in a corner the better part of an hour and then looked up to see her leaning against the counter on her forearms. Her breasts were large and they puffed out over her folded arms.

"You're not bad," she said and her voice was pale and flat like stale beer. "But I can make you better." She had a pale yellow smile like late winter sun and the corners of her mouth turned down instead of up.

The Indians filed out and Fergus started marking prices on some silver bracelets.

"Can you sing?" she asked.

"Sure." His voice hadn't cracked in over a year.

"I've got to make lunch," she said. "But I'll listen to you. I know a thing or two about music. Maybe I can help you." She started through a back door and jerked her head for him to come. He looked at Fergus but he was squatting behind a glass case putting the bracelets in it so Julián shrugged and followed her across the dirt to the house behind the store.

He went through his repertoire in the kitchen and from time to time she walked over to reposition his fingers with her long hard hands or take the guitar from him and replay a passage and when Fergus came to lunch Julián was still there.

"There's plenty, you can stay," she said.

After that he hung around more or less regularly. Sometimes he helped Fergus in the store and sometimes Val made him do chores around the house. Once she asked him if he should be skipping school so much but he told her he wasn't passing anything anyway. She shrugged and said okay, then he might as well be useful.

Fergus paid him when he did odd jobs. When summer came it grew into a more or less steady job except when Julián had to run the tractor for Antonio or the neighbors he hired out to and everyone said he was finally going to amount to something.

He soon became a permanent fixture at the post and often tended it when Fergus was trading on the reservation. Sometimes he even went with him. "You need to learn to trade," Fergus said, and Julián learned the art of sharp dealing. "They'll cheat you," the trader drawled. "You're a fool if you don't return the compliment. They expect it."

Julián found he had great talent; and sometimes he traded a little on his own and brought back pieces of cheap jewelry which he sold to the tourists when Fergus was out and kept the money and thought, *Why not?* He'd learned the philosophy from Fergus.

He finally dropped high school altogether.

Julián bedded Soledad when he felt like it and stayed at her house part of the time. He'd probably marry her when he got around to it—she already swelled with his seed—but there was no hurry. *Poco tiempo.*

She didn't prod him. Too, there were certain rumors about her. She learned healing arts and herb magic from old Teresita who was a *bruja* and some said she learned the black arts as well though he didn't really believe it. Unlike Teresita, Soledad attended mass regularly, though it seemed somewhat to bore her.

Meanwhile, Julián enjoyed both worlds.

Val had stacks of records and whenever she and Fergus went to Santa Fé or Albuquerque they bought more or if he went alone he got them for her because Fergus would stand on his head if Val said to. It only made him look an ass, Julián thought. That wasn't how to handle a woman but it wasn't his worry and he did like to hear the music, or some of it. The operas bored him but some of the symphonies had good parts stuffed in between a lot of cactus land. He listened to classical and Spanish guitar for hours, especially Segovia, sprawled on the floor by the stereo with his head against the plaid cushions of the ranch-style sofa Fergus had bought for Val's birthday from the Sears Roebuck store in Albuquerque. ("I hate that sofa," she said once to Julián.) He'd listen and then he'd play the same songs on his own guitar and Val would come on him, see his self-satisfied grin, and tell him he wasn't that good.

"And never will be if you don't work harder. You're lazy as hell," she would say and he always agreed. Then she'd get mad and cuss at him which always made Julián laugh because she cussed so poorly. Those words in her mouth always sounded like an Anglo trying to speak Mexican when all he knew was book Spanish. Then she'd get madder and call him an asshole.

"So when are you going to get to work?" she asked.

Always he promised, "*Mañana.*"

"Don't know why I bother with you," she said one day. "You start thinking you're so damn good, nobody else will." Fergus had gone to the reservation and she'd been tending the post but it was quitting time and she walked in and stood listening in the door.

"I play for the *bailes*. They think I'm good."

"You can do better than that. You want to stay in Descanso all your life?" She lit a cigarette and tossed the match in a glass ashtray. A piece of cellophane wrapper burned a little and the smell floated in the air.

"*¿Por qué no?* Our fields are good. We own the tractor—I get good money hiring out. I make good money here. So someday I marry Soledad and settle down. Why not?"

She insisted he could be good—really good—and she took up her own guitar and sat on the floor beside him. "Listen," she said. "Hold my cigarette." She played the passage.

"Keep going," he said. She played the whole piece.

He put his own guitar aside, leaned against the couch, and smoked her cigarette. He inhaled with deep breaths. He watched her long straight hands, *guitarrista's* hands with hard calluses on her fingertips. He looked at her face with her long yellow hair falling forward. When she played she got a sensuous look that she never had any other time. He wondered if she ever got that look in bed with Fergus. Mostly her face didn't change much; she just looked at Fergus in that flat way she looked at everyone else and her voice didn't change much either. Only when she played her guitar or the grand piano at the end of her living room did her face come to life like a late sunrise on a winter morning—that or when she got mad and yelled at Julián.

He watched her hands move. He listened to the soft throb of an old song and something swirled inside his loins like the deep-inhaled smoke in his lungs.

When she finished he looked at her, a hard long look from the corners of his long eyes. "Ever do it with a Mexican?" he asked.

▲

Julián's sun blazed brightly. He worked when he felt like it and made love when he felt like it, to Soledad when the blood boiled hot or to Val when he wanted to laze in placid shallows when Fergus wasn't about, and some days to both. He listened to records and he made his own music, and only one small fly buzzed at his table: Kitty.

Kitty was enormous, tiger-striped, and male. No one knew where he came from. Val started feeding him, eventually got close enough to pet him, and finally enticed him inside one night during a blizzard. Except for his occasional nocturnal pursuits of lust, Kitty hadn't left since.

Julián hated that cat. He yowled above Julián's music. He rubbed against his ankles. If Julián decided to play around with Val, Kitty planted himself between them and snarled. In the way of male cats, he sometimes sprayed the wall.

54

But Val felt some strange attraction for the unlovely animal. Fergus tolerated him and Kitty largely ignored Fergus; but the minute Julián appeared, there also appeared Kitty. He stalked Julián, he sprang at him from behind furniture, thrashing his serpent tail, snarling and yowling and rubbing. *Dios*, how Julián hated that cat. Val just smiled lazily downward and stroked the beast.

She liked to be stroked too. Once when Fergus was on the reservation, Val closed the post early during a heavy snow storm and went to the house where Julián built a fire. They sprawled on the floor, leaned against the couch, and Julián began to stroke her with long slow caresses.

Suddenly Kitty sprang and lit squarely on Val's big breast, his obscene furry tail writhing in triumph. She laughed. Something snapped in Julián like a busted guitar string. He grabbed the overgrown mass of striped fur, strode across the floor with Kitty snarling and biting, kicked open the door, and grabbing the animal by his monstrous tail, hurled him into the snow.

"You son-of-a-bitch," said Val. But her face got the smoldering look he thought only her music could arouse and it was Val who made the advances that night.

Next day Julián felt almost kind toward that cat and when he was sure no one saw him, he fed him a tin of sardines he had taken from his papa's store.

▲

In the school yard they played. The smell of roast *cabrito* floated in the air and Julián filled with emotion. This was the last time he'd play here. He was going to bigger, better things, and he filled with his own importance but he felt a loneliness too and a big love expanded inside him for his own people. He saw his father who was finally proud of him and he planned a time when his parents would travel to Taos and come to the fine *restaurante* and hear the fine audience in their fine clothes clapping for him, Julián, and his father would say, "*¡Bueno, mi hijo!*" He looked at Soledad and at his two sons and thought tonight he would make another and later he would come home famous and build his family a big house and marry Soledad.

Then he saw Emilio arrive with his family from Pájaro and his heart hurt and the dark anger blew back like heavy smoke and he switched to an angry song. Val looked at him surprised before she changed her song to fit his but something came into her flat blue eyes and he knew she understood his mood.

It was a successful party. After Padre Lorenzo blessed the food, everyone stuffed himself and the men made frequent trips to the pickups to pass around the bottles of *tequila* and *aguardiente* and some smoked the marijuana—among other pleasures, it guarded one against witches—and the women gossiped around the long table and sat on the blankets. Doña Rosàlía shook her frizzled head dolefully and said she'd had a sign. She'd spilled salt that day. Bad luck would follow.

Old Doña Felicia sniffed and said it was a sign of nothing but Rosalía's own clumsiness.

Pilar Archuleta undulated from one group to another and cast eyes outlined in heavy black stuff toward the men who came and went to the pickup and back, especially José Villareál, who leered back; and the baleful eyes of the less seductive females cast themselves on Pilar.

By dusk there had been three good fist fights and several dog fights; Pedro Villareál and Tonito Valdez had a spitting contest using a Prince Albert can for a target; and Alarico Vicente even played a few of the old songs on his guitar which he didn't do much anymore because of the arthritis in his hands.

The fireworks were the big show though not exactly as planned. For a while some of the men tossed firecrackers at each other and the dogs on the periphery howled. Then when it got dark enough the women gathered up the children and everyone sat expectantly on blankets in a wide circle and awaited the show.

Diego Salazar and Fergus took charge of the center arena and carefully spaced the eruptions of light and noise. The smell of burning powder drifted lazily around and everyone was happy. Each golden fountain received its shrill accolades, each loud bang its squeals and laughs. From behind the tables Luis Valdez shot Roman candles over everyone's head.

Perhaps it was the dark or maybe the last few healthy swigs of *tequila* Luis had consumed. Or maybe the thing was defective. Whatever the cause, Luis lowered his trajectory, the red ball of fire plunged to the stage, lit dead center in the pile of unlit explosives, and detonated volleys and colors and flashes and booms, sending simultaneous but unsynchronized showers of sparks in all directions into the scattering crowd. Fergus and Diego were the first to scatter. Everyone shrieked and when the first surprise was over, they laughed and hollered and clapped. It was a great show.

But it wasn't over yet. Luis still had a few missiles left and, determined not to waste them, began aiming toward the new moon whose crescent was just rising from behind Cipriano Pacheco's hay shed which it silhouetted across a broad weed field.

Luis missed the moon but he hit the hay shed. No one knew it until a small but rapidly expanding blaze upstaged the moon and then eclipsed it entirely.

"*¡Fuego!*" The cry ascended. Everyone rushed in a roughly circular pattern for a few confused minutes and then the men raced for the pickups and piled thickly therein. The more provident grabbed cans of Coors as they ran. Tonito and Pedro, in their hurry to get there first, rammed their vehicles into each other and chalked up a few more notches in their war-scarred fenders. The men raced to the fire.

Doña Rosalía shook her head and her chins waggled. "I knew when I spilled the salt. . . ."

"Cipriano's falling-down barn isn't any loss," snapped Doña Felicia.

"Well," said Rosalía, and her small eyes flashed inside their folds of flesh, "it wasn't much salt!"

They didn't save the shed but it wasn't for lack of energy. Some dipped buckets from Cipriano's well; others filled vessels from his kitchen sink, though this was largely ineffective because there was never any pressure and the trickle was as slow as Cipriano's father who was hell-bent on coming too, though he had to be lifted into the pickup and lifted out, and he insisted on directing operations and kept yelling "*¡Santiago!*" as loud as his quavery voice could yell.

Some ran for Diego Salazar's well, which was the closest, and attempted to pass buckets along a line but the chain kept breaking because no one would stay in place long enough to wait for the buckets.

The shed was gone. There wasn't much hay left from the winter anyhow, Cipriano said. What was burning with such gusto was in reality four months' garbage which he'd piled up through the winter and this providential fire saved him the trouble of carting it off. Everyone sat back on his haunches to watch the blaze and those who had grabbed beers popped the tops and democratically shared with those who hadn't been so foresighted.

When the flame was spent and settling into senile smolders and the beer reduced to belches, they threw their cans onto the smoking heap like soil on a coffin, uttered a final eulogy, and proceeded back to the party. It was time for the dancing to begin and if, from time to time, some couples were to stray for a little lovemaking out behind the *alamos* feathering the moonlit *acequia*'s edge, they all knew the wise old eyes of Padre Lorenzo would grow vague and turn from those lighthearted lapses of nature.

They headed back for the *baile*. Unfortunately, just as the procession rolled down the dirt trail to the schoolhouse, Cipriano's three goats managed to break their single tether and were trotting belatedly and arrogantly up the same trail toward home. Each parade met the other head on and the lead goat, a cocky billy named Diablo, pranced into the single wavering headlight of Tonito's truck too late for Tonito to apply what was left of his brake pedal which only worked if he pumped it rapidly.

The sharp collision caused several in the back end to lose their balance. José fell over the side into the dirt but he'd been leaning out pounding on the sides loudly and probably would have fallen out anyway. His only injury was a torn sleeve.

Diablo wasn't so lucky. The edge of Tonito's bent fender caught him a breast-piercing impact in mid-prance and threw him into the air before he fell heavily. As the blood began to flow from his sinewy chest he held up his head in the single headlight's beam and gave one surprised beat of agony before he died.

Later Drake Cavanaugh found himself sketching the surprised goat as it leapt in the headlight. Its face looked like Julián's.

5

"So what about the money?" Joe asked. "What happened to it?"

"Nothing," said Drake. "He spent some. Gave some away."

"And hid the rest?"

"Didn't have to. They never stole from him."

"Show me a Mes'can that won't steal whatever isn't nailed down. . . ."

"Have it your way. What about the money he left here?"

"What's it to you?"

"Just curious."

"I bet you are." Joe squinted his eyes the way he used to when he looked at his hole card. He was still thinking about the ante. "I guess if he's interested he better come check it out himself."

Drake grinned. "He just might."

Joe kept looking at his watch. "Look, Mr.—whoever you are. . ."

"Call me Ishmael," he started, but Joe looked blank. "Forget it," he said.

". . . you expect me to believe Drake Cananaugh just disappeared from the face of the earth . . ."

"No, he went back to the earth."

". . . to some burg that doesn't exist . . ."

"No," said Drake. "I didn't say it doesn't exist. You said it doesn't exist."

". . . that Drake Cavanaugh who was a solid citizen turned his back on civilization . . ."

"No, that's what he was looking for."

"Bullshit."

"He found some of that too."

". . . that he abandoned his wife and practice for no reason . . . ?"

"They turned him off," said Drake. "He was just goddamned bored. Law'd become a farce."

"And his wife?"

"She was a farce too. Why is it," he mused, "when so many women decide to become virtuous they no longer find it necessary to be charming?"

Joe looked at his watch again. "I've gotta get back."

"You poor bastard," said Drake.

They paid their bills and walked into the gray wet where a half-hearted rain collected in black puddles. The wind flapped a soggy sheet of old newspaper against Drake's ankle but he didn't notice because he was looking up at the sign. The billboard reared atop a flat-roofed mock-adobe complex that housed the Gas Company of New Mexico, the Sugar-and-Spice Totsy Shoppe, and the Last Frontier Package Store. From that billboard cold gray eyes looked down at him, still condescending, and a message in patriotic red and blue urged all to VOTE FOR LEONA STONE.

"She's running for the legislature," said Joe.

"She always liked her maiden name best," said Drake.

▲

He always remembered when he first saw the Rincón Secreto and the fire they made there.

It was the day after Tonito drove Julián to Española to catch the bus for Taos. Everyone gathered in front of Romero's and some jumped in the back of the pickup. Julián threw in his rope-tied suitcase and guitar and pranced about and laughed and made jokes and bragged about the girls he would screw in Taos and all the time he kept cutting his goat-eyes at Soledad to see if she acted jealous.

Tonito raced his engine and told Julián to get his ass in gear. He said goodbye again and jumped for the cab just as Tonito let up on the clutch pedal which threw him against the door. Drake thought for a moment he looked like the sacrificial goat Diablo in the headlight's beam.

Those in the pickup laughed and shouted, Julián jumped in, and they roared down the road shooting dust and gravel behind them.

In the doorway of Romero's store stood the hunched figure of Teresita and

60

a small strange smile lifted the seamed lips. The hooded eyes kept their own secrets.

▲

She would go to the Rincón for roots and herbs, Soledad told Drake. Did he want to go?

He did, though it was a long trek and he was still weak. They would leave early and sleep that night in the old cabin that sheltered those who took their sheep and goats to graze in the *ciénega*.

They tied food in blankets, and with a bottle of red wine Drake bought from Tomás and in a pickup borrowed from Segundo, they bumped up a trail which was nothing but ruts and brushy growth and spring puddles, through piñons and junipers and scrub oak into an aspen grove until a fallen tree halted them.

They tied the food on their backs and started the walk through the white light of an aspen grove that shimmered and quivered with the delicate life of ever-dancing leaves and throngs of white butterflies rose like bubbles. The way climbed gently for a while, then cut through a log fence into an open expanse where a rancher, a *rico* from the other side of the mountain, pastured horses. They heard the noise of crashing foliage and arrogant neighing and stopped by the edge of a clearing. A bay stallion pawed the ground about his mare and after the neck-biting hoof-flying foreplay, mounted her in a massive mating of sweating flesh and sinew and wild-thrown mane and fire burned behind his white-edged eyes.

Soledad stood straight and she watched Drake and smiled.

They cut through the fence and followed an old Indian trail, little used now. Indefinite as a lingering ghost, it stole through the aspen, then steepened and they left the bright aspen-light and climbed into the pines, the dark militant battalions that guarded the upper slopes. The climb grew steep and the air thin and Drake had to stop often.

Pine needles crunched beneath their footsteps. Quick-darting chipmunks scolded as they passed and raucous birds protested.

He felt intrusive. A deep unease spread through him. Somewhere in the bowels of this brooding forest still strode dark unemasculate gods who sucked the distilled air deep into cavernous chests and breathed out the drunk-making resinous god-breath. Here somewhere still pulsed the promise of a fecund New World.

They crossed a haunted emptiness of black skeletons where fire gods had swept a path and the lonely spirits of dead trees cracked in the moving quiet. Yet already life fed on death and the green of newborn forest pushed like hope through the black ghosts.

Then they came to living pines and beyond them they clambered through a gray rockslide toward the top of the world. He followed, watched the calves of her sleek hard legs push over the rocks with steady rhythm, watched her wide skirt swing from her wide hips, saw her lithe strong silhouette rise above the gray brow.

They stopped the rise and he gasped. There it glimmered, a crag-guarded crater where once, when the old gods were young, fire shot from the mountain's core to the firmament to burn as stars where now the winter snows drained into its deep black cold. They looked down into a *ciénega* where rainbows began, or ended, to the flowered meadow and the lustral pool where the old dark gods still gathered.

Above, the high peaks walled the eyrie and from their snow-patched crevices, from the giant god-gashed cross, icy rivulets sought the lake.

As the seasons circled Drake returned many times to the lake-set Rincón; many times in the timeless time while his life quickened in Descanso he ascended to the high Rincón where grew the god-grown plants that Soledad gathered; and each time it entered him more strongly and he absorbed the Rincón's strength.

But it struck him numb this first time. He couldn't comprehend it yet. He sensed powerful secrets, groped for meanings; he could feel the colors and the quivering emotion. A nearly unbearable yearning washed through him but he didn't know what he yearned for. He stood unmoving.

Soledad let the strength of the Rincón flow up through the soles of her feet into her limbs and loins and watched his awe. She pointed to the pine-fringed edge of the *ciénega* where sagged the cabin, ghost-colored with age and the weight of seasons.

"The horse thieves used it in the old days," she said. No door hung from the rusty hinges but the roof still held over the single room where they lifted the packed blankets from their backs.

Then, carrying burlap bags, they began to dig their harvest from the meadow's soft floor. Soledad showed him what to look for, how to know the feathery flowers of the *yerbe del pescado* with its dark green leaves that flashed white undersides in the rushy air, and the stiff-leaved *inmortal* and the bright-leaved *cañaigre* and the soft-eared *cebadilla*. They gathered branches of the *altamisa*, dug roots of the *yerbas*. Drake watched her move through the gentle-tough fecundity and she, too, seemed gentle-tough and sap-full and soil-sprung.

It was sweat-making work and the sun god poured yellow heat over them and when he reached his noon throne, they rested by the lake. Soledad spread the blanket and opened tins of sardines. They cupped water from the lake and drank from their hands and the great vitality of quiet seemed to rise from that dark lake-womb and suffuse him. He thought of the stallion and his mare. He saw the sunlight pour into the lake, saw its white stream pierce the dark womb, and thought, *Here is the mating place of sky and earth.*

Suddenly, because he could not see beneath the dark lake surface, he knew he must dive into that womb; some instinct deep inside him was drawn by its deep fertility. He unlaced his boots, kicked them off, unbuttoned his flannel shirt, and stripped off his jeans.

Soledad's eyes rippled. "The lake is cold."

He grinned. "My ancestors were Vikings."

She watched him with her deep Indian eyes. He pulled off socks and shorts and thrust birth-naked into the burning-cold ice-black depths and sought the cruel goddess.

He swam deep and crawled blue and breathless onto the spiny grass. Soledad gestured toward the blanket, watched him wrap his quivering new-born body in its cotton folds. She watched him strike a match and cup it in shaking fingers to a cigarette. A light cut through her well-eyes as he had cut through the dark lake and she smiled.

He drew deeply on the cigarette. "The Indians say we emerged from the center in a place like this."

She shrugged. "*¿Quién sabe?* I think so."

"But you're a Catholic. You don't worship the old gods."

"There are many spirits, Carlos."

He laughed. "You sip at the springs of your cross religion, I think. And then you skitter back into the forest and dance with some dark cousin of Pan's."

"I don't know what you mean." Unconcerned, she wrapped a sardine in a tortilla and ate.

As he warmed he tingled. His veins throbbed with rushing blood and the puffy ridges the lion made were purple against his pale shoulder flesh. Above them reared the sharp cross-gashed phallus of the peak. He felt as if he were swimming still in the hot-pouring sun and the immense throbbing quiet. He lay back and closed his eyes and inhaled the blue smoke.

She stared at the herb-healed lion-gashed ridges, he threw off the blanket, and they both saw his reborn potence. Neither moved. The knowledge lay quivering between them like heat waves in white air.

"Are you a *bruja*?" he asked.

"Do you think so?"

"I think so." He smiled his one-sided smile and sucked in another breath of smoke. "And you also belong to Julián."

"I belong to nobody, Carlos." Her husky voice vibrated like a cello and he thought it was true. Like the crimson hollyhocks in her patio, she offered her pollen to whatever bees alit. She was the Mother herself and her fecund earth yielded to whoever would plow.

She pulled the comb from her hair, shook the nightfall around her, and spread her arms in a woman gesture. "*Y acabo*—Julián's gone."

It was a mating place.

Many spirits moved in this silence, moved inside the wall of the thrusting mountain tower, moved deep in the dark lake, in its hidden woman-center, and he hungered for such a center, for some deep woman-soul, deeper than mind, warmer than thought, as he had thrust his tensing body into the lake water, without thought, without will.

Dark and lake-quiet and life-throbbing she sat and waited motionless until he moved to her.

▲

They caught trout for their supper and kindled a fire at the lake's edge. They watched the last rays of the spent day linger on the glistening monolith thrusting above; they saw its deep scars darken. Drake stoked the blaze and, half in jest, poured a splash of wine into the flame and it hissed and rose in a gulp of dark smoke.

"Why did you do that?"

"A libation for the gods." He grinned. "Man learned to ferment the grape soon after Prometheus gave him fire. It was the fittest offering he could invent.

¿Vino, querida? Wouldst tipple with the divine company?" He passed her the bottle and then he drank. It had a thin dark taste, only a step beyond the fruit.

He watched Soledad move about the fire, watched her set out the bread and dip the clear water from the lake for coffee; it would take its time to boil at this altitude. He squatted on the lake edge and cleaned the fish; he sliced sharply up their white bellies and returned the guts to the clear water to settle slowly back into the placental richness.

They drank again. He let the red wine trickle down his throat, into his pumping bloodstream, and he breathed deeply of the winey air in the purpling Rincón, heard the rushy murmur of the rivulet that overflowed the lap of the lake. He absorbed the thickening night.

They drank the red wine and ate the fish and chewed the bread Soledad had baked. "You can't buy real bread anymore," he said. "Not back in civilization."

"Julián likes store bread."

"Puff-stuff slop. Remember the dough that collapsed the day of the party? That you threw to the chickens?"

"It was dead."

"Yes, well, that's what happened to the world. There was a dream once and it rose like the dough, only we forgot it and it collapsed on itself."

He cupped a handful of fire-warmed sand and let it run through his fingers a long moment and thought of generals who weren't allowed to win wars, and laws to protect the guilty, and women who weren't women and schools that couldn't teach and symphony halls where wood-faced musicians played Beethoven's Seventh to deaf diamond-studded ears. "'In the room the women come and go Talking of Michelangelo.'"

"What?"

"Nothing. Do you know why I came to Descanso?"

"Julián brought you. You died almost."

"I did die. I died and was resurrected. I could go back now. I should. By every standard I held before I died, I should go back. But I'm not, Soledad. I'm not going back!"

"You will. When you're well. When it's time."

"I am well. But it's not time. It never will be. There's nothing to go back to, Soledad."

"You got a wife?"

"Not really. Though I'm married."

"You had a wife? And don't any more?"

"Maybe I never did have one." She looked puzzled, and Drake laughed. "We drifted apart."

"She was not a good wife?"

"I was a lousy husband. We didn't like each other much."

"Why did you get married?"

Because she was pretty and lively and fun to take to the Officers' Club; and then when her parents were killed in the car wreck she'd had to cope alone and she was only eighteen and she seemed stunned and soft and sometimes her voice sounded like tears.

"I wanted to take care of her," he said.

"She didn't like that?"

"For a while." Leona had enjoyed being Mrs. Charles Drake Cavanaugh with the money and the prestige but his conversation bored her. She joined clubs and got elected to boards of directors and joined women's lib movements.

"What I called protection she called chauvinism," he said. "There's nothing left. The dream's gone. There's only plastic wrappers of puff-stuff bread that isn't bread, it's just flatulence."

"What?"

"Men came to America great with dreams and they laid blue eggs of promise and they hatched great men." His voice vibrated with its new life. "But then the reformers came and built their institutions and they smothered them. They didn't want real men. So they broke the great blue eggs into fragments and there was no center left."

Soledad giggled. "You make a lot of big words, Carlos!"

"I'm a lawyer." He grinned, reached for the coffee, and poured some into the rusty cups they'd found in the cabin. They let the strong hot liquid warm them inside and they sat closer to the fire, pulled into the small round chamber of its glow. He picked up her square hand, held it between his, and felt the dark pulse in her wrist. They looked into the red flame and the watching became a ritual, a silent reverence as the jets from earth's center were released in sparks that flew toward the fiery stars, the strong male stars, primeval explosions of passion somewhere beyond the gods, stars that would be a long time burning.

An owl hooted softly and she shuddered. *"Bruja,"* she whispered.

"Are you afraid of *brujas*?"

"Everyone is afraid of *brujas*."

"Isn't Teresita a *bruja*?" He smiled.

"Don't laugh, Carlos," she said quickly.

Still he teased her. "Doesn't Teresita teach you the dark arts?"

She crossed herself quickly. "I go to the church." She drew the blanket around her shoulders. Again the owl hooted.

The bowl-shaped moon rose, orange and female—a wet moon, Soledad said. "It tilts, it spills." They drank a little more *vino* and looked to the lake where stars grew deep and the pointed moon gave birth to ripple children.

"Don't look up for the stars, Soledad," he said. "Men can't fly to the stars. We're earthbound. But we can dive to them. Look, they grow deep in the lake, they grow from the earth's core. That's where man finds his stars, *querida*. In the earth."

"I don't know what you're talking about."

"Neither do I." They laughed but it was only a softness in the quiet. They drank more *vino*. They heard the high moan that was far wind above the mountain and they breathed the pregnant smell of rain. The lake grew smoky and the stars submerged in cloud. The cold pierced them in the great loneliness and they fed the fire. He watched Soledad, watched the firelight reflect from her face and shine in her eyes like candlelight through tawny wine and knew she was moonripe. He pulled her to him and once more, like sun-hot hungry earth, she received his seed.

They rolled themselves in blankets, the man and the woman, and slept in the cabin before the storm attacked. They awoke simultaneously with the first brutal crash.

"*¡Ay, válgame Dios!*" she shrieked. "*¡San Bartolomé! ¡Santa Bárbara!*" In the explosion of light he saw her cross herself and clutch her blanket around her, saw her black hair falling about her shoulders. They huddled as far from the doorless opening as they could shrink and gut fear clutched him.

Repeated detonations shook the world. Balls of furious fire boiled and spilled down the steely rock, rolled about the walled Rincón, and raped the roiling lake. Thick black covered them briefly before it was jerked away by the wild demons of brilliance.

Yet in some strange way, with all the destroying forces of the universe crashing about him, Drake thought of creation. *This is how it was in earth's beginning, before the Beginning was even the Word. This is the great renewal of the life-force.* He knew the old gods still bellowed and raged and lusted on these heights, knew it was an act of hubris that he and the woman had dared come to the Rincón. A strange elation washed through him because they had.

The rain came suddenly. It broke against the face of the peak, it choked the deep fissures, it funneled through the chasms to inundate the earth, to fill her deep secret caverns with seminal water. The trickle that had gently sought the lake became a roaring gorge demanding entry. It charged into the frail shelter where the man and woman huddled and somewhere, he knew, it invaded a rocky cave where a tawny-eyed lioness crouched burning with her mate in primeval otherness.

Lyon, lyon, burning bright in the forest of the night. . . .

It poured through the doorway and the explosions of fire and fury reverberated off the mountain walls and tore open the firmament beyond. The only dimension of existence was wind and water and streaming stone and rocking explosion.

Sometime it abated, sometime it was over. The boiling cauldrons of fire swung down the mountain, spent gods rumbled sullenly into distance, tender air sneaked back in the water's wake.

The man and the woman slept again in their sodden nest.

▲

Day rose from somewhere beyond the mountain. It stood naked and morning-washed on the desert floor, shone pink and fresh on the storm-swollen river, climbed gold and young up the mountain and through the aspen, over the dark pines and the slaty rain-glistening rocks, it spilled red and glowing over the purple mountain and into the Rincón.

Soledad stood in the morning, solid and lithe, and her hair fell straight and black. She greeted the dawn for a silent moment as her bronze forebears had stood for centuries on pueblo walls. She twisted the glossy mane into a rope and anchored the knot with her comb.

Drake remembered from some murky past Leona's ritual of alarm clock and shower and hair-dryer and hot curlers and suddenly he laughed aloud. He hadn't laughed in the dawn since boyhood. Soledad turned and smiled.

▲

Drake walked to the little house at the end of Francisco's orchard, stood looking a long moment, turned the knob, and stepped across his own threshold. The supplies that Tonito Valdez had picked up for him lay in a heap on the bare floor. He began to unwrap and stash things—a couple of skillets, kerosene lamp, bedroll, saw, hammer, nails, cans of food, mousetraps.

He looked at the cloudy windows, the dirt-caked corners. There was a lot to do. The challenge of physical work was a new vigor in him and the summer stretched ahead and then the golden autumn. There was time to make tight his house before snowfall.

He didn't examine his actions, didn't look for motives, and beyond acknowledging that he was a complete son-of-a-bitch, didn't want to probe the dank secret corners of his mind where poison spiders spun sticky guilt. He wanted to shed the old knowledge, to refute the old false discarded world.

He wasn't ready yet to question. The physical challenge was enough. Now he only wanted to go back to some instinctual level, to caulk his own shelter and do it with his own sweat, to solve the simple problems of fire and food. Perhaps, entrenched inside this timeless fastness, he would learn to read the minds inside it like maps to his own, to hunt out its mystery and their mysteries, to translate it into charcoal lines and shadings on a virgin page. He would gaze at what he'd caught and try to understand it.

"*¿Qué tal, Carlos?*" Segundo came to help him clean and caulk and calcimine. He'd been promising since the *acequia* was cleared. *Mañana* he'd come, always *mañana*.

In time they would refloor and reroof. Later they'd make adobe bricks, add a bathroom and wire for electricity, and put in a butane tank and a new stove. The transaction bettered them both. He paid Segundo good money and he learned to spin his own cocoon in this old-new world.

Francisco benefited too, for Drake would improve the property and pay good rent. The house had been his father's, had begun to crumble after his mother and then his father made their slow journeys to the *camposanto*. Now it would come alive again.

They took off their shirts to work and Drake pretended not to see the scars on Segundo's back.

"You soon grow black like a *mexicano!*" he teased Drake.

At noon they ate corned beef and crackers and at the end of the afternoon Drake sent one of Segundo's kids for a six-pack and they looked at their work and knocked off for the day. Still later Soledad brought him cheese and a pail of goat's milk and they ate and drank and lay on his bedroll.

When she had gone he lit the kerosene lantern, but it drew clots of millers so he turned it off and washed in cold water and sat on his *portal* and smoked a cigarette. He felt good about the work.

▲

The moon grew full and waned and died and from the dark it was born again and once more filled and shrank. He darkened in the sun and his muscles hardened. He began to know the villagers as he reached for them in their own language. He had studied Spanish when he was an undergraduate but it was head-learned. Now he learned it in the heart.

He talked a lot to Francisco. Sometimes he watched him carve the *santos*, watched the old man's sensitive fingers play across the wood to search the saint inside before he began to carve, watched the shape emerge and the life come, and Francisco talking to it all the time.

"I don' make the *santo*, Carlos. I only just let out what's inside."

Sometimes he helped Francisco irrigate his garden or his orchard and watched the fruit swell. He saw the shaggy black bears that sometimes came down to eat the raspberries from the bushes, the bears that looked so fierce and nibbled so daintily.

"Next year you need ditch-rights," said the old man. "A man must plant his own garden, *¿no es verdad?*"

Meanwhile Drake bought from his neighbors. Sometimes he bought *cerveza* from Tomás and took it to the old man's and together they sat under a tree and smoked and drank the cool brew. Sometimes Francisco reached out his strong gentle hands as if to feel the air, lifted his head to breathe of it deeply, and chatted with the passing birds. The six-pack dwindled and a neat pile of crushed cans grew. Peace began to sink into the soul of Carlos Cavanaugh as the quiet water settled into Francisco's fields.

Other times he walked to Soledad's or he saw her skirt swinging above her strong legs as she wound around the orchard to his house and he knew the fire for him leaped inside her.

He walked sometimes to the trader's, down the rutted road that wasn't much more than a trail, down to where it met the graded access road. The trading post stood in the Y, and a little farther down the back road from the pueblo it meandered up and joined it. He talked to Fergus or watched the Indians who came to trade. A few times he went with him to the reservations. Fergus and Val never asked questions and they marketed for him when they went to Santa Fé or Albuquerque.

Sometimes he had them bring items for his neighbors. "Don't play Santa Claus," Fergus warned. "They got pride. And they'll never trust you if you act like a *rico* trying to buy your way."

So he bought things, ostensibly for himself, that he let them use—a chain saw, or parts for Tonito's pickup or Romero's tractor, because, he explained, he used them too. He bought a butane heater, said it was the wrong kind for his house, gave it to Soledad and paid Segundo to install it.

The summer grew old and he walked along the *acequia*. He watched the beans spread, the chiles grow long and green; he walked by the alfalfa fields and sometimes he glimpsed tarantulas in the tangled fronds; he watched the apples and squashes ripen.

Often he walked to the edge of the cliff, lowered himself to a small ledge that overlooked the valley below where the Quemado sought the Río Grande and the dark mesas beyond that rose from the desert floor like prehistoric beasts; and always he felt its uncreated state, as if the Mover had flung in passion great masses of sheer force and then stood back from his work appalled, awed at the immense living force, afraid to mold it into anything the gods had yet envisioned.

He drew the distant flat-topped mesas. They seemed to promise a leveling off where passions could rest but then they plunged again sheer into the vast infinity of moving desert and laughed at the promise. With his hand he drew, but his soul could not yet comprehend the air so clear it seemed a vacuum, yet shimmered so full with changing light.

The desert had always fascinated him. He'd bought a Cessna soon after he married and loved to watch the desert below. Leona didn't care for it except to get from Point A to Point B; but he loved its feel, loved to watch mesas and hills and sand flow beneath him, loved the moving cloud shadows that stippled the desert and the eternally changing colors.

He sat on his ledge and drew the wind as it rolled across the desert below in overlapping waves, each dust-laden crest swallowing the one before it, watched as it rolled toward them, rose in swells, engulfed Descanso behind him and Pájaro above, and broke against the great immovable peak and bellowed and broke again.

Often he carried his drawing pad to the little church when no service filled it. He drew the blue wooden railing and the altar behind it flanked by the crude, ornate *reredos*, too heartfelt to seem garish. He drew the wood-burning stove with its tin pipe that crawled black up the wall and the long tables that ran at angles to the altar with their patiently embroidered linens and their little families of saints.

He sat on long benches that were stern and hard like the faith they demanded and he heard the whitewashed silence. He copied the *santos* who hung on the wall—San Rafael with the gentle face; the crucified San Acacio; San Cristóbal with his holy burden—and the *bultos* in tin *nichos*. The Virgin of Guadalupe he drew and the *Santo Niño* and the central figure, San Juan keeper of secrets. He drew the *bambolete* that hung from the uneven *vigas* that supported the ceiling with its crossed pine boards where candles gave dim light to the room and life to the *santos* who lived there.

He tried to comprehend the faith that breathed within.

September came, and expanses of yellow aspen forests blazed, brilliant against the pines' dark sobriety. The nights grew chill.

The earth bore chiles and he helped the men pick, helped them haul the mountains of fiery pods for the women to roast. He breathed the sweet aroma that rode the hovering piñon smoke as it rose from chimneys and *hornos*, the intimate piñon smoke that catalyzed the village.

Francisco's apple trees bowed heavy with their load and he helped him fill baskets with the sweet globes. The bristly piñons on the hills below bore thick clusters of tiny sweet nuts and he heard the children sing as they raced the darting chipmunks to gather the bounty.

"*Pepenando piñoncito,*
Para el pobre coyotito."

As the chiles reddened and the apples swelled and the piñons clustered, Drake felt the village swell with its own life. He felt the energy that pumped from the fields and through the *placita* and in the cubic houses molded of the earth herself. He felt the village breathe, felt its sap flow alive in its own center. He felt the life within the node.

He spoke sometimes to the big German priest with the burning blue eyes and the beaked ascetic nose, Father Andreas, who lived in Colinas and flew in a Super Cub a wealthy Santa Fé parishioner provided. One day when the plane landed Drake walked to the *prado*.

"Neat rig you've got, Padre."

"Saves me a bunch of driving. I cover lots of miles." Drake was examining the plane. "You fly?"

"Korea. Air Force."

"Pilot? So was I. Before seminary."

That started their friendship. Drake helped tie down and they traded stories. The priest said one day soon he'd let him take her up. They were two Anglos in a Spanish world, drawn by education and a common war and, though they shared no religious bond, they enjoyed an occasional intellectual chat and sometimes the priest came to Drake's house for a drink of good Scotch whiskey.

The days shortened. "Soon it will snow," said Francisco. He and Drake drove Tomás Archuleta's pickup into the hills for wood. They descended into the valley, followed the river, then cut up the sandy *arroyo* to where the junipers twisted tough arms against the wind.

They came to a weathered board nailed crooked to a tree. "No woodcutting without permit." Francisco spread his hands and grinned. *"No comprendo inglés."* Drake shrugged, shifted the snarling gears, and they bumped past it in second up the rutted trail.

After several hours on the chain saw Francisco said, "I show you something," and they followed the rut up a steep wash. They topped a rise and approached the site from the rear. The weed-strangled remains of a gravel road angled northeast to connect eventually with the road to Las Vegas. They looked down to the *casa grande* where the *rico* had once lived. They left the pickup and walked down the hill. They circled the house, a large two-storied structure of remodeled territorial style, where now the plaster clung like spreading scabs and paneless windows gaped blankly like the eyes of an amnesiac. Beneath a sag-roofed *portal* they squatted to smoke.

"Must have been quite a place once."

"*Sí*. No one was living here a long time until a *rico* came and bought it. That was twenty years ago. He bought apples from my papa and wood. He hired many workmen and repaired the *casa*. But then he went away again."

"Why?"

"*No sé.*"

"It's a lonely place."

"*Sí*. There are ghosts." Francisco drew on his cigarette, blew the smoke curling into the sad air, and his eyes brooded dark. "I made a great sin here once," he said. "Long time ago. Some day I tell you when our wood piles grow tall and the snow comes and the days go slow."

In silence they climbed to the pickup.

One day they pruned Francisco's trees. The scream of the chain saw sliced the cold air. Drake's hands grew numb and it seemed to him Francisco took forever to decide which branches would go. He fingered each, talked to it, debated.

Drake saw a low-hanging branch and angled the saw to cut. Francisco put a hand on his arm. "Not that one." He pointed a crooked strained finger to an old nest. "They worked hard to build that home." His smile was gentle. "They come back in the spring."

The days wound by and then a new knowledge came to Drake-Carlos Cavanaugh.

Soledad came with eggs one afternoon as the sun rode low toward the far valley. They drank some wine and heated beans and fried the eggs. They talked and he listened to her husky laugh. He kindled a fire and, squatting before it, watched it blaze high and remembered the high *ciénega*.

He turned to Soledad. "Do you remember the fire we made at the Rincón? By the lake?"

Yes, she remembered. She closed the curtains she had made for him. The ritual always amused him and he laughed. "Who'd see in?"

"It keeps out the *brujas*."

"No it doesn't," he said. "I've got one right here with me!"

He came up behind her and cupped her full breasts, slid his hands down her waist, over her belly. And then he felt its hardness, felt a thickening, and with a cold wash of horror he knew she swelled with life-seed. The smell of piñon smoke was sharp.

He couldn't speak but only continued to move his hands over her gently swelling belly. His hands comprehended what his mind was not yet ready to acknowledge. They stopped moving, they rested on the small living node, and still he couldn't speak. He breathed the burning piñon smell deeply.

"*Sí*, Carlos." She laughed. "I remember the fire we made at the Rincón!"

6

"*E*ver know a witch?" asked Drake.

"Sure," said Joe, "my secretary. Sometimes Drake called Leona a witch."

"That was before he met a real one. Real witches have style."

"What are you talking about?"

"Witches," said Drake. "*Brujas*. It isn't a word to use lightly."

Joe said he guessed vacuum cleaners had put most of them out of business. He laughed at his joke.

"They don't ride broomsticks," said Drake. "They travel in fireballs. Or become owls."

"You an expert?"

"I knew one," said Drake. "In Descanso lived a witch."

"Oh, sure."

"An old woman. Nobody knew the whole story. But before she died she told an earful to Soledad."

"To who?" asked Joe.

"Soledad. She saved Drake."

"She a witch too?" asked Joe.

"Some people said so," said Drake. "Some people called her a *bruja*. She might have been. I don't know."

▲

On the night Soledad went to the Rincón, Catalina's baby started pushing its way into the world and Segundo fetched Teresita.

Two hours later they quaffed the *vino*, dark like blood. Catalina and the new baby slept in the next room as the rain sluiced across the village. Teresita sat at the table still littered with supper and drank the red wine with Segundo. She didn't know why Segundo always made so much of a new baby, not with all he had already, but they drank the wine to the small new life and then he poured two more cups.

"For you, *vieja*," he said, "that you may still be alive for the next one!"

She clutched the cup with knotty claws and laughed again, a high cackle of age and secret knowledge. "I'll be here for the next," she said, but it wasn't Catalina's next one she thought of. It was the one that she willed might be just beginning this night at the high Rincón. "Old Teresita is not too old to pull another *niño* into the world." She had guided many souls through the dark lonely passages between lives, new souls entering and old souls departing, and she no longer distinguished much between the two. "*Ay, sí*, I'll see the next one in."

The next one would be Soledad's.

She'd told Soledad to take the Anglo to the Rincón. "It is time," she said and grinned with her three teeth showing. "You will finish his cure where the high spirits live!"

She cackled again and looked at Segundo and he sidled his eyes to the crucifix on the wall. *Ay*, they always did. They called her when they needed her help as they had called her for sixty years; but they feared her eyes. After they passed her in the *placita* they crossed themselves, afraid of the *mal ojo*, afraid of the unnatural blue eyes in her dark Indian face, eyes like misplaced pockets of sky in the earth, eyes without expression that saw all and told nothing. Still they fetched her though they hung strips of garlic to guard against the *bruja*.

Fools, she thought, *they think Teresita can't see!*

"You came quick tonight," said Segundo.

"*Ay*, I knew it was her time. Teresita knows these things." She'd seen Catalina in the *placita* early that morning; her hooded old eyes, still sharp like winter sky, noted the drop of Catalina's belly, watched the way she walked, and knew Segundo would come loping down the road that night. When the purple thunder began to roll beneath the mountain and send clouds in sullen clots she knew the time was close.

Things were happening on the mountain and in the valley below. Forces of life were loosening. She waited.

Teresita drained the *vino* from her cup. Through the window the lightning sliced the night, the peak caught its fire, and she felt the power in her, felt it still rise in her bony body, in her blue-knotted hands that curled like claws around the cup.

The thunder crackled and one of the sleeping children cried out but none awakened.

In time the rain tired and the spent storm limped down the valley and left only low clouds that swathed the black village in dun folds. Teresita wound the *rebozo* about her, pulled it around her humped shoulders and over her brow and mouth; her beaked nose and hooded eyes showed sharp between the folds like those of a crag-hovering vulture.

In her own hut she lit a lantern and in its flicker the spirits moved quietly in the herb fronds that hung from her *vigas*; in the hillocks of leafy debris they breathed in deep window and dark corner; in fragments of hoof and bone; in the sheep skull and in the fangs and rattles from the *biberón*, the giant poison snake. Everything has its use and only fools pass by the instruments left by the silent spirits. *Ay*, she thought, *it is true, what is waste for a fool is wealth for the wise.*

Some of it she strewed for its effect on those like Segundo who came for her help. He'd noted it well and paid her accordingly. She turned the rusty key in the carved chest in the corner behind her bed, pulled from it a coffee can, and deposited the money on top of the wad inside.

Ay, válgame, she was spent. The power had drained from her but she was not ready for sleep. Her knotty blue veins still throbbed with the dying vibrations as a chicken flops when the head is gone and the life jerks slowly out. She poked at the coals in her stove until they glowed orange and she set the dented tin pot of old coffee in beside them until it warmed. She poured it into the stained cup.

It helped drive the night chill from her bones. *Ay*, Soledad and the Anglo would sleep in a wet nest tonight! She grinned: Soledad's young blood would warm them!

Her power had been strong this day. She'd boiled the *toloache* with the fangs of the rattlesnake and measured it with care. She took the long rope of twisted yucca fiber from its peg on the wall, curled it into a large ring, and sat in the center. She rubbed the stone over her body and looked deep into its eye, blue like her own, until the spirit flowed between them and her soul left her body and flew with the owl and she was among the aspens beckoning Soledad and the Anglo up through its golden light, on to the pasture where the horses ran, where with all her energy she willed their spirits to mate, to quicken the sluggish blood of the man that he might be cured that day.

Her spirit grew lighter as she traveled up through the pine forest, over the rockslide; she floated over the shimmering *ciénega*, over the lake reaching deep into the secret earth caverns.

The Rincón was a strong place, a high place where spirits lived and her own powers fused with theirs. She led the man and woman to the herbs, not as strong as in the autumn but strong enough, let them inhale her will through their pale dusty scents. She glided fishlike through the water, deep into the dark center. She grew young again in its arcane deep, ripe and desirable, and she glinted golden, blue, beckoned the man to her. She saw through the darkness with the eyes of the owl. . . .

All her powers poured into the Rincón before they returned to her motionless body; and still they surged through her when it grew night and the storm brewed on the peak and her spell was done.

The strong coffee flowed through her drained body. She was old, lonely, tired—too tired for the great force of will she yet needed before the life spirit left her body to join the life at the other end of the gray passage. She had not yet awakened the untapped spirits in Soledad, had not yet generated their life, like flame, by friction of her will. This she still must do before she could pass the polished blue sky-stone to her.

Teresita kicked her shoes under the bed, peeled the thick stockings from her vein-knotted legs, and hung her black skirt from the peg above her bed. She lay in a small bony heap and slept.

▲

The power had first entered her when she was a girl and her blood was hot for the young man at the pueblo. But Juan was afraid of her; they all were. They thought her ugly and strange because of her startling blue eyes. When she was born her mother, seeing the infant's pale stare fixed on her face, fell sick and died and the people said she was witch-entered, though her father, who was a *cacique*—a leader of the healers—told her it was ignorance that made such talk.

Juan avoided her and let his dark eyes follow Placida and passionately Teresita willed evil to the girl. "May something strike her dead!" she cried.

Her father, squatting on the dirt floor in their dark room, spoke sharply. "Angry spirits may hear your dark thoughts," he said. "Such words can fly on evil wings," and he made a prayer stick to drive away any lurking *sawish* and warned her not to listen to Coyote.

She said no more, but her blue eyes followed Placida sullenly.

A few weeks later a rattlesnake struck Placida as she carried water from the ditch and though the priests waved eagle feathers over her and intoned the aid of the bear and the badger, after many hours of agony she died screaming.

Teresita ran terrified and hid in a willow clump by the river. One cannot run from one's own dark heart, she learned; and as she huddled on the sandy bank her terror receded, her natural toughness of soul began to rally and her sharp mind to work. She had not caused this thing, she reasoned; she lacked the knowledge. Had a witch heard and done her bidding? She gazed into the river where witches live. She crept to the edge, scooped a handful of sand, and tossed it into the stream. Nothing came. She must learn the ways to summon them.

Could there be within her some unusual strength of will that sped like a strong-shot arrow, gathered life as it flew, and became a deed? Then should she not learn to use it? Should she not fine her skill as the hunter perfects his aim?

Some looked at her darkly, remembering her strange sullen looks. She heard the whispers and stood apart. She looked with scorn at those of weaker wills and blunter minds, watched them with secret eyes, observed their ways, and noted their weaknesses. She learned to live with the loneliness.

Her father sensed these strange thoughts and latent powers, knew they must be channeled, and began to teach her the healing properties of the plants, the magic of bone and feather and fang. He directed the forces within her toward the good spirits that abide in everything.

"Learn the ways of the birds," he said. "Become an eagle if you would soar and see. Learn the ways of the human heart if you could cure it."

In time he gave her the sky-stone. "It is sacred," he said. "Sun Father impregnated Earth and left his blue sky-seeds in her. The serpent Awanyu guards the water-wombs and sometimes he gives the precious stones to men of healing. Use it well and know it must return one day to the deep waters to be given again. Know its spirit and use it only for good."

For the most part she had.

Her knowledge of herbs and of the human heart grew vast. As a rule she healed with the white arts but the dark heart calls for darker skills; sometimes, when passion or necessity drove her, she summoned the dark spirits though it was a great deal more trouble. She learned the art of the *mal ojo* and the ways of hooting owls; and only a fool would be deaf to Coyote as well as the Eagle. She passed no medicine by.

▲

Soledad came down from the Rincón with bags of herbs and certain roots and a tired and sunburned Carlos. When dark settled, Teresita walked to her granddaughter's house and peered silently in the window, a hunched figure with beaked nose and hooded eyes. While she waited, Soledad, followed by Carlos, came from the kitchen and pulled shut the white curtains. The sharp old eyes had seen what they searched for.

Teresita smiled.

The Anglo's cure had been a long one and a less skilled *curandera* would not have managed it. She put all her knowledge into it, bent all her will, summoned her deepest energies and sent them beating into his own thin pulse. Though Soledad used the right treatments, Teresita called the spirits.

Soledad was no *simplona* though sometimes she acted one. She had the powers. Teresita could feel them, had recognized the wells within her even when she was a *niña*, had known they flowed deep. Of her five grandchildren Soledad was the one with promise and she took her into the mountains and valleys, along *acequia* and *arroyo* and *río*, into high *ciénega* and flat desert, and taught her every plant that grew. She showed her the creatures living and dead, talked of the spirits that pervaded the earth, and waited for the girl to awaken to them.

She watched her grow and learn. She was the only thing in the universe that Teresita loved.

Soledad remained unaware of her own untapped forces. She'd had things too easy, thought the old woman. She'd never been isolate, never had to peer darkly into the human soul that her own might survive.

She had never known the loneliness.

▲

When Teresita was still a girl a mysterious sickness killed many. A *cacique* blamed it on *brujas*; some saw the balls of fire they traveled in. A number of people were questioned, among them Teresita, because of long suspicion and the blue eyes and because her father was one who died.

She stood silent before the *cacique* and her emptiness swelled in her breast like a malignant knot. She remembered the sad patient eyes of her father as he watched strutting *mexicanos* through the years and the crude Anglos who came to his land and swaggered in his pueblo; and he learned the sadness of change. "It is spun into our lives, little one," he told her. "One cannot remove it without tearing the web of life." He counseled silence when the heart is sore. "The snake who shakes his rattles is the quickest killed."

She remembered and stood straight and endured the ache and held her words inside.

They would have flogged her but the tall priest in the brown robes forbade it and sent her off to the mission school.

She stood apart there, too.

When she was hired out to serve at the table of a rich *ranchero*, she ran off in defiance and tossed away her virginity to the *mexicano* who drove the cattle. After a week he deserted her in Colinas but she hid in a barn and stole enough to eat until Patricio discovered her.

Ay, she'd learned enough of humans to know both sides of the heart.

▲

Autumn came and Soledad dug roots along the river and brought them to her grandmother.

The old lady patted the soft roundness of her belly. "You caught a *niño* at the Rincón?" She grinned.

Soledad shrugged. "There or from Julián."

"Fool! The Anglo is rich." She put coffee on to warm. "It was the Rincón," she snapped. "You think Teresita doesn't know?"

"If I don't, how can you?" Soledad sat on the bed and watched Teresita poke at the fire. "It makes no difference who plants the field."

"*¡Mal ajo!* To have such a fool of a granddaughter! Drink the coffee and listen to me." She sucked up her own brew greedily. "I am old, *nieta*, and tired. I would see you a grand lady, if you do as I say. I have seen into Carlos, I read his heart. He will atone with money. . . ."

"Not for Julián's get."

"It is not Julián's," she screeched. "Do you think Teresita doesn't know when the seed was sown? Do you think I was not there? That I did not ride high with you in the Rincón?"

Soledad's eyes grew afraid.

"Would I fail you with my powers?" She let her blue eyes bore into Soledad's. She walked to the chest, pulled the key from her deep pocket, and turned it in the lock. She watched the girl cross the room and put her cup on the table. She pulled the blue stone from its cache, followed Soledad, and held it before her face. "Do you think I don't see well with this sacred eye?"

She saw Soledad's eyes widen with the old fear and put a claw on her arm. "It is good power, *amada*. One day it will be yours."

Soledad pulled away. "It is evil!"

"Not evil, *carita*. Touch it, feel its power." She told how it came from the deep water, how the serpent gave it to her father for healing, how he would someday take it back. "But until he does, *amada*, its power is ours!"

Soledad crossed herself and backed toward the door.

"Come back, *carita*. It is for you old Teresita works."

Soledad ran from the hut.

The ancient loneliness swept through Teresita. One could not force the power. Soledad must accept it, must open her soul and let it swell through.

Ay, much yet to do, and she was so tired, so lonely.

She sat and rubbed the smooth blue stone.

▲

It had frightened her the first time, too.

Before her father died, she walked along the river hunting an elusive plant. About to return defeated, she fingered the stone. It felt warm, alive. She pulled it from her pocket, looked deep into its god-eye, and let the blue stream flow between them.

She knew her own eyes were weak, that she must see with the far-scanning eye of the eagle. Wondering, she inscribed a circle in the sand as her father had taught her and sat in its eye. She passed the stone over her body that the all-spirit might envelop her, gazed into it until she saw the tawny eagle, until she merged with him, mounted his high-soaring magnificence, until she swept high above the river, and circled its littoral for the small white blossom . . . until she knew where to walk.

When she found the plant an eagle feather lay golden beside it in the sun. She carried strong medicine back to her father.

82

He looked into her eyes, new-wise with sight, and smiled his spare smile. "You have accepted the gift," he said. "But great gifts work only in lonely souls. You must receive them together."

She feared this power that consumed her.

▲

October came with false gold and morning ice.

Teresita hobbled bent-backed through the *placita*. Doña Rosalía nodded, pulled her *rebozo* closer, slid her small fat eyes from Teresita's, and hurried nervously on her way. José Villareál slouching outside the wall around the churchyard straightened and swaggered but fear darkened his brooding eyes. She grinned and let her three yellow fangs show. José crossed himself.

In front of the store Julián pranced. His summer was a great success, he told his friends; the people came to the *restaurante* just to hear him and they stayed late and bought many drinks, caught in his moods and rhythms, charmed with his goat-eyes that overbrimmed with the melancholy strains and laughed with the lively ones. His music stirred the ladies with seductive anticipation so they looked warm-eyed at their escorts who invited him to their tables between songs and bought him many drinks.

Bernie Weinfeld was keeping him on through the winter; he had a week's vacation in which to radiate glory on Descanso.

Teresita hobbled on, watching from her hooded eyes, willing his attention. This *cabrón* wasn't going to ruin her plans. She turned into his papa's store and knew he would follow.

Antonio made a pleasantry about the cold mornings.

"I see Julián is home," she observed.

"*Pues*, not for long." Julián came in and Teresita moved toward the rear shelves and watched them both. "He is too important now to help his old papa," Antonio complained.

"*Mañana*," Julián promised. "*Mañana* I cut wood." He cut his eyes to Teresita who reached for coffee. "*Buenos días, vieja.*"

"You go to Taos again?"

"*Sí.*"

"*Ay*, just as well. As things are." She fixed her blue stare hard on him.

"What do you mean?" He walked toward her a few steps.

"You have seen Soledad?"

"But, *sí*!" He grinned widely. She continued to fix him with her sharp knowing eyes. "What do you mean, *abuela*?" He said it low with an oblique look at his father who listened behind the counter.

"I mean nothing, Julián," she whined. "I'm only an old woman."

"An old woman who sees much."

She pulled a knotted rag from her pocket and counted out coins for her coffee. "Good day to you, Antonio." She turned and looked hard at Julián a moment before she left.

Ay, he would come to Teresita before the day was out! She grinned.

▲

She couldn't remember when they first called her *bruja* in the village but it was after Patricio had gone. It was Patricio who had taken her to Descanso.

He had found her in Colinas after the *vaquero* abandoned her, where in the early dark of autumn she sought creature warmth with a nursing goat and shared its milk with her kid. Teresita must have made a human noise as he saw to his mule in the next stall for he walked around a partition, a tall stern *mexicano*, and the lantern accentuated the sharp planes of his face.

He jerked her toward him. "What the devil? *¿Qué va?*"

She was frightened but she stood tall and looked at him mocking and said nothing.

"Answer me!" he commanded. Still she stood quiet but tears welled in her strange blue eyes and his voice gentled. "You're only a child," he said.

Her anger flared. "Look again, *señor*," she snapped, and he threw back his head and laughed. "And don't make so much noise," she said. "You'll call the ghosts from their graves!"

"How did you get here?"

"By my own will and none of yours!"

"But, *por Dios*, by mine you'll answer! Have you run away?" She didn't answer. "Are you hungry?"

"What do you care?"

"*¡Por Dios!* Because I'll see you're fed!"

He pulled her across the frost-hardened soil and in the kitchen's yellow light she saw he was handsome, more handsome than any man she had ever seen.

84

"Porfirio," he called, and as she jerked back he tightened his hold. "Stop snarling," he said. "He's my uncle. It's his house."

An old man came through the door. "Bless me, Patricio, what's this?"

"I've caught a little night bird, *tío*, nesting in your barn."

As they pondered what to do with her she devoured the hot stew, absorbed the fire's heat, and watched the planes of Patricio's face change like a tall crag when the lightning dances about it.

They learned as much as she wished them to know: that she had never known a mother, that her father had quit this earth, that she had no home. Porfirio mentioned the mission school and without thought she blurted, "No!"

So that's the way it was. "It's no place for a wild little bird," said Patricio slowly. "Sleep tonight, *pajarita*, you're safe with us." They made her a bed of blankets by the fire.

After they went to their own beds she watched the fire burn itself out and she saw in it the mobile face of Patricio. She clutched the blue stone in her pocket and turned all her energies toward him where he slept in the next room.

Not knowing what else to do with her, Patricio took her to Descanso to his mother who had neither room nor use for her and she berated Patricio for burdening her with this stray, until Teresita cured Emilia Gonzales's child of running sores even the *curandera* from Pájaro had been unable to heal. After that the villagers accepted the Indian girl with the strange eyes who could cure their maladies, though they remained uneasy in her presence.

▲

"Beware the *toloache*," her father told her once. "Too much can kill. Use only in extreme necessity." It opened the mind, she knew, to visions of delight or horror which could be directed by knowing suggestion.

She gathered the dust-green plants with the bell-shaped flowers and dried them carefully in the corner of Señora Matta's long kitchen. She kept her straight slim body clean and she washed her hair in the *amole* root which made it shine like the high lake at midnight. She made herself useful for Señora Matta and desirable for Patricio. She pulled two hairs from her head, cut them in tiny pieces, dropped them in his red wine, and waited.

When the red rash appeared and their throats swelled painfully she dosed several of the villagers and when Patricio grew ill she nursed him. As the fever lightened she made a broth and boiled it in the *toloache*. She administered it carefully and guided certain thoughts into his ripening vision, conjured certain images in his expanding desire, and he saw her as a woman.

In the fall they were married in the little church—though when Patricio said his vows he did not look at her eyes.

Within the year Teresita bore a son. During the next years several pregnancies terminated abruptly until finally a puny daughter made her apathetic way into the world. By that time Patricio often slept apart. Her mother-in-law smirked.

Teresita and Dolores Matta fought over the boy and each carried her complaints to Patricio who began to wish all women to the devil. He sided increasingly with his mother and each time his wife miscarried he looked at her strange eyes which now seemed to him veiled and a devil question plagued him.

She knew his growing revulsion and tried to pull him close though she was by nature isolate. Twice she boiled the *toloache* for him and each time she conceived. But when she miscarried the questions again invaded his mind. He began to avoid her sharp blue gaze.

Once more she conceived by this trickery, but it was the last time. Distaste grew to fear, and only whiskey gave Patricio courage; and often to prove he wasn't afraid he grew violent.

His mother blamed Teresita. "Never before was he this way," she spat. "The *bruja* has cast a spell on him!" Her neighbors shook their heads and agreed. They began to turn from her and to cross themselves when she passed by.

Still they called for her when they were sick.

One night Teresita and Patricio quarreled violently. "*¡Bruja!*" he screamed, and then with widening eyes he repeated it in a whisper. "*¡Bruja!*" The next morning he was gone, and their son with him.

They never saw Patricio or the boy again. His mother shrieked and railed and accused "the Indian slut" for days until Teresita picked up the infant girl and moved into the tiny shack she called home after that. No one contested her possession; the hut was ghost-ridden and long deserted. She caulked the holes, covered the leaks with flattened tin cans, and grew conversant with the ghosts.

She went less often to the church. She had no use for its spells—her own were more potent—and she cultivated her isolation. In time she no longer went at all.

The whispers began. Though the villagers sought her cures, they believed she also cast spells, and lips began to frame the word her mother-in-law had heard Patricio scream, and repeated: *¡Bruja!*

▲

Julián came as the deep scars in the mountain filled with purple and the crags gleamed in the dying sun.

Teresita sat in the only chair. Through the dirty window the rusty light of old sun threw an orange beam on the sheep skull on the hearth. She looked at him sharply and saw signs of the life he led in Taos. He puffed above his tight jeans and soft flesh was beginning to pouch beneath his eyes

"You've come to plague old Teresita," she grumbled.

"No, *abuela*. I pay you my respects."

"Bah," she said,. "Do you think old Teresita doesn't know you're here to raise ghosts best left in peace? Go your way."

"You think I should know something?"

"I think you should know a great many things you'll never learn. The light mind only floats on air."

"You hinted at something. . . ."

"I've forgotten." She lowered the dry lids over her eyes.

"Tell me, *abuela*."

"Best to leave things alone."

"Tell me."

"You'd have me speak ill of my own. . . ."

"Ah, of Soledad!" He smirked. "Tell me!"

"I am old," she whined. "I am no longer certain of things. My eyes grow dim."

"You see everything." He crossed the room and recrossed. Twigs crunched beneath his boots and released their pungent dust. He stood above her sitting bent-shouldered in the straight tall chair. "What of Soledad?"

"Use your own eyes, *cabrón*." She raised her eyelids and looked him full in the face until he turned away and her words followed him across the graying room. "You have seen her."

"*Sí.*"

"What did you see?"

"She swells with my son!" He flashed the arrogant grin.

"*Ay*, she swells."

"It was the night before I left," he bragged.

She cackled. "You look and cannot see."

"What do you mean, *abuela*?" He turned toward her suddenly.

"That men should see with more than their eyes."

"You've dark knowledge."

"Is it dark knowledge you want?" Her eyes gleamed like fireballs. "Then go to Soledad. But leave the curtain open. Don't shut out the *bruja* if you would borrow her eyes! Now leave an old woman in peace."

She'd sown the dark seed. Let it sprout in the soil of his own mind.

▲

Ay, verdad, the trouble men caused! Julián wasn't the first she'd managed.

Teresita had felt the old loneliness after Patricio left. She supposed she had loved him and there was the humiliation of desertion. She grew more isolate.

It was the last time she would try to enter the heart of another or open her own to any man. Once more she donned the loneliness like an old coat. She would live apart; she would rear the child and do well for her but she would never let her come into the inner rooms of her own secret soul.

She came and went about the village. She cured the ill and delivered the babies and sometimes the young girls came to her secretly for spells to cast on indifferent young men or faithless lovers. Always she watched. She put on the eyes of the eagle to read men's thoughts and when the eagle soared too high she learned to see with the eye of the hawk, to swoop on the rotting stinks of darker secrets. Her flesh grew thin and her beak sharpened. She hooded her blue gaze under heavy lids and she began to stoop. She became the most skilled *médica* in the hills, the best *partera*, and she mastered the black arts, too.

Some said the sickness that flew through the villages after the Great War was witch-spread and some looked at her in terror. Fools! But the greater their fear the greater her power.

She plied her trade and reared her daughter Juanita who was a fool who could never fend for herself. The saints and devils knew she needed a man to depend on but no man sought Juanita. She was too placid. She lacked the heat that could have dispelled their fears of Teresita. Then Panfilio Quintero came from Santa Fé on a handsome black horse, built himself a house, and began to look about for a woman to cook his food and warm his bed.

Here was a man who feared not man nor *bruja*! She turned her strong will on him. Here was the man to sire her grandchildren.

All the girls giggled when Panfilio rode through the *placita*. They sighed and let their dark eyes invite him. He looked through them and went about his business which often took him off for days.

He rode off on Bello, sometimes straight toward the peaks, with gear for hard riding and sleeping on the trail, and it was told that he knew all the hidden passages through the mountains. He always returned with money and bought drinks for everyone at the *cantina*. He got drunk with them but he never said where he went, though some suspected, and when they made insinuations he grinned widely, winked a laughing eye, and let his fame grow on speculation.

It was a technique Teresita appreciated. She watched him and she waited and she timed his trips; when he rode for the mountain on a yellow July day she calculated his return.

For three days she gathered plants along the trail until she heard hooves tearing through dry underbrush; when he came jogging down the path at an easy pace, over-assured and smoking a corn-husk cigarette, she crouched by the path smiling. As Bello came abreast, she straightened. The black horse shied and Panfilio landed on his shoulder cursing.

Teresita laughed aloud. "You ride like a woman!"

"You cackle like a *bruja*," he growled.

"Let me feel your shoulder."

"It will mend itself." He limped toward Bello.

She turned her blue gaze full on him. "Whose herd grew smaller this trip?"

He looked straight back at her. "What do you know of my business?"

"That you are the most skillful horse thief in these mountains. That you sell them for high prices in the north!"

He laughed. "And do you move in the fireball and see through the eye of the eagle?"

"Or his cousin the owl. Did you bring much money?"

"Enough." A woodpecker hammered a pine above them and the clatter echoed in the forest. Brush crackled under Bello's restless feet.

"Go your way," she said. "I have medicines to gather. Come tonight and I'll poultice your shoulder."

"It will mend. I'm no woman."

"You're afraid of me like the rest," she taunted. "The shoulder will swell."

It did and he came. Their eyes saluted each other, acknowledged the other's professionalism. Juanita, neat, placid, and unaware, followed Teresita's instruction. Her hand was steady on the poultices and she was quiet. Here was one who neither talked nor giggled.

Teresita watched and smiled her secret smile.

▲

Only the last of the five children born to Juanita and Panfilio smoldered with his intelligence and animal fire. Marta was a fool and the three boys obedient and dull but Soledad moved to her own sensuous rhythm. She followed Teresita's movements with solemn dark eyes and preferred her grandmother's hut to the comfortable house Panfilio built with paned windows and wooden floors and smooth walls that embraced a patio.

Teresita taught her how to find the herbs in hidden places, how to dry them, and which to use for what. And she showed her the blue stone. Soledad never liked to touch it. She feared it as she feared to touch a still snake lest it suddenly writhe with life. Teresita smiled. It was only a turquoise to others but some sleeping power in Soledad sensed that which slept within the stone.

Teresita smiled and waited and something in her own lonely life awakened as a withered desert plant uncurls when at last the rain falls. Her heart expanded, her sharp eyes softened as she watched the child grow like a small animal, and her soul exulted as she saw her grow to sensuous maturity. *Ay*, here was the woman-soul!

Then Soledad married Filemón—a nobody, fumed Teresita, a fool. *Ay*, well, a fool sets his own snare and a little push could spring it.

Even Panfilio, who was no fool, had shaped his own. Grown sleek from the grass of other men's pastures, he bought a shiny red automobile. One freezing night he drove with Juanita up the mountain from Española. Over-assured, as he had been the day Teresita unseated him from Bello, he drove too fast, slid on an icy curve, and plunged to the desert below. They both died instantly.

Soledad and Filemón moved into Panfilio's house.

Filemón liked to play the big man in the *cantina*. He had a weak head when he drank, a loud mouth, and a wild temper and, like many weak men, he was alert to slights. A few words from Teresita hinting at some sneer from one of his friends could arouse his insulted honor. After a few drinks he usually sought a fight; fights in Descanso could turn ugly and violent.

Teresita waited.

The time came and she planted the seeds, and Filemón's own nature destroyed him. He did as she had known he would.

▲

Julián did not take the straight path from Teresita's to Soledad's but walked toward the church, circled it, and turned toward Soledad's. Teresita, her old bones wrapped against the autumn cold, watched his circuitous progress and made her way by another route.

One with the night, she stood silent behind a thick cottonwood and watched him approach Soledad's door and stand clenching his fists until he flung inside. In the shadow Teresita moved silently to a window and waited bent like a vulture on a limb. She smelled the sharp cold and the piñon smoke. Her claw rested on the rough wooden sill. An owl hooted.

Soledad moved to feed the fire. Julián watched her silhouetted against the light, looked again at the swell of her ripening belly, and his eyes tightened minutely at the corners. He followed her, let his hands move over her shoulders and breasts. She moved sensuously against him as a cat moves. He reached for the *santo* to turn it to the wall but then his hand stopped and through the window Teresita saw his eyes tense again. She saw him remember her words as Soledad moved toward the window and grasped the white curtain.

"No!" he barked. "Leave it open!"

Soledad turned her head toward him, her hand still on the curtain. "I heard the owl hoot."

"Are you afraid of *brujas*, Soledad?" he asked softly.

"*Brujas* see inside."

"What are you afraid they'll see?" He strode toward her. "Tonight it stays open!" He tore the material from her hand and it made a ripping noise. His voice grated. "Tonight I will borrow the *bruja*'s eyes!"

Teresita smiled in the night.

Soledad stood ripening and sensuous and her full mouth curved taunting. "What are you trying to see, Julián?"

"Whose seed swells in your belly? Whose?"

She smiled. "Yours, maybe."

"And maybe. . . ?"

"Ask the *bruja*, Julián!" she taunted. "Or the *santo*. But he won't tell, will he?"

He slapped her once, hard, and her face streaked red but she only stood there taunting. Then she spit at him, a great mouthful of scorn aimed hard at his face and she laughed while the spit ran down his cheek. He strode to the fireplace. He grabbed the *santo* and screamed out a curse. He pounded the little statue furiously against the fireplace; he beat it until its pulpy chunks lay lifeless on the hearth. Its colors streaked the white plaster like smears of blood. One battered eye stared up.

Julián's hands trembled and his eyes filled. "*¡Bruja!*" he shouted. He was hoarse and his goat-eyes held pain.

Teresita smiled. She hobbled home clutching the warm stone in her cold claw.

▲

Soledad was brushing up the *santo*'s remains when Teresita arrived next morning. Her sharp eyes darted while Soledad fetched coffee; they noted the pile of lifeless wood, the marks like blood on the white plaster, the curtain that drooped torn and sad. "That Julián!" said Teresita. "What a tantrum!"

"What do you know of it, *abuela*?" Soledad's husky voice was sharp.

"I still have eyes, *bella*. They say he was wild at the *cantina* last night." She drank the coffee with little sucking noises. "His father is angry."

"His father is always angry."

"He goes back to Taos. Today."

Soledad shrugged. "He feels important there."

"Julián bloats on his own magnificence." Teresita carried her cup into the kitchen and she was there when Julián came around bloodshot and stubble-chinned. She stood quietly out of sight and listened.

"I'll mix *trementina* and *punche* for your head," said Soledad.

He hadn't come for that, he said. He was repentant. He would believe Soledad if only she would tell him. He hadn't meant to snatch the curtain.

The curtain would mend.

He had let in the *bruja*. It was the *bruja* who had poisoned his mind. "Here, I'll keep her out," he said. He made a cross of two splinters from the hearth, fastened them with a thread from the curtain, and put it under the small rug inside the door. "She can't come in now." Everyone knows witches cannot walk over a cross. "And the *santo*. . . ."

It was too late to save the *santo*—but she'd thrown a splinter of him into the fire. San Juan had kept the secret.

Julián would never know!

Teresita stole quietly out the kitchen door.

Soledad went to her in the afternoon. "What do you know of it, *abuela*?" Her voice was low and harsh. "Julián is gone. He would have married me."

"And burdened you with another weakling like Filemón."

"Julián needs my strength. They'll swallow him in Taos. His new friends and the new life and his new importance—he can't handle that world, *abuela*!" Small streams flowed down her cheeks.

"And you think you'll save him?" Her voice was scornful. "You want to save someone?" Her voice crooned, and she smiled and her three teeth were pointed. "Save someone who can be useful, Soledad. Carlos can make you a fine lady."

"I don't want to be a fine lady and I don't want Carlos. And he doesn't want me."

"He'd like his son."

"How do you know it's his?"

"*¡Basta!* I know."

"Yes, you're working your old dark powers again, and Julián. . . ."

"Julián works his own dark powers. You think you love Julián? It's a stupid word, a word for fools!" The words hung crimson in the air.

Her voice softened. "I had a father once, *carita*. I loved him as a puppy follows his mother. He was a good man. He taught me many things. But I warmed in his warmth, I used his strength. I did not grow strong until he died. I learned then to gather the hidden secrets I might have passed by.

"I thought I loved Patricio, your grandfather. I did not mind that he slept with other women. Men do. But he left—he ran away, he took my son. He shamed me in the village. I learned to do without the opinions of the village. I grew stronger! As you must do!"

"No, *abuela*. You grew bitter, you turned to evil powers."

"The powers are within." Her voice rose and cracked. "They are in me and they are in you, Soledad. You must take them, you must use them!" Her eyes bore into Soledad's.

"No!" Soledad's voice sank, and she whispered as she backed to the door. "I will not! I will never come near your powers! Leave me be, *abuela*, don't touch me again!"

She was gone.

Teresita stared at the empty door. She sank into her rigid chair, clasped its arms with her knotted hands, and her beaked head bent forward. She was old, old. She talked of love, of strength. But her strength ebbed weakly now. The only thing she loved had run away.

A long time after, Soledad told these things to Drake.

"Was she really a *bruja*?" he asked.

Soledad didn't answer.

7

"*L*eona's speaking tonight," Joe said. "At the high school."

"Maybe I'll go."

Joe said, "See you around," and turned into the bank. Its jaws closed over him. Drake limped on through the tired rain and wondered what cause Leona was riding now and thought maybe he really would go listen to her speech. First he'd get a motel room.

He grinned and thought about the speeches he used to make when he was a desirable citizen—until the last one.

It was a Chamber of Commerce dinner. They'd hosted a realtors' and developers' convention and he was MC and bored as hell. He didn't like developers because they were the bastards that were slicing up the world and peddling it like chunks of watermelon. He said, "Welcome to the Land of Enchantment," and then he'd led off with a funny story which was the right formula but the wrong story.

"The Garden of Eden was right here along the Río Grande," he said. "One day Eve was pruning the roses while Adam was out hunting arrowheads, useless as always, and suddenly a serpent slithered up and handed her his card and said, 'Eve, you're letting a good piece of property go to waste.'

"'What do you mean?' asked Eve.

"'I mean, if you'd subdivide this place and get it zoned right and build a few condominiums, it would sell like apples.'

"'What are apples?' asked Eve.

"'Like the Big Apple,' said the serpent. 'And you need a good boutique. Your buyers won't want to go around in fig leaves. You could make this place real uptown. We can call it Plutopia.'

"'You got a realtor's license?' asked Eve. 'Well, I've got power of attorney.' And by the time Adam got home she'd contracted it out, installed parking meters, and named it Albuquerque. And God moved out and let them have it."

"That was the worst story I ever heard," Leona said when they got home. "It was in very poor taste, and I've never been so humiliated in my life. I don't know what's wrong with you."

Nothing at all, he said, he was just a genuine card-carrying bastard, and she said as irresponsible as he'd gotten it was a blessing God had denied them children.

"It wasn't God," he said, "it was the Pill."

"That's just another example of your bad taste."

He said, maybe so, but he didn't think she ought to lay it on God because she was too busy with Mental Health and Planned Parenthood and the Country Club Board of Directors to have time for children. Or sex either.

She didn't speak for about a week which wasn't unusual or even particularly inconvenient. Besides, she was right, he was a son-of-a-bitch. The trouble came when she decided to forgive him.

She bought a new nightgown, a black thing with yards of nylon. He'd just as soon make love to DuPont Chemical Company, he thought, though he didn't say so; but it had all the zing of a flat Alka-Seltzer and he just couldn't get it on.

"You can't plan a seduction scene," he said, "like a country club board of directors meeting. We will now come to order and read the minutes of the last meeting. There weren't any, said the secretary. Nothing happened."

"You are not funny," said Leona.

"But the treasurer has a report. Purchased: one black nightgown of DuPont nylon costing eighty-nine dollars and ninety-five cents."

"A hundred and fifty," said Leona, "if you're going to be nasty."

"And since there's no new business, I move we adjourn the meeting."

"Very funny," she'd said.

Maybe he would go hear her speech.

He threw his bag on the luggage rack and thought all motel rooms were like all the others—even their special features. The color television in this one had remote control and a quarter in the bed's headboard produced a massage.

▲

96

By dark it had begun in earnest.

The snow hid the mountain above and the valley below. Descanso drew into itself and the old gods slept deep in the earth. The only sound against the rush of the wind was the gaunt crunch of the man's boots that broke the frozen crust and made black depressions which filled again as he passed.

Drake wished his black thoughts could fill white as easily.

Soledad grew large with the child Teresita said was his. If so, what was he going to do about it? He had fathered a bastard, a child of neither race nor of either of their worlds.

The wind shot arrow-tipped ice crystals into his face. He leaned into it and concentrated on the immediate goal which obliterated the larger one of ultimate decision as the driving snow obliterated the reality of the world beyond it. He groped toward the gold that would be Francisco's window and a fellow creature.

"I will carve for you a *santo*, Carlos," said Francisco. The little saints stood about on table and shelf and cast their moving shadows against the quiet walls. The men spoke of the snow which seemed to cover the world and didn't, and of life's problems which seemed particular and doubtless covered the world. They smoked and drank red wine, watched the fire, and from time to time Francisco spoke to his small saints to include them in the talk. Always both men were aware of the great quiet-making peace outside.

"But it isn't real. The peace, I mean. It's just a cover, like the snow."

"It's real if you let it in, Carlos."

"Easy for you."

"Faith is never easy. I was a long time learning. You start by talking to the little saints—they're easier than God. I shall carve for you a *santo*, Carlos."

"They're only art objects to me, not faith symbols."

"Are they not the same? Do you see San Ysidro?" He crossed to the patient saint flanked by his angel-driven oxen on their shelf. "This one was a long time coming." He gently touched the red hat, ran his stained finger softly over the long face with its patient dark eyes so like his own, down over the long blue coat. "You were a stubborn one, weren't you, Ysidro? For a long time I couldn't find you."

He walked to the window, gazed at the white night beyond. He grasped a log in his strong stained fingers and threw it on the flame. Explosions of sparks leaped out.

"Do you remember the big house I showed you when we gathered wood?

I committed a terrible sin there and I have carried its burden for twenty years. Never do we find peace, Carlos, until we die. But we learn to bear our guilt with patience.

"Ysidro, my little *santo* who took so long in coming, knew. He plagued me whenever I looked at him. He would not let me forget. I locked him in a trunk but still he knew.

"Mine was a sin of passion," Francisco continued. "It started with the *rico* who bought wood from my father. Once he came here looking for him and he brought his wife, slender and white like an altar candle, and her face was like wax that might melt under her hair that burned like a candle's flame. Did I have a San Ysidro, she asked, like the one she had seen once in my father's home? No, I said, but I would show her some others.

"But her husband was impatient and said he wanted none of that Catholic nonsense.

"Some months later I buried my father. I brought from his house the San Ysidro I had carved for him, that he cherished so. The little saint had hardly made himself comfortable when the *rico* came, alone this time, looking again for my father."

▲

Francisco's tale unfolded.

"I overpaid your father for apples last fall," the *rico* said, "and I paid him for five cords of wood last spring. He brought only three. Where is he?"

"Leave me in peace," Francisco shouted. "You would find my father? Then you must go to the *camposanto*. He lies there now."

He said he hadn't known, that he was sorry.

"You are sorry! And that will bring him back? Go and tell his good friends you are sorry. Tell those who dug his grave, who sat all night at his *velorio*, that carried him on his last journey! Tell them you are sorry!"

The *rico* tried to speak but Francisco kept on. "Do you want to know how he died, *señor*?"

"If it will ease you."

"Then I will tell you. He died because you killed him!"

The man's mouth dropped but the *santero* kept on. "My father was old and worn with work. You wouldn't know about that, about the heavy work, and how cruel the earth can be. The poor man cannot rest, *señor*. Always he must labor.

"You overpaid him for the apples, you say. Do you know the years he gave to those apples? Do you know about the bad years when the freezes kill the fruit and sometimes the trees themselves? Do you know about the years the *acequias* run dry and everything parches and dies?"

Francisco dashed a tear from his eye. "But he promised you the wood, you said, and twice you came to remind him. You couldn't wait though there was yet time before the frost and he was harvesting from dawn until starshine. But you must have your wood so he left his fields at midday and together we went to cut your wood.

"He gave out, *señor*. He tried to straighten up. He gasped for air but he sagged forward and fell. And I watched him die there on the ground."

"I didn't know." The *rico* bowed his head. "I'm truly sorry. If there's anything I can do. . . ."

"You can leave me in peace." He turned away and Francisco followed him outside. "I will bring your wood."

"No," said the *rico*. "It doesn't matter."

"It mattered enough to kill my father. I will pay his debt."

Francisco had one of his own to pay.

He turned San Ysidro to the wall so the little saint's eyes wouldn't follow or accuse him as old Ramón had so often said: "Lessons not learned must be repeated."

▲

Francisco was very young when he decided to be a saintmaker. He journeyed once with his parents to Santa Fé which seemed as far as heaven and there he learned in the great cathedral how small was the church at Descanso and how shabby their *santos*. "I will carve fine ones," he vowed, "for our church." Though he was ashamed of Descanso's saints, his father said the prayers of the poor *santos* rose to heaven as quickly as those of the fine ones.

At home his mother dusted the simple saints carefully and mended the Virgin's robes. She told her small secrets to San Juan and she spoke gently to the *Santo Niño*, though sometimes she scolded Him. "Your cheek is smudged, naughty one," she said as she cleaned it. "You've come too close to the candle again." She could never have talked to intimately to the grand saints the little boy planned.

Once Francisco took the *Santo Niño* from his manger where he waited for

Christmas Mass. His mother didn't discover the little statue in her son's arms until they got home.

"What have you done, Francisco!" she cried.

"The baby is cold," he said. "I will warm him at our fire."

"Then warm him quickly," she said, "before his mother sees he's gone!"

The boy began to carve cottonwood chunks but his efforts were clumsy and his brothers made fun of them. One he worked especially hard on—San Francisco, his name saint—but he was lopsided and the child cried with frustration.

"You can't carve a San Francisco," his father said, "because you don't know him."

"How can anyone know a saint?"

"Talk with him. The birds did. Can't you listen as well as they?"

His mother loved the crooked statue. One day she took her son's hand and they carried the figure up the steep trail to Pájaro to show to old Ramón the *santero*. He peered at the little saint from under his eyebrows that joined together above his nose and hung over his eyes. Flames burned behind those eyes and Francisco was afraid his eyebrows would catch fire.

"So you want to make saints!" His thin voice sounded like the tamarisk when it scrapes the walls in cold wind. "Then you may come to me."

The boy puffed his chest. "Do you like my saint?"

"No, he is very bad. So you must come to me."

Francisco began to climb to Ramón's house to learn the ways of saintmaking. For a long time the old man didn't speak to the boy, though he talked continually in his high singing voice to the figures he worked on. Francisco watched all his movements.

One day he glared and said his apprentice might as well be useful. "If you want to make saints," he said, "you must start with the stink," and he set him stirring the hooves and horns and skins to make glue in the iron pot over the fire by his corral. "Saints and saintmakers need humility."

The boy learned to choose the wood, to examine it from all sides with his hands and his eyes. He learned to handle the knife, to powder the gypsum and boil the *yeso*, to mix the colors from earth and bark and root and flower. He made brushes of yucca fiber and chicken feathers.

Ramón told him about the saints as he worked, which ones carried certain objects or bore certain marks. He talked whether Francisco was in or out of the room and seemed not to notice the boy's inattention. But sometimes after a tale of miracle or martyrdom he saw his tale had gone unheard. Then he scolded and began again.

He was like a log at the back of the fire that, though not burning, is hot inside and smokes until it is ready to burst into flame. So old Ramón worked with heat inside and words like smoke and when the boy didn't listen the flames jumped from his eyes. "Lessons not learned must be repeated."

Once Francisco gathered red clay from the cliff face. He could have cut the same color from a bank up the *arroyo* but the walk was tiresome and the slight danger on the ledge made the color seem brighter and the deed grander. More concerned to paint his own performance than to color the saint, his feat grew perilous in the telling until the flame behind Ramón's eyes snapped sparks. "It is the color that matters," he snapped. "Not the gatherer."

▲

Francisco smiled telling of his youth and then returned to his tale of the *rico* and of the plan he formed after the man drove off.

He chopped the man's wood, made sure the amount exceeded the debt, and with the last load prepared his own payment.

He hunted until he found a nest of poison spiders, caught them in a jar, and watched them swarm inside the glass with their strange red marks like drops of blood. After he stacked the last of the wood at the *rico*'s house he smashed the jar and watched them scatter and disappear into the woodpile.

It was a senseless plan but he could think of no better. He prayed to San Jorge who gives success in battle to guide one of the poison things to its target. The man might be rich and important, he thought, but he, Francisco, was allied with saints!

He had forgotten he was not of their company but only their servant. He forgot, too, that rich men do not carry their own firewood.

"Your wood is here, *señor*," he said. "You will find all you paid for. And more."

"I will pay for the extra."

Francisco would not take his money. "It is enough," he said, "to know my father's debt is paid!"

But as he wound his way home uneasy thoughts began to gather like heavy clouds and darken his heart. When he reached Descanso he tied his burro and went inside to the church. His prayers did not lighten his heart.

Crossing the village, he breathed the sweet scent of burning piñon and thought as he always did that it was the smell of people's lives. It cooked their food and warmed their bodies and lightened the darkness and rose like incense from the sacrament of living. Always he had thought God must warm His hands over it and smile at the odor of humble people at peace in their hearts. But it gave Francisco no comfort that day.

At home he turned San Ysidro to face him. "*Bueno*," he said. "It is done now, so have your say!"

The little figure did not speak.

"I did it for my father," Francisco cried, "because I loved him!" The little saint seemed to stare beyond into the fields and past them to heaven itself, until finally Francisco thought he spoke and his voice was sad. "Lessons not learned must be repeated."

He looked to the Blessed Virgin in her *nicho* over the fireplace and thought she nodded at Ysidro's words. The San Cristóbal that had been his mother's looked from another wall as he shouldered the little Cristo. "I carry my burden with pride, Francisco," he seemed to say. "You must carry yours."

All the saints in heaven were against Francisco.

▲

"Make me a San Ysidro," his father had said so often. But Francisco carved warriors. No farmer saint for him. And that too had come to haunt him.

For though he carved warriors, he learned he could be none. *Santero* he was, but it was his brothers Eliseo and Gilberto who were called to be heroes. The Great War had come and he was only fifteen years old!

He burned that they should go on the great adventure while he, a better shot than either, must stay at home because God had let him be born too late.

He made tiny San Cristóbals for each to wear and the carving was a prayer for he loved his brothers. But he also burned with envy and when he finished he took his father's shotgun to the river and killed three jackrabbits. They were poor substitutes for Germans.

"It is God's will," his father said.

"Always you accept what comes," the boy cried out. "What good has it done you? When the frosts kill your trees you say, 'It is God's will.' When the storms wash out your bean fields and when the *acequias* dry in the summer you say, 'It is God's will.' Have we no wills of our own?"

The day before his brothers left, he and Eliseo sat beside the *acequia* for the last time in private discussion. Envy made him surly.

"Francisco," said Eliseo, "I been thinking." He tossed a stone into the ditch.

"Don't wear out your brain."

"I went to the *morada* last night with Papa and Gilberto." He plopped another rock into the water. "I made a vow. If I come home from the war I will become an *Hermano*."

"Then I will make my vow too," cried Francisco in a rush of strong feeling and not to be outdone. "Eliseo, if you don't come home, then I will take your place!"

They joined hands in the secret handclasp they had practiced as children and then, embarrassed, they scuffled, rolling in the dirt laughing and pummeling each other until they were out of breath.

"Anyway," said Francisco, "you'll be back."

"Sure. I got San Cristóbal!" Still. . . ." He sank another rock. "You never can tell."

Neither came back. Gilberto died of appendicitis and Eliseo lay dead on a battlefield in France whose name they couldn't pronounce.

"God's will be done," said their father.

Francisco spoke to no one and began to look to himself. Had he carved the images that his brothers wore in too much anger? Had he thought of his own will and offended San Cristóbal?

Lessons not learned must be repeated.

▲

Francisco thought of these things when he returned from the *rico*'s and he turned to San Cristóbal again. "How can I carry this burden I have loosed?" he begged. "How can I pray?"

"To work is to pray," he heard. "*Oremos*."

He picked up a chunk he had saved from the *rico*'s wood, a knotted shape with a life inside that begged release. He turned it this way and that and felt its shape. It was a large piece with two branches. Perhaps the large one was a riding saint, the lesser the head of his horse. It would make a fine *bulto* with arms attached if he knew who was inside. But no saint spoke.

He was still studying it when Padre Lorenzo came to visit. He had been Descanso's priest then for a dozen years and unlike Father Andreas later, he lived in the village. "I can't find the saint in this one," Francisco complained.

"Perhaps you don't listen," said the priest. "You storm over your father's death when you should rejoice in his release."

"Eternity is so long, Father. What must it be like?"

"Look around you," said Padre Lorenzo in his voice like a high wind—even then the asthma plagued him. "We're in the middle of eternity. It's in the wood you hold." He knew his friend's burden. "Which saint speaks in it?"

"Maybe Santiago. See—here is his horse, his spear."

"You listen to your own warlike heart, *amigo*. Perhaps he's a humble saint who says, 'Forgive your enemies.'"

Francisco put the piece aside.

Several weeks later the *rico* came again. He looked haggard. "I've come to buy my wife a *santo*."

"You refused her one before."

"She insists," he said. "It's become an obsession. But that isn't your concern. Would you show me what you have?"

"There are other *santeros* in the valley."

"But she likes yours. Please," he said. "Please sell me this one." He pointed to San Ysidro. "She liked this one."

"He isn't for sale."

"I will pay whatever you ask."

"He's not for sale, *señor*. I've nothing to sell to you."

"My wife is very ill," he said slowly. "And lonely. It would be company when she returns from the hospital. Please."

Francisco nearly agreed for he liked the lady, but the *rico* kept on talking. "I'm sorry about your father," he said. "I'm trying to be your friend."

"*Ricos* don't become friends with poor men. The *santos* are not for sale."

The *rico* carried his burden, too, Francisco knew. But he would not help him. He bore his own. Let the rich man do the same. Let him learn his own humility.

After the man had driven off in his shiny car Francisco began to think of the pale fire-haired lady, ill and lonely for a *santo* in the white hospital in Santa Fé, and before that in the lonely house where he imagined her held prisoner. He remembered his father's patient humility, his patient 'God's will be done,' how he had for so long begged Francisco to carve him a San Ysidro.

He remembered his father standing in a ruined field. The *acequia* ran low for lack of snowmelt—for, he always said, it takes a hard winter to make a happy summer—and no summer rains swelled the *arroyos*. The fields grew parched. The men prayed and clouds massed every afternoon but none gave rain.

Finally they carried San Juan from the church into the fields that he might bring the rain. The clouds built, grew heavy, darkened and churned, and the lightning forked through them. In the night it came.

"Blessed be San Juan!" cried his father when he heard the first drops. The rain swept heavy, then savage, and heaven had no bottom. It cut ditches through the paths and the fields which grew to chasms and then to running rivers.

By morning the fields were gone. The beans, the chiles, even the tough squash vines lay beaten, their roots bared, and the corn lay flat and broken. The people stood silently and many wept. His father stood, tired and sad, and he raised his face to heaven, washed blue in the morning sun.

"God's will be done," he said.

The night after the *rico* drove off, Francisco had a dream and the dream was as it had happened.

"Make me a San Ysidro," said his father. Through the years Francisco had tried to carve his father's saint but Ysidro would not come.

"I can't! You shouldn't ask me now!" he cried for he was mourning his own lovely Adela who looked like an angel and loved like a woman and now lay pale and dead while the son whose birth had killed her lived. She had been Francisco's wife not yet a year.

He wouldn't look at the baby. Teresita took the infant to Clara Vigil who nursed one baby and had milk for two. When that grew scant Teresita let him suck rags soaked in goat's milk.

"We must christen him," said the priest. "You must choose godparents."

"Choose whom you will," said Francisco, and when his father asked what he would name his son he shrugged. "I don't care."

"We shall call him Ysidro," said his father.

Weeks passed. Francisco wouldn't see the child and carved no saints.

What good were they? He went to the *morada* but the *hermanos* could not ease his bitterness. He sat at his bench and picked up a piece of wood, then another, but no saint spoke.

And then in his dream he and his father turned the *acequia* into their field. It was spring and Francisco thought of Adela again and the tears ran. He felt his father's arm on his.

"I can't carve you anything!" he cried and crying awoke in the dark. The dream was still warm. He lay and remembered how he had gone to the *camposanto* and stood a long time at Adela's grave and wished she would speak. A small brown wren lit on her grave. She and Francisco had often talked to the birds and to each other through them. The little creature cocked his head and cast a round eye from beneath a white eyebrow and his tail bobbed as he went about his business as Adela would be telling him to go about his. The bird had no time to talk. He pulled an insect from some stubble and flew off with it to his nest. To care for his young.

Francisco walked slowly toward his house. Then he stopped. He turned and started for Clara's and once his direction was set he walked faster until he ran.

"I've come for my son."

That night he took up his knife again. The saint had spoken. At the end of the week he carried the little statue to his father. "Here is your San Ysidro."

▲

Francisco arose from his memories and the tight hatred had gone. He thought of the sad lady with her flame of hair that burned about her white face. He would make her a *santo*.

That evening the troublesome piece of wood with its odd shape seemed to beg for release and then he knew her. "Santa Bárbara," he said and thought of her, the maiden whose wicked father locked her in a tower and, jealous of her faith, drew his sword and cut her head from her body.

He began to carve. Here she stood, little Santa Bárbara with long dark eyes and her hair falling down her neck. She wore a crown. Behind her the knot Francisco had thought a horse's head became her tower.

He worked all night. Later he would powder the gypsum and mix the glue. He would fasten her arms and make her pedestal. He would coat her well and leave her to dry while he ground his colors and mixed his paints.

Soon she lived. The tiniest smile curved her lips as the flame-haired lady's smile had curved when she looked on Francisco's *santos*.

He carried her on his little burro, down the steep path to the gorge and along the sandy *arroyo* to the trail through the piñons of the *rico's ranchito* and as he rode he thought of the flame-haired lady and of Adela and of his son Ysidro.

He remembered how Clara had watched the baby during the days until he grew large enough to follow Francisco to the field with sturdy legs and round cheeks. He was a gentle child and the two grew close as the years passed. He grew tall and slender like his mother and had her soft eyes.

Francisco carved many *santos* and gained some fame and Ysidro too learned the craft. "You will be a finer *santero* than I," said his father, "for your heart is nearer the saints by nature."

But God had yet to test Francisco.

For Ysidro, like Gilberto and Eliseo, was called for a soldier. "He is not meant for soldiering!" his father cried to his *santos*. "He is too gentle!" But the wings of war beat over the mountains again and cast their shadows over the villages. Their country needed men. Alarico Vicente went too. He was older and said he'd look after Ysidro as much as any man can do.

As Francisco plodded toward the *rico's* he thought then of the strange thing that had happened before Ysidro left for the army. The boy wore a San Cristóbal he bought in Española but he asked for one of his father's. Francisco thought of those he had made for his brothers so many years before and a fear arose in him. But he carved him carefully and when Ysidro held the little figure in his slender hand his eyes were soft. "Papa, I made a vow last night. When the war is over I will join the *hermandad*. If I come home."

Eliseo had made the same vow.

"Of course you will come back," said Francisco huskily, and then, even in a voice like Eliseo's, Ysidro said the same words. "Sure, I got San Cristóbal. Still—you never can tell."

Francisco later believed his fear prophetic. For Ysidro was trapped in a place called Bataan.

For long months no word came. "It is my own sin that imprisons him," he cried to Padre Lorenzo. "When he was born I wanted no son who had killed my Adela. Now God remembers and takes him from me!"

"Then you must do more penance."

"I will lash myself."

"No," the priest said quietly. "You must plant apricot trees"—the trees of faith, he called them—"for they are the first to bloom and their children, the little flowers, are so often taken from them in the cruel spring. To plant any tree is an act of faith. But to plant an apricot is the greatest faith. You will learn to accept if their fruit is killed and look to another spring and your faith will be renewed.

"Besides," he added, "your orchard marches right up against the *camposanto*. I think the little trees will cheer the lonely ones who lie there." Of course the spirit had flown he added quickly and, lest he sound impious, crossed himself.

Francisco planted the trees. But it didn't bring back Ysidro.

Even that terrible time dulled. He went into his little grove and cared for the apricots without thought because it was his habit. Slowly he found peace in them. The birds came and they talked and finally he accepted.

▲

Francisco, telling these things to Drake, was quiet long moments. Then he finished his tale of the *rico*.

"I carried Santa Bárbara with peace in my heart. I had thrust out the anger and released the saint. I had done good work.

"But my peace did not last. As a small cloud is caught on the mountain and gathers others, gray thoughts gathered in my mind and grew into dark fear. I remembered the tiny black spiders and in my mind I saw one clinging to a log, borne to a lady's room.

"What had caused her illness? What horror might I have made?

"I clutched the *santa* and found myself repeating the rhyme of my childhood.

> *Santa Bárbara dancella,*
> *Libra nos del tiyo y a la centella.*
> *(Free us, Santa Barbara,*
> *From the fires of storm and passion.)*

"I held her tightly all the way.

108

"'*Vaya*,' said the fat cook. 'We want nothing here.' She slammed the door.

"I walked to the front and knocked again. 'I wish to see the *patrón*.'

"'He won't see you,' said the servant girl.

"'Tell him Francisco has brought the *santa*.'

"'He will not see you.'

"'Then call the lady,' I said, 'if she's back from the hospital.'

"She threw her apron over her face. 'Go away!'

"Behind her the *rico* appeared, gaunt and white with the life inside him frozen. 'Invite him in,' he said.

"I knew before he told me I had brought the *santa* too late. I thrust it at him. 'She is Santa Bárbara,' I said. 'She was locked in a tower. She died true to her faith.'

"He took the *santa*, looked at her face. Then, for the first time he looked at mine. 'Would you like to see her, Francisco?' He led me to where she lay in a blue coffin. The room smelled of candle wax.

"'I will take her east but we will have a service here first.' He talked not so much to me as to any listening ear. 'I don't hold with it but it was her wish.'

"'Did she know she was going to die?'

"'We had known a long time.'

"'May I say a prayer?'

"'If you like. I'll leave the saint here. She'd have liked it. It looks a little like her.'

"The hall was deserted when I left so I let myself out. He stood on the *portal* in the wind. Before I left I asked one more question. 'Her illness. It was no—sudden thing?'

"'She'd been ill since our little son was born,' he told me. 'The doctors could not save him and she had been fragile since. For a bit we hoped—I brought her here where I thought the pure high air might help her.'

"*Gracias a Dios!* A rush of weakness washed through me. I didn't know what to say, Carlos. I was ashamed. And grateful. God had not punished me with her death.

"The *rico* too had lost a wife and son and I felt compassion and humility. The spiders had not carried out my murderous intent.

"The *patrón* insisted I drink a glass of wine before I started home. So we drank a *copita*, not saying much, both of us stiff with our own guilt, I suppose.

"'We've had more than our share of deaths lately,' he said. 'Did you know

Jesús Espinosa? A good man, Jesús was. Took care of the horses, did repairs, brought in the wood.

"'Only last week he became violently ill. He swelled in his neck and face and became delirious. I sent for a doctor in Las Vegas but Jesús was dead before he could get here.'

"The wine grew sour in my mouth as the *patrón* finished.

"'His arm and neck were a mass of bites. He must have disturbed a whole colony of black widow spiders.'"

▲

Francisco ended his tale. He gazed through the fire and its light moved gently on his face and softened the chasms of time. Drake threw another log on the blaze and released sparks like a shower of comets. Outside the snow deepened and the quiet enclosed them. He turned from the cosmos beyond to the presence at hand. He contemplated the little San Ysidro with the angel-driven team and when he finally spoke it was to the dreaming figure.

"Why were you so stubborn, little saint?" He touched the smooth surface, warm in the fire's comfort.

Francisco saw the gesture and smiled. "San Ysidro made God Himself wait! Do you see how much larger he is than his oxen? That's because men's prayers are greater than their labors. Ysidro was slow to learn that for it was his habit to plow on Sunday. He was more concerned to plant his corn and chiles than to honor the giver of the seed.

"So God sent an angel who said to stop that Sunday plowing or He'd send hail to kill his crops. Ysidro plowed on. God could wait better than the seeds.

"The storm came and killed the plants. The next Sunday he plowed and another angel said a summer drought would parch his crops. But Ysidro said, 'The *acequia* flows. Tell the Lord a drought is no worse than a late planting.'

"Then a third angel said, 'Ysidro, God has reached the end of His patience. If you continue to plow on Sunday He will send you a bad neighbor!'

"Ysidro pulled on his reins and threw them down. 'You win,' he told the angel. 'Nature's moods subside, but an ill-tempered man never changes!'"

"And now I've come," said Drake, "and you have the bad neighbor."

"I was the bad neighbor, Carlos, and I killed an innocent man. I have borne that guilt for twenty years."

"As I must bear mine?"

"You can't push water back uphill."

"I never fathered a child." Drake's words flowed slowly like an ice-choked stream. "Now I have one and haven't one. To have and not hold from this day forward."

"You don't know it's yours."

"What if I've burdened a child with the loneliness of belonging to no world? Look at Teresita—an Indian with a white ancestor somewhere who gave her blue eyes and because of that she's been stigmatized, called a witch, for God's sake!"

"It may look like Julián. Wait and see." The old man walked to the window. "God sends the winter so the earth can rest. The Indians call it the Time for Staying Still."

"Your religion has absorbed many elements. *Brujas* mix with saints, and Christian myths with Indian myths, and your *alabados* are Moorish."

"The church has wide arms. 'Many trails wind up the mountain,' the Indians say. 'But they all lead to the top.'"

"And those of us who choose no road never get there at all."

"*¿Quién sabe?* But I think the going is harder."

Drake pulled on his thick jacket and looked again at San Ysidro. "I still don't know why he hid so long."

"I sought the wrong saint. What saint do you seek, Carlos?"

Which saint and which road up the mountain? What was he doing here anyhow, why had he fled the civilized world? "I think I just want something to believe in," he said. He turned from the golden warmth into the night, into the black night so strangely lit by its own driving snow.

Something to believe in as he'd once believed in civilization that now he fled because it had grown blind. He fought through a dark icy nothingness in a village that shouldn't even exist, where saints and witches lived side by side and talked to each other every day. *How are you, how's the saint business, whose fields will you water today? I go well, thank you, how's the witch business, whose fields do you curse?* Where men pass by in strange wordless procession and the ghosts of their dead brothers with them and they beat themselves with yucca whips and the flute wails high and a man is hung on a cross each year. Where Indian chants to arcane gods beat their rhythms alongside Moorish *alabados* and men entreat the Christian God and placate the old gods of the mountain. Where now the Earth

Mother sleeps, or is it Mary the Virgin who looks like an Indian maiden in these dark mountains?

It all hung together somehow. Her arms are wide, Francisco said.

Drake fought through the wind and snow and, in the orchard, he stopped a moment. He placed his thick-gloved hand on the bole of a tree. Was it apple or plum or gentle apricot, or did it matter while its sap lay deep in the root held in the Mother's dark arms?

The wind softened in the grove and he looked at the gray above and the white below. He knew somewhere in the eternal black beyond rose the mountain. The god of the mountain shrouded himself in the gray storm and Drake thought, *You'll find no God up here tonight*. Even the Christian God had crawled into the mountain. He'd gone to the Mother.

It was the Time for Staying Still.

No trail to the top of the mountain tonight, he thought. Suddenly he saw them again, his gray mind remembered again, those burning amber eyes of the lioness—Lyon lyon burning bright in the forests of the night. *She's warm*, he thought, *she's curled with her mate, far back in her warm cave that winds deep into the womb. She knows where her gods sleep, where they stay still.* He saw her eyes again and they were the eyes of Francisco's saint who knew where his God was, where he breathed warm in his earth.

He pushed on toward his own shelter to his center where he would make fire and release the spirits to warm his formless soul. He would curl warm in his center and know where they were. He would know the time for staying still.

He had not fled civilization. He had come back to its roots, to his own soulroots, if he could find them, had come where men still had the vision, where something still lived, something worth saving, a center where sparks flew out and gods lived.

8

*H*e sat beside a tweedy lady whose flesh escaped from her corset in localized puddles. She had a determined breastline and her arm kept spilling over his.

"Her husband was killed, you know," she said. She smelled of hair spray and lilac cologne.

Her friend said, "Yes, they never could find him. But he'd started acting strange before that."

On the stage a firm-voiced woman led the pledge of allegiance and the fat lady next to Drake laid her right hand over her bosomy heart and recited ardently, except she stumbled over the "under God" part.

A bulb-nosed man with a cleft in his chin asked blessings on the gathering, the democratic process, the speaker, her cause, her supporters, the after-speech coffee, the cookies, the collective communicants, and a Democratic victory at the polls, Amen, and the fat lady glared at Drake who didn't bow his head.

Leona had kept her figure. She didn't look much different and she talked the same. Her voice crackled around the edges and sounded compassionate and vulnerable the way she had always sounded when she was most hell-bent, the way a kitten gets fluffy and purrs so one forgets about nine lives and claws. Drake didn't listen to her words—he never had—but some came through anyhow.

"Job opportunities are NOT the same for women," she said. "I know. I was left a widow, alone," and her voice trembled and Drake thought, *Yes, a widow alone with four million dollars*, and he grinned. The fat lady glared at him but he kept grinning.

"But I am not running as a wife or a widow," said Leona in her brave soft voice. "I run as a person in my own right and I run on the name I was born with, Leona Stone!"

On the front row a skinny blonde with round glasses leaped up and thrust high a poster on a tall stick. It read LIBERALS LOVE LEONA in red and blue letters and a few people cheered raggedly.

"And I will work for equal rights for all races and all creeds," Leona said. "We must eliminate discrimination against our Hispanics."

Sure, when you make them just like us. But you can't leave them alone, can you, to go their own way? thought Drake, and he said, "Balls," not very loud but the fat lady glared.

Leona said it again. "I will work for equal rights for all races and all creeds AND FOR BOTH SEXES," she said, and her voice grew stronger but Drake didn't listen any more. All he could see were the cold gray eyes, like rocks in winter.

▲

Juan Tafoya led him to the lions.

Some of the Indians came to the post to trade and others just to hang around, especially in bad weather, and they squatted around the wood stove and the big room smelled like wet wool; but when Juan came, he was usually after Little Caesar. Juan followed the old ways.

"He been here?"

"'Bout an hour ago. Fergus has him." Val tossed Drake the keys to the station wagon. "Drive Juan down to Lupe's," she said in her flat voice. "Watch the brakes, they're loose."

It was the usual routine. César got drunk and wild and roared up the back road from the pueblo in the war-scarred pickup to get money from Fergus who tried to detain him until his father could catch a ride to the post. Fergus couldn't refuse César his money—they all had it coming on trade items and drew as they wanted—but he'd stall until Little Caesar was hell-bent to leave and then take him to the bar down the road and have a few with him until Juan got there.

They drove through the vapors of old snow-ghosts that rose toward the sun and Drake glanced at Juan's profile, sharp like wind-carved rock.

"Men get sons they get trouble," the old Indian said and Drake thought of the dark-eyed son of Soledad's born in the spring, the *niño* that might be his, that he did and didn't wish were his. Soledad and Francisco told him to leave well enough alone and he did though he visited often and he was still Tío Carlos who drew pictures for Mario and Alberto and brought them gifts. When he looked at the soft-eyed baby with the long lashes, his throat grew tight and Soledad smiled. Then he'd go back and work with the charcoal, driven to catch the living village, to push the lonely out, though it always came again.

"Plenty sons, plenty trouble," said Juan. "One son plenty trouble too."

"Yeah," said Drake. "I guess so."

When César saw Juan he broke to run and it took all three of them to pack him in his pickup between Juan and Fergus. Drake followed in the station wagon and at the pueblo helped incarcerate César in his own house with enough hootch to placate him until he passed out.

"Hunt dance next week," said Juan. "You be there?" Fergus said he might. "You too," Juan said to Drake.

"Ever been to a dance?" Fergus asked on the way back.

"Not here. I'd like to."

Fergus said Juan had been in to buy red ochre. "That means he and his *compañeros*'ll be going to the Lion Shrine. Some of 'em still practice the old religion. Go in before the hunt dances."

"What do they do there?"

"Never watched 'em." He grinned. "But I'm a honorary warrior."

"Which means?"

"Means they trust me. Also, I killed a eagle once. They got the feathers, I paid the fine." He ran his finger around the snake band on his hat. "Want to go in there?"

"Would they let us?"

"Might."

Fergus drove with Juan beside him. Drake was wedged in the back seat between two elderly Indians of ample flesh and thick clothing. The heater clanked and blew and before they crossed the river the temperature was one degree short of hell. Drake pointed to the button that controlled the automatic window—his companions couldn't or wouldn't speak English or Spanish either—and he pushed it in pantomime from his center position. They grinned, nodded vigorously, and resumed their frontal stares. Their faces poured heavy bronze sweat. The heater blew on. Neither Fergus nor Juan seemed to notice.

They crossed the river, black between banks covered with thin snow like old torn lace. Drake leaned across and punched the button. Nothing happened. He punched it again. He tried the other.

"They don't work," said Fergus. "Warm back there?" He punched the master control. Nothing happened. He shrugged.

"Guess I'm having hot flashes," Drake said and Fergus laughed his thin laugh and that triggered the Indians to join in. For the next stretch of river they cackled gleefully.

They left the river and started the sharp climb west up toward the high plateau on "The Hill" where perched Los Alamos, that strange artificial town where the white man had released forces the Indian had always known.

"Funny thing," said Drake. "The Creator went to all that trouble to engineer the atom—building block for the whole damned universe—packed every force known inside. Love and hate and reason and propagation and everything in between—the whole works, the germ of everything. And a gang up there smashed it apart."

"I reckon when they're finished," said Fergus, "the Lord can start over again."

"If He thinks it worth the effort."

The air grew denser. Drake pulled off his sweater and the Indians joined in. Off came jackets and heavy shirts. The pile of clothing in the back grew. The hot air kept blowing and everyone kept sweating and Drake felt like a marshmallow between two melting chocolate bars.

They turned off the highway, sharp left. Suddenly Fergus swerved to miss a rock in the road, hit a shoulder, and they fell into a hole, lurched to a violent stop. The Indians started laughing again. Fergus swore, shifted, backed out, shifted again, and resumed momentum. No harm done.

Some mysterious life, however, released by the jolt began to flow through the window mechanism. Suddenly, smoothly, the two rear windows and then the front one slid down and a rush of air washed through the close quarters.

"What in the name of seven shades of billy hell. . . ?" began Fergus and one of the Indians said something in Indian and they all began to laugh again.

They wound through the lip of the canyon. The icy air rolled in over Drake's bared arms, over his companions' naked chests. He leaned over to close the window. It didn't budge. Fergus tried the master. Frigid air continued to inundate them and the Indians kept laughing.

They left the car beneath the towering ruins of the ancient cliff homes, the smoke-blackened caves where Juan's ancestors had once lived in their hidden valley, had burrowed into the gray pumice of sun-warmed cliff, molded mud homes on the floor beneath where, rock-protected, they grew beans and corn and squash in their fertile fields, watered by the *rito*. There they had lived in the midst of a beauty that filled their being, safe until the Tewas from the north drove them from their Eden. A long day's march south they traveled, through canyons and past mesas to build new homes on the high *potreros* where the five men journeyed this day.

They trekked single file. Three old Indians, dark faces rutted with canyons and mesas like their ancient home, set the pace, steady, unbroken by rest or talk down the towering crags into gorges cut by lonely streams which sought passage to the great river, the Río Grande, life-giver to the pueblos' breast-suckling fields; up the forbidding rose-glowing walls to the *potreros*, those grim sentinel wedges which soared aloof between the canyons; up through rock and scrub oak, through piñon and juniper they wound, through silent forests of fir and pine, toward the ancient shrine where the red man still paid homage to the Beast Gods.

Behind them tramped the white men. Drake, with half-formulated thoughts, groped toward some communion of life with life, toward some touching of the pale intellectualized mind of the white man with the dark blood-throbbing instinct of the Indian, toward some penetrating of the cloud-spirits of mesa and canyon and earth and sky whence came their life. Deep they wound through the misty forests where myth and history steal hand in hand, to recapture some memory of Eden, or at least some memory of its wonder.

The white man can't do it, Drake knew. *Once weaned, we never regain the taste for mother's milk. The delight of the spoken word is dulled when we learn to read; the beautiful sound-shape of the word disappears when we see its sight-shape formed; and Pan died when Christ was born. Or did he migrate to the pristine new world, the great dark spreading mass of the Americas? Did he wind, ever westward, beyond and beyonder, up into these lonely canyon-furrowed fastnesses, and does he hide here yet waiting for resurrection in this yet-uncreated wild?*

Drake pushed on with an old unshaped expectation like that he had felt as a boy when a fish tugged his line from its arcane depth, like a soul about to be pulled into the light. He pushed on behind the leaders of this strange procession with their square straight backs and their thick gray braids.

They saw wild turkeys in an opening by a stream. Men and birds contemplated each other a moment until the flocks disappeared into the brush and the men pushed on. Gopher tunnels mounded the earth and the Indians pointed to tracks of coyote and deer and to the peculiar X of the roadrunner.

Browsing mule deer looked at them curiously, softly wiggled their great white ears, and kept on foraging and Drake thought, *for all their gentleness they're more destructive than the fierce bears who pirate the berry bushes. Like the do-gooders,* he thought, *who would strip the bark off civilization and destroy it more thoroughly than all the world's fierce weapons.*

Juan led. Each time they came on other life he stopped, hand up, and men and beasts eyed one another, separate in their otherness, one in their communion of pulsing life in the immense stillness. Tall above, the straight pines crackled as they swayed in the high rushy air; birds signaled in round soprano notes; the tiny feet of darting chipmunks made skittering noises as they raced up and down the tough bark; a woodpecker's persistent tap echoed. The drone of an occasional plane from another age invaded and retreated and always the deep silence won. Once a skunk ambled across their path unhurried. A gray fox flashed through the muhly grass. The moving air above misted all sounds in its soft mysterious whisper.

Suddenly they came on it, the last god-gashed chasm they must cross. They started at the appalling might of the canyon, looked from craggy heights deep into the fissure, gazed across at the sheer, rose-red crags opposite them, watched a wheeling raven glide through the gorge below, glossy-black like obsidian in the brilliant light.

They began their descent. Drake looked neither up nor down but measured their progress by the opposite walls which they must scale. On the canyon floor they followed the stream bed, started the lung-searing ascent, pulled up and up the rocks, vermilion against the blue air, until sometime they gained the top. Drake gasped, felt the winey air rush into his lungs and mingle with his own breath, felt the life whirl in him.

Here piñons clung tough and tenacious and junipers thrust contorted limbs in strange motionless dance, wild and resolute creatures of the earth, defiant in the high winds.

Another *arroyo*, another rise; and still they climbed on the arching roof of the *potrero* until finally they reached the ruined walls of the dead pueblo atop the high silent tableland amid the wind-warped trees.

"Yapashi," said Juan. "You wait here. Come later."

The Indians headed on to perform their rites which were sacred and private and the white men squatted by the rubble of the ancient walls and smoked and heard the living spirits of the silent dead.

"You can get just so close to an Indian," said Fergus. "Only the old ones still come over here much, I guess. The Beast Gods live here. Mountain Lion Man's their head honcho. Juan's ancestors built this town and the shrine—they're up there now smearing red ochre on those lions' eyes and then on their own—makes 'em see better, spot the game faster they say—and they put it on their feet, too. To run faster. And they spread sacred cornmeal and breathe the lion's breath.

"Yet they're Christians."

"Sure. Go to mass, pray to Saint Whosis, whichever one's their village *patrón*—but the Christian God's one of many and the *santos* just that many more kachinas."

"I wonder how deep the Christian thing goes."

"Deeper than ours, I reckon. Indians are big on ceremony. Never let it all hang out. Take out the mystery and it ain't religion to an Indian. They don't dig the notion of hell and damnation, either. Can't comprehend sin. Their bag's to keep the natural order, be part of it. Through the mystery—that's where the power is. That's why they don't want us up there—whole thing would lose its power. Any leak in the balloon and the power seeps out."

Drake lay back against a rock. He rubbed the bum leg and sucked the high cold air deep and felt the sun-warmed rock against his back and the cold beneath his buttocks. To the southwest purple clouds mustered and through the silence of brooding centuries the low rumble of thunder reminded them that the mountain gods still rule.

Man up here was one with the mystery inside the sleeping female earth. Up here man didn't have to speculate where he came from or where he'd go because up here he knew. Up here he knew the enormous mystery of life that makes the reality bearable.

Fergus said the Indians might tell them about their lions and share the legend as long as he didn't ask. Or they might not. But it wasn't a question of words, Drake knew, or explanations, or doctrine.

After a time they followed to the shrine carved from native rock with the instinctual knowledge of all art and all faith, that the creation outlives the mortal creator.

Drake had seen pictures of the Stone Lions, had thought them mildly interesting. The reality startled him. The ancients had not carved these crouching beasts on the high *potrero* for scholar's eye or anthropologist's translation. By his patient hewing with obsidian knife or stone axe, the ancient sculptor made communion in stone with the spirit of the Beast Gods and it was a strong, sure summoning of their earthly incarnation, for life breathed in this weathered stone. The lions' sinews knotted in the haunches as the lithe stealthy beasts, two of them, gathered to spring, the long tails barely arrested in their serpentine motion. In the still, high world Drake felt the great hearts beating, felt the sharp eyes newly red like blood with the ochre which man from earliest times had smeared to renew life in his insensate dead, felt the *anima* that gave swiftness to the feet to follow the deer, felt behind those seeing eyes and the great mind force that willed the game into the sacred enclosure of stone and strewn meal.

In the Beginning was the Word. Was it *Lyon*, and did He speak it in an Indian tongue?

He stood at Shipapolima where lived still the Beast Gods below, guarded by the lions who face the east whence rises each day the power.

The white men sat cross-legged beside the life-sized beasts. Around them lay mounds of antlers, thank offerings for the game, deposited through the years; and before the beasts stood fine Indian pots, a few still whole, most crumbled to shards. One burnished bowl shone black, carved with the imperfect grace of love that goes beyond symmetry and curling about its rim wound the old Plumed Serpent, bringer of water like the snake-formed lightning, guardian of water like the undulating river, symbol of eternal life and of the water that nourishes it. Peering into the hollow, Drake saw it held water from recent rain. *Like a baptismal font*, he thought.

A piñon tree bent over the shrine and from its winter-living branches hung prayers sticks.

The living still kept faith.

They waited, quiet. They felt the silent energy that rose in waves about them. They inhaled the silence and absorbed the throbbing life.

Clouds moved over them, tented the shrine in shadow, and Drake felt a nearness, a breathing force—not personified nonsense like guardian ghosts but an essence, a life principle that enclosed them under that cloud-tent with the energy below, made them one with the rushing *élan* of the universe and with its still eye-center and they breathed the vapors and knew the pagan powers were not dead.

After a time Juan told the legend.

"Poshaiyanne come from waters under the earth, he born to Shayako great giant lady." The story fell from his mouth in the old round-shaped words, colored words like the worlds they told of, words of pigment and mystery and for a long time after Juan finished the words rolled over them in waves, yellow like the mountain light, blue like the canyon shadow.

It was the stark story of a small tough band who wandered in a cruel land, burrowed into its crags and crevices, and committed seeds into its soil womb in the ultimate act of faith. Their ancestors wandered foe-driven through the primeval silence where the rattlesnake coiled and the lion tracked his prey and the eagle soared and the legend shaped, of Poshaiyanne who came from the waters below the earth to live at Shipapolima, who went to Sun Father and begged that he might lead his people from the center as the plants shoot from the earth, to dwell in Sun Father's light. So it was that the great War Twins led the people up to their home on earth.

They led them from the east opening of the red world of fire, where they acquired the heat of life. They passed into the blue world of air and acquired the breath of life and from there proceeded out of its south opening into the yellow world where flow the waters of life, where cloud becomes rain and river and enters man and flows through his own blood. Finally, like the dry land that thrust from the waters, man, with heat and breath and blood, emerged into the white world of light where he now lives; led by burrowing badger, he climbed up the tall Douglas fir through the west opening as the Indian climbs the ladder from the subterranean kiva into the world of sun, the white world that opens to the north.

Among those who emerged were the first medicine men whom the War Twins took to Shipapolima that Poshaiyanne might give them keener senses to see and hear and smell more sharply and protect the people.

Here Poshaiyanne transformed them into the Beast Gods and gave them each a sacred direction to guard. Chief of all is Mountain Lion, god of the North, who lives at Shipapolima together with Poshaiyanne. Here also lives Kochinaka, Mother of Kachinas; here she keeps the game.

Here the five men sat and breathed in the life on the high *potrero* now as on the first day and here they quickened to the pervasive energy of peace that rose like invisible smoke.

Here Drake Cavanaugh felt the first faint stirring of his own psychic energy.

They resumed the trek on the silent trail.

They slept in the cliff-hung canyon where the ancients had made their third village, Tse-ki-tán-yi, but before they slept they sat in a circle of fire. Drawn together into its light, they shared its mystic life as men have done since the first hunters learned to release its yellow magic.

"Always my people were pursued," Juan began. "On a high mesa above Cuá-pa they carved more lions." The firelight reflected on Juan's dark eyes and moved on his dark face and he looked like one of Francisco's *santos* whose faces wore Indian casts.

Many trails wind up the mountain, Francisco had said, *but they all lead to the top*.

Juan's words rolled on.

Six times they moved. Each time they reared their walls and sank their kivas into the earth and in each a small hole passed through the floor, led deep into Shipapu. They dug pits round like the kivas to store their corn in the earth's womb, so like the tomb, for the living seed to lie as dead until it would once again grow from the warm Earth Mother and emerge into the light from the eternal center as all life did.

Six times they dug new fields and planted their seeds, their beans and squash and melons, and always the corn, the green corn which through the summers grew straight and tall like the Corn Maiden herself; they watched their own maidens grow straight and tall with black hair that hung glossy like the corn tassels until they would take husbands and grow their seed like the corn that nourished their lives.

Their lions guarded the game and life was good. The centuries rolled unmarked by history's ferreting eyes.

Then on great plunging beasts came the Spaniards with sun-flashing skins of armor and their long-robed medicine men with the God of the Cross which the people honored with their own gods until the blue-robes told them they must kill the old gods and worship only one. They joined the rebellion that swept from Taos. They killed the long-robes and the silver warriors and settled again along the river to till the fields and tend their gods.

The Spaniards returned. The people moved again to their old high fortress. They carried the sacred instruments of their ceremonies with them, the turquoise sky-stone and the bits of gold that are seeds of the sun, and they hid these things. The *cacique* in proper secrecy dug beneath the *rito* and hid the sacred treasures; but in the fighting he was killed and none could find the treasure again.

"Not so long ago," Juan finished, "somebody decide the treasure is under them lions at Cuá-pa. He set dynamite. So now only one lion guards that last shrine. The white man blow the other one up.

"But the treasure still hides!"

Drake lay beneath the overhanging cliff, wrapped like the others against the cold. Shadows moved large about them and the ancient gods moved as silently in the fireglow. Drake felt the presence of Mountain Lion Man and Poshaiyanne and he lay trying to ponder with words not yet born.

He thought of Poshaiyanne who, like Christ, knew not an earthly father, who died and lived again, and he thought of Dumuzi and Adonis and Osiris and of other gods who were resurrected since man invented religion; it occurred to him here in the spirit-quickening dark that many eyes have glimpsed the same eternal life principle they knew in the sprouting seed which rises from the dark earth, in the green principle of the forest on the same mountain they all climbed.

Somewhere on its high slopes perhaps Poshaiyanne rested. Perhaps he smoked a corn-husk cigarette and chatted with Jahweh and maybe they both listened to the distant serpentine notes of Pan that wound from the depths of a rocky cleft, soft music, feminine, that rose from the phallic flute. Here they called him Kokopelli and said he was hump-backed. By whatever name he calls the butterflies of spring and the flowers of summer and in whatever form, goat-hoofed or bent-backed, his phallus rises to propagate life, to swell the clouds that bear the rain and the crops that bear the fruit and the women who bear the brown babies.

Maybe they rest, Jahweh and Poshaiyanne, by a woman–lake in a high rincón, or beneath a faith-filled apricot tree. Maybe sometimes the paths converge, maybe you could follow the flute up any path.

But first, he thought, *you've got to find the mountain.*

The Indians greeted the day. They stood tall and looked to the east and received the emerging sun and the white men watched, silent.

They climbed to the cave. They saw the paintings, pure strong pigment, black, white, red in the bright hard light of new day, saw them fresh with the newness of untamed men who called their spirits by making their forms.

Here, in these colors, Sun Father pours the light of life onto the earth. Here kachinas forever dance their prayers and call the spirits whose masks they wear. Here the striped *koshares* weave in and about like prayer threads. Here, summoned, the animals run.

On these walls they enter the Otherness. They call the clouds and the serpent-thrust lightning to release the rain. And over them all stretches the serpent. Arrested in the long moment of eternity, he guards the flowing stream, he sends the mystic river of intuition flowing through the eyes of the beholder into his soul.

The snake, Drake thought, *always symbolizes eternal life. It sloughs its old skin and emerges new, resurrected. They say he's blind while he's shedding it, but the process still goes on; he gets new sight with new form. He's a phallus, too, and beneficent. It's only the Christians who make him the Eden-invading devil.*

Below him another serpent winds from the center and guards the deep pools that eddy from the spirit world as kachinas wind from the kiva, as dancers wind from Shipapu.

Drake, staring, felt his psyche whirl down into the spirit pool. His consciousness wound back to the Beginning before the Word and he saw the thing before a name attached, the essence before the substance when it was still concept, not percept. He saw the serpent in the clear water and followed it down through the clean smooth well, past its walls of rock before they were pitted with intellectualist holes. His spirit swam deep into the formless caverns, into the center where amorphous faith not yet pounded into dogma seethed rich and placental.

But I can't stay here, he knew. Immersed, he gasped for breath. Man lost his gills when he came from the center but Drake felt their vestiges tremble. *You can't go back to the womb.* Up he pushed, up and up, his heart tearing back to the air and Adam named his mate Woman, he named the Otherness and, naming, gave it a form and each was split forever, a lonely half of the whirling transcendental wholeness that is the great life.

He followed the serpent out and up into the air they rose. He flew on its back as Moctezuma and Malinche flew once before time from Cicuyé and followed the eagle in the path of Father Sun and dropped the seeds of life that grew to be pueblos. Far and farther south they flew on the feathered serpent to where they call him Quetzalcoatl.

On his back Drake flew.

He alit in the cave again and saw another figure he had not seen before. He saw time alight in the timelessness for in the center of the long frieze thrust a cross, a Christian cross, tall atop a mission altar.

The paths converged for a time on their climb up the mountain and empty snake skins lay discarded along the way.

"Kind of incredible, ain't it?" said Fergus.

The sun rode west as they topped the last *potrero* before they would descend from their high altar to where time would rise, take shape in roads and cars and buildings and telephone lines. Below them to the east the Río Grande snaked silently through its deep rift, widened into the glitter that was Cochiti Lake. Across the chasm towered the Sangre de Cristos, silent, shimmering, mass on mass they rose, arrogant, lonely, snow-prisoned peaks, rose-red in the dying light.

An eagle wheeled golden through the airy space, or maybe it was a spirit that rose free toward the isolate peaks. *But man must climb, must find the path at the bottom. We can't start in the middle*, he thought. *The significance is in the whole journey. Maybe the lions do guard the secret. Maybe the path does start there. Or maybe it begins in our awareness.*

Suddenly Drake sensed the strange quick moment of *déjà vu*, or prescience maybe, and he knew the words before they formed in Juan's mouth, the image before they came upon it.

"Mountain lion." Juan pointed to the half-eaten carcass of the deer in the old snow beneath the ledge, his blood congealing dark, his back snapped by the powerful spring of the tawny beast. Drake saw it before he looked, felt the strong pull of the deer who also knew the beast's claw. He knew somewhere with serpentine tail lurked the beast with burning eyes, knew she saw him, and the old hunt-lust surged through him again as it had before.

Did He who made the Lamb make thee? Even God was two, or maybe especially God: the oneness contained the otherness.

They filed down the trail to pavements and people and patterns.

Four days later the white men went to the dance.

They left early to reach the pueblo before light and the three of them bumped shivering through the pre-dawn black. Drake was glad Fergus had fixed the windows.

In the plaza they huddled in the icy black and the wind slashed through their clothes and into their veins.

"The animal dancers left the kiva already," said Fergus. "They're putting on their horns in the hills and the hunters are rounding them up for the dance."

"Oh christ," said Val.

Villagers began to clot the square. A cluster or so of Anglos looked uncertainly around and drew together. A couple from Dallas roughed the cold in Neiman-Marcus western wear. A fire-cheeked young woman from New Jersey with a tiny camera concealed in her jacket announced she was finishing her thesis. "On the psychology of primitive masks as seen in Southwestern ritual drama."

"Oh christ," said Val.

"Seen many dances?" asked Fergus.

"This is my first but I've got two weeks."

"Reckon you're a heap smarter'n me," said Fergus. "I been here twenty years and still don't savvy them dances." Drake grinned. Fergus's grammar tended to fracture around certain kinds of people.

"Well, of course I know what to look for."

"Lotsa dances to cover in two weeks. All of 'em different."

"The pattern's the same. See one and you've seen them all."

"That so?"

"Sure. And I'll interview some Indians."

"Liable to get your leg pulled."

"Not if you ask the right questions. Oh, darn, where'd I put my other film? You have to know how to talk to them, you know. On their level."

"Oh," said Fergus.

"Well, what are they *hung* on?" shrilled the Dallas blonde. "Don't they know we're *waiting*?"

They climbed a ladder, settled on a rooftop, and dangled their legs.

They waited for the dancers who for four days in the kiva had fasted and purged and kept themselves from women. Four days they had summoned the life forces in their own beings, had joined with them in powerful ceremonies about which the uninitiated can only wonder. Four days they let the life which is one flow, up from the center, down from the Father, in varying degrees through the

126

gods and the beasts and the spirits of the dead and the living. Then they filed up from the center and donned the power with the masks. Life in its varying forms had mingled four days, the Oneness and the Otherness, before the streams of dancers emerged as man had come through the levels of existence, up through the great birth canal of Earth into the four directions, and became the beasts who guarded these directions.

It was nearly time.

On the mud walls the watchers waited.

Streaks of cloud paled in the east. The new dust of snow caught the growing light and the black shapes of house and kiva grayed. The scattered talk hushed. Then, as the mud houses caught the first yellow glimmer on adobe they blazed, orange earth and shining snow crystal, and a soft gasp opened the closed throats.

From the hills they came galloping with jangling ankle bells, these animal men. Two buffalo led the herds, noble and ponderous, great-headed, massive-shouldered, curve-horned. Two, where once they outnumbered all the others, they acquired the tragedy and grandeur of the doomed which is to say of the universe.

Around them raced the other game. Half-a-hundred—elk, mountain sheep, mostly deer—they ran into the plaza, bare torsos bent over the sticks that were their forelegs, their backs draped with the pale hides of the winter deer. They raised their antlered heads proudly; they ran in all directions, unstructured, as the deer run loose in the hills. Sometimes they leaned on their sticks and let their belled hindlegs kick out.

Behind ran the Game Mother, lithe, young, arrow-darting among them, and with her came the hunters. Through the fleeing game, shaking her gourd, darted the maiden. Sometimes she touched one with her wand of eagle feather and evergreen, commanding until she and the hunters forced them up the dozen steps onto the round flat top of the kiva with its ladder shafts like lances that pierced the sunrise, aboriginal lightning rods that conducted the power. Down into the secret depths the dancers streamed.

The sun blazed on the plaza, on the glistening snow-powder, on the earthen mounds of the *hornos*, on the cross-topped mission church and the few stunted trees with their west-swept branches, on the brush-poled corral.

Those beneath the earth in the round kiva must perform rites before the dance could begin. For the waiting Val had stashed doughnuts and a thermos of coffee. They crawled from the roof with the rest, to eat or wander or socialize.

At midmorning it began.

PMMM-pmmm, PMMM-pmmm, PMMM-pmmm, PMMM-pmmm.

The drummers led.

HEH-yah, HEH-yah, YAH-HEH-YO.

The chorus followed.

From the kiva they streamed behind the war-bonneted chief. From the center throbbed the slow pulse of earth. Its cadence invaded each person, compelled each heartbeat into its rhythm. Low, insistent, it marshalled the throbs of cosmos and earth, it synchronized the beats of man and spirit, earth and sun, beast and man, so all pulsed together in the great One, the powerful energy of the universe.

The drums grew louder.

PMMM-pmmm, PMMM-pmmm, PMMM-pmmm, PMMM-pmmm.

HEH-yah, HEH-yah, YAH-HEH-YO.

The Game Mother danced in white deerskin, her leggings and moccasins edged with skunk fur—"to keep out the witches," Fergus said—and against the white dress gleamed turquoise jewelry and a red sash like a gash of blood. Her feather-topped hair straight, long, black-gleaming in the strong cold sun, she danced slowly, sideways, step-slide, step-slide, to the right, to the left, her gourd rattle aloft, ceaseless. She danced in the center with the buffalo, their faces and torsos painted black beneath the shaggy, heavy, eagle-feathered heads. The gourd rattle of command in one hand, the bow and feathered arrows of the hunt in the other, they danced upright, more spirit than game. Knees high-lifting, they were lords but always subject to the Maiden Mother, the eternal female principle. Maiden and buffalo danced slowly—close and retreat, close and retreat—pulled by the bond of huntress and quarry, isolate in their otherness, touching only through the tip of her green fir branch. As formal as a minuet, as wild as the untamed beasts, the dance was solemn, deeply moving.

Val leaned forward. Her face was intense; one strong hand clutched the roof edge tightly, red, gloveless, and her eyes watered.

HEH-ya, HEH-ya, YAH-HEH-YO.

The rhythm changed abruptly.

Pmmm-pmmm PMMM, pmmm-pmmm PMMM.

Ha-ya-NO, ha-ya-NO.

The dance accelerated.

Val inhaled sharply, alert to the alien rhythm, not yet comprehending.

"Cold, baby?" asked Fergus. He put his arm about her shoulder.

The tension broke. "No," she said, her voice flat.

The antlered game wove complex patterns, in and out, crossing, winding, circling. The hunt chief led the buffalo. The maiden commanded. Incessant rattling. Step-slide, step-slide.

Abruptly the drums ceased. Silence hung in the air for a staggering moment and then the beat resumed. The first rhythm pounded again. The dancers filed into the kiva.

The turquoise people had performed, the summer people, the male sky-people, and returned to their center. The squash people filed from their kiva, the winter, female, earth people, and the dance commenced again. As one season ends another begins.

All day they alternated, summer, winter, as the seasons turn.

HEH-ya, HEH-ya, YAH-HEH-YO.

Four times before the sun was high, four times after he began his descending journey.

Ha-ya-NO, ha-ya-NO.

Always the *koshares* broke the solemnity even as they served the practical ends of helping the dancers, of securing loosening bits of paraphernalia, of scooping up a tiny deer (who must not have seen over five years) when he tired.

"Oh, isn't he *cute!*" shrieked the Dallas blonde.

Naked except for breechcloths, jangling bells on wrists and ankles, the white-painted clowns, black-striped, their hair bunched in stiff top-knots tied with corn shucks, they wove like unseen spirits, unnoticed by the other dancers, and in the intervals between dances they clowned outrageously. They chased each other, they dragged one another through the snow-powdered dirt.

They caricatured the white hunter. One carried a pine branch. The other, thinking it a deer, shot, then paraded it for all to see. The Indians looked slyly to see if their Anglo guests laughed.

"What are they *doin*'?" squealed the blonde.

By mid-afternoon, the formal dances were done. The ritual would soon begin.

In bounded the *koshares*, relief before the grim drama and again they acted the white man. A corn-tufted 'game warden' accosted a gun-toting 'hunter' who, after much searching in pockets, produced a paper (hunting permit?), then a whiskey bottle. They drank and tussled.

Other clowns climbed to rooftops and heckled the spectators. Sometimes they snatched a delighted child who squealed as they ran with him before the hunters returned him to his mother.

Another *koshare* became a woman. 'She' carried a camera and aimed it at the crowd at the kiva, finally at the 'hunter' and the 'warden,' who reeled to either side of her and began to make humping sexual motions.

"Ain't they *cute!*" screamed the 'woman' *koshare*.

The crowd roared.

"What they *doin'*?" 'she' yelled.

Inexorably the drama of life proceeds.

In bounded the game, panicking, hiding, driven by the buffalo—once the herded, now the gods. *We suffered our fate as you must suffer yours.* The dancers moved as the wild game moves, the antler-tossing deer, the bounding elk, the ponderous buffalo.

The crowd grew tense.

The hunters followed. The chase began. The game circled wildly through the plaza. The hunters streaked close behind and all knew death inevitably would follow.

The hunter raised his bow. He nocked his feathered arrow and let fly the shaft. Up leaped the flying deer. Heart-hit he fell heavily. He thrashed convulsively until dead and limp. The victorious hunter slung him over a shoulder and bore him into the kiva.

The bonneted war chief, mad to kill, raged through the game. The hunters followed. A chaos of lust and fear clouded the plaza and the din of cries and shouts until, one by one, the hunters triumphed and they carried off the animals, the limp dead prey.

Over it all and through it all beat the drums.

From out of the confusion reappeared the maiden, the eternal woman, mother of man and game, sad and serene, and one was aware now only of buffalo and maiden mother. The rest were insignificant. There were only the maiden and buffalo—only the woman, gentle, inexorable, the enduring principle—and the beasts, the sons, noble, mortal, at bay.

Beasts and woman faced each other, total in their Otherness.

She reached out her arm. She touched one and the other with the wand, with the green branch of life, with the eagle feather that flies in the sun: the sentence, necessary that the people may live. The gesture of fate, of death. But also of life, of resurrection, for life flows from the sacrificial dead into the living: death sustains life.

Neither cringed. They faced their fate unflinching. They nodded: Acceptance? Compassion? Forgiveness?

Mother, forgive them, they know what they do.

"They didn't quite follow the pattern," said the thesis-writer. "But on the whole it was satisfactory."

Later, in Juan's home, Drake, Val, and Fergus ate mutton stew and the ash-flavored saltless pueblo bread that came from the *hornos*. The dancers had submerged, had returned to the center where they left their cosmic beings and emerged men again. Juan, who chanted in the chorus with the old men who no longer danced, returned to the world where men grow hungry, where they acknowledge friends and women and mutton stew.

The folds that spread from Juan's deep eyes and down-turned mouth changed direction. They pulled up and he made jokes with his guests. César brought his wife and sons and after they ate the two small boys danced. They imitated their elders and Juan laughed at their antics.

Val helped Juan's wife with the dishes and the men settled back for a smoke. Drake waited, hoping his host would talk about the dance, about its symbols and significance.

Juan belched. "Was a good dance," he said.

"That's close as you'll ever get to a Indian," Fergus said as they shot through the dark, shot on rubber tires from the aboriginal center in the American time machine. "Stars up there over the plateau are closer."

"Juan's friendly enough. Talkative."

"Sure, the stoic stuff's for the tourists. Indians talk. Not about the important stuff, though. That's why so much shit gets written about 'em by eastern anthropologists. They'll answer that Vassar broad's questions with any kind of malarkey they can dream up and it'll likely get published as gospel."

"I was hoping Juan might explain it to me."

"Why?" asked Val. "It either gets through or it doesn't."

She's right, he thought. *It doesn't work unless the participation is mutual. Like sex. Or art. Or religion. The guest has to throw his own thing in the stew, too.*

Val sat between them and stared ahead into the vast dark. She smoked continually and in the light of the glowing ends of the cigarettes, or the flaring matches, he could see something lurking behind her flat expression. He'd seen it during the dance but it always ducked back inside and hid.

"Turn the heater down, Fergus," she said.

"Sure, baby."

They drove on through the dark, along stretches where they glimpsed the snow-banked river where stars bobbed like phosphorescent ice chunks.

"Oh, yeah," said Fergus. "Juan sent you something." He arched back in his seat and reached into his pants pocket. "Nearly forgot." Across Val he passed a closed fist and dropped two flesh-warmed objects into Drake's hand, two small carved stones.

"What are they?"

"Fetishes. They trade for 'em over at Zuni."

"Why for me?"

"I told him you tangled with the lion. That was your hiking ticket to the shrine. He's acknowledging you."

"As what?"

"Friend, maybe. Hunter, or fool."

Drake tried to see them in the dark. "What are they?"

"They are two genu-ine mountain lions, son. They help hunters. Reckon he figures you need it."

They turned off the main road, started up the ascent, and hit a sudden bump, a small one, but enough to awaken the sluggish god of mechanisms. The front windows slid smoothly, obediently, down and all the icy breath of the lonely universe rushed in on them. *Deus ex machina.*

"Oh christ," said Val.

Drake warmed the little lions in his hand.

9

*A*fter the speech three women in red, white, and blue aprons served coffee and cookies the cleft-chinned man had blessed and Leona smiled and mingled and vote-fished and Drake leaned against a wall and folded his arms across his chest and grinned and wondered if she'd recognize him any more than Joe Emmons had (or show it if she did), but she didn't glance his way because he looked like a crummy wetback.

He considered ambling up and shaking her hand casually. ("It's been a long time and you don't look a day older.") He didn't. A recognition scene might amuse his sardonic demon but it would be bad taste. Some people would say cruelty but Leona wasn't the victim type. *You can't smash a marble statue with a fly swatter*, he thought. *But you could smear it with squashed fly guts and that is bad taste.* He hung that idea on a nail and leaned against a wall and watched the tribal rites and wondered where aesthetics had gone, why high-school auditoriums had to look so institutional, especially the new ones with folding metal chairs in primary colors and vinyl floors and a wall painted crotch high with the school's screaming color. This one was red like fire engines, rah-rah-rah.

He declined a cookie and ducked out past the misspelled obscenities in the halls into the night heavy with gray mist and gray smog. He walked back to the motel.

He hadn't read newspapers in Descanso. Up there it hadn't mattered what insanities spun like faceless dervishes in the vacuum world he'd left but now he sprawled across the bed and opened out the first sheet he'd skimmed since he'd shucked the old serpent skin and left it lying in the path that hadn't been a path after all, just a shallow pit he'd slithered round and round in. The first paper he'd read since he'd crawled blind and grown a new skin.

Van Winkle in the modern world, he thought—they'd both traded nightmares for dreams, he and Rip—only Rip had come back to a king booted out on his buns. He'd missed out on the ass-kicking, didn't even know about it. Maybe shots had been fired while Drake was in Descanso but pop-guns weren't heard 'round the world, not in the flap-doodle world he'd left. Dear Abby solved the world's problems and the comic page sated literary thirst and the daily horoscope provided a plan of life.

The ad lay innocent in a left-hand corner like a snake in the sun. "Ruin your weekend," it read. "Come to Los Alamos." Special package, salute old Indian ruins, guided hikes, square dance lessons, slide shows.

Christ, they still chased Poor Lo's ghosts. And slide shows, or is it side shows? And square dancing. HEH-yah HEH-yah YAH-HEH-YO is passé, positively aboriginal my dear. Swing-your-partner-and-do-se-do is in, and a hellacious sight more comprehensible, especially for Dallas blondes and Ivy League anthropologists, besides being closer to sanitized rest rooms.

It isn't chemical warfare or nuclear holocaust that will destroy civilization, he thought. *We're perishing from terminal tackiness.*

He showered again to wash away the stale smell of the high school and then across the steam-clouded mirror he traced a plumed serpent.

▲

The bells, they feared, would soon toll for Padre Lorenzo. They prayed for him in the church and they talked of him in the post office and the *cantina* and Doña Rosalía saw omens. He was indeed very ill; all, they agreed, because of the bells.

The bells marked the great events of their lives. Their weddings, baptisms, and funeral masses grew larger when the rich tones of the large bell sang from the church tower and the ancient celebrations of the Savior's birth and ascension became new and immediate.

The other bell, the old one they called La Campana, brayed hoarse-voiced like a burro from a *jacal* but they waited each Christmas and Easter for her voice and it was her they loved best.

Soledad tended the old priest in his illness and Drake saw to the wood for the fires and bit by bit he learned the story of the bells which is to say that of Padre Lorenzo.

Some blamed Alarico Vicente for the padre's illness. Alarico was too old and crippled to be *sacristán*, they said. His joints were so swollen he could scarcely move and they'd seen his face when the pain, like an electric current, ran through his feet from the beri-beri he'd suffered in the Japanese prison camp during the war.

He only snorted that the young men were worthless. He'd been *sacristán* thirty years, he said. It was his Christmas duty to light the *farolitos* that lit the way for the Santo Niño to ready the church and to ring the bells.

Padre Lorenzo told Alarico he must relinquish the midnight post.

"I fought in the war, Padre," he said. "You forget."

"No one forgets. You won't let them."

"Soldiers don't desert their duties."

"Old soldiers do," rasped Lorenzo. "They get laid off. We're both of us last year's cottonwood leaves, Alarico. We only clog the *acequia*."

Alarico would not back down.

When midnight approached the old priest waited for his friend at the church. Mass wasn't until morning—though Padre Lorenzo had always held it at midnight, the new priest wouldn't arrive until day—but the bell would ring. Wheezing and coughing in the cold he watched as Alarico tried to force one foot and then the other onto the high rung.

He hitched up his robe. "Give me a boost, Alarico."

It seemed a year to Alarico, huddled below in frigid humiliation, before the first faint tap and then the deep peal, as full and rich as Christmas itself, rolled joyfully over the dark village.

Lorenzo blew his nose hard in his bright bandanna when he reached the bottom. He gasped from the cold and wiped his eyes but triumph laughed in his thin voice. "Only two dead cottonwood leaves," he wheezed. "But while the young men slept, Alarico, we rang the bell!"

The padre rang the other bell at icy daybreak, too, as he had done for many years and promised he always would. Each Christmas he rang La Campana in a shed, a *jacal* like that where Christ was born. When the new priest first came he frowned on the custom, called it superstition and said Lorenzo coddled the people like spoiled children. (Alarico overheard the conversation.)

"I ring it for the beasts," the old priest answered. "The lowly beasts who worshiped at the manger, that they too might know it is Christmas. And at Easter to tell the birds He is risen!"

"A heathenish custom."

"To share our Lord with the birds and beasts? The founder of our order wouldn't have thought so, Father." He had mulishly stuck to the custom.

"Yes, Alarico, we rang the bells." He had rung La Campana at dawn, too, though as he later admitted, his throat burned, the fire was deep in his chest after his midnight climb, and by the time he had made his frail way at dawn the frozen air sliced his lungs like a knife. By dusk his voice was a wraith and fever alternately burned and chilled him so he shook the cot he lay on.

"But the bells rang," he rasped to Alarico and Francisco at his bedside. "La Campana sang for the animals!" For a long time he lay as if asleep and Francisco stood to leave. Then his eyes opened. "San Francisco," he wheezed. "He was always my favorite saint. Make me a San Francisco."

He turned to Alarico. "Two old cottonwood trees! And La Campana, too." The old wispy grin flitted across his face as it always had when he had conspired with God against the new priest. Then his eyes looked vague and the grin faded to the wistful smile of a lost angel. "Father Andreas doesn't approve."

"He doesn't understand."

The grin flew by again like a scurrying ghost. "But the animals do," he whispered.

Soledad nursed him and Luz prayed by his bedside until she fainted. Drake and Enrique Peralta hauled wood, passed pleasantries with the villagers who filed in and out and visited with Alarico and Francisco who came twice daily. It became a ritual.

It also seemed a time for introspection.

Alarico suffered worst. "It was my stubborn pride," he kept repeating. "If I wasn't so hell-bent to ring that bell. . . ."

He relived the war during these anxious days. "I failed then, too," he told whoever would listen. "I didn't bring Ysidro home." In Padre Lorenzo's small *sala* they drank the coffee Soledad made and from time to time Alarico pulled at his sad slim *mustachio*, gray but still gallant.

"I promised Francisco. Ysidro wasn't cut out for no soldier. Not scared—didn't have enough sense to be scared. No soldier sense. Brain full of dreams.

"Telling Francisco about his boy was worse than facing Japs." He rolled a cigarette in shaking fingers and Drake wished he had his sketch pad.

"Ysidro was brave. He wasn't no more scared than we all was when them Jap planes first hit us at Clark Field or on our retreat to Bataan with them bastards strafing us all the way. He didn't complain down there when we was trapped and starving and all the supplies they promised us didn't come.

"Once he was listening to our radio in the jungle and they was talking about all the factories at home pouring out guns and planes and tanks. Only thing was, they was all crossing the Atlantic. 'They got their oceans mixed up,' I said.

"Ysidro just looked gentle-eyed like he always done and said he heard Columbus sailed the wrong way too, once.

"We got hungrier and our ammunition ran out and then we had to surrender. We all had malaria and dysentery—*ooh-eeh*! Ysidro and me help each other on that Death March. That's what killed him.

"The Japs wouldn't let us get water but one time. I was all bent over with dysentery and he filled my canteen. But when he tried to give me some a guard knocked it to the ground and cracked his rifle butt across Ysidro's kidney. The water all ran out on the ground.

"He never got over that blow. It did something to his insides. He was barefoot, too, and the blisters bust and the skin was all gone. We carried him far as we could.

"Then he had a dysentery attack and stumbled off the road—and a filthy Jap bayoneted Ysidro. Ran him through, and then put a foot on him to pull out his bayonet."

The recounting was in the nature of confession and seemed to lighten Alarico's load.

▲

The third day Padre Lorenzo grew worse. All Descanso prayed for a miracle which Soledad said it would take and they gathered in small clumps and repeated anecdotes which the others had already heard. Drake and Enrique stacked the padre's wood and ducked into the *cantina* after to drink a *cerveza* and report his condition. "*No bueno,*" said Enrique.

Tomás opened their cans sadly behind the bar, wiped his head with a dirty handkerchief, and remarked on the frailty of all men and of the padre in particular. Then he grinned. "Remember the time he let the Indian get away?"

A few chuckles ran about the room and those inside remembered when the state police had come up their mountain three years before. The Indian, in for murder, had escaped the state prison, they advised. He was believed in these mountains and dangerous.

"Maybe in the mountains," Sheriff Garcia, picking his teeth, told Tonito down in Colinas. "But he ain't dangerous." Tonito was deputized and sometimes, after he got through tending bar on Saturday nights, he helped Garcia on the force. "Indian only stabbed a Anglo in a fair fight," the sheriff said. "In a Indian bar. Where that hippy shouldn't of been in the first place."

The state police, getting little cooperation from Garcia, were on the Indian's trail and Father Andreas was in Descanso when they came. He stayed with Padre Lorenzo in his tiny house and the two priests supped with Doña Rosalía, Enrique, and Luz.

"Tonito said it wasn't really murder," their hostess said. "Garcia told him. Just an ordinary Indian." She primped her permanent.

"A convict," said Father Andreas and pledged his cooperation. He told his parishioners to double-check their *jacals* that night and after supper he proposed to look about that of his hosts, just in case. "No need for you to come," he told Father Lorenzo, who came along anyhow.

He'd also padlock the church, he decided. The old padre was amazed. The church was never locked.

"Can't be offering haven to criminals, Father."

"The church isn't for sinners? Oh my, Father!"

They left then and Enrique didn't hear the rest of the conversation. They locked the church door, though. That much he knew.

In the morning the lock hung open and the key was gone from the table in Father Lorenzo's kitchen where they left it. Someone had been in the church. Large footprints muddied the floor and the altar cloth had a smudge and hung crooked.

Had someone hidden there until the state troopers were gone? How had he gotten in?

Could whoever took the key have let him in, relocked it, and let him out after the police left?

(Luz, sweeping the padre's kitchen, overheard the conversation and told Doña Rosalía and her father later.)

"I went in late to pray," the old priest said vaguely. "I often do. Someone could have slipped in."

"You certainly would have known."

"In deep prayer? Oh my, Father!"

"You locked the door when you left? Did you not go out again?"

"Oh yes. I often do. Before it is light."

Had he gone to the church?

He passed by on the way to the *camposanto*. Nothing seemed amiss.

"Yet the door was open this morning, and the key was gone."

"I must have misplaced it, Father."

"It was your responsibility, Father."

And then—the men in the *cantina* always loved to hear Enrique tell the end—then Padre Lorenzo, looking innocent like an *angelito*, said, oh yes, he knew that—but after all, even Saint Peter had once lost the keys to Heaven! The old man crossed himself quickly and gusted off with vague mutters.

Later that day when Luz and Doña Rosalía went to get the altar cloth to wash off the smudge they found the key resting innocently under San Juan Nepomuceno. "The keeper of secrets," Luz said softly.

"Dear, dear," muttered Padre Lorenzo and a small hoarse giggle surfaced and turned into a cough. "For shame, San Juan," he wheezed and then crossed himself quickly.

Though none ever knew the truth, they all had their opinions.

▲

While Soledad tended Padre Lorenzo, Marta kept her sons, three since the birth of Pepito, whom she sometimes brought by the priest's house. He was a square little boy of two, built like his mother. Emotion stabbed Drake each time he saw the child and the question blazed in his mind though he didn't ask it. She would only smile that womansmile, he knew.

He had gone to Soledad's the day the child was born and his eyes were cloud-scudded as he looked at the miracle of new life, miniature but complete. "He even has fingernails," he said.

Soledad laughed. "He'll need them to scratch his way in the world."

"Soledad." He leaned over her, started to touch the soft black fuzz on the baby's head, then with a light finger he traced a long frond of hers instead that fanned the pillow. "Soledad, is he mine? Is he my son?"

"*¿Quién sabe?*" She shrugged and laughed again. "Does it matter who drops the seed in the soil?"

"It matters whether it's a corn seed or a melon—a *grano* or a *pepita*."

"We'll see how he grows," she said carelessly. "Come in, Father."

Padre Lorenzo gusted in and his vague smile wafted over them all. "May

God and the Blessed Virgin smile on all the little ones." He signed a cross. "Carlos! What brings you here!"

He knows damned well why I'm here, thought Drake. "Look here, Father, there's something I want to say."

"Men talk too much," complained the priest mildly. "It causes much trouble. Little ones like this stay pure until they learn to speak."

"Words get to the bottom of things."

"Disturb the bottom of the *acequia*," said the old man, "and the mud rises."

Teresita hobbled into the room. Soledad had stayed away from her grandmother for weeks after Julián's visit, but the rift seemed healed. The old woman picked up the baby and he opened his cloudy eyes to a world in which he saw only light. She watched Carlos closely. "His eyes. . . ."

"Will be like his mother's," wheezed the priest firmly.

Soledad spoke before Teresita could. "We were only asking," she said, "whether he is more like a corn seed or a melon."

Padre Lorenzo's laugh blew the clouds from the room. "Right now," he said, "he looks like a small round *pepita*!"

Though they christened him Juan, they called him Pepito.

▲

Drake drank coffee with Soledad after he stacked the padre's wood.

"I hope Father Andreas comes soon," she said. Her patient grew weaker.

"The padre can't have much to confess," said Drake.

"Not like some," she said, and told him about her grandmother's death.

Teresita had left her life as Pepito was barely getting into his; and, leaving, pressed the blue stone into Soledad's hand. "For the first time I wasn't afraid when I felt its life and knew its power was mine.

"She told me dark things then and when she was through I ran for Padre Lorenzo. She was dead when we got there. She never confessed her sins."

And there were sins, Soledad knew, that pressed on the soul of the old woman who had given her the strange love she withheld from everyone else, who lay with the life gone out, so tiny it seemed impossible she had housed the great flame of her spirit. *Ay*, there had been sins.

The villagers remembered them.

Once a stranger came to her door at night and was gone the next day. No one knew where he came from and none saw him leave; the footprints of a bear were seen clearly outside Teresita's door.

Another time, called to the Villareáls' to attend an illness, she entered and left through the kitchen. Catalina wondered why she hadn't used the front door until she remembered the little cross of needles under the rug. Everyone knew witches couldn't walk over a cross.

There was the time Doña Rosalía told Delfina Romero that Soledad wasn't good enough for Julián. They didn't see Teresita crouching by a shelf in the back of the store until too late. After that Doña Rosalía's hens suddenly stopped laying.

The villagers whispered these things and Soledad heard the whispers. *Ay*, there had been sins.

"But not witchcraft," the old priest told her. "She ministered to all of us." It was June and things bloomed that made him sneeze—things, he observed, that she turned into cures for others. "One man's medicine is another man's sneeze," he said. "She was a good woman."

Some crossed themselves and said she shouldn't lie in sacred soil, Soledad remembered. "But he buried her in the *camposanto*. And later, when the new priest got here, Padre told him she had died confessed!

"But then," Soledad laughed. "Then he crossed himself—fast!"

Padre Lorenzo rallied and Drake brought him apricot brandy which made speech less painful, he said.

"Soon," he wheezed, "I go to join old friends in the *camposanto*. *Es bueno*. There you and I first spoke, *¿no es verdad*, Carlos?"

Drake remembered. He'd first seen him among the graves, a steeple-shaped man with wispy hair like thin clouds caught on a dark spire. Wandering among the dead, he talked to himself or them in a voice like an asthmatic ghost. He hailed Drake, they exchanged pleasantries, and the old man continued his discourse with no pause or change of tone. Drake was never sure whether he was addressing him or his invisible audience.

They chatted often in the *placita* or in the churchyard or on the bank of the *acequia*. Sometimes Drake found him with Francisco in his orchard—the rock and the wind, he called them—and as their friendship deepened he often shared a *copita* with the padre and lazy conversation.

The old priest could relax in his company, Drake thought. He didn't have to be on duty around him, to try and sell his religion. "Because I'm not a customer, Padre. Though I'm not knocking it. What cures one man causes an allergic reaction in another."

"And were you never a believer?" the priest had asked on a day of high blue summer. They sat in Drake's small patio and watched the bee-clotted hollyhocks Soledad had planted against the sun-baked wall and they watched Goso, the awkward adolescent puppy Catalina Sifuentes had given Drake, as he chased the yellow butterflies that bubbled about. The father loved butterflies. "One of God's happiest miracles," he called them. He sneezed with allergies and wiped his nose with the red bandanna. "You've never believed?"

"I used to go through the motions. Another splash of brandy? Guess I fell by the wayside long ago."

"And so do we all," sighed the old priest. "Too often I neglect my God for His people."

"Isn't there something about ministering to the least of them?"

"But not about twisting canon law to suit them. What fine brandy this is! One can smell the apricots. When I was a young man I pointed my feet straight for heaven. I wouldn't dawdle on the way." He wiped his eyes again. "But one day it occurred to me that it was impolite to rush so through the scenery God made for us to enjoy. I slowed my race toward heaven and listened to the people on the way. I was in less hurry to complete my journey. People are more needful of my attention than angels, you know. And livelier company."

He crossed himself hurriedly as he always did when he was afraid he'd uttered an irreverent thought and wasn't quite sure and his quick rueful smile flitted like sporadic sunlight through blowing lace clouds.

A gray-striped cat dropped over the wall, and a fountain of butterflies rose like golden dust. Goso ran to Drake and pressed against his legs. Cats terrified him.

Drake laughed lazily, held the bottle toward his friend, and refilled his glass. For a moment only the drone of bees, the soft splash of the brandy, and Padre Lorenzo's occasional sniffles bobbled in the sun-gilt silence.

"I haven't the learning Father Andreas has," he said. "There is much I don't understand." His voice wandered off vaguely.

"You seem to hold your own. Like when the Indian got away."

"You've heard that story?"

"More than once. The people believe you helped him."

"They also believe I can make a miracle."

"You let him in the church?"

"I went to pray. If someone else felt the same need, could I deny him?"

"The troopers must have checked the church."

"I locked it when I left."

"He couldn't let himself out."

"How do you know he was there?"

"Oh come on, Padre, it's over and done. Wasn't he?"

"*¿Quién sabe?* Some affairs are best left in God's hands."

"Like fugitives?"

"And miracles."

The distant hum of a single-engine plane mounted the air and grew louder.

"The prop-driven priest arriveth," said Drake. "On the Holy Ghost Airline."

The roar grew. The fragile peace collapsed like a soapbubble. Father Andreas's plane shot from behind them over the house and banked sharply toward the pasture.

"Like a defecation from heaven," said Father Lorenzo and immediately crossed himself. "I should not have said that."

Drake laughed.

"I should not even have thought that." He made a circular motion with his glass and watched the amber eddy. "But," he said, "one can't push the bubbles back into the spring." He swallowed the last of his brandy, gazed sadly at the glass, empty like an expired peace treaty. He deposited it on the table, tightened his cincture, sneezed twice, and wafted off to meet Father Andreas.

Later Drake remembered how a butterfly landed on the rim of the empty glass and balanced delicately with slow wings.

▲

Francisco smelled the brandy's sweet aroma before he entered the room. Carlos, leaving, gestured toward the bottle. "Summer's essence," he said. "We were toasting summer and butterflies."

How the Padre loves them, Francisco thought. He poured himself a measure, inhaled its soul, and remembered the last time they had walked in the orchard and a butterfly rested on the priest's full brown sleeve. "How fragile all life is," Lorenzo had said. "Even an angel must weigh more!" He laughed in his quavery voice and relieved a limb of three golden apricots. Two he placed in the tub Francisco was filling. The third he ate.

Francisco had never known anyone with such a passion for apricots. In anyone else, he thought, it would be the sin of gluttony. In Father Lorenzo it became a hymn of praise.

When they rested in the shade the old priest mopped his forehead and then his watery eyes with his ragged bandanna and from time to time he popped another sun-filled fruit into his mouth.

"The fruits of sin," he said.

Francisco was startled. "You called them fruits of faith!"

"¡Ay, verdad! From man's sin is born his faith." He leaned against the trunk, ate another, and wiped his juice-blessed lips. "Do you remember when I told you to plant them?"

"Sí. My heart was dark with losing Ysidro. 'They are the earliest to bloom,' you said, and their children, the little blossoms, so often taken by the cruel spring—like my Ysidro. The trees of faith, you called them. As they have been."

"As your faith made them," said the priest, "and my sin." Another fruit disappeared between his lips. He closed his eyes and savored it. "I used your grief for my gain, Francisco. 'Plant them,' I said."

"For faith."

"I said that. But did I think of faith or the delicious fruit?" He ate another. "I fear it was my own passion I indulged," he said sadly. "And I don't even grow my own. I eat yours."

Had he not done his share of work on them, Francisco asked, even when the dust blew and the cottonwood seeds scattered their fluff like sins and his nose plagued him unmercifully?

That was his penance.

"And the years they get killed back. We are never certain."

"No more are we certain of salvation. But then, if we were certain, we'd need no faith!" He sneezed. "Do you suppose each apricot is for a sin forgiven? Then I need many apricots!" He ate another sun-warm token, crossed himself, and closed his eyes in the fragrant peace amid the yellow butterflies that danced their silent prayers.

Ay, no butterflies in December. Francisco breathed his own prayer and stood to leave.

A faint smile lifted Lorenzo's face. "*Por favor,*" he whispered. "Make me a San Francisco."

▲

A small white bird had perched on her window, Doña Rosalía said at the post office, and a candle guttered low: double signs of death. She feared the father would not last long. "And all to ring the bells," she sighed.

"What of that bell?" Drake asked. "The old one—La Campana?"

Rosalía loved to tell the tale. "It started with Doña Felicia," she began. "Long ago when she was young and beautiful. She told it to me this way:"

Felicia was sixteen when she first saw Amado Romero ride through the high *portal* into her father's *placita*, a tall man with slant eyes and a bold nose, a guitar over his shoulder and a rifle in his hand. The sun gleamed on the black horse and on the rider's black hair and something else gleamed in his black eyes and she was suddenly aware of her own woman shape and though he couldn't see her behind the vines that screened the long veranda, she sucked in her waist and thrust out her breasts and tossed her black mane as the snorting horse did his. She heard him ask in an arrogant voice for Don Diego and she ducked inside when her father strode into the *placita*.

That night the stranger was at dinner and he brought distance and daring with him. He came from Descanso over the mountain and he carried a letter from the priest there, *muy importante*, which seemed to displease her father.

"You may tell the good padre I know nothing about his bell," said Don Diego.

Amado Romero had been a *soldado* and had ridden into Mexico with those who chased Pancho Villa. Along with her sisters Felicia listened with lively eyes and dancing blood as his voice rose and fell like flame and even her mother's masked eyes crinkled a little at the corners.

Don Diego was cold and courteous.

The next morning the visitor was still there and on the next he rode with her father to the high pasture. After that Don Diego seemed more friendly toward Amado.

"Papa thinks you stole Premio," Felicia said, giggling, when Amado rubbed the stallion down at the end of a day working cattle. With talk of war so many of the men had gone off to join the army and September was busy. He stayed to help, not really a guest but not a hired hand either. Felicia hung around the stables, watched for him, gave unusual attention to her own small bay mare. "He thinks you stole Premio from the army."

He laughed loudly and cut his oblique eyes at her. "Say I captured him! He belonged to one of Villa's *capitánes*."

"Did you kill the *capitán*?"

"No. Though one could say he was dead. Dead drunk!" Often the two armies camped very close and the *soldados* visited at night. "We drank their tequila and played cards."

"You didn't fight battles?"

"Sometimes. Not much."

"Why did you become a *soldado*?"

"Why does anyone? To find adventure! When I was at home—Descanso is a very poor village—I had to hoe beans and plow fields and go to mass on Sundays."

"Were there no *bailes, señor*? Or pretty girls?"

"Some." He laughed. "Call me Amado."

"Amado." Suddenly she wished he were her *amador* and she blushed and he saw it and laughed across Premio's back and gave her a long slow look that promised something, and dared her too.

"So what about Premio?"

"I was the best card player in the army. I won him."

"From the drunk *capitán*?"

"From the groom I played with. *Ay*, I had a time hiding him, too. But things were confused and then there was a battle at Carrizal."

"You were a hero?"

He came around Premio, looked down into her face. "No, *querida*," and he laughed softly. "I was hung over. I missed the battle! But so, I imagine, did the groom. He'd bet his *capitán*'s horse!"

She giggled. "Why did you come here?"

"I'll tell you. Later." He came out of the stall and looked down at her. He smelled of horse sweat, a good male smell.

He kissed her gently at first there in the stable which smelled of horses and dust and alfalfa hay. Her lips opened under his and then a rush of heat flooded through her and she flung back to him his dare.

Later he told her about the bell.

It came from Spain and hung in the mission church. For two centuries it tolled the births and deaths and due to some mysterious phenomenon of acoustics or angelic manipulation—for it was a small bell—its strange sweet voice carried up the *río*, resounding against the plum-colored mountain, and flooded the village which had no bell.

The distant tolling filled the canyon and stole into their lives, a soft voice in a hard wilderness.

Utes and Comanches began to raid their valley until they abandoned their village and fled to the mountain and many of the *genízaros* from the pueblo fled with them. The isolates gradually merged their blood and became one.

In time the danger lessened. People began to come down into the valleys again where their crops could thrive and some settled along the *prado* that overlooked the old village site. They called the new village Descanso because of the miracle.

It was a good spot except for one thing: they could only hear the bell on very clear days.

In the pueblo below the mission church crumbled despite constant repairs and when a new church was begun a rich *gringo* gave them a finer bell. *José, María, y Santo Niño!* Heaven smiled on Descanso for they were promised the old bell as soon as the new one arrived, the old bell which their ancestors had brought and to which their *abuelos* listened, the bell whose golden tones had entered their souls before they were conceived in their mothers' wombs.

Then one night it disappeared.

At sunset its glint reflected the western rays. At daybreak its silhouette no longer hung black against the dawn-red streaks from the east which now flooded free through the hollow of the empty tower.

Ladrones had stolen their bell!

Some said it was *brujas* for no dogs barked and they discovered no footprints save their own.

Others asked what sin they had committed that God should punish them so.

Still others remembered a soft-spoken young *hidalgo* who, some days before, rode through from a war with Cuba toward his papa's *rancho* across the mountain. He had stopped to watch the work on the new church, heard the talk of a fine new bell, and asked casually about the old one.

A year passed. They heard of an *hidalgo*'s son over toward Mora who had brought his bride a present, a souvenir of the land of his ancestors, a bell which he hung in the chapel to ring for his marriage and for the birth of his first child.

"That child was you, Felicia," Amado said.

She laughed and lights played in her eyes. "Are they sure it's the same one?"

"Oh, yes. They just don't know how to get it back."

"And that's why you came?"

"*Ay*, I came for the bell. But I stay for you."

Don Diego said the bell was his. "It came from Segovia, the home of my ancestors. When I found it, it was abandoned."

"It was promised to Descanso."

"Then why did you not send for it?"

"You wouldn't answer letters or see any messengers. Until I came."

"Strutting like an *hidalgo*."

"But you saw me." Amado sent a lance-eyed look from his long eyes. "And I believe you a man of honor."

"In return for the bell, *señor*, I vowed to the Blessed Virgin that it would ring for the marriage of my first child. You wouldn't have me break my vow."

"No, *señor*." Amado spoke slowly. "A vow must be kept. The bell must ring for Señorita Felicia."

He stayed through the winter. Don Diego grew fond of the brash young man and often on winter nights they played at cards.

"I cannot understand," said Amado once, "how you can so often win. No one in Mexico could beat me."

"Ah, but in Cuba," said Don Diego, "no one could beat me!"

Amado continued to lose and to meet Felicia in the dark.

Don Diego arranged his daughter's marriage. Felicia would marry the son of Don Pedro Gonzales y Luna, an old friend whose land adjoined his. The boy was handsome, personable, and pious. The families were well pleased.

Only Felicia rebelled.

Don Diego was quiet and gentle and unmoving when she defied him. "And whom would you choose?" he asked reasonably.

She only cried.

"Look around you," he said. "So few real *hidalgos* are left. Who else is there?" He cast for a joke. "Would you have someone like—like Amado Romero?"

She wiped her eyes which only brimmed again and jutted her chin at him.

"He would do quite well, Papa!" she said.

He laughed at the absurdity.

The card games continued. "Always you beat me," Amado lamented one evening. "Soon I must return to Descanso. With no bell and no winnings."

"But you are an excellent player," Don Diego said. "You should not give up."

"I'm no match for you, Don Diego."

"We'll play one last game! This one for real stakes!"

"What have I to put up?"

"Premio!"

"Premio!" He gasped. "Against—what?"

"What is worthy of him?"

"He's a fine horse." Amado thought a long moment. Then he said slowly, "The bell, Don Diego. Descanso's bell!"

"My bell," he corrected. "And it must ring for Felicia's wedding."

"It was your challenge, *señor.*"

"You'd have me risk my vow to the Virgin?"

Amado shrugged. "If the Blessed Mother is on your side," he said, "that should give you the edge."

Don Diego's pride flared. True, he had the strength of the vow. Besides, he always won. "Done!" he said. "We'll let the Virgin decide."

"I think," said Amado softly, "you have no worry. The bell, I'm certain, will ring at Felicia's wedding!"

Don Diego, the letter read. *Knowing you, a man of honor, will honor your loss, I have taken the bell. I have also taken Felicia. I too am a man of honor: your vow to the Virgin will not be broken: the bell will ring at our marriage!*

On the night they eloped, Felicia, with the horses and burros, waited for Amado and the Indian boy outside the walls. Excitement warmed her against the driving March wind until they arrived with the bell between them.

They had trouble, Amado told her later, digging the chain from which it hung out of the tower wall and when at last its anchoring gave, it fell with a crash. Though the wind covered the noise it was a bad moment.

In Descanso the people were jubilant when Amado came down the mountain with the lovely *señorita* and the bell they had awaited so long. They listened delighted to Amado's tale of how they had fallen in love; they laughed when he recounted the card game he had so carefully set up through the winter of deliberate losing; they gasped when he told how he stole the bell, of the crash it made, and of the trek over the mountain with the bell-laden burros swinging it between them, its clapper wrapped.

They gave thanks when they hung La Campana. At the wedding they sucked in their collective breaths to hear for the first time her incredibly sweet voice of whose legendary beauty they had dreamed.

The first tones rang out. Startled looks glanced through the congregation. Disbelief became consternation.

Had the legend been distorted, the angelic tones exaggerated?

Was the Virgin angry?

Some alchemy of sound had turned the golden notes to base metal!

Why would the Virgin be angry? They had done no wrong. The bell was theirs by right. Amado had won her fairly and honored the vow.

It was the crash when it dropped, they said, a natural accident. Besides, the tone really wasn't so bad. They had expected too much. The bell, like themselves, was of this earth. She reminded them of their own imperfections. She kept them humble. They prized her for that.

Above all, La Campana was theirs.

They grew to love the small imperfect bell so like themselves; when the bishop sent a new one they were dismayed. Everyone agreed the new bell had a fine pure tone but it was La Campana they loved. She was their conscience and their soul.

Meanwhile Padre Lorenzo had come to Descanso, a funny man with his odd loping walk and his squeaky voice and vague manner. At first they laughed but then they loved him for he, like their bell, admitted his own faults freely. He could not be stern with them and they soon learned that when he acted most austere he was trying hardest not to laugh.

It was Father Lorenzo who settled the problem of La Campana.

Why shouldn't Descanso have two bells? he asked. Let the proud new bell chime in her tower. La Campana could hang lower, closer to her own people, and he would ring her at special times. It began the custom they had followed since.

She hung on a crossbar that rested on forked juniper posts, shoulder-high to a man, in the courtyard of the church. Twice a year she still sang to them.

"Our Saviour was born in a stable," the padre said, "where the lowly beasts could worship Him. Should our beasts do no less?"

So it was that each year in a different *jacal* the stable manger was readied and in it they placed the figures Francisco had carved: *José*, *María*, and the *Santo Niño*, the shepherds and the Magi.

One year when Cipriano Pacheco's barn was honored a Wise Man unwisely stood too close to the stall and one of Cipriano's goats ate his robe and a hunk of his posterior. Francisco patched the wound but the scar reminded them that even wise men can be foolish, that even the mighty suffer infirmities and they honored him the more.

They carried La Campana to the *jacal* and on Christmas morning she rang for the beasts of Descanso.

During the forty days of Lent they veiled her in purple and turned their thoughts on mortifying their own flesh.

On Easter Eve they unveiled her, carried her through the *placita*, out to where Francisco's apricot trees affirmed their faith next to the *camposanto*, so near that the floating petals drifted over and softened the graves in spring. There in the branches they hung her and the padre said prayers to Saint Francis, his favorite saint and benefactor of his order, and he prayed for the birds he loved.

When morning flamed pink with new life and light, La Campana with her human faults and hoarse voice proclaimed the He is risen.

▲

A large sigh enveloped Doña Rosalía. Her small fat hands that danced with her words now signed a cross. "Never once has our bell failed us. But now— the new priest looks down his long nose at her. And who besides our own padre is saintly enough to ring her?"

"He isn't gone yet, Doña Rosalía."

"*Ay.* But Carlos—the white bird came this morning!"

That same night—it was Epiphany—sometime between midnight and dawn the wispy ghost of the old priest slipped quietly from its trembling shell. For the last time he and La Campana had welcomed the Santo Niño.

10

*D*rake slept raggedly because the heat kept blowing all night to spite the central control so in the morning he showered again and threw the towel on the bed and in the mirror he saw his naked whiteness where the brown left off, like part of him had never gone home again but the brown part still belonged to Descanso. He saw how gray his hair was, too, which he already knew but he hadn't paid much attention to.

In the coffee shop he ordered eggs and juice in English and made small talk in Spanish with the Mexican behind the cash register and the only other customer was watching him from down the counter so he said good morning to him too.

"Rain's over," the man said. He talked like Brooklyn with a Harvard varnish and he wore a green tie. A briefcase lay next to his cup. "Come from around here?"

"More or less," said Drake.

"Interesting country." The man pulled a card from the case and handed it down the counter. Arthur Foxe, Ph.D., Associate Professor of Cultural Anthropology.

"I took some anthro," said Drake, "in my undergrad days." The waitress brought his eggs and poured them both more coffee.

Doctor Foxe looked surprised and when Drake said Yale he looked even more surprised. "Law," said Drake. "But I don't have a card. Only these." He pulled the stone fetishes from his pocket and put them on the counter. "Genuine artifacts," he said.

"Interesting," said the professor. "Yale, you say?"

"My family had oil money and an Ivy League complex."

"Where do you practice?" asked the professor.

"I don't," said Drake.

"Where do you live?"

"Nowhere," he said. "I'm in a state of becoming, not being, Professor," he added.

"Call me Art," he said. He swished his coffee in his mouth before he swallowed it. "I suppose I am too," he said. "I'm on sabbatical. Studying Southwest cultures."

"Yeah?" said Drake.

"Yes," said Art. "Which I would guess you know something about."

"Not much," said Drake. "But I've talked to some experts. There was a guy spent some time up at a trading post where I hung out. He was an expert. From Washington. Did demographic reports on Indians or some damn thing. BLM guy brought him up and he latched on to me. I went to a couple of pueblos with him." He laughed and pulled the plastic cover from the jelly packet. "Their farming methods upset him. Thought they needed modernizing."

"Don't they?" Art swished his coffee again.

"Maybe," said Drake. "I don't know. You'd be tampering with their religion. This guy was hung up on economy. I showed him some piñon trees, showed him how the little nuts grow in clusters in the cones. It's a big part of their economy, I told him.

"So he went back to Washington, wrote up his report. The BLM guy showed it to the trader and he showed it to me. Know what the stupid son-of-a-bitch wrote?" asked Drake. "In the official government report he wrote it: 'The Southwest Indians,' he wrote, 'exploited and poverty-stricken, are reduced to eating pine cones.'

"That's what the lint-brained bastard wrote."

"I'm not working for the government," said Art. "And I'm not interested in economic reports. What I'm really interested in are the Penitentes."

"Yeah," said Drake. "They all are."

"Know anything about them?"

"Enough to mind my own business," said Drake.

▲

Always they begged for a miracle—just a small one as befitted their humble lives.

"They're all around you," Padre Lorenzo had always insisted and he cited spiders' webs and yellow butterflies and newborn creatures and apricot trees.

Of course, they assured him, they were grateful for these but they wanted a special miracle—a small one would do—just for Descanso, to assure them that God (unlike the *políticos* in Santa Fé) knew they were here, that He had once rested in their sunny *placita* for one small moment of eternity if only to remove a cactus prickle from a heavenly toe.

"Make for us a miracle, Father," they begged. "A miracle for Descanso."

"It is from your own faith that God makes miracles." He chided them, but gently; while he lived, Father Lorenzo had hoped he could effect, or find, a special miracle—even a small one—for his people.

Later they said he did.

▲

He had a wish, too, a small request, much smaller than a miracle. He had served them when he lived and wished to be buried among them when he died. He would lie at the edge of the *camposanto* where the shade of an apricot crept as the day grew old, where its roots might someday pierce his heart and feed on his flesh and suck him up to become blossoms and sweet fruit—which, he reflected, would be in itself a miracle, one of the ordinary ones he loved. It was a small and simple wish.

When the time came it seemed not so simple.

The news rolled like purple thunder over the village.

Father Lorenzo was dead!

The people wept. They would miss the frail old priest who had lingered so long on earth like a sidetracked angel in brown Franciscan habit; but death is not the end and they prepared his *velorio* and thought of the new cross soon to spread its white arms in the *camposanto*.

The thick thunder rolled again.

Father Andreas would give him higher honor than the humble *camposanto*. He would find eternal rest beneath the altar at which he served so many years. Father Andreas was happy so to honor the old priest.

They tried to explain. It was not the padre's wish.

It was proper that he should lie there.

But it was not his wish.

It was the greatest honor.

But it was not his wish.

Anger made Father Andreas stubborn. "In any event," he snapped, "it is only an empty shell we bury. His spirit has flown."

Then why, they wondered, *is the altar so important?* They grew sad. Only the miracle they had always begged for would commit the padre to the *camposanto* as he and they desired.

January encased the village in crystalline cold and no miracles lit the night—not even the ordinary ones. No rainbow arced, no butterflies bubbled, no apricot blossomed, no baby creature wriggled with new life. Even the spiderwebs were swept clean from Doña Rosalía's home where they kept vigil through the night with their padre before he would be sealed from them forever beneath the altar where the shaft, already hollowed, gaped waiting.

The candles shone yellow around the table where he lay in Doña Rosalía's *cuarto de adorno* and the flames jumped at each breeze that slipped in with those who passed in and out to join the prayers the *rezador* led; they made the padre's face seem to move with the thin ghostly smile that had frolicked across his feathers when he lived. His missal with its puppy-gnawed corner was clasped in the waxen hands more solidly than in life. He'd always left it lying about. Only the red bandanna he had always tucked up his sleeve was missing. Wouldn't he need it?

"*Angeles* don't need to wipe their noses," Doña Rosalía said.

"Padre Lorenzo will," said Alarico morosely.

It was on account of that eternally dripping nose that Padre Lorenzo lay dead now Alarico thought; that and his own stubborn pride. He knelt by the thin still body and begged for forgiveness. He looked into the coffin and the quiet face moved in the light, or he thought it did.

"Two old cottonwood leaves in the *acequia*, Alarico. But we rang the bells while the young men slept!"

Alarico wondered if angels could giggle.

"*En el nombre del Padre, del Hijo, y el Espiritu Santo*," the *rezador* intoned. Another *alabado* pierced the night. Kneeling in the corner, Luz Peralta, soft-glowing, looked like a candle molded of white wax.

Alarico left his vigil and others took his place. The women chattered in the kitchen where they readied the *chilorio*, the midnight supper, and the men congregated about the great fire outside. At intervals the *alabados* wailed from within and then they resumed their talk and it was of ordinary things and sometimes of Padre Lorenzo.

"Remember the time he let the Indian get away?" They told the story again and laughter jogged comfortably about the fire as they thought of the troopers searching for their quarry who was locked secretly inside all the time.

Then they sobered. It was Father Lorenzo who would be locked inside after this night. They didn't want their beloved padre to lie in the church encased, away from those he loved.

Someone sneezed and it sounded like the padre and an uncertain laugh played around the fire.

Across the village Drake heard surges of wailing *alabados* ride high on the cold wind. He threw another log on the fire, poured himself a whiskey, wondered again if he should make an appearance at the *velorio*, and for the third time decided he should not. He was still an outsider.

Besides, he needed to ready the extra room. Father Andreas would arrive in the morning for the funeral. When in Descanso he'd been staying with Drake since Father Lorenzo's illness, partly to avoid the rivalry between Doña Rosalía and Delfina Romero over who would do the honors and partly, Drake suspected, because it was more comfortable; though the priest who seemed to have a compulsion for hair shirts was likely unaware of that motive.

Goso put his head on Drake's knee. He fondled the dog, looked around and, remembering the deserted shell he'd moved into his first summer, contrasted it to the snug nest he'd made it. Segundo had poured the adobe floor, now covered thickly with Indian rugs Drake got from Fergus. He'd added a bathroom and installed butane and electricity though he often sat with just the light of the fire moving like quiet butterflies on the walls either by choice or because the power failed. He was well stocked with the small comforts Val and Fergus got him in Española or Santa Fé—records, books, and good hootch.

On the mantel stood Francisco's Virgin and beside it the tiny mountain lions Juan gave him. A carved *trastero* held his dishes; a Dasburg painting Fergus had found ennobled the wall. In the deep windows the geraniums Soledad brought in coffee cans bloomed against the white curtains she made him.

"Always close them at night," she warned, "to keep out the *brujas*." He seldom did, though. He liked to stare out to infinity where stood patiently the crosses of the *camposanto* and beyond them, above the *morada*, rose the Calvario and beyond that and into the stars soared the cross-gashed mountain.

He turned back to the warmth inside. Slow-growing like everything in Descanso, his small adobe had shaped itself to his life like a comforting old sweater. Anglo impatience sometimes rose in him when Segundo's promises to help him *mañana*—always *mañana*—stretched into weeks; but sooner or later he always came and the house was no worse for the waiting. *Mañana* was forever.

His neighbors were his friends and here the word had meaning. Still, the Otherness was always there and he grew lonely though he supposed loneliness was part of any man who would know himself—and here he knew peace.

He stroked Goso's ears again. Catalina's bitch was as prolific as Catalina and she'd brought him the puppy from last spring's litter. He tracked mud and he slept with Drake which would have horrified Leona. God had given this dog a glossy copper sheen but before Drake owned him two hours he displayed a proclivity for rolling in mud, horribly and completely coating himself, a talent he soon honed into a career. Drake named him *Cienegoso*—'Muddy'—and abridged it to sound like *Gozo*, and that was equally apt, for Goso's life was one of complete joy.

It was Goso who had gnawed the corner off Father Lorenzo's leather missal while the padre enjoyed a glass of the apricot brandy Drake kept especially for him; they laughed over Doña Rosalía's recent encounter with the ghost which turned out to be only Tonito who'd slipped into the *jacal* to sleep off the effects of too much *aguardiente*.

Drake was apologetic.

"*De nada*, Carlos," the old priest had wheezed. "The word of God can stand a few teeth marks from one of his own creatures."

Through the icy night the *alabado* rose again and Drake's sense of obligation with it. He drained his glass, sighed, and picked up his sheepskin jacket.

He stepped into the cutting cold, saw the crosses of the *camposanto* rear moon-pearled against the night. *Too bad the padre can't be buried there*, he thought, *where he wanted. Where his people want him. Where he belongs.*

Christ, it was cold. *No butterflies now*, he thought, and wondered why one always remembered the irrelevant things. Or maybe nothing was irrelevant; maybe the act of remembering made it significant.

He cut across the *placita* toward the bonfire. A few boys chased each other in its light and dogs ran with them.

"*¡Qué tal, Carlos!*" That was Tomás Archuleta. Drake squatted with them, talked some, but mostly listened.

Sometimes a ribald joke defied the night and laughter ran like sparks into the airy black. Other times growls crawled low to the ground like a cold-stunted centipede and Drake sensed an unarticulated resentment toward Father Andreas.

Inside he paid respects to the living and the dead, first of all to Señor Romero's ancient mother who sat like a tiny old mandarin and held her cane like a scepter. One always greeted Doña Felicia first, wondered what dart her keen little tongue would shoot, then watched to see the glee that lit the black eyes and deepened the millions of fine wrinkles that ran in all directions like shattering glass.

▲

From her corner Doña Felicia watched the mourners file in and out. They were only moving shapes, the faces shrouded unless they were very close, and sometimes she thought she recognized people who had rested in the *camposanto* for many years.

¡Ay, Dios! One's life passes through as the shapes pass through the room, she thought, *and we rejoice when they come and cry when they depart (though it should be the other way around) and we love them at birth and at death but not always in between.*

They were all a little afraid of her, especially her own family; her son Antonio and his placid ewe-wife, Delfina, and all their sons except Julián who followed his own impulses—only he hadn't the hide to see them through. Julián might have been interesting, might have been like his grandfather Amado, like herself even, but he was boneless inside. Julián was like a goat, smart and noisy, prancing after the gringo ways, the gringo ideas, tasting them all, but he didn't have the goat's stomach and his horns were all paper that would crumple the first time he butted a soft juniper post. Well, at least he'd butt. None of the others would.

She watched the figures file into the room where Padre Lorenzo lay and come out clutching their rosaries. She could feel, she could almost smell, the yearning. Prayers they would say for his soul but they couldn't bury his body where he wanted to lie.

158

"*Ay*, if there was any way," someone whined to her then came close and it was Cipriano Pacheco. His father shuffled beside him with his fly open but Domingo still had more feist in him than Cipriano ever had.

She bowed her head over the cane she held with both hands, closed the dry lids over her eyes, then opened them again and spurred a black look straight at him. "Why can't you?" she snapped. "There are ways of getting around the German priest. If any of you are men there are ways. *¿Cómo se no*, Domingo?" *Ways*, she mused, *that would amuse her padre, who had his own ways.*

Only Padre Lorenzo knew the whole story of the bell.

When they heard the new bell was coming, Amado had told him the story, not in the confessional but in the padre's home so that Felicia could hear it too.

"It's very kind of the bishop," he said. He sat stiffly and pressed his hands between his knees. "But we love La Campana."

"We are forever plagued," said Father Lorenzo, "by our own sins and other people's charities. But," he added, "the new bell will have a better tone."

"*Sí.*"

Father Lorenzo sat quietly. *You can't hatch an egg before its time*, he thought.

Amado pecked from inside his shell until it finally cracked. "Because it's my fault, Father. My fault La Campana lost her voice."

Yes, he knew the story.

"No. It wasn't the dropping that did it. She isn't cracked."

"Cracks don't always show."

"She lost her purity because of me. Because of how I got her."

"In fair contest."

"No, Father. Not fair." He slanted his eyes at the priest then at Felicia and then at heaven. "Not fair." His eyes sidled to the floor. "Don Diego didn't see the card I slipped from my cuff! But the Virgin did."

Felicia's tart tongue was faster than her thought. "Then the Virgin shouldn't have been looking over your shoulder!"

Father Lorenzo began to cough but not soon enough to cover the giggle he couldn't contain. He crossed himself quickly.

The years passed softly. When Amado lay dying Padre Lorenzo came. "Maybe when I'm gone, Father, La Campana's voice will be whole again." His sharp nose jutted imperiously toward heaven. Even in death Amado could not be totally humble. "It was my deceit that made her hoarse."

"Maybe," said the priest. "Though I doubt it." He laughed. "My voice was once whole, too, but now it has invisible cracks. I, too, have sinned. I have plucked too many pleasures on my way to heaven. You only cheated your father-in-law," he said. "But I have cheated the Father!"

Doña Felicia, remembering, felt a tear slide down her fine-seamed face for Padre Lorenzo and for La Campana who would not ring again, she supposed—not even for Padre Lorenzo who would not lie among his people.

"Fools!" she snapped. Could no one outwit the German priest? "Amado!" she called out imperiously. "It is up to you!"

Doña Felicia was slipping into the past again, they said and sighed. *Ay*, it would soon be her *velorio* they held.

Soledad took coffee to her. "Here, *abuelita*, it's strong and hot." She saw the old eyes focus and felt their recognition.

"Where is my grandson? Where is Julián?"

"Gone to Taos, Doña Felicia."

"*Ay, sí. Válgame*, what a fool! Outwitted by Teresita. *Ay*, I know whose son toddles in your kitchen! Julián should have beat you first and married you after. And run the gringo out."

A bubble like a sudden giggle in church popped in the old lady's eyes. "It did Teresita no good, did it?" she gloated. She sucked her coffee. "*Sí*, Teresita lost that game. I must remember to tell Amado. He'll laugh."

▲

No, thought Soledad, *my grandmother did not snare Carlos, though she caused him doubts.* He still had them she knew. His eyes clouded when he looked her way as he was doing this night. Padre Lorenzo had calmed the storm. Soledad knelt by the coffin beside Luz, reached into her pocket for her rosary, and felt the blue stone. It was hers now. She no longer feared its power.

She had run from Teresita's house in dark fear that night after Julián left and through the winter she did not go to her house or let the *bruja* into her own.

In spring when the dust blew high Padre Lorenzo gusted through the sagging gate. "Your grandmother grieves," he said. He watched Soledad walk heavily to the well and helped her pull the bucket up. "It is not for you to judge," he said. "It is easy for us to call out '*bruja*' to cover our own sins. She works much good." He drank from the bucket, wiped his lips with the red handkerchief, and mopped his eyes, red from dust.

She would fix him *contrayerba* for his eyes, she said.

He smiled vaguely. His was a mild punishment for his many sins, he said. "Teresita has cared for us all, with love."

"She does not believe in love, Father."

"She loves you." He left the thought hanging between them like vibrations of a just-rung bell and drifted out the gate. His thin white hair lifted in the driving wind.

She went to Teresita after that, saw how bony and shrunken she was, and took her claw-curled hand in her own.

"*Ay*, you'll need me soon," whined the old woman. She felt Soledad's belly. "The night he was conceived I said I would bring him."

Soledad looked about the little hut. She saw the thinness of its treasures, the bare cot with its shabby blanket and the rusty black *rebozo* on the peg, the little trunk that secured the meager hoard in the cans inside. Her young eyes swept across the fireless stove, they rested on the sheep skull, the snakeskin, the gray lace curtain full of holes which sagged at the window, and her heart felt heavy like her belly. These were the remains of a life. If there had been witchcraft, there had also been good and that life had nurtured her.

She embraced the bent old crone and felt the thin body yield for the time of a breath before she stiffened. "Forgive me, *abuela*," she whispered. "I love you."

"I don't expect love," said Teresita. "I expect some sense!" She probed at Soledad's belly with gnarled, knowing old hands, and she cackled. "Soon! Soon little Carlos comes!"

Soledad looked into the blue eyes that had trapped some small piece of infinity in them. "His name will be Juan," she said.

Padre Lorenzo christened him Juan, the baby they called Pepito, and soon after he buried Teresita in the *camposanto* where, for all her sins, she lay; where he, for all his goodness, was denied.

José Villareál knelt beside Soledad with his own memories and some itched like wool in a hot room. Luz raised her eyes and let them pause a moment on him, softly like candlelight.

"*Ave María llena de gracia*," he gabbled but the words kept butting against the coffin and the flames shook like giggles and Padre Lorenzo's mouth seemed to quiver at the corners too with the little smile that had always escaped like a puff of smoke through a crack.

The father will be paying for those smiles now, José thought and the image of the frail old man in Purgatory made him pray harder, though he didn't believe the padre's sins were enough to keep him there long. Still, one never knew.

José was afraid of Purgatory. He heard the dark horses thunder and he thought of his own sins and he squeezed his eyes shut so he wouldn't see Pilar Archuleta, and when he opened them the padre's lips seemed to smile again and fear washed through José. Then he saw Carlos looking at him and tried to look jaunty. He shrugged and tried to make his face say what his voice couldn't. *¡Qué importa!*

He'd said it often enough when the priest rebuked him. They often made fun of the old padre when they were boys, especially José. They imitated his wind-pushed walk; often they assumed an idiotic stare and talked nonsense to presences they pretended to see in the air.

Once José had his friends tittering as he alternately talked to a tamarisk tree and gasped loudly as if to sneeze, like the father. "Ahhh . . . ahh. . . ." He pawed up one sleeve, then the other, as if fishing for a handkerchief. "Ahhh . . . ahh. . . ."

Carried away with his own performance he failed to notice when his audience quit laughing. Over his shoulder a red bandanna appeared in a long thin hand.

"Here, my son, use mine!" said a wheezy voice.

It was an awful moment. Crimson shame washed over him, and revulsion, as he had to take that soggy rag. The other boys stood like lightning-struck pines until the old father ambled on. Then a snicker popped out and another answered it and the giggles grew to guffaws and it was José they were laughing at. He lit into Tonito Valdez with pumping fists and reaped a bloody nose.

They made fun of the father but they ran to him for help. He saved José once when the boy was small and feared the *abuelos*, those fearful ghouls who take away the naughty children.

"If you aren't good I'll let the *abuelos* have you," José's mama threatened and he hid in a *jacal*.

Padre Lorenzo found him hours later shaking with cold and fright, explained the *abuelos* were only men and led him home the back way so none

162

would laugh at him.

He felt guilty thinking how he'd laughed at the wispy old priest. He guessed the padre knew they laughed. Sometimes in church he made a pronouncement and then looked surprised as a titter pranced through the people; then he laughed too, ignorant of the joke but delighting in felicity.

"If God didn't enjoy a bit of fun," he often said, "He would not have made laughter. And if I am its cause," he sometimes added a bit wryly, "I am God's chosen instrument!"

Other times he laughed at some private humor and after Father Andreas came the old priest often and innocently let quick words spurt like the lively little flames that play lights on a dark wall. José seldom understood the gist but he saw the quiver of the old priest's mouth come, then hide quickly from the glance the young one shot and he would cross himself and smile at some invisible angel hanging from a *viga* above and José would sense a gnat of humor.

¡Pues! That gnat eventually landed on him, and stung. He still squirmed to remember it.

It was at confession in October a year ago. José recounted the usual string of transgressions then added, "And I have stolen."

"Again?" A soft sigh ruffled the curtain like a ghost shrugging. "From Tomás?"

"No, Father. Not even a beer. Tomás watches too close. Like he don't trust me!"

"You stole money?"

"No, Father! Just a *rebozo*. For my mama. It didn't belong to nobody; it was in a store." José got the righteous tone he used to get at the school in Colinas when the Anglo teacher accused him of copying Angelita Sedillo's paper. *Chite*, it hadn't been Angelita's paper he peered over her shoulder at; it was the front of her dress he looked down. She let him, too. That was before he got too old for school and quit to work—when he felt like it—on the railroad at Española.

José waited for his penance, prepared to tell endless beads. The padre had other ideas.

He'd stolen a *rebozo*—he should wear it!

Like a woman!

Each morning for a week he must cross the *placita* to join the others who rode to Española to work. Each day for a week José must ride in the back of a pickup for all the world and his friends to taunt with that black *rebozo* over his head like a woman and every afternoon he must return to recross the *placita* for all Descanso to view.

He must not clown and he must not explain.

Pilar Archuleta undulated her way across the *placita* each afternoon. She flaunted her ripe breasts deliberately at him, let her sensuous eyes crawl over his shameful headgear, and then she giggled. She let the giggles roll over him until he burned inside.

Once Luz Peralta slipped through the *placita* like a small shy ghost, let her madonna eyes rest on him lightly, and he saw her shy mouth soften before she hurried on.

That was the worst of all.

¡Santa María! He wouldn't steal again! Not a *rebozo*, anyhow.

Next time it would be a good pair of boots!

The *rezador* finished the rosary. José stood, looked down at the silent face, and waited for a hoarse high voice to protest mildly against his sinful thoughts. Behind the gentle laughter in the imagined voice he heard a sadness he hadn't recognized when the voice lived.

Tears filled his chest and rose to his eyes. They blurred the room and lit the candleglow with colors and in the silence a rainbow formed in the tears and lifted the heart of José Villareál.

"I will not make you sad again, Father," he whispered, and this time he meant it.

José had seen a rainbow.

▲

The jumping candle flames sent yellow butterflies flitting over the room. They rested gently on the dead priest's face and Francisco remembered again how the fragile yellow wings beat the air currents fragrant with the smell of ripe apricots and the aroma had more substance than the airy little creatures.

Francisco prayed a long time for he had many memories. *Ay*, his old friend had died doing God's work like the holy martyrs although he'd always insisted he hadn't the courage to be a martyr, or the persistence. He didn't desire the next world so quickly or the painful trip, either, for that matter.

Father Andreas had the stuff of sainthood, he said once. "Like a silver chalice overbrimming with the Holy Spirit. While I—" he laughed, "—I'm just a rusty old cup carrying alkaline water to the scraggly gourds at the edge of the patch!"

"Gourds are part of God's purpose, too," Francisco said.

Father Andreas thought the old priest lacked proper respect for ecclesiastical authority.

Once they bought materials in Colinas to repair the church roof with the understanding that they could return what they didn't use. Padre Lorenzo, however, seeing the large quantity left over, distributed it to his parishioners and explained later to an irate Father Andreas that their roofs needed mending too.

The young priest's eyes spurted blue flame. "The refund for the returned materials," he snapped, "should have reverted to the church fund."

An innocence like that of an April lamb shone from Lorenzo's eyes. Had not San Lorenzo, his own name saint, distributed the church's money among the poor rather than give it to the Roman emperor?

"There is no analogy whatever, Father," Andreas said, and his voice was still angry but it also sounded tired.

Francisco, too, knew the story of San Lorenzo who was roasted on a grill for his audacity and, they said, gave the cook directions in the process. "So you do follow the holy martyr's way," he had insisted.

Lorenzo wiped his watery eyes. The penalties were hardly the same, he said. Then a wispy smile flitted. "Though the wrath of Father Andreas has its own bit of fire!"

▲

Each communed with his ghosts and filed into Doña Rosalía's *sala* where the electric light burned the ghosts away. They ate the feast and drank the *vino* and bantered in the kitchen or out by the fire and they felt the comfort of their padre's presence.

Then they thought of the waiting altar. An uneasy cold crept into their veins; some fingered their rosaries; and Doña Rosalía looked for a sign.

All she saw was a persistent spider in a high corner, spinning his web beyond the light.

Father Andreas arrived mid-morning. Furtive looks crept about the church as he intoned the funeral mass.

She would be next, thought Doña Felicia; she or Domingo Pacheco who hunched on the bench opposite her and his fly hung open and so did his mouth and he drooled, and his bony wrists poked from ragged cuffs. *Ay, and we'll lie in the camposanto without our padre. Why doesn't Amado do something?*

Soledad thought of Teresita lying in the *camposanto* in hallowed ground. Padre Lorenzo had seen to it, had even lied and taken it on his own soul to save hers. *Why can't someone. . . ?*

His old friend couldn't smell the apricot trees beneath the altar, thought Francisco. He wouldn't feel their shade creep over his grave when the sun grew hot or hear the gentle plop as a ripe fruit fell to the warm earth or feel the sweet tokens of God's forgiveness.

How often he'd helped Francisco fertilize, had tossed spadefuls of the end and the beginning of life, and when he passed through the *placita* he carried the faint odor of apricots and manure and incense his parishioners associated with sanctity. *If only we could find some way.*

We rang the bells, Father, thought Alarico. *But La Campana won't ring again. Her husky voice that carried all our faults for us won't sing again. Ójala.* He knelt on swollen knees in the cold church.

Always the padre talked of miracles, thought José. *Of butterflies and babies and spiders' webs and of apricot trees and rainbows. They were miracles, he said.* José remembered the private rainbow of his own tears and thought how, in the *camposanto*, the padre would have lain beneath the arcing miracle of promise in every rainbow. *But here?*

As Father Andreas said the ancient words he thought, *the Church is the rock,* and felt its solidity encase him like a fortress wall against the arrows of their medieval ignorance. It was right that the old priest should rest beneath the altar where he had served. The thought of lying so protected when his own time came gave Andreas a comfort.

"You know, of course," Drake had told him at breakfast, "the people want him in the *camposanto*."

He knew. But he wouldn't give in to their superstitions. God knew how he fought it. In the dark confessional of his mind he remembered the imagined sins of his own youth and his own superstitions. Sometimes he looked at his congregation and knowing their confessions he saw his own sins leer at him as from a mirror and then he felt the anger surge and he sought haven in the rock-bound solidity of the Church.

He did right to bury the old priest here.

"Seems pretty hard-nosed," Drake had said earlier. "But it's none of my business."

Andreas agreed it wasn't.

"They're praying for a miracle," Drake added.

Yes, it was part of the thing the old priest had encouraged—part of the subtle tug-of-war they'd engaged in since Andreas had first been sent to take over the old man's duties, to add his parish to his own larger territory.

"Mine are gentle people," Lorenzo said. "You're too harsh on them."

"We must mortify the flesh to serve the spirit."

"Yet you chastise the *Hermanos* for mortifying theirs."

He thought of the dull sounds of yucca whips on bloody flesh and an urgency to feel the exquisite pain on his own back, to feel his own blood run, washed through him almost like a sexual urge and as sinful, and the shrill notes of the *pito* pierced his mind and he exploded in crimson rage and a hatred like that of hell consumed him and he imagined what secret things happened in the *morada*.

"Men must not hide their secrets. Not from the Church."

"I think all men hide some. In corners of the mind like the hidden places in caves where we're afraid to probe because dark hairy things might crawl out."

Those same dark thoughts swarmed beneath the surface in the church this day. Andreas intoned the ancient words and sought the solidity.

Splitting wood behind his house, Drake heard the bell toll its sad sweet dirge. New dark sorrow brooded inside the church with that strange Spanish mysticism that neither he nor Father Andreas could penetrate, that Otherness that was always there.

He cleaned the *acequia* alongside the rest and drank with them at the *cantina* and danced at their *bailes* and followed their *santo*-led processions and sometimes attended mass in their church that he might comprehend that Otherness that he tried to preserve in his sketches.

He didn't go to the funeral mass. This was their private grief.

It was part of the loneliness—of winter and of isolation and of wanting the child he couldn't acknowledge. In the long days of summer he could work on his own house and soil or in the fields of his neighbors. Winter was the silent time when his uselessness echoed in his hollow rooms.

Yet here at least the whole world wasn't useless and empty. Here life had a purpose. It was a sacrament and good and therefore to be cherished so that its own energy of survival was its ultimate morality. *The morality the whole world had once*, he supposed, *before it went a-whoring*. But here it still survived and, determined to fathom it, he learned to perceive.

He learned the feel of a 'dobe wall warm in the sun, learned the sting of snow against his face, learned the smells of resinous air and piñon smoke and storm-bearing clouds and of the goats. He saw the shape of things apart from their functions and the changing colors of hours and days. He saw the people, studied their moods, and sought their souls. He heard the nuances in voices and the soft rush of spirits and all the minute sounds of the vast stillness. He heard the silence.

He worked for hours each day. His sketches that had begun as dilettante diversion shaped into craft. He came to believe in the importance of what he was doing, of documenting Descanso, of catching its eternality embedded like a fly speck in amber before the outside world would rush in and smash it as it had smashed its own morality; the routine of work fit around him like a heavy coat and—sometimes—it kept out the loneliness.

There was always the child, Pepito. He saw him with his mother in the *placita* or at her house when he went to visit Soledad and to carry on solemn conversations with Mario and draw pictures for the boys. He watched the child grow, saw his early steps as he followed his brothers on small unsure legs, heard his curly laugh as he caught a butterfly, his howl of rage when he fell. The little ache was always there but he grew used to it like the loneliness.

The bell tolled again. He leaned on his axe, saw his breath waft in the cold toward the little wooden crosses in the *camposanto* and dissipate like a priestly ghost. He watched Goso bound in excited circles in his own energy of joy that overbrimmed in happy yaps and that was a morality too.

The bell tones rolled over the valley, collided with the cliff, tumbled back in round echoes and split in melodic shards over the dead and the living.

He knew inside the church they tried not to look at the gaping devouring altar, because it was too late.

They'd dreamed of miracles.

Their padre had seen them daily.

Drake began to chop again and felt the good feel of muscles pulling in long hard strokes. He, too, wished for a miracle.

▲

Even miracles need time to grow.

Look into your own hearts. They heard him yet. *It is from your faith God can make miracles.* Through the winter, into Lent, the seeds lay beneath the ice in the warm soil of their thought.

Strange things began to happen.

Enrique and Alarico, working in the church on a Friday, said they heard wheezy breathing from the altar and an unmistakable sneeze.

Two of Segundo's sons, serving as acolytes the following Sunday, swore they heard knocking noises from under the altar and that a candlestick moved as if disturbed.

Luz went to clean in Father Lorenzo's little house as she had done when he lived and found his missal lying on his pillow. She knew it was his because of the corner Goso had gnawed. She reported it whisper-voiced to her Tía Rosalía who spread it through the village.

Had not the missal been buried with him?

They'd seen his thin hands folded over it at the *velorio!*

Four of the *hermanos* went inside the little rectory to see this thing and came out crossing themselves. The tooth-marked missal was indeed on the pillow, they told the villagers clumped outside. No one would touch it. The people looked dart-eyed at one another. The silence around their thoughts began to thaw and whispers ran in melting rivulets for seedlings to poke through.

On Ash Wednesday they draped La Campana in her purple shroud and gave the honor to Luz who first saw the missal. The women clutched their *rebozos* close about their heads and shoulders, huddled against the freezing February knife wind, watched solemn-eyed as Luz stepped to La Campana hanging from the low crossbar in the churchyard, where no spring melt yet softened the ice-warped village.

They saw it. It was a sign, they said.

Directly beneath the bell, melted, liquid in the frozen world around them, a small pool glistened. Luz knelt, touched its surface, looked up at the dark silent eyes and her face shone.

"It is warm," she said, falter-voiced like La Campana. "Warm—like tears!"

Like homeless little ghosts in the tamarisk trees, the words rustled uneasily through the *placita*, over the frozen *acequia*, about the low houses and through the silent 'dobe walls.

"She cries," they said. "La Campana cries because she can ring no more."

None of them was saintly enough to ring her. Only Padre Lorenzo had ever done so, and. . . .

The padre lay sealed beneath the altar.

▲

From the *morada* the sounds of Holy Week wailed high on the cold wind. Young men like Tonito and José who had not joined the *Hermandad* slunk shamefaced through the *placita* or strutted defensively. Except for them, Descanso seemed a village without men. Should an out-of-season *turista* or an indiscreet state trooper stray up the rutted road he would be told they had gone into the mountains for wood, as they told the gringo bosses in Colinas or Española. It was as if every man in every village in these mountains suddenly needed wood.

The women cooked *panocha* to give strength to the men and carried it across the *acequia* and through the *prado* up the rock-stippled hill to the *morada*. Some sang *alabados*.

Above the wailing voices the *pito* dropped notes like tears, and the *matracas* perforated the wails with their own grisly rhythm.

▲

Delfina Romero sold several pairs of white cotton *calzones* such as the *hermanos* wore at their rites. She tended the store that week. Antonio had duties in the low *morada* where dark secrets like trapped smoke thickened the air.

Processions wound over the frozen ruts of Descanso on Thursday and again on Friday and they dragged the fearful *carreta de la muerte*, the crude cart with its heavy wooden wheels. In it rode the leering skeleton and in her long bony hands she clutched her arrow-nocked bow.

Drake watched from his window and drew the thing and smiled mockingly but the grin was thin armor and a cold crept in. Above it all the wailing soared and dipped like demented furies. It pierced one's ears, one's mind, one's soul, and even after the *alabado* died the notes rode the air, eerie echoes in the canyon.

As the sad sunlight, old and dust-screened, lingered on hill and *morada* walls and yellowed the great cross, a line of white-trousered men filed from the *morada*. Some bent their backs beneath heavy crosses and the soft dull *thwuck* of weighted yucca whips cut into bared flesh. They topped the rim of the hill and disappeared.

One would hang on a cross that night.

▲

Sometime during the solemn week they had made a decision. They adopted an extra obligation for this night of sacrifice.

Sometime in the moonless night they fulfilled it.

A few wakeful eyes saw dark shapes move toward the church, saw the glow of lanterns through the door as it opened from time to time. A few listening ears heard the dull clink of metal on stone.

From the *camposanto* came sounds of heavy feet bearing a solid burden, the scrape of shovels in rocky ground.

By morning new plaster covered the altar and it matched the fresh-plastered wall that awaited Easter, innocent and clean.

Many walked through the *camposanto* on Saturday, over by the edge, close to where the apricot trees leaned winter-bare branches over the new-made grave the people pretended not to see.

That night they carried La Campana as they had always done on Easter Eve and they hung her from the brittle branches of the little tree closest the *camposanto* that guarded their dead and even though they knew she would not ring this Easter morning, they smiled and carried in their hearts the peace of an act of love fulfilled.

▲

The miracle happened at dawn.

In the night a high wind swept from the cross-gashed peak and behind it swirled a white-robed host that crusted the earth with snow.

Drake Cavanaugh knew when the wind stilled, reached for another blanket, sensed the whiteness glowing from beyond the window, and went back to sleep.

Across the village Soledad felt the earth's rhythm change subtly, got up to peer outside, and transferred Pepito to her own warm bed.

Doña Rosalía heard Perdido growl and went to the window. Toward the *camposanto* a glow of light moved through the falling snow.

Francisco heard the light snow tap against the window and passed a hand over his bristle-stubbed face. He lit the lantern beside his bed and began to pull on his clothes. He buttoned his sheepskin jacket and picked up a newly carved San Francisco. He had a promise to keep. Carrying the *santo* he cut through the orchard and saw his breath white in the glow of the lantern he held. He carried his gift to the last small apricot tree where La Campana hung, right at the edge of the *camposanto* where it reached the last-made grave where Padre Lorenzo lay at last.

He knelt and prayed and stood again, watched the snow fill the depression his knees had made, saw it dust onto the *santo*, and he thanked his maker for the life inside the wood. It was like the Resurrection. *Ay*, the tree must die before the saint inside can live. A light lit the old man's fine-carved face. "'*Sta bueno*," he said.

By the time he warmed by his own fire the falling snow covered his footprints.

It stopped after a bit. The air cleared and the sky behind the mountain grayed; the peaks took shape and thin plumes of blue smoke began to rise from snow-sheathed chimneys. Soon the bell would ring from the church tower to greet the Easter dawn. Only one bell would herald Easter news this year, and though she was pure-toned they still felt the emptiness of an abandoned friend.

Dawn neared.

Catalina Sifuentes who was pregnant again was setting the coffee pot on her wood stove which crackled with lusty morning fire. Segundo was in the *jacal* breaking ice from the trough.

Soledad at the *fogón* dipped a rag in warm milk and let a fresh-born kid suckle, too early mothered and too soon orphaned.

Alarico sat before his fire half-dressed and rubbed his swollen ankles and knees. He'd rung his last bell.

Enrique Peralta left tracks in the snow as he strode toward the church; he climbed into the tower, stood a moment in the icy air and watched. When the first red fire streaked the east he pulled the rope, released the clear sweet tones, and when the rose notes faded he stood a moment, looked over the village, rose-sparkled, blue-sparkled, looked to the purple cross gashed in the jagged mountain above and the dark silhouette of Pájaro crouched above like a hungry beast. He looked over the rim of their valley to the canyon below, gazed toward the great gorge where the river cut toward the southern desert, brought his soaring gaze circling back like the eagle to the nearer view, to the earthen walls of Descanso with its curling smoke, its stirring life.

Suddenly it sounded—a bell, and her notes were hoarse and joyous.

La Campana rang!

Drake sat up in bed. "What the hell. . . ?"

Soledad threw a coat over her head, ran into her patio, and clutched the blue stone in her pocket. She picked up the striped cat that purred at her ankles and stood listening.

Catalina put down the pan she had just lifted from the stove and the baby moved within her.

Cipriano stood with hay-filled fork in his hands.

Luz knelt by her window; she raised her hand toward the cross-gashed mountain and smiled at something beyond.

José sat in the outhouse, astonished when La Campana's voice flowed in.

Doña Felicia sat in the kitchen and put down the coffee cup her daughter-in-law had just brought her. She called out in her high treble, "*¡Escucha*, Amado! La Campana rings!"

Doña Rosalía knew immediately it was a miracle. She'd seen the ghostly light.

Francisco, warmed by fire and accomplishment, heard it and wondered. He crossed to San Ysidro and touched his wooden oxen. Could it be the wind?

The wind was still.

Or—a whisper nibbled at his thoughts—*could it be Saint Francis?*

San Ysidro looked into space with large dark eyes and behind his black beard he smiled a secret smile.

La Campana's vibrations still pulsed as the villagers began to converge in her direction. Who had run the bell? Little groups wound through the thin snow around Francisco's orchard toward the edge of the *camposanto* where La Campana hung from the little apricot tree and then they stopped and gasped and some cried out. "*¡Mira, mira!*" and they crossed themselves and looked at each other and at what they saw.

They stopped short of the tree and the bell and no foot tracks neared it. Light feathery marks like those of a tiny scurrying creature—or a ghost— disturbed the snow around the new-mounded grave and under the tree where La Campana hung.

A beam of early sun touched her. A few feet away beside the wooden cross that marked the newest grave stood the newly carved San Francisco. A small brown bird with a white crest perched on his arm and it seemed to some he resembled the dead padre.

Francisco had put the *santo* there. But. . . .

He had not rung the bell.

He had not placed the snow-dusted missal beneath the tree, a missal with a worn corner a puppy had once chewed. From beneath the little book flapped the frayed edges of a faded red bandanna.

No human footprints marked the snow.

"*¡Es el milagro!*" Descanso had its miracle.

The people smiled. They knew who had rung their bell.

Slowly they began to file back toward their homes to prepare for a joyous Easter mass as soon as the new priest came flying in. Only Francisco stayed behind. His lips moved in prayer and his eyes filled and as he wiped them clear with his gloved hand he saw what the others had missed.

On a snow-dusted branch of the bare little apricot tree a single tiny bud swelled, with foolhardy courage . . . or faith.

11

"*E*ver hear of the Penitentes?" asked Art.

"I lived with them," said Drake. He drained his cup and said he was going for air.

"Mind if I come?" asked Art. "I like a constitutional after breakfast." He carried a black umbrella.

The sky had cleared. The wind blew chill and smelled of exhaust fumes.

"Do they really flagellate themselves?" asked Art.

"Yes they do."

"And crucify someone?"

"So they say," said Drake. "I never saw it."

"Hard to believe that kind of savagery still exists."

Drake looked at him. "Depends on what you call savagery, I guess. They kept religion going back in the early days when the church pulled out."

"In a perverted form," said Art. "I've read a great deal about them."

"Yeah, a lot of shit's been written."

"But to crucify people. . . ."

Drake said they usually didn't die. "I never knew one to die," he said.

"That's because it's secret," said Art. "They just don't tell you. Any way you look at it, it isn't civilized."

A brown Chevy riding low on its bumper advanced slowly. Its windows were closed but still the cacophony of rock-and-roll split the morning. Adolescent faces laughed out at them from beneath slicked-down hair. "That what you mean by civilized?" asked Drake.

A small dog with matted gray hair lifted his leg and peed against a fire hydrant, then cocked a floppy ear toward Drake and Art, worked his back legs importantly like a little kid who's just answered the question right, and started his busy way across the street.

The crawling low car with its blaring antimusic accelerated suddenly, spurted, swerved toward the little dog, ran it down, hit it square with a pulpy thud. They raced away and their laughs and the noise went with them. On the rear bumper a sticker read LUV YA JESUS.

The dog lifted its flop-eared head from the crushed body and Drake ran toward it. He stroked an ear. He cupped the round little face in his hand and his own throat felt thick. The little fellow struggled horribly for a moment, then his head fell, and a line of blood ran from his mouth onto the wet pavement. A hind leg still twitched.

"Sons-of-bitches," Drake yelled. A car blared its horn at him and he jumped back. It ran square over the small gray body.

"Sons-of-bitches," he said again.

▲

"You tell that *gavilán* get his ass outa here and not come back never!" The call roared from the back of the *cantina* and swept over the person of José Villareál and everybody laughed. But José only took another long swig of his *cerveza*, wiped the back of his hand across his mouth, then on the new red T-shirt, leaned back, belched loudly, and grinned. José had white even teeth and grinned a lot. He was used to Tomás ordering him to leave because that *hombre*'s daughter, Pilar, was always in heat and José flashed a white grin and an evil eye and slicked his shiny hair straight back and he walked with a swagger that made everyone forget he was small. To be ordered out was the highest flattery.

Besides, he knew when he left Pilar would follow him.

He grinned and shrugged. "*¡Qué importa!*" he said to his buddy, Tonito, who was watching the bar for Tomás. Sometimes Tonito also tended bar at Colinas and sometimes after that he went on police duty when Sheriff Garcia would let him and then he arrested his earlier customers, especially the gringos, for DWI. On the nights Tonito wasn't enforcing law and order he went carousing with José—drinking tequila and chasing girls and fighting cocks. They went down the mountain in Doña Rosalía's pickup; they had always borrowed Pedro's until he went to Colinas and took it with him.

Tonito flashed a grin at José who took another long drink and was letting it wash the dust out of his throat when Tomás came raging from the back like a Brahma bull out of the chute and Tonito said, "He be one mad *hombre, amigo*. You hadn't oughta throw fingers at Pilar when he's looking."

José said Pilar shouldn't twitch her ass at him when *he* was looking and then he grinned and said, "Okay, okay, Tomás," in his lazy voice. "You don't want my money, I take it down the road."

"An' start takin' it now," roared Tomás. "*¡Pronto!*"

"When I finish my *cerveza*." He passed his fingers sensuously over the sweating can.

"*¡Nombre de Dios!* The rest of his *cerveza*, he says!"

"You get my money, I get my beer."

"You come in here, insult my Pilar. . . ."

José thought it would be pretty hard to insult Pilar Archuleta but decided it wouldn't be a tactful thing to say to a mad bull so he drained his Coors, squeezed his hands around the can, felt it crumple, and swaggered out in his red shirt and his tight jeans, all macho, leaving the can on the counter.

"And don't come back!" Tomás roared. He grabbed the crushed can and let it fly, right past José's head.

The departing guest turned at the door and grinned his macho grin, threw a defiant finger at no one in particular and, laughing, ducked out the door.

Drake laughed along with the rest, the way they always did. Everyone already knew the punch line, because it happened this way with slight variations just about every Saturday night when José swaggered in from Colinas with his week's pay and his fidget eyes and Pilar would twitch through and José would signify by comment or gesture that she'd made contact and Tomás would throw him out. There wasn't any bad blood between them, not even a personal quarrel. Tomás knew Pilar stirred up the chile pot deliberately, but he had to go through the motions of protecting her questionable virginity. His protests gave José a chance to go through his macho act; each maintained his reputation; and the performance entertained his clientele before they settled collectively to serious drinking.

Drake knew they'd seen the last of Pilar for the evening. He ordered another whiskey and waited for the bets on José's chances that night. It was about even that in an hour or so he'd come roaring in looking for Tonito, cursing all women and proposing they go down the hill in chase of more.

Then both young cocks would swagger into church next day and, self-consciously out of grace, abstain from mass which was their way of proclaiming to the congregation at large and Pilar in particular their successes with the girls in Colinas or Española.

Though Francisco called José *un hombre sin oscuro*—a man of no soul—Drake sometimes saw the quick shadows of fear cross the unfurrowed face, as a hawk will cast his circling shadow over the desert floor, saw him cross himself as if he heard black horses thundering in the sudden short storms of his mind, before he recovered his arrogance and laughed and showed his fine white teeth and said loudly, "*¡Qué importa!*" Big deal!

Drake didn't know what José hunted but whatever it was he didn't find it in the girls he screwed which would be like stalking a mountain lion and trapping a rabbit and he thought, *It's what a man hunts, not what he finds, that carves his soul.*

If a man did find what he hunted, what then? Did he find the symbol or the thing behind it? Or nothing at all? Which was the reality anyhow, the lion or his secret power? José's girls, or the arcane depths of the female earth?

Or was he getting drunk and assigning shadows to José because he'd seen him in a few moments when fear washed over him and exposed a deformity in his nakedness? Well, drunk or not, he'd seen it; and though he didn't know what José sought, he knew what he feared, which is coming close.

He remembered the time they'd gone fishing. José loved to pull trout from the shaggy-shored streams and he knew where the deep pools were. When they left, his gaunt mama was shrieking like a wind in a winter chimney.

She'd had another dream. "It was your papa again," she mourned. "He gets no rest in Purgatory because he has sons who won't pray for him!" Morality always hung like heavy perfume in the air around Atiliana Villareál.

"*Sí*, Mama, okay. *Mañana* I will light him a candle."

"*Mañana*, he says! *Mañana!* Always he says *mañana*, he thinks only of catching the fish while his papa suffers. *Ay, válgame*, soon enough you'll be there too, you'll need prayers from your sons. If ever you have any." A new rise of tears washed her eyes. "If ever you find a good girl to marry."

She hit a nerve, though, and José went to light another candle before they went fishing. Drake, waiting in the back of the church, saw José's shaking hand that lit the candle in its red glass, saw the haunt-eyed face when he turned to leave, and remembered the same look at Padre Lorenzo's *velorio*.

On a side wall toward the back of the church hung a *retablo* of a saint

178

carrying a string of fish. "San Rafael," explained José. "The patron of fishermen." He made an obeisance to the *santo*. "Now we catch fish!"

As they left the church they met Luz Peralta coming in with a mended robe for a *santo*. José looked at her as if she were the Blessed Virgin herself. Drake heard the deference in his voice when he greeted her, saw her quick shy smile, and noted her fragility.

"There's a girl for you!" he said.

"She's not a girl," said José hoarsely. "That's Luz Peralta. Gonna be a nun."
Maybe so, thought Drake, *but she sure looked soft-eyed at José.*

In the sun again, José threw off his dark mood with an eloquent shrug and delivered his favorite formula to dispel the threat of Tomás, the taunts of Pilar, and the awful fears of Purgatory. "*¡Qué importa!*"

Remembering, Drake grinned and started to leave the bar but just then Enrique Peralta came in so he ordered two more *copitas*.

Pilar Archuleta knew José's hot eyes followed her through the door into the back part of the *cantina* where she and Tomás lived. She giggled softly and waited in the bedroom until her father roared out; then she threw a purple *tápalo* around her shoulders and slipped into the dark. She sauntered—let José grow hot waiting for her in the *jacal* behind his house. Thinking about José's hands that went all over her, his warm fingers that played like kittens' paws over her flesh, her veins rippled like small *arroyos*.

She laughed, thinking how she would tease him and leave him just before he could do anything. She'd show him he wasn't going to screw her again until he learned his lesson. She'd make him quit talking about the girls in Colinas and Española!

She got nearly as much fun hearing him howl as she did when she let him go all the way. She never saw a man go so wild when he didn't get it as José.

She slipped into the *jacal* with its rich manure smell and the soft satisfied noises of animals at night and, pretending she didn't see José's dark outline, ran into him deliberately, let his hard bare arms feel the yielding softness of her pointed breasts—she had the best pair in Descanso and she made sure all the young cocks and some of the old ones too were kept constantly aware of it.

She giggled. "Someday Tomás gonna kill you!"

"With empty beer cans?" He grabbed for her, let his hands begin their sensuous roaming.

"Don't be in such a hurry." She started her usual routine, to tease and retreat, advance and withdraw.

"Pew!" he said. "What stinks?"

"You don't like my perfume? I know somebody that does."

He laughed lazily and, though she couldn't see his teeth, she knew they were white in the dark. She leaned against a post and he cupped her round bottom in his hands, pulled her fleshy hips toward his flat ones, fell under her on a bed of baled alfalfa. *Her hair always smells stale like the grease you fry tortillas in*, he thought. It was a disgusting smell, it infuriated him, and at the same time stimulated his lust. His hands grew more urgent.

She rolled away. "*¡Tonto!* That Concha Chavez has got to be pretty hard up!"

He propped himself on an elbow. "How do you know about Concha?"

"You brag all the time, that's how." She grabbed a straw, tickled his face with it until he sneezed and leaned over him, letting her breasts hang just in reach. "She got what I got?"

"She got everything you got, *gatita*, you just got more of it!"

"Well, you get no more of it, *zopo!*"

He sneezed again. "Goddamn it!" He snatched the straw, held her wrists, and rolled on top of her while she giggled. She felt him against her, felt his hot hands under her skirt, knew he was tired of talk and she let her body undulate slowly until she knew he couldn't stand it any longer.

Then suddenly, deliberately, she bit him, let her teeth sink into his lip until the blood welled wet and salty.

"*¡Zorra!*" he roared. "*¡Puta!* Whore!"

She slipped from beneath him and darted across the *jacal*. "*¡Gallo!* she taunted. "*¡O, qué mucho gallo! ¡Qué mucho macho!*" She laughed loudly and let the mocking sound hang in the dark between them. "Go give it to that skinny Concha Chavez."

"*¡Puta!* I'll show you what a man is. . . ."

". . . or Luz Peralta!"

He jumped toward her, grabbed, held her wrists in one hard hand. With the other he slapped her. "*Putas* don't talk about saints," he said in a low hard voice.

"Saint!" She yelled with laughter. "Just because she lied about some water under that stupid bell."

He drew back to slap her again but she jerked her head back and her hair with its greasy smell flipped in his face and stung his eyes. He still held her wrists. The burro in his stall protested his interrupted sleep.

"Luz Peralta feels sorry for you! She laughs behind your back like everybody else. *¡Señor Macho!*" She laughed again, looked at him long and taunting, then spit full in his face and jerked loose.

José wiped the spit from his cheek and cracked his fist into a post. "*¡Puta!*" he roared.

The burro brayed.

Pilar, still laughing, ran up the road.

▲

"Go away! *¡Vamos!*" Enrique called from his window.

"We can't, compadre," yelled Tonito. He and José fell against each other in drunken glee. "They've locked us out!"

José doubled up again, rolled in the dirt, and punched his fists against the door. "Oh, *Dios*, it was so funny," he gasped. "That li'l fat pig. . . ."

Tonito howled "'*Cerdo cerdoso*,' you tell him. 'I like to see a *gordito* like you throw us out!' Oh, *Jesús*, it was so funny!"

"Hey, you know som'thin'?" José grabbed the door handle and managed to pull himself upright. "He did it! That *gordito* butted our asses out!" They collapsed again at the hilarious enormity of it all and Tonito reached over his sagging friend and began to pound the door again.

"Go sleep it off in the *jacal*," yelled Enrique.

"We're hungry. You want we should starve, *compadre*?"

Suddenly José felt the strains of music swell in his soul.

"*Si quiéres que te quiéra de corazón,*
   Procotón-tón-tón, procotón-tón-tón . . ." he howled. Tonito kept pounding on the door.

Suddenly it gave and José fell into the room. This was unbelievably funny and caused another laughing fit.

Doña Rosalía in her long nightgown was not amused. "Where's the pickup?" she demanded. "*¡Borrachos!*"

They were indeed *muy borracho*, they admitted solemnly. Very drunk. *Muy, muy borracho!*

"What have you done with the pickup?"

Tonito inspected the floor and then the ceiling. He contemplated the matter. The vehicle in question was in fact mired deep in sand off the rutted trail that branched from the Colinas Road. Just how it left the trail neither could remember but they'd stumbled home serenading whatever lucky spirits listened in the sweet summer night.

> *"Cuand' una niña baile con un panzón,*
> *Procotón-tón-tón, procotón-tón-tón. . . ."*

Ay, there wasn't nothing like a few snorts of *mescal* to comfort a man's wounded spirit! José hadn't been singing earlier. When Pilar left him in the *jacal* he went into a red rage, smashed his fist against a post, kicked a cat that came too close, and roared back to the *cantina* with blood on his knuckles and murder in his eye.

Tonito was waiting in front with the pickup revved up. They scattered dirt and stones as they deepened the ruts toward the Colinas road and José kept volleying salvos against the entire female sex. Tonito passed him a quarter-full bottle of *mescal* from time to time so they were half-oiled before they even got to town. They proceeded to get kicked out of the Colinas bar and then out of another one a few miles down the road. By the time they found a couple of willing girls they were too drunk to do anything about it but they were also by then too full of joviality and love of mankind to care.

"*Mañana*," said Tonito, "we'll dig out the truck. Tonight we let it rest."

> "*-tón, procotón-tón-tón. . . .*"

"*Nombre de Dios*, will you shut up that noise!" Enrique in the doorway looked even funnier in his night shirt than his lumpy sister and the boys began again to guffaw. "You wanna wake up my Luz? You wanna talk in this house, you talk quiet," he said. "She don't like nothin' but sof' words!"

Contrition swept through José's soul and Tonito began to back from the room. He respected his *prima*. Luz wasn't like ordinary people.

Doña Rosalía sighed heavily, pushed them into her kitchen, and set cold tortillas and goat cheese on the table. "Then you sleep in the *jacal*. I want no *borrachos* in my house!"

It was Luz who brought coffee to the *jacal* when the morning sun burned through their eyeballs and seared their brains. When José muttered apologies she smiled gently. "It was Pilar made you do it," she whispered. "Always Pilar. I understand, José. I will pray for you."

Always Pilar. It was easy to agree. *Verdad*, wasn't there always a woman behind men's sins when a man got drunk, went whoring, fell from grace?

Always there was Luz to pray for him. To hell with Pilar Archuleta. Luz didn't laugh behind his back—he didn't think. When he got to Purgatory she'd light him a candle—lots of candles. It would take lots for him!

He remembered once when they were small they gave a children's version of *Los Pastores*. Padre Lorenzo assigned the children their roles and each afternoon for the week before Christmas they practiced under his careful coaching. Luz was the Blessed Virgin and she was so terrified of her awesome honor that she knelt each day and implored Santa María to give her courage to perform. Tonito played Saint Joseph and Padre Lorenzo was forever scolding him because he couldn't stand still. He kept scratching.

José was a wise man with one line to say and on the second day of practice he screwed it up,. "I bring you *mirra*," was his line; but it came out "*mora*" which made more sense anyhow. Even a *tonto* would know better than to bring myrrh to a baby. "If I was that baby I'd rather have good berries to eat than any old perfume," he said when Father Lorenzo corrected him. Everyone laughed and after that he purposely said it wrong each day.

"This wise man brings the gift of laughter," said Padre, "which is indeed a greater gift than myrrh." He crossed himself hastily. "But you must learn it right and not embarrass us all."

Pilar was the first angel, the one who brought glad tidings which everyone thought immensely funny and, when the *padre* and the principals were busy practicing the big scenes, she entertained the wise men and shepherds in the back of the church with dirty stories she overheard at the *cantina*. The other angels sat piously apart. Pilar produced coins she picked up in the mornings from the floor and even some she filched from the cigar box Tomás kept behind the bar.

"I could steal *aguardiente*, too," she bragged, "if there was anybody macho enough to drink it!"

José bit. "You steal it, I drink it."

"Pooh, you couldn't drink even a *traguillo!*"

"Dare you, José!"

"Show her, *amiguito!*"

"Bet?"

"Bet!"

The shepherds and the other wise men placed their bets with the lead angel, the dare expanded, and the rules were set. Pilar would filch the bottle and José would drink its contents in view of the sojourners to Bethlehem without Padre Lorenzo's knowing.

It was only the tag end of a bottle of tequila Pilar was able to produce but it sufficed. "Behold," she said with a giggle, "I bring you good tidings of great joy," and when she said the lines later during practice the shepherds sniggered. They hid the bottle outside and if Father Lorenzo wondered at the excessive mirth in the back of the church and the frequent trips some of his shepherds and wise men made in and out the door, he found out its cause soon enough when a very drunk little wise man lurched down the aisle, opened his mouth to deliver his line, and threw up.

"Behold!" whispered Pilar giggling.

They wouldn't let him be in the play after that. José's mother cried enough tears to irrigate a three-acre bean field and Pedro wouldn't speak to him because he had to take his brother's place in a "little kids'" play—and in fact, when he strode glumly down the aisle, he did look like a Douglas fir among stocky little piñons. José's accomplices forgot their gleeful participation and expressed pain and shock that their friend and fellow actor would so profane a holy trust and Pilar with widened eyes asked where on earth he'd gotten the nasty stuff. Only José's father was amused but Procopio Villareál was himself a hell-raiser. Like father, like son, said many. *¡Otro que tal!*

The children performed on Christmas afternoon to a packed church. José, between his parents, watched sullen-eyed as the innkeeper said there was no room, saw Joseph struggling to keep still and not scratch. He watched the shepherds and wise men walk solemnly, innocent-faced down the aisle, and clenched his small fists in fury when Pilar appeared, and all the adults exclaimed what a beautiful little angel she was.

"Behold," she said in sweet ringing tones, "I bring you good tidings of great joy!" The line triggered giggles which the shepherds tried hard to suppress but the harder they fought the more explosive they became until they were convulsed. The congregation smiled tolerantly and Pilar stood, solemn, beautiful, and innocent.

Everyone praised the children afterward. Parents and grandparents and godparents glowed with wet-eyed pride; the actors smirked; Pilar accepted accolades like the Queen of Heaven; and José, blinking back the tears, reached out a surreptitious hand and pinched the most beautiful angel, hard, right on her little round behind.

Luz slipped over to him in his disgrace and put her small hand in his. "It was Pilar made you do it," she whispered. "I understand, José. I will pray for you."

▲

Now, hungover in the *jacal*, he thought about Luz and about salvation and about his own wickedness. He thought also about Father Lorenzo, how he lay lifeless at the *velorio* with the candlelight around him, and how he, José, had promised to straighten up and how the dead padre sent him a rainbow in a tear which meant he could still be saved maybe—with a rainbow and Luz to pray for him—except for Pilar.

Always Pilar was there to taunt him. Once when they were children she'd dared him to walk through the *camposanto* alone at night, mocked his fear, and proclaimed to everyone, "José is a girl!" until he swaggered to its edge and walked inside. He felt the spirits breathing behind him but, knowing she watched, he willed himself not to run though his legs washed weak with terror.

He pinched her bottom once they were safely away and said, "*Qué importa*," but his voice quavered and the spirits darkened his dreams for nights.

The terrors that preyed on the child gave way to the lusts of the man, but still it was Pilar.

Always it was Pilar. "Some day I might kill her," he muttered, "with her smelly old hair." He held his head. "*¡Ay, Jesús!*"

He moaned all the searing way to the pickup and all the time they were digging it out of the sand and all the brain-jouncing way back to Descanso; his fury mounted all week so by Saturday night he roared into the *cantina* like an intense fire. He wore new jeans and his red T-shirt, and a knotted bandanna around his thick bull neck.

Drake sat with Enrique when José charged into the *cantina*, scooped up the can of Coors Tonito slid down the bar to him, and waved at Enrique.

"*¡Qué tal, señores?*" He flashed his white grin and swaggered over to their table.

"You gonna wake up the *camposanto* again tonight?" asked Enrique. José said no, he had other plans, threw a finger, and laughed at various suggestions yelled at him from around the bar. His eyes didn't laugh, though, Drake noticed, but tightened at the corners like a warning.

"You better get it tonight, *amigo*," said Tonito, "'Cause I can't go drinkin' with you." He pulled his deputy's badge from his breast pocket, polished it against his leg. "Sheriff wants me," he said importantly. "Down Colinas."

"I'll get it tonight, *compañero*," José said. "Oh, will I get it! And then throw aside that *puta* an' go find another. . . ."

"I'm working, I told you."

"Got my own wheels tonight." Pedro was up for the weekend, he said, and Pedro always went to bed early and left the keys in his pickup. José crumpled his can and ordered another.

"Well, don't come my way in it. Don't wanta have to take you in. Hate to arrest my best friend!" Tonito returned the badge to his pocket.

"When you gonna grow up," grumbled Enrique, "and quit playing macho?"

Drake saw the eyes tense again. Then José grinned "*Mañana*," he said. "Maybe. Hey—last week—I didn't mean to wake up Luz."

"You better act right around my Luz. An' talk low. Because she don't understand loud words!"

Drake changed the subject. "Know those geodes Fergus sells?" José nodded. "Hard stones outside like a thick skull. But porous. Sometimes water gets through, eats out the center, so it's lined with beautiful crystals."

"Not all of 'em," said José. "Some are solid."

"Like some brains. Some make crystals, others stay rock."

"Like mine?" José grinned.

Drake shrugged. "*¿Quién sabe?* Maybe it's not too late for either of us to grow some crystals."

"*¡Qué importa!*"

In a little while Pilar flounced out and swept her eyes slowly around the room. "Papa's finishing his supper," she said to Tonito. "He said when you got to leave?"

"Hour or so."

She looked around again, hand on hip, sauntered toward Felipe Sifuentes at the far end of the bar and let her breasts push against Tonito as she squeezed past. She leaned on the bar and made low conversation with Felipe and suggestive laughter lapped around the room.

186

José stalked to the bar and ordered another Coors.

A heaviness hung in the *cantina.*

"*Hola,* José." She leaned toward him. "Seein' Concha tonight?"

"Maybe. Later. First I got some business."

"What kind of business?"

"Unfinished. We got something to settle, *gatita.*"

"You'll be talkin' to yourself!"

"You scared of a real man?"

"That'll be the day!"

Tomás came in from the back and belched. Pilar wiped a spot from the bar and snaked toward the door. "Night, Papa," she said, and he sighed, and José threw a finger and the usual routine followed.

"*Ójala,*" said Enrique. "That José. A wild one. He got two sides, an' they fight. A wild side like Procopio. But his Mama's religious. Not like my Luz—she got a saint inside her. But Atiliana Villareál, she got to talk about it all the time."

"Yeah, still praying her husband out of Purgatory."

"*Sí.* Always Procopio get mad and blow up. That's how he got himself killed. Fighting. Over a woman up in Pájaro. José a lot like Procopio. But he got his mama inside too. An' working down to Colinas—he make gringo money, get gringo ideas."

"Like Julián Romero. Turning into a wino, I hear."

"No, it's different. Like those rock brains you talk about, maybe. Julián, he got a mind full of those shiny crystals. Too soft. José, he got a hard mind."

"Not all hard." Drake remembered the day they went fishing. They'd seen a squirrel struggling in the rushing water and José waded in and pulled it out. He said *qué importa* but he was gentle-eyed. "Not all hard."

"José going to explode some day." Enrique drained his *cerveza.* "Like his papa."

On the table between them the beer can lay crumpled.

Pilar placed a red hollyhock behind one ear and poured a flood of perfume down the canyon between her breasts. José pretended he didn't like it but it drove him wild.

She wondered how long she could tease him tonight. Not very long, she guessed. He was getting to the crazy-wild point. She smiled in her mirror, smeared some dark lipstick on her full lips, and smiled again.

Maybe she'd let him have some tonight, she thought, and then changed her mind: *Let him get wild! So wild he'll forget Concha Chavez and all the others and want to marry me in the church.*

Pilar intended to catch José Villareál.

Bueno. He'd waited long enough. She threw the purple *tápalo* over her shoulders and slipped into the dark. A new moon whitened the 'dobe walls and a faint breeze stirred. It would carry her perfume ahead of her to José. Maybe she'd promise him things and make him walk her down by the *'cequia* tonight, down under the cottonwoods in shadows where silver light filtered through. She'd drive him crazy-wild tonight. He was already boiling hot.

She smiled and snaked her sinuous way toward the *jacal.*

▲

Enrique smoked his *cigarillo* in the *sala* his sister had cluttered with junk she'd bought in Española through the years. Rosalía sat in the light of the electric lamp she was so proud of—the first in Descanso—and he watched her knit. The flesh on her upper arms jiggled each time she threw a loop of pink yarn over the needle.

Luz sat in a corner. Her hands lay softly in her lap. She was like her dead mother, he thought, but more like a spirit made of air in her white cotton dress. Not like that Pilar Archuleta. Enrique didn't envy Tomás that one.

"She goin' to make big trouble one day," he said and Doña Rosalía looked up from her knitting and asked who.

"Pilar," he answered slowly. He remembered how she pranced through the *cantina* earlier that evening like a mare in heat. "And that José a wild stallion. They are like fire and *gasolina.*"

Luz watched her father with dark eyes.

Rosalía sighed. "Well, I hope he and Tonito don't come pounding here again!"

"Tonito's on the force tonight."

"Good. José will have to find his own trouble."

"I think he may find some tonight. Got the devil in his eye. That Pilar got him burning and he's got Pedro's pickup." Everyone knew how José drove when the devil was in him. "That boy goin' to kill somebody some day."

"Or himself." Doña Rosalía counted her stitches.

Luz crossed herself.

Doña Rosalía looked up. She stared at Enrique with eyes that remembered something and finally said with conviction, almost with relish, that something bad would happen that night. "I heard a coyote this afternoon," she said. "A coyote howled. In daylight." Everyone knew a coyote's cry in daylight foretold a death. "This afternoon I heard it." She resumed knitting. "José better stay away from that wheel tonight."

"Carlos says he's got a mind like one of those round rocks Fergus sells. The kind that got no shiny jewels inside."

"How can he tell," asked Luz softly, "without seeing inside? I think God puts some jewels inside everyone."

"Well, he hides 'em pretty well in some people," Enrique said darkly. "*Sí*, José chase trouble tonight I think."

▲

At the window in her dark room Luz looked toward the peak and saw the glitter the slim moon struck on the high snow that hadn't melted from winter. It shone pure like an altar candle and she said a prayer to the Virgin.

She thought of José. Pilar made him do terrible things. She knew he mustn't drive careening down the steep road, not in the wild anger Pilar put into him; she knew no one would stop him.

Unless. . . .

Unless she might! She was the only one. If she could get to the pickup before he did. If he hadn't already.

Her heart raced and she felt afraid but she had nothing to be afraid of. The saints weren't afraid, even in real, terrible danger, and they drew strength from their faith. She faced no danger, nothing at all except Tía Rosalía's anger if she knew.

She wouldn't know. Luz clutched her rosary, pulled her dark *rebozo* over her head, and softly stepped into the moon-paled night.

▲

God damn to everlasting fiery hell the whole female sex, thought José. The bitch had done it again—acted on fire for him, led him along the *acequia*—and then she'd thrust a sharp quick knee to his crotch, rolled from under him, and was gone before he could recover.

He crashed his fist into a cottonwood trunk, felt the pain race up his arm, and stood with bloody fists. *Damn the puta! Damn all women!*

She'd run off laughing. The whole village was laughing—even Luz, Pilar said—but Pilar was a liar. Luz didn't laugh at him.

¡Ahhh, qué importa! He'd go find Concha—Pedro's truck was parked at the end of the *placita* behind the church wall. Or maybe he'd go to Española. He needed a woman or he needed to kill somebody and maybe it would be Pilar. Meanwhile he'd floorboard it. The devil roared inside. He began to run.

Two sliver-moons showed in the cracked windshield and, as he ran closer, two of himself glared back fire-eyed.

"Stop, José!" It was only a whisper but it pierced the roaring in his head. *What the hell?* He stopped, his eyes still focused on the double image. A flash of white floated behind him and a face like a ghost shone in the glass, a face nun-draped in a black shawl, and it was a single image.

He turned. "Luz! What are you doing?"

"*Gracias a Dios*, I got here in time." She had run, and she breathed hard. "I was afraid. . . ."

"Afraid of what?" He was impatient. His devil whipped him. "Pray for me tomorrow, tonight I got business." He started around the truck and put his hand on the door.

She followed, put a moon-white hand on his, so soft it felt weightless, but it clung like a spider's web. "Please stay, José."

"Go home, Luz, you're meddling. Go home, for God's sake!"

"What's wrong, José?" Still her hand rested weblike on his.

"Something you wouldn't understand. Go home!"

"I do understand, José. It's Pilar again."

He looked down at her and for the first time her nun-eyes looked like woman-eyes. She smiled. Her breath caught in a nervous little laugh and when he heard the sound the red rage boiled inside him again and Pilar's words seethed through the devil-pierced mind.

Laughs behind your back like everyone else.

Even Luz! The little nun-girl he'd thought pure like the Blessed Virgin herself. They were all the same, all women were *putas*, and the thick red rage rolled through him like the greasy smoke of hell.

"Whore!" he screamed. He scraped off the clinging hand. He slapped her hard. All women were *putas*. His fingers clutched her thin shoulders. He snatched the *rebozo* and threw it from her. His fingers tore at her clothes, dug into her flesh. He flung her hard onto the gray dirt, and there he assaulted her, in great floods of crimson rage.

▲

Tonito stepped from the *cantina*. He pulled his badge from his pocket, puffed warm breath on it, and rubbed it on his pants leg. He pinned it on his shirt. He looked forward to the night. It made him feel important working on the force on the Saturday nights the sheriff needed him, important and responsible, giving tickets to drivers of shiny cars. Wearing that badge did something for a man. No matter how much hell he raised other times, when he put on that badge he was a man. He'd even arrest his own friends if he had to—though he was glad he was important only part time.

He strode the length of the *placita* to the far side where Descanso's few vehicles parked. At the far end stood Pedro's, still parked. He was glad of that. He started to climb into his own.

Then he heard it. "*Ayyyeeee!*" Tonito grabbed his shotgun from the cab and ran toward the sound.

Through the night silence rode loud sobs, strong male sobs, and words poured from the anguish of a homeless soul.

"Talk to me, please talk to me!" It was José's voice and the words were dammed by terrible sobs. "Oh god oh god! Talk to me. Oh Luz please talk! *Ayyyeeee!*" The high wail mounted the air.

In the silvered space beside the pickup José stood on wide-planted uncertain legs. In the pale light tears glinted on his cheeks. Below him, like a broken doll, a frail white figure lay crumpled and from a face as white as mist black eyes stared like sightless caverns.

Tonito stopped stunned, then ran toward her. "*¡Prima!*"

Slowly she turned her white face toward him as he lifted her shoulders but nothing showed in the eyes which stared but did not see.

He laid her head gently on the *rebozo*, stood, turned toward José whose fists clenched and unclenched. They had dried blood on them. He reached for Tonito and gabbled out words. "Tonito, I did it, I didn't know I did it—I didn't know nothing—until—Tonito. . . ." Tears covered his face.

Tonito gasped.

"Make her speak, Tonito." He fell to his knees beside her and sobbed. "There were two of me, Tonito. Tonight in the window there were two of me. But Luz was always one. Luz, you didn't laugh. I know you didn't. Luz, forgive me." Deep terrible sobs tore from his chest. "Oh pray for me, Luz!"

"Get up!" Tonito's voice cracked like a pistol.

Slowly José stood. He faced his friend. "Take me in," he mumbled. "Take me in, Tonito."

"No," said Tonito. "No. It's a family matter." He talked thickly, remembered the time the dog that was his own had gone mad and he knew he had to kill it but he tried to put it off and he walked slowly to it, like now. His words came out one step at a time. "A family matter."

José's eyes flicked to the badge—the man badge—and Tonito knew it flashed silver as his chest moved and José's eyes, moon-glinting, followed the gun barrel as Tonito raised it and aimed at his friend; the eyes slid to the frail broken doll with the staring eyes and a plea wrenched from his empty chest.

"Pray for me!" His voice rose like a trapped lion's and sliced the night. "Pray for me, Luz!"

José looked back to Tonito. He stood straight then and forced a harsh laugh. "*¡Qué importa!*" Fear burned his eyes but he stood with courage.

For an instant old comradeship pulsed between them. Then running steps pounded the ground and yells ripped the moment. "*¿Qué pasa?*"

"*¿Quién es?*"

"*¡Hola! ¿Qué es ese?*"

Tonito fired.

▲

Drake sat on the floor of the cold church and copied the *retablo* of San Rafael. His sketch pad rested on a bench. Strange how hard it was to capture the clean lines. Flat crude *retablos* painted by unskilled artists should be easy to copy. Francisco said it took faith to free the life inside.

Hell, he wasn't trying to accomplish a work of art, only of documentation. Still, the cleanness eluded him.

He thought of José who invoked San Rafael's aid for the fishing trip. *Must have worked*, he thought. *We got fish*. He remembered José's terrors of Purgatory and his final brutal act. Drake laid down his charcoal, left the unfinished attempt on the bench, and walked about the church. He flexed his cold fingers. For the hundredth time he studied the *bultos* and *retablos* and marveled at the untrained artistry of faith.

He kept seeing José's eyes—the haunt-eyes he had turned from the altar that day, the gentle-eyes the time he'd fished the squirrel from the stream.

At the altar rail and before several of the *santos*, votive candles burned in their squat glasses. It was All Souls' Day. The candles were burning prayers for those in Purgatory. *Well*, he thought, *no harm in that, if you can believe it, if it gives comfort to anybody.*

None burned for José.

Even his own mother would not light a candle for a son who had died from so bestial a sin.

José did not lie in the consecrated soil of the *camposanto*. The Church does not bury with blessings one who has raped a saint. His was a lonely grave on a rock hill, marked by no cross.

Luz had not spoken since and her blank face continually reminded everyone of that brutality. She knew no one. Her eyes were empty votive glasses whose flame had died.

Drake stood at the altar rail. Images of that terrible night came back to him and the sounds of José's anguished cry. He heard the scattered shouts of the alerted village, the single explosion of the shot, and the shards of its thousand echoes. He felt the night air on his face as he ran toward the spot with the others. He remembered the animal fear that contorted José's face, that slowly drained from his eyes as the vibrancy fled the young body, and Tonito leaning over a fender vomiting. The screams of the villagers as they saw the awful thing came to him and the tolling of the bell.

He saw again Enrique's trembling hands, gentle on his daughter's shoulders as he led his dazed child home, remembered how he turned to admonish his neighbors for the din they made. "You wanna talk 'round my Luz, you talk quiet." His voice shook. "Saints don't hear nothin' but soft words!"

Drake went back to the *retablo* and examined its clean primitive lines. San Rafael was a thin saint, elongated, almost El Greco-like. His long body, his long wings, the long string of fish he held were all outlined in hard black paint and a pointed black beard lengthened his ascetic face. The colors that filled the lines were dark and primitive. San Rafael, patron of fishermen, and also the guide of lost travelers and a healer of the blind, Francisco said.

Drake returned to his sketch pad.

From time to time someone entered the church. None disturbed him. Each nodded, lit a candle for his dead, and said a quiet prayer.

None prayed for José.

Except for these quiet visits, the church was still, its silence shaded only by the scratches of Drake's charcoal. Thoughts roamed without pattern in his mind and he followed their progress with an almost visual sense. One idea made him smile as it passed by and then he looked at it more closely. He shrugged. *Why not?*

He laid down his charcoal and stood. He looked at San Rafael, patron of travelers lost on their way, healer of blindness, and he winked at the skinny fellow. He ran his finger over the rough wood on the *retablo* and loosened a splinter as he'd seen Soledad do.

He didn't know why he did what he did.

He walked to the back of the church, put a dollar in the little box beside the door, and took a candle. He carried it to the altar rail, held the splinter from San Rafael in the flame of a live candle, lit his own from it, and dropped it still ablaze on the wax.

He set it beneath San Rafael, still grinning his half-grin, and he mocked his own strange impulse.

"*¡Qué importa!*" he said.

"What are you doing, Carlos?" Soledad led Pepito by his small hand and Drake saw the child and felt the old pang of love.

He hadn't heard them come in. His face burned. "For José," he said, and she gave him the deep well-look. "Seems sort of too bad to think of a chap in his fix without even a candle."

12

Cars sped people to work and breathed exhaust fumes into the morning as Drake said, "So long, I've got to split."

"But the Penitentes. You were going to tell me about the Penitentes."

"No," said Drake, "I wasn't. Besides, you're right, *señor*, they're barbarians. We're all barbarians, only some of us are civilized barbarians."

"What does that mean?"

"*¿Quién sabe?*" Drake remembered the little dog. *Poor little bastard.*

He rounded a corner toward his old office and came to the auditorium he had contributed to in his civilized days. *Welcome home, Drake–Carlos, welcome back among the civilized barbarians who are your own kind now. You can go to the civic symphony and hear Beethoven's Ninth which is all about courage and triumph and you can look around the auditorium at all the Sweeneys with black ties and blank faces waiting for it to be over so they can have their martinis at the country club and make up the next day's foursome.*

You're back now, you've got to make it legal. Hell, you can't even get a passport to leave again without producing Drake Cavanaugh out of a hat.

He walked through the well-tended streets of Rancho Ribera where leash laws were enforced with such strict authority and no pile of doggy-do ever spotted the petunia beds because no doggies ran loose to do or if they broke out they got eliminated by low-riding Chevys.

For a couple of hours he walked until the day had a chance to get started. He passed the church he once attended with Leona on civilized Sundays, all in expensive good taste. It wasn't heated with a wood stove or lit by a crude *bambolete* hanging from uneven *vigas* and it wasn't cluttered with crude *santos* or garish *reredos* or tin *nichos* or crowded with dark heads in black *rebozos*.

A jogger puffed down the street. His ass jiggled and he wore headphones to seal him from the worldsound. A meter maid added diversion to someone's life with a parking ticket. A woman consulted her shopping list with serious concentration. Across the street people pushed carts from a supermarket. The everydayness of life engrossed everyone and kept the mystery at bay.

A siren wailed, grew louder, screamed past, and turned down a side street. It splashed dirty water on a boy who should have been in school.

"Cocksucker," shouted the kid.

The fire truck stopped not far down the street. It couldn't turn in to where the house burned because an empty car blocked the way. People gushed from doors and hurried toward the fire.

Finally the firemen found the owner of the car. He said he'd put it there to keep curious people from getting in the firemen's way.

They hooked up the hose and battered in the door and one ran in to see if anyone was inside but no one was. Someone said the owner was named Ernie and he was at work.

"But I called him," said a shrill woman with a fat voice. She wore a dirty housecoat and rhinestone earrings and last night's makeup. "I called him first off," she said. She wore her importance like the emperor's new clothes. "I called him even before I called the fire station."

Everyone offered suggestions to the firemen and got in their way and the fat woman with the earrings wondered if Ernie had insurance.

After a while the flames subsided and the people started home in laughing loitering clots to call their friends who'd missed the fun. It was a spot of color in their dun-colored lives.

Drake walked on to the mock-territorial building with the blue woodwork and the heavy paneled doors and the brass plate that read Hendricks, Cavanaugh, McBurnham, and Fremont, or at least that's what it read once. Leona hadn't liked that office much. She said a firm with their prestige needed a larger suite in a swankier place and the other wives tended to agree and while he was thinking this he saw that the heavy doors were gone and the brass plate, too, so the wives must have gotten their way.

He looked through the glass doors into a chrome-plated cavern gutted of its old partitions and a long line of bowling lanes accommodated a ladies' league getting in its morning games. Peals of distant thunder that rumbled from the hollows were the thunders of civilization.

Better to get on with it. He should see Leona first. The wife shouldn't be the last to know. He lit a cigarette, flipped the match onto the pavement, and departed the thunder to go face Dame Cavanaugh.

Looked like it might rain again, or snow.

▲

"Once upon a time," said Drake, "the head, the heart, and the penis all lived together in harmony. Then Prometheus brought fire and industry, departmentalized the peaceable kingdom, and man's faculties have been at war with each other since. Or, if you prefer, call him the serpent in Eden. It's the same legend."

"No it isn't," said Father Andreas.

"They both brought knowledge and so they were both do-gooders. The worst corruptors of mankind are the do-gooders, gathering souls like so many scalps, to save their own. The world's greatest danger is not sin, Father, it's charity."

A green horsefly buzzed and after Drake swatted him another disappeared into the curtain folds. Drake looked outside. "And you are socked in but good so we might as well have a drink."

All day the mountain had been sullen. By afternoon it grew cold. Clouds like yeast rose in the crater beneath the peak, thickened and darkened, spilled down the slopes, and veiled the village. The wind hit with furious force, and demons of ice began to whirl. Darkness fell with the snow.

"All bloody hell breaketh loose, Father," he said. "I told you to get out early if you wanted out."

"I had a baptism, a catechism class. . . ."

"Ah, the sins of charity. You know, if you didn't wear those skirts, Father, you'd look like Odin." Drake mixed the drinks. Andreas did look like a red-lipped Nordic god even with the robes. On either side of his beaked nose cheeks flamed like the geraniums in the village windows and his eyes snapped blue sparks.

"Skoal!" Drake began to scratch idly at his pad to catch the likeness of the priest.

Since the old padre's death Andreas spent his nights in Descanso with Drake. He enjoyed the good Scotch whiskey—one of his few indulgences—and both men enjoyed the repartee.

Through his drink Drake squinted at the fire. "Yes," he mused, "the original sin was altruism and not Eve's for trying a new dish. Or Pandora's for opening a jar. Curiosity isn't a sin. Though one should beware serpents bearing apples or gods bearing fire."

"Satan—an altruist?"

"He brought knowledge. But take Prometheus if you'd rather. The Greeks were at least as intelligent as the Hebrews and a hell of a lot more fun."

"Prometheus had better intentions."

"Prometheus was history's first grand-scale do-gooder and he deserved what he got. Though I suspect he suffered less from his punishment than from that stream of sympathizers. It's bitter to be judged by one's inferiors.

"Anyway we've been plagued since. With all sorts of problems—charity among them. And charity's price is dependence. Satan and Prometheus hawked knowledge at the price of common sense. That's where you churchmen go wrong. Your brains are so stuffed with dogma there's not a cranny left for an original thought."

"Don't blame the religion because of its practitioners."

"Don't you ever get bored with the same old tired themes?"

"I find my Lord excellent company."

"But can He say the same about yours?"

"Don't be blasphemous. Would you fix me another drink?"

"Sure. You churchmen credit God with everything except a sense of humor. Anything intelligent enough to fashion man—a mistake in judgment, perhaps, but you must admit it took engineering genius—a God that original can't be such an ass as to sit around waiting to be worshiped and adored all the time. I'm not as conversant with Him as you, of course, but I would assume He created man hoping for some intelligent conversation. And when He didn't get it He sent the flood."

The green fly buzzing like an invitation to sin dive-bombed Goso who snapped twice, missed, and resumed his nap by the fire.

"I believe," said the priest drily, "the scripture mentions sin?"

"The Hebrews always tacked on sin. Anyhow, they lifted the story. In the original the gods were bored with man's ceaseless babble. 'We're gonna wash these men right outa our hair,' sang Anu, and let her rip. In the Greek version, of course, it was sheer spite—Zeus was a vengeful bastard. Sin wasn't the issue until the Hebrews came along and took the fun out of everything. Anyhow, it was not the pious man but the clever one who put his ass in gear, built a boat, and got saved."

Andreas laughed.

Drake crossed to mix another drink. "You know, the Greeks really had it over us. They amused their gods—offered them theatre instead of church. An extremely civilized practice. Theatre and good conversation."

"What do you believe in?"

"The great god Pan, I suppose. Who, by the way, had a terrific sense of humor though he did have a temper. They say when he heard Christ was born he died. More likely, he just went underground to sulk and still lives somewhere, like in these pagan New World mountains."

"We agree on the paganism." The priest sighed. "Mine is a losing battle."

"Why? You've got the field to yourself. You marry them and bury them and baptize their babies, and teach them their catechism. . . ."

"Which they buzz back like that fly and often with as much comprehension." Andreas paced to the window, watched the snow, and drank a long draft. "It's their superstitions." He turned. His eyes crackled and his red mouth curled. "Ghosts, *brujas*—medieval poppycock!"

"Oh, come on. You represent the world's greatest medieval institution!"

"It goes back a bit farther. You've heard of Christ? Thinking churchmen have always appealed for reason. Abélard, Erasmus. . . ."

"And got their knuckles rapped severely, I believe. You can't reconcile faith with reason. Not any more. Though I think it was possible once, when your religion still stuck to Christ, and men listened to nightingales instead of priests. Haven't you ever questioned the hierarchical doctrines?"

Father Andreas toyed with his cincture. "Yes. I even considered—at one time—leaving the Church. That was before seminary. I was in pre-med. My father expected me to take over his practice."

"They siphoned me into law. But I took some art classes and anthro and archaeology because it seemed to me even then that if civilization was ever going to work we'd better not forget where it came from. And I used to read poetry. I liked Eliot though I couldn't understand him. Maybe that's why I liked him— he left some mystery in. I always thought poets were of more consequence than lawyers. But I was told to stow that crap and get on with my studies."

"And you did?"

"Oh yes. For years I stood firmly by duty. What a word—duty: the curse of the thinking classes."

"Well, there's no thinking class up here. Just that barbaric 'brotherhood.' Surely you can't be unaware. . . ."

"I don't consider it my business. You tell me not to condemn religion because of its practitioners. Well, don't you condemn the practitioners because of their religion."

"I don't. Lord knows, I try to get through to them."

"But it's a one-way conversation. Try listening—you might learn something from them. I have. Let's have another drink. *In vino veritas* and in good Glenlivet is more *veritas*."

"Just don't forget supper."

"I'm never too oiled to toss an omelet. Padre Lorenzo took them on their own terms."

"He was one of them. I'm not."

"Neither am I." Drake spoke with the careful articulation of the mildly mellowed. "But I've opened up to them. So could you if you'd take off that damned hair shirt. Here's your drink."

Drake threw a piñon stick on the fire. He listened to its quick hot crackles and Goso's steady snore against the night wind beyond. He set his drink on the mantel and fingered the Virgin Francisco had carved him.

"I feel a profound spirit of place here, in this forgotten pocket of God's overalls. The crust of earth is thinner in some places. The shrine at Delphi. The mists of Avalon. The Salisbury Plain. . . ."

"And here? Come off it, Cavanaugh."

"Most of all here. The Rincón and an Indian shrine Juan Tafoya took me to. These mountains—places not all paved over with modernism, maybe, I don't know. In some places the earth still breathes. The great Neolithic Earth Mother still sends up waves of life—call it psychic energy."

"Rot."

"I should take you one day to that shrine, Padre. Two stone lions on a high *potrero* and they guard the entrance to the center of the world."

"They still believe it, don't they?"

"You'd better believe they do. There were fresh prayer sticks and offerings. And artifacts—some very ancient—and all strangely undisturbed. No one dares touch them."

"Antiquity laws."

"It's more than that. Some powerful force protects it. I call it spirit-of-place."

"I call it nonsense."

"You should go see those lions, Father. It's a hell of a long trek. But the search for religion always is, I suppose."

"If you want to call it religion."

Drake shrugged. "The Indians say these mountains cover the center of the world. The Place of Emergence. Hell, how do we know we didn't emerge from the center of the earth? It's nothing more than birth from the womb in macrocosm."

"You don't believe all that gibberish?"

Drake shrugged. "I don't disbelieve it. Neither do I disbelieve your religion, though I don't go for the organization."

"At least you believe in some sort of a religion."

"Not a single religion—more in its allness. Religion's like a great primeval ocean whose tides sweep the universe. A sort of psychic awareness. The Indians still comprehend the oneness. It's pure truth, not separate truths all conflicting with one another—moral versus scientific versus religious versus philosophic, or heart versus head versus penis. It's pure wisdom, before man split it into narrow fragments of knowledge—like splitting the atom, it causes all hell to break loose. Besides, the division's only an illusion. You can divide the Atlantic from the Pacific—but they're still connected, they're all one. Can you say the Atlantic is the only real ocean? If so, you've missed the whole concept. I can't believe in individual oceans—but I have to believe in oceanity."

"Let us pursue the argument with one more drink. Do you believe in the Holy Trinity?"

"I believe in the Holy Ghost—the mystery in all religion. The mysterious flow between you and me, and between us and the earth, and between the earth and the universe." He carried their glasses to the *trastero*.

"That's transcendentalism."

"There's no such thing. The minute you call it an *ism* you bottle it in dogma and it smothers. Maybe that's the secret of Pan—he didn't have formal cults but he was the oldest god and the spirit in the others. Maybe he's your Holy Ghost with a happy laugh and happy pipes and the hooves of a happy goat!"

"A libidinous god of sexual excesses."

"The dichotomy of the universe is sexual. Hell, Father, even Christ was 'begotten not made.'"

"Not by man."

"By the Holy Ghost—Pan, if you will, being libidinous. Yes, I believe in a spirit—or spirits. Here's your libation. Did it ever occur to you that these people's ghosts and *brujas* might actually exist?" He picked up the sketch pad, then threw it down. "Damn that fly!"

He turned, swatter in hand. "Do you know, just before José Villareál was killed, Doña Rosalía heard a coyote howl? In daylight?"

"So?"

"Coyotes rarely howl in daylight."

"Did she even hear it? Or only remember it after the event? Was it from the metaphysical world or her own mind?"

"What difference does it make? Where does your own Holy Ghost come from? Let's eat."

Goso followed them into the kitchen, swept an arc on the floor with his tail, and watched Drake break the eggs.

"It's the mystery—the Holy Ghost or Doña Rosalía's signs—that divides religion from science. One proves, the other suggests. If it were proven there'd be no virtue in believing and no selectivity in heaven. Everyone would get in and it would become a democratic institution and cease to be heaven."

The fly buzzed like the universal question.

Father Andreas tilted his glass, smiled into its shallowing depths, and settled his big frame on a kitchen chair. "Oh, now you're condemning democracy!"

"I condemn what we've made of it. Stuffed it into do-gooder *isms* and smothered the concept which was based on the belief in man's rationality. Catalina brought me fresh tortillas today. We'll have a feast." He lit the butane under the chile pot.

"Old Ben Franklin warned us. 'We've given you a republic,' he said, and then challenged us to keep it. And of course we haven't."

"But it was still man's noblest experiment." The priest's deep voice boomed. "And it's still noble and still an experiment and, like religion, it demands faith. You believed in it once, Charles Drake Cavanaugh—enough to fight for it—and what did you do? You copped out. Why?"

"Because we've become the great sterility. Paternalism has gobbled up

202

individual integrity and they perpetrate all their *isms* in the false name of human rights, which adds hypocrisy to greed. And we reap the predictable end of democracy—the welfare state. The mediocre shall inherit the earth. And only the turds of civilization are left. That's why I'm here. I couldn't bear to watch it any longer."

"You're a cynic."

"Call me a romantic. It was a romantic who first got up off of all fours. He believed in something better. So do I."

"And you expect to find it here?"

"I believe if civilization is going to be preserved—if it was worth getting up off the ground—we've got to go back and find out what it is. For six thousand years men have sensed something greater beyond us—some promise in their lives, some basic truth inside us, some spark of the transcendental divine, if you will. I believe civilization—the real article, not its rotting carcass—is a chain, a chain of intellectual fire stolen from Olympos and that each man must find that fire—not sit on his ass and wait for a handout from Prometheus—and kindle his own flame from the old embers."

"And you think you'll find Olympos here?"

"*¿Quién sabe?* We've all got to find our own and then start up the trail to the top. That's where the faith comes in. Or the blind hope Prometheus plagued us with when he gave us the fire. We've got to believe there is a fire up there.

"Dish up the chile while I pour the wine. I've a pretty fair claret."

"I'm not sure we need any."

Suddenly the electricity blinked, sputtered, and blacked out.

"Another fuse." Drake laughed and fumbled for a lantern. "Segundo wired it." The smell of kerosene joined that of hot chile and the room glowed orange. Goso pushed his pan across the floor pursuing his third of the omelet. Fingers of frozen snow tapped against the window.

"Have you found. . .?"

"What?"

"Whatever it is you're hunting."

"No. Maybe—like Columbus—I hunted one thing and bumped into another, of greater value. I don't swallow the superstitions of these people or share their beliefs. But I've looked on pure faith. I know it exists. I know there's a mountain somewhere—and that it's worth hunting." He smiled. "I've even helped hunt. Have I shown you my fetishes?"

"No."

"Two little carved mountain lions. Juan Tafoya gave them to me—I'm not sure why. They're supposed to help the hunter sight his quarry. There's no democracy on a hunt, Father. It takes excellence to outwit the game. Democracy—or its socialistic result—discourages excellence. That's why it's basically immoral. Here, you're out of wine."

"I'm also out of chile." The big man refilled his bowl. "What a fine bishop you'd have made," he said, "if only you believed in God."

"Oh, is that necessary?"

"There's your fly." The sluggish creature hit against the stove, crawled on its surface, and took off heavily. "As elusive as the questions we ask." The priest's hand tightened around the stem of his glass. "It seems to me you're making an awfully intense search for something you don't believe exists."

"I believe it once did before the organization killed the spirit. So did civilization back when a Bach fugue was more important than a flush toilet."

"You installed plumbing quickly enough."

"Who am I to shun comfort? But I don't confuse it with the elevation of the soul. We've put the terror at bay—electricity's hard on ghosts and *brujas* and things don't go bump in the night much anymore. But we've also lost the mystery. And the vision. Without the terror the peace at the end doesn't mean much. Terror is proud and clean because it demands courage. Without courage the peace has no definition, it's all mush. The Question has to come first. Today we know all the answers—and no Question. Let's finish our wine in the other room."

Drake set the lantern in the front window, poked up the fire, and lit the candles on the mantel by the Virgin. "I too have a saint, Father. Francisco made her for me."

"It's hardly lovely."

"It's honest."

"It's crude, vulgar, and an insult to the Blessed Virgin."

"How do you know what the Virgin looks like? Have you seen her?"

"Has Francisco?"

"I think very likely he has."

The wind had settled to a soft moan. The snow fell heavily. Inside the fly droned again.

Drake handed his Virgin to the priest. "Have you ever wondered what this is she stands on?"

"It looks like a crescent moon."

"It is. Or the horns of a cow. Both fertility symbols, used interchangeably in the ancient world. The Earth Mother again—goddess of the womb and the tomb. She presides over our emergence from the soil and our return to it through the ancient horned gate. She has many faces but she's always the same—she's all of them—Ninhursag, Inanna, Ishtar, Hathor; all the neolithic goddesses wore crowned horns. In the New World, mother-goddesses have been found from the Andes to the Sangre de Cristos. And they're all fulfilled in the Guadalupe Virgin on her crescent of fertility."

"To so corrupt the image of the Blessed Virgin—"

"I think it strengthens your argument. That over the globe and through the centuries, men have perceived the same principles—it's pretty incredible, really. It doesn't prove any of it true but it supports the principles. Why can't religion have universal laws like physics?"

"And there's another plus." Drake replaced the Virgin. "Great religions inspire great art."

"Which for you justifies religion?"

"Why not? Art's the basis for civilization."

"But can art save souls?"

"It very possibly saves more than religion." Drake's voice was dry. "At least it makes the journey more pleasant."

"I'm not interested in men's comfort in this world but in their final destination."

"But getting there's half the fun! Who do you think has the better chance of getting in heaven, the priest or the artist? Or is heaven, like the Renaissance papacy, the spoils of the politicians—say, Alexander the whichever? The Borgia?"

"Those Renaissance popes were great art patrons."

"Is that how they breached the gates? How is it done—in your fashion, with battering rams made of saved souls? Or does one sneak in with a wooden horse offered in the name of art patronage? Or can't one just climb the mountain and enjoy the hike and hope there's an intellectual flame at the top? I'll meet you up there and we'll see who gets invited in first. I'll bet on the poets! You talk about discipline. . . ."

"Moral discipline."

"Balls. Any clod can be moral. Even a bishop. Hell, I was moral for years, in your sense of the word. Real moral discipline, the kind the artist needs, is in looking—really looking—at things and people and the universe. Real looking, that demands honest questions that won't let you look away, that imposes choices—not between right and wrong, any fool can make those—but between right and right and knowing full well the desperate price of each. It takes courage to be an artist. Especially a poet. Of all the arts only poetry rated three muses."

He began to sketch again. Andreas had a fluid mouth.

"Then with so many muses, why aren't there more poets?"

"Why aren't there any nightingales in America? Their song's too subtle for socialism. That's why Pan left the civilized world. The market was too restricted. No one would listen except the poets. We send Sweeneys to Congress and consider plumbers more useful than poets."

"Perhaps to the majority they are."

"But the majority is usually wrong. The majority doesn't think at all, which is why collectivism is immoral. It was the majority who crucified your leader, Father. Majorities hear neither nightingales nor poets. But on one point alone art wins over science or religion."

"Even over plumbers?"

"Only in art can reason and faith be reunited. Only in art can man find again the duality he knew before the fall—the perfect tension, the balance of heaven and earth. The totality of opposites.

"Even religion was still an art to Padre Lorenzo and not a scholarly treatise. It was still pure. His Virgin was an Earth Mother. He understood the balance, the totality.

"When I came here my life was fragmented like a thousand little spigots all drawing from the source, draining the soil, lowering the water table to no good end. My basin was going dry. So I cut off the thousand spigots that drained my psychic well. I cut them off and found a source.

"The Indians call it the Time for Staying Still. For recharging. Descanso's mine."

"To what end?"

Drake shrugged. "Maybe those sketches I've worked on will be some small way of recording a fragment of the civilization here. One little link with the source. *¿Quién sabe?* I think Padre Lorenzo understood what I'm trying to show. These people. . . ."

"And their miracles? Do you suppose he really believed he could be the agent of some local wonder?"

"I don't think he'd have presumed that much."

"He presumed often enough to disregard the bishop's specific instructions. Said neither the bishop nor Rome understood his parishioners." Father Andreas erupted from his chair, strode to the window, then turned and his eyes burned blue. "A priest must not try to be God!"

"But all of you do. You presume to make His judgments. The good padre wouldn't have refused to bury José in the *camposanto*, for instance. He'd have let the Lord decide José's eternity. He must have had some good—José, I mean. And he loved the old man. I saw him at the *velorio*. I saw all of them there."

"And did you listen to their plots?"

"I didn't hear any."

"Oh, you needn't hide it." Andreas sounded tired. He crossed to the *trastero* and poured more wine. "They plotted."

"They didn't confide in me. I'm an outsider."

"Yes, and you always will be. Get out, go back to the world you belong in! You talk about Erasmus and reason—well, apply it to yourself. What makes men human instead of animal? Reason. Mind. That's man's function, to think. It's what humanism's all about. And you sit up here indulging yourself, you shirk all responsibility.

"You talk about civilization." The priest's eyes snapped. "Well, if it ever existed—in your sense—it's still there, while you throw away your humanity—your mind—you let it rot up here."

"Man does not live by head alone."

"You're denying your own intellectual responsibilities. You're cutting yourself off, the music and the art and the libraries that preserve the best of that six thousand years you say are going down the drain. Go back. To your own world—because it is your world, like it or not."

"Yes." Drake walked to the window and stood a long time. When he turned he spoke slowly. "You're right, of course. And I will go back. Someday. When I've found where the trail begins. I guess I've known that all along." He threw another log on the fire. "This isn't my world. But neither is it yours, *amigo*."

"I'm here for a reason. It's part of my discipline. I'm fighting the ignorance. Do you think I don't know where Father Lorenzo's body lies?" Andreas carried his glass to the window, peered again into the snow, and brooded dark-souled.

"What difference does it make?" Drake shrugged. "If it gives them comfort."

"Because it leads to more ignorance. More superstition. It's like your electricity—they take charge of their own religion the way they wired your house, without knowledge, and overload the circuit, so the least little thing blows the fuse." He walked to the *fogón*, pulled at his clerical collar, and threw a log on the flame. "And the cure is discipline. Relax it once and you invite infractions. Suppose I'd given José holy burial—wouldn't that have made a mockery of all morals? Wouldn't it have said to the whole village, 'Go and sin, it doesn't matter, you'll be indulged'?"

Drake swallowed the last of his wine and crossed to the *trastero*. "What are you running from, Padre?" His voice was quiet.

"What do you mean?"

"We're both alien exiles here. I ran away—I admit it—I walked out of a society I couldn't tolerate any longer." The wine gurgled as he poured. "I've found an island of peace here. A sense of decency. A feeling of history, of something worth preserving, and I'm trying to document it in my clumsy way. But I'm still the coward who ran away." He walked to the window and looked into the gray. The fly droned. "Why are you here?"

"That's obvious, isn't it?"

"You hate these mountains, these people. Yet you specifically asked for this assignment. What were you running from?" He lit a cigarette.

Father Andreas put his glass on the mantel with a snap. He picked up the little Virgin, fingered the crescent she stood on, and put her down again. He examined the fetishes. He paced to the window and clenched his big hands and when he turned to Drake his blue stare glittered and it was almost hypnotic. Above his collar the veins corded in his neck; his red mouth flared, and his voice was tight.

"That's what I ask myself." He picked up his glass from the mantel and sat again and his eyes reflected the fire. "I was in pre-med before Korea but after I got home I began to realize men's souls were more important than their bodies. And more lasting."

"Debatable. But it doesn't explain Descanso."

"After seminary I went to a midwestern community and soon had a parish of my own. Life was pleasant. But I was restless. I felt superfluous."

"Oh. You were unhappy because you weren't unhappy!"

"Would you have been content if you'd never gotten beyond drawing up powers of attorney? I wanted a challenge. I wanted—I needed—to take God's work where the going wasn't so easy, where. . . ."

"Where you could wear a hair shirt? I never understood the missionary compulsion."

"Then why did you go to Korea?"

"For adventure, I suppose. I was young."

"Ideals had nothing to do with it?"

Drake took a long drag from his cigarette, then threw it into the fire. He grinned. "Okay, you win that round. Sure, I was fired up. Go lick the Commie bastards. God, Mom, and the flag. I still believe in what they used to mean."

"And you believe it's still there, down beneath. You said yourself you were disgusted with the cowards—the 'yellow bastards' you called them—that wouldn't go to Nam—"

"Damn right. Belong to the club, pay your dues. Hell yes, I was disgusted."

"—so you ran away. You quit paying your dues because some of the junior members wouldn't pay theirs."

"I told you—I lack the missionary complex. You're here to save souls—principally your own. Which brings us back to my question: why is your soul in such almighty danger? What are you running from?"

The priest grabbed the swatter and began to prowl the room. He looked at the Dasburg on the wall. "Did your father like you?"

"I guess so."

"Mine didn't. Not much. Mama overdid it the other way. Everything I did was better than what any other kid did."

"Were you their only child?"

"The only boy. The girls were older. I grew up hating women."

"And your father?"

"He was a doctor and my hero when I was a kid. He and John Brown. I used to go on calls with him in the country out from the little Kansas town where we lived. I'd play along the creeks and pretend I was John Brown massacring slavery men. Papa disapproved. Naturally."

"Normal kid stuff."

"Playing at murder? Anyhow, I still played the game and then felt like a sinner for hiding it. I committed other sins in secret, too, as I grew older, some you'd never suspect—"

"I imagine I would."

"—but the guiltier I felt the more I sinned. And I used to hope they'd catch me and punish me dreadfully."

"Didn't they ever?"

"Sometimes. Mama would cry, if it was really bad, and hold me on her lap and press me against her puffy breasts and the smell of her perfume made me sick. She always blamed it on some other kid. Papa threatened to punish me and we'd go to the garage and I'd think, 'this time I'm going to get it,' and I'd be afraid and my stomach would feel thrills the way it did when we'd go to Kansas City and I'd watch the roller coaster at the amusement park and try to get up nerve to ride it so I could show how brave I was."

"And then?"

"He never followed through. We'd go off in the car and he'd be grumpy and say we were surrounded by too many females and what I needed was some man talk. And then he'd say coarse vulgar things and laugh—only it was put on and we were both self-conscious and I'd just feel sick."

"You said he didn't like you."

"He thought he did. But—except for my moral lapses—he never approved anything I did. It's funny—he encouraged my naughtiness but he made fun of anything good I did. If I made a B in school he asked why it wasn't an A. If I confided an ambition he'd laugh and say I wasn't smart enough. I can still hear him with his heavy voice—there was still a trace of German in it. 'Oh,' he'd say, very sarcastic, 'you vant to be a surgeon, vit your great clumsy hands!' Or, 'Listen to him, Mama: he vill fly aeroplanes, he vill be a great ace pilot! He forgets he was so afraid of the roller coaster he vet his pants!' I used to dream of Papa saying 'Goot chob, Andreas,' and his eyes shining with pride."

"That's why you went to med school?"

"I didn't get beyond pre-med. Korea came up."

"Did he approve?"

"No. I came home on leave, pretty puffed up, after I got my wings. I was going to war and be very brave. Papa said I was playing hero. 'I grow old,' he said, 'keeping my practice until you can help me. So vhat do you do? You qvit the school I am paying for to strut about in your new uniform!' It made me angry—and guilty again. Because it turned out he had a heart condition. I was overseas when he died."

"So you've scourged yourself since. Which is stupid. After all, you went for a principle."

"Did I? Or just to prove a point, find an excuse to quit school, to get out of medicine without Papa calling me a quitter? I don't know."

"Who does? Is there such a thing as a pure motive?"

"The holy martyrs. . . ."

"Were often damn fools. Martyrdom is unsufferably arrogant. Like your John Brown. 'Look at me,' it says, 'I am God's anointed. See how holy I am, how brave.' And to what end? What good are you serving here? You don't like these people, or their ways, or their villages. One of their own would be more acceptable and likely do more good. How many souls are you saving up here?"

"My own, maybe."

"Couldn't you save it by just leading a normally decent life without flagellating yourself for some childish peccadilloes and a daddy complex?"

"It was more than that."

"Well get it off your chest. 'Forgive me, Father Drake, for I have sinned. . . .'"

"Forgive me, Drake, I'm a great bore."

"You are, somewhat. Confession is a minor form of martyrdom. A pious way to brag, another 'look-at-me' game. And interesting only in proportion to the sins confessed. Haven't you a real corker to tell?"

"I very likely would have without the discipline I find here."

"Let me guess: you've lusted in your heart. . . ."

"I have hated my Papa."

"Because he was hard to please and you think he didn't like you? Good God, Padre."

Andreas jumped to his feet "Because he was my hero and he debased himself." he shouted. His words began to boil like lava from a long-smoldering crater. "His coarse talk grew worse as I grew older. He used to ask me if I'd been with women. He said that was what I needed. He prodded me to give in to shameful feelings. He pushed me at women until I hated them. But I still had those physical compulsions and I hated myself." His eyes glinted. "I hated my Papa because he made me feel I wasn't a man. When I came home on leave I felt manly at least—heroic even—I was a pilot, headed for combat. A man. But he wasn't impressed. You say I'm trying to save my soul—yes, Drake, I am!"

"And you're still looking for penance, aren't you, Father?" Drake said slowly. "I wish I could give you one. I wish I could say 'Go and sin no more.'

Unfortunately, I haven't the credentials."

Andreas plunged out into the snow. The crimson words hung heavy in the air and Drake wondered if they'd still be friends when morning came or if the devil-scourged priest would hate him because he heard these things.

The sky cleared by morning and the birds were noisy and the brilliance pierced the eye painfully. Andreas had already washed the dishes and made coffee, had grabbed the axe and was attacking the woodpile as if it were sin.

They both had mild hangovers. "We won't shrive our souls any more," said the priest with his red smile when he came in for coffee. "Though I did all the confessing. I still don't know why you stay here."

"Neither do I," said Drake.

Andreas left the next afternoon and as they loosed the plane from its moorings he turned to Drake. "Just one question," he said. "Do you really believe all that nonsense you were babbling?"

"When I drink a lot I talk a lot."

"You don't really defend their superstitions?"

"Hell, no!"

"It was all just banter?"

"Sound without fury."

"I'll get you out of here yet."

"But you want to know something, Father? That afternoon—just before José was killed—when Doña Rosalía heard the coyote?"

"Yes, what about it?"

"Nothing. Only—I heard it too!"

Drake walked back toward the house through Francisco's orchard, bare now, and gray, and Goso raced in great joyous circles. The drone of the plane faded and the old loneliness closed in. Andreas might be screwed up but who wasn't? It was a long time between good conversations and after each he hungered as after one canapé. But there was no intellect left in the world he'd left, either, not in the tyranny of collective thought, not in herd madness, not in the follow-the-leader psychoses of the men who ruled the world but couldn't read a book, only an occasional editorial that swept everyone's thought in one direction like so many tumbleweeds against a fence. No salvation there. Andreas was wrong.

He saw Francisco at his woodpile, waved to the sturdy little man of giant faith, and walked on.

He threw sticks for Goso for awhile. He scattered some grain for the tough little mountain birds who weathered the winter and asked no quarter. He split some kindling and burned some trash and smelled the sharp sweet smoke. He threw more sticks and watched the bounding poetry of Goso's rhythm until the sadness of winter afternoon closed in.

Clouds shuttered the sky again but a thin cold band of orange probed like courage through the gathering gray and lit the snow-gilded landscape. He carried kindling, laid a fire, and retreated to the comforts of hot bath and fire-crackling room.

Inside, like the Question, the green fly buzzed.

13

*I*n the afternoon he decided to get it over with. Leona still lived in the same house and had the same phone number but it was listed under Stone now. A man in the yard was cutting back the chrysanthemums for winter and when Drake walked up he asked, "Are you the new man?"

"No," answered Drake, "the old one. They call me Carlos."

"We were expecting a man to come transplant some trees."

"Does he leave the birds' nests?"

"I really don't know. Does it matter?"

"Only to the birds," he said. "And an old man I knew."

"Could I help you?"

"I doubt it," said Drake. "I'm looking for the lady of the house. For Leona," he added, so the man wouldn't think he was selling subscriptions.

"She's in Santa Fé today," the man said. "But I'm her husband. Would I do?" He looked at Drake and Drake's clothes the way he'd eye a frog in the champagne punch.

"Oh," said Drake. "I didn't know she'd married again."

"You must not have been around for a while," Leona's husband said. "I'm Jim. Jim Lackey. Her first husband was killed, you know."

"Yes," said Drake. "I've heard. Was it suicide?"

"No," said Jim, "though he made some strange remarks the night before he died. They say he'd gotten most peculiar." He moved to another clump. "I didn't know him myself."

"I did," said Drake. "That's what I need to see Leona about."

Jim surveyed Drake's clothes again. "Were you—friends?"

"You might say so."

"Then I shouldn't have said that," said Jim. "About him being peculiar."

"Oh, I don't mind. He was peculiar."

"A fine lawyer, I understand."

"I guess so," said Drake. "As far as lawyers go. But a lousy husband. Mind if I smoke?"

"Just don't throw the butts in the yard. Know him well?"

"As well as anyone."

"This is my last bunch. Well—since you're a friend of the family—come in for a beer?" he asked. "Though I don't expect Leona for another hour or so."

The invitation was perfunctory but Drake said, "Thanks," and Jim gathered up his tools and put them away neatly in the tool shed and left his yard shoes on the stoop.

In the kitchen he hunted for an ashtray. "We don't smoke," he said. "Have you talked to Leona since Drake was killed?"

"No."

"She bore up very bravely. Of course she'd been through a lot before the accident. He was not only peculiar, he was extremely difficult. I could tell you any number of things Leona has told me."

"I'm sure you could."

"She was better off without him."

It occurred to Drake that coming back from the dead was like seeing yourself in a three-way mirror and that made him grin and Jim asked what amused him.

"I was thinking of mirrors," he said.

"Mirrors?"

"Yes," said Drake. "Most people like to see themselves straight on in their best pose with their proper smiles. It's the angled mirrors—the three-way ones—that tell the whole truth."

"Oh," said Jim, as if the frog in the punch had begun to speak French. He took the glasses from the cabinet. "Shall we go in the den?"

"Mirrors are funny things," said Drake.

Jim said he guessed so but you could see his heart wasn't in the topic, besides which he didn't parlez-vous the language.

"Versailles is full of them. Ever see the Hall of Mirrors?"

"No," said Jim.

"Leona did. Drake took her. Told her he kept thinking of all the diplomats sitting there deciding which way they'd make the world turn. Surrounded by all those mirrors that caught them from all directions. He said he kept wondering if they could view their own asses from behind or only those of the other diplomats. Leona didn't appreciate his comments. Said he couldn't understand true elegance and had no appreciation of the finer things."

"He was like that," said Jim.

"It has always been my impression," said Drake, "that diplomacy is the art of observing other people's asses while successfully hiding your own."

"I suppose so," Jim said politely.

"That's why so many diplomats are lawyers," said Drake. "They're good ass-hiders."

"Drake was a lawyer," said Jim. "But he wasn't good at diplomacy."

"Maybe that's why he stopped being a lawyer," said Drake.

Jim looked at him sidelong. "He didn't stop. He died."

"Same thing."

Jim began to look like a man with an itch where he couldn't scratch. "Yes, well look, Mr. . . ."

"Carlos," said Drake.

"Your business with Leona—it has something to do with Drake Cavanaugh?"

"I'm afraid so."

"Maybe you'd better tell me."

"Maybe I had. But there won't be any trouble. A minor legal adjustment. . . ."

"What are you talking about?"

"Drake. Something's turned up."

"Oh? The money, maybe?"

"More than that," said Drake. "He has."

"You mean—they've found the body? But, good Lord, man, it's been—ten years!"

"Nine," said Drake. "But he plans to leave again. He won't make trouble. All he wants is a passport."

"Are you trying to tell me Charles Drake Cavanaugh is alive?"

"And peculiar as ever."

"Have you seen him?"

"Yes."

"Where?"

Drake grinned on one side. "In a mirror," he said. "Front, side, and ass!"

▲

Doña Rosalía couldn't wait to spread the word when the trader's wife disappeared. Tonito brought the news with the mail which she glanced through quickly and bundled into a corner to sort later. Then she locked the door and, followed by a grumpy Perdido, set out for the *placita*.

"Nobody knows where she went, Fergus least of all," she told Antonio Romero who was swatting August flies behind his counter. Antonio only listened with half his mind because his mama lay dying for the third time and Soledad said this time it was real, there was nothing she could do for Doña Felicia and it was just as well Julián had come.

"Fergus won't talk to nobody," Rosalía elaborated to Alarico who was drinking strawberry pop on the shady side of the store. "She was there yesterday," she said to Cipriano and Tomás who were passing the time of day in front of the *cantina*. "Fergus got back from the reservation late last night and the old pickup was gone and her with it and Garcia found it down on the Colinas road where the bus stops! And the keys still in it!"

Then Doña Rosalía sent Tonito back to the trading post to scout out the particulars. "It could be foul play," she said and pulled in several of her chins sternly. Doña Rosalía went to the movies every time she journeyed to Española and she was an expert on crime.

"Find out what she was last seen wearing, how she acted yesterday, what she did, and who was at the trading post. Too bad you quit your police work— you might of found out a lot from Garcia." Doña Rosalía sighed loudly and watched Tonito drive off scattering rocks.

She worried about him. For a while there had been the danger—remote but possible—that the *políticos* and the state *policía* might decide to poke their noses into the affair of poor José and give Tonito a bad time but Sheriff Garcia in Colinas passed the word to Alfredo Garcia, who was the coroner and also the sheriff's *primo*, who in turn pronounced José's death the result of natural causes which ended the matter before it got to the gringo police. Such a verdict was more or less routine when a killing was an unfortunate accident growing from an overflow of high spirits in a Saturday night fight or when it was a matter of family justice—a thing outsiders rarely understood. Sheriff Garcia knew justice was best served within the villages themselves and his was generally what Carlos called a lazy-fair policy. Doña Rosalía liked the word and memorized it.

This was one reason Garcia had been re-elected for twenty-three consecutive years; the other was that no one ever bothered to run against him except once, in 1958, when Onie Martinez (who had just been fired by the Safeway manager) decided he'd like the job. Onie made a lot of speeches but the week before the election his wife chased him down the street with a broom. He'd been burning trash and, as he explained later, while he was in his neighbor's house having one friendly *cerveza* that *puto* fire jumped the fence and burned the shed which in turn brought his wife's ire—and her broom—crashing around his ears.

After this public humiliation he withdrew from the race. No one contested Garcia again, though from time to time he lazily wished someone would, to give the job importance—besides, he liked the speech-making. For the most part, though, he was content to run the department with as much efficiency as possible—efficiency being an absence of red tape, interference, and trouble. On the whole most arrests were confined to speeding tourists, Saturday-night traffic accidents, and the hippies up the canyon. For the rest, the sheriff was blessed with the divine faculty of minding his own business.

Doña Rosalía's worry wasn't from fear of repercussions but from Tonito's own gloom. After that terrible tragedy of José he wouldn't speak to anyone for a month and then he turned in his badge. The sheriff tilted his chair back, unbuttoned his waistband, picked his teeth, and listened to Tonito's explanation. He was most understanding.

Tonito quit working at the *cantina*—he couldn't stand to watch Pilar twitching her ass like nothing had happened, he said.

"He'll be back," Doña Rosalía told Tomás. "*Poco tiempo.*"

After a year, however, Tonito still brooded. He drove the truck for mail as always, he attended the *bailes* on Saturdays and mass on Sundays—but he didn't laugh as much or get as drunk and he joined the *hermandad*. The chile had gone out of his life.

¡Ójala! She couldn't stand around thinking about Tonito, not with people hungry for news. *Ay*, and didn't the good Lord send children to plague everyone? There was Doña Felicia dying and that sot Julián adding shame to his papa's

worries. *Sí*, children were a plague. But she wasted time. She still had to inform Carlos.

Drake sat at the patio table, a beer in one hand and a stick of charcoal in the other. He contemplated his sketch pad and occasionally stroked in a bit of shading but it was desultory. He had been weeding his onion patch in the midday summer sun and his concentration centered on the *cerveza* cold and foamy which he imbibed with the sweaty gratification of a job completed.

He was thinking his own thoughts and listening to the hum of the bees in the pink hollyhocks when Doña Rosalía puffed around the side of the house like an overburdened locomotive on a steep grade.

Goso charged. Perdido stood his ground hackle-swollen; they exchanged a few rounds of black insults and then lay facing each other in armed truce.

Drake turned the sketch face down, greeted Doña Rosalía, and hoped the canvas chair wouldn't give as she eased her wideness into it.

Would she join him for a beer?

No, *gracias*, but she'd take a Coke and when he returned with it she was examining the drawing. Something seemed to excite her. "*¡A redo vaya!*" she cried. "Do you know what this is?"

"Well," he said, "it's supposed to be Val White."

"But do you know what it means?" Her fat hands rose, palms out, like two exclamation marks. "You heard about Val?"

"What about her?"

"*¡Ay, válgame!* You don't know!" Doña Rosalía's hands arced into space, then commenced fanning their owner and conveying Coca-Cola to her parched person as she recited the sad litany of Val's sudden and mysterious disappearance. "And to think that this time only yesterday she was alive and well!" Her eyes filled with tears.

"She probably still is. Went shopping or something."

"Leave the post with Fergus gone?" she shrilled. "And not even a note!"

"How do you know?"

"Because Fergus is out of his mind! Went tearing out in all directions!"

Drake doubted the latter feat but didn't say so. It was a sign, declared Doña Rosalía, a miraculous, unmistakable omen. "Because why else would you just happen to be drawing a picture of her, just now?"

"Why not?"

"It was a sign!" Doña Rosalía didn't believe in coincidence. "Maybe it was her ghost and that's why you were thinking of her!"

Drake laughed. "Oh come on, Doña Rosalía, I make sketches of everyone. I did one of you—remember?"

She was diverted a moment remembering. "But I sat right before you!" Her eyes gleamed. "Always you look at people when you draw them!"

"Not always."

"But in your mind you see them!" The exclamation marks rose again on either side of her face. "She was here," she announced. "In spirit!" Her eyes grew round as the thought swelled. "Her spirit flew to you. She calls for help, Carlos! I know a sign when I see one. You wait, something has happened to poor little Val!"

It was hard to think of Val as little—she was a good six inches taller than Doña Rosalía—but that lady's diminutives had nothing to do with size. "*Ay,* something has happened to poor little Val!"

She gulped the last of her Coke and stood to leave. Perdido delivered a few parting snarls at Goso. Doña Rosalía took a step, then turned again to the sketch. "That funny thing around her neck," she said thoughtfully. "That jewelry. I never seen her wear that before." She promised to report any developments. "And if she comes into your eyes again, Carlos, you pay her attention, *¿comprende?* And then you come tell me!" She puffed off toward the *placita.*

The truth was Drake knew more about Val's disappearance than Doña Rosalía would ever suspect.

He drained the last of his beer, contemplated the foamy residue, and picked up the charcoal. He shaded the stone in the pendant, looked at the sketch a moment, and wished he'd left the damned thing inside. Then he went for another beer.

Twenty-four hours earlier his life had been full of peace. It was Francisco's day to irrigate and Drake spent a pleasant afternoon helping him. They talked and smoked as they leaned on their spades and watched the water flow through the orchard and at the end his soul felt as quenched as the trees. Goso bounded gleefully through the water, rolled in the dirt, and trotted home gloriously, ecstatically, filthy.

That evening in his patio Drake watched the sky pale and the trees catch the flame of the low sun. Across the clearing rose the weathered crosses of the *camposanto,* quiet and patient. The glow died from the crosses and then from the trees and his eyes moved upward with the dusk to the peak from which shafts of rose fire gleamed.

Goso rested his velvet chin on Drake's knee and drooled with delicate tact and Drake scratched the soft place behind his ears and the two of them inhaled the odors of goat manure and simmering chile and pine pitch, the earthy odors of life that hovered over Descanso. They felt the chill of evening and heard the calls of the women to one another and the raucous cry of a circling hawk above the drowsy night-nested day birds and the rustling of the spirit world through the branches of piñon and tamarisk.

From the bank of the *acequia* beyond the trees the plaintive chords of Julián's guitar rose from time to time—he had come for Doña Felicia's last days—and the notes were sad and soft. *Julián still has the old magic, the muse still touches his ruined soul, and he knows—he knows,* Drake thought. *That is our tragedy, that we must always know,* and he felt the throbs of guitar strings like those of the heart.

A goat bell clanged through the *prado* and reedy voices quavered in counterpoint against the high calls of the children who drove them home. Among them, Drake knew, rose the shrill voice of the four-year-old Pepito as he ran sturdy-limbed behind his brothers.

The old yearning went through him like the throb of Julián's guitar; but he'd learned to accept it now, to leave it alone. He visited Soledad and the boys like a friendly if eccentric Tío Carlos. He watched Pepito with the little burro Drake had given him; the child's gentle love of all creatures made his own tears come. He thought of him and smiled; he looked at the mountain and thanked its gods for the profound peace.

Later he wore his euphoric state like a robe into the bathroom, wrestled with the plumbing, and congratulated himself—it was like a ritual—for his ingenuity in rigging a shower. With Segundo's help he had installed a pump and pressure tank, a contraption with a manual switch that he had to remember to cut on and off, but the shower worked—usually.

He stood in the luxury of falling water and rising steam, felt the soapsuds cascade over his skin, and knew a fine soft contentment.

Suddenly a shadow darkened the mist and a form loomed just beyond the plastic door. He turned off the taps, felt a gush of icy water which dribbled off with a clanking shudder. Soapy rivulets still slid down his shanks.

"Don't mind me," said Val White. He stood in dripping disadvantage and patches of soap began to dry on his skin. She tossed him a towel and flipped cigarette ashes into the toilet. "Finish your shower, I'll wait."

He knotted the towel around him, stepped onto the mat, and thought she looked strange wearing a dress. "May I offer you a drink?" He felt like an ass.

"I'll fix it," she said. "Though this isn't a social call." Still she stood there. She leaned against the door, took a long drag on her cigarette, and eyed him like a slave on an auction block. "Better dry off before you catch cold."

"Well, damn it, get out so I can."

She smiled and looked him up and down again. "I'd of come earlier but I didn't want to be seen."

"Where's Fergus?"

"Reservation. You need a shave."

"Go fix some drinks."

She leaned across him to throw her cigarette in the toilet and lost her balance. He reached out to steady her, the knot loosened, and the towel dropped.

She laughed loudly. "So what are you trying to hide? You're okay."

He snatched up the towel. "I really prefer to display myself on my own terms."

She was sprawled on the sofa with a bourbon and Coke when he appeared in the living room. "Your drink's over there."

"You said this wasn't a social visit."

"No, but I'll be sociable. I closed the curtains."

"Afraid of *brujas*?"

"I don't want to be seen."

"I might have said the same a few minutes ago." He sipped his Scotch. "Well?"

"I've left Fergus," she said calmly. "Or I'm in the process."

He was surprised and not surprised. She never seemed particularly turned on by Fergus but Val never seemed particularly turned on by anything.

"Why'd you come here?"

"For money."

He picked up his sketch pad, began to doodle, and waited for her to go on.

"I somehow didn't want to help myself to his."

"It's yours, too."

"Yeah." She held her long-ashed cigarette and looked around. He handed her an ashtray. "I guess I just want to leave on my own."

He watched how her blonde hair fell in front of her shoulder and began idly to sketch its flowing line. "What happened?"

"Nothing." She snorted a one-syllable laugh. "Maybe that's the problem." She stubbed her cigarette and pulled another from her pack.

"How'd you get here?" He lit her cigarette and saw the flash of the red stone in her pendant as she leaned forward.

"Walked the last bit. Left the pickup in some piñons."

"Protecting my unsullied reputation?"

"Maybe." The smoke circled her head and softened the flat planes of her face.

He sketched seriously now. "How much do you need?"

"Enough to last till I get a job."

"Where'll you go?"

"Do you care?"

"No."

"Not back to Saint Louis." He could have guessed that. She'd told him before how she ran off with Fergus, abandoned the musical career her father promoted so zealously that he practically cloistered her, and how he went into a rage when she told him she was going to marry Fergus and finally drove them out threatening Fergus with murder, mayhem, or emasculation.

"I guess he was right," she said. "I shouldn't of married Fergus in the first place. But I'll never tell Daddy that."

"Why not? Parents soften."

"That's what I'm afraid of. If Daddy went the forgiveness route, he'd just shrivel up. There wouldn't be anything left for him." She leaned forward, elbows on knees in the posture of a woman unused to skirts and drew heavily, several times, on her cigarette. "Or me either, I guess," she added. "Because then he wouldn't be Daddy anymore."

Val had an odd mouth, he thought. She didn't smile often and when she did the corners curved down. "What'll you do for a living?"

"I don't know. Go back to music, I guess."

"You've already blown that, haven't you?"

She paced, then stopped and looked at the Dasburg. She lit another cigarette. "I guess so. For the big time, anyhow."

"Was there ever any big time in the offing?"

"Yes." She turned toward him and squinted her eyes against the smoke. "I was good. Damned good."

"You smoke too much."

"I know it." She turned back to the Dasburg. "What in hell do you see in this thing?"

He shrugged.

"Oh, screw it." She ground out the cigarette. "But I was good. Damned good."

▲

Julián sucked the last drop of tequila from the bottle, let his tongue slide around its mouth, and hurled it across the *acequia*. He leaned against the cottonwood tree and shivered but the mountain chill was better than going back to where his little old *abuela* was dying, better than having his mama cry and his papa's eyes snap disapproving every time he looked at him. It was better than seeing Soledad.

Maybe tomorrow he'd go see Val. She'd give him hell. She'd say what they all said, that he was a drunk, a bum, he'd blown it. By God, he still played the best guitar in Taos, or Santa Fé or Albuquerque, for that matter. Just because he liked a little swig now and then. Had to drink with the patrons. Julián Romero was welcome in any drinking group, too. He'd learned a thing or two since he'd left this *puta* town that couldn't tell its ass from a posthole.

Val would understand. *¡Uta!* She'd still give him hell but she'd give him a little ass, too. Just wait, *querida*, he thought, and then said it aloud. "*¡Ay, querida!*"

"Were you calling me?" said Pilar Archuleta.

He started. "No," he grinned. "But you'll do! *Ay, caramba*, you'll do! What you doing?"

"Looking for you." He'd seen her black-rimmed eyes on him when he bought the bottle from Tomás earlier. "Can I sit down?"

"Sit close, I'll warm you!" He flashed his white grin.

She sat crosslegged and spread her red skirt full about her. "Your songs," she said breathlessly. "They turn me on."

"You turn me on, *querida*!" He wished he hadn't drunk so much of that tequila, that the edges of things weren't so fuzzy, that *pinche* didn't take so much effort.

Pilar leaned across to grab his hands, stroked the calluses on his fingers, let him get a good look down her blouse. She said how long his fingers were, caressed them with her soft ones, and laughed low in her throat. "But you grow fat!" She patted his stomach, let her fingers glide across his belly.

"*Un panzón.*" Her skirt rode above her cocked knees and she didn't have any panties on and he thought lazily, *It's there to take.* His goat mouth smiled and his long eyes cut across to look at her wide ones lined with the dark stuff.

Ay, the little bitch was ready. He'd give her what she wanted; he was an expert at the love business. He pulled her across his lap and she giggled and they both rolled over and lay on the stiff grass under the cottonwoods. She moved sensuously against him or was it the earth that moved beneath him? His head swirled and he wished again he hadn't finished off that tequila so fast; but he wasn't drunk, it was that god-awful perfume she wore. His head would clear in a minute.

She was all over him and he thought how good a woman's body felt and this one was all woman, *una mujerota.*

Suddenly the dark smell of her perfume washed through his swirling head into his swirling stomach. Gut-wrenching spasms tore through him and the great stud of the western mountains began to puke.

He came to later, dimly remembered Pilar's presence, or he'd dreamed it. He sat with his head on his knees to let a dizzy spell pass, finally pulled to his feet, threw his guitar over his shoulder, and headed home. He'd see Val tomorrow. To hell with these perfumed fillies.

A light shone through the curtained window where Carlos lived. He guessed he'd been wrong to be so jealous.

He stood outside. *Por Dios*, he felt putrid. Just one drink would settle his belly. Maybe he'd go in and drink a *copita* with Carlos. Then he heard voices and one was a woman's.

"I was good. Damned good," she was saying and it was Val's voice. So that's the way it was. Julián walked on.

▲

"Bullshit," said Drake. "If you'd had it you'd have stuck with it."

"Maybe." Her voice was flat. "You don't know a damned thing about it."

"Fix me a drink," he said, "while you're up. And you could use another yourself."

"I told you, this isn't a social call."

"But I haven't given you the money yet."

"You will. I don't have all night."

"The bus doesn't go by Colinas road until after dawn."

"Who says I'm taking the bus?"

"You don't have much choice."

"Here's your drink."

"And sit down, you make me nervous."

"Sorry." She lit another cigarette.

"You're always in smoke." He began to sketch again. "Like a halo. Madonna of the Stinking Weed. Now drink up and let's figure options. You may have to go home again."

"Mark that one off."

"You want to tell Uncle Carlos about it?"

"No."

"Suit yourself." He continued to draw. "I never saw that necklace."

"I never wear it." She fingered the pendant. "I won it. In high school, in a contest at the conservatory. That started Daddy's obsession."

"You weren't so keen?"

"Keen enough. Not neurotic, like he was."

"Tell me about him." He started another sketch and Val talked and smoked and toyed with her drink and a picture began to form.

▲

Valentine Larsen, named for the day of her birth, was the only daughter of a Scandinavian factory worker who alternately indulged and terrified her. She was her Daddy's pet; on her he concentrated his great pride and equally great fears—pride in her ruddy blondeness and in the musical talent she'd inherited from her mother who gave piano lessons to augment the family income; and fear that some man would come along and sully her virginity. Valentine adored her daddy but she was terrified of him, particularly when he stopped for a few drinks after work on Fridays and came back home fancying his pale wife was carrying on behind his back. Then, roaring with rage, he beat her with his belt, locked the bedroom door, and proceeded to show her who was boss. Val wasn't sure what went on behind the door but her mother, nursing bruises, carried her head in high pride after those sessions and her eyes shone and she declared it showed how much he loved her.

Though Val always hid during those outbursts, her father seemed to her magnificent, greater than anything human. Sometimes she committed small mischiefs just to put him in a rage. He never struck her but it thrilled her to hear him bellow and curse and stamp noisily through the house.

She dreamed that such a bigger-than-life man might some day appear and carry her off, someone as ferocious and wonderful as Daddy. She grew older and the career loomed, and she largely gave up the fantasy along with other childish fairy tales until the night Fergus White strode into their living room, lanky and drawling and incredibly romantic in cowboy boots and a battered Stetson with a rattlesnake band.

He came with Val's brother. Nils was installing shelves in a shop that sold Native American artifacts when the trader rolled in from New Mexico in a '52 Plymouth station wagon with Indian jewelry, rugs, and pots. He made the trip yearly after the tourists left. They began to talk, had a few beers at quitting time, and Nils brought him home to supper.

Fergus was thirty-five years old. He'd done an army hitch, gone to college a couple of years on the GI Bill, knocked around the country since, and decided Indian trading was for him. He had no room in his life for women—not the permanent kind anyhow—until he saw Val.

When he came into their house that night—it was October and drizzly gray outside—she was nineteen, freckled, and oversized for a woman. She'd never had a date or worked for a living except to help teach scales to the uninspired children who afflicted her mother. Each day she attended the conservatory where she'd won a scholarship and a large pendant in the form of a treble clef set with a genuine garnet which she had worn on a gold chain around her neck since.

Each time her father looked at the pendant it winked its red eye of promise and proved his ambition had foundation, that those who knew recognized Val's talent. He neither understood nor even listened to the music that cascaded from her long strong hands but the flashing pendant symbolized the higher life attainable by the talent-blessed; Nils Larsen Senior pledged to the God he didn't quite believe in that he would guard that talent against any possible deterrent—principally male—that might hinder its fulfillment.

She went nowhere alone except the conservatory and the neighborhood grocery. She worked hard and loved her music though she lacked the white burning flame of determination that forges professionalism and the cold driving discipline that tempers it. If she would not be great, she knew she could be good, perhaps even make the minor concert circuit or a good civic symphony.

She became more than proficient on the piano, she mastered the classical guitar, was better than average on the violin, and was for the most part satisfied with the prospects. She forgot her youthful dreams of a man who would carry her off, who would make love to her with the passion her mother inspired, a passion whose occasional violence was that of Olympian desire.

Then Fergus White suddenly stood with Nils in the golden lamplight as she pulled the galoshes onto the last small pupil of the day.

"Howdy, Ma'am," he said.

He talked that evening about Indians and Penitentes and other wild species in the Southwestern spaces and even her father was spellbound. It never occurred to him that the middle-aged Fergus could threaten his plans for Val.

He'd be in Saint Louis a couple of days, he said. Could they recommend a modest rooming house?

There was one close by, clean and reasonable. "But the cooking's sad," said Enid Larsen who was proud of her own. So he lodged down the street and boarded with the Larsens for the better part of a week before he went on to Chicago.

In seven days he was back on their doorstep "to tend to some business." He didn't say what and they didn't ask. He enlivened their meals and he praised Enid's cooking and he seldom spoke to Val though he offered to drive her to the conservatory and pick her up while he was in town. His business, he declared, took him that way, anyhow.

The art of flirtation was unknown to Val. She knew no men beyond her own family, the grocer, and some instructors at the conservatory. But, young as she was and old as Fergus was, she knew he was the man she'd awaited and despaired of ever knowing. Excited feelings chased through her when she heard his drawling voice or looked at his weathered face like the chasms he described that cut through the vast Indian country he lived in. She hated the freckles that made her seem young and trivial.

The rides to the conservatory and back, alone with Fergus, were agonizing and exciting though she looked coolly out the window of the rattling station wagon, kept her chin high and—she hoped—her eyes disdainful. She clutched her sheaf of music tightly to keep her hands from shaking but she sounded calm as she asked him where his hatband came from.

"Rattlesnake," he said. "Killed him myself. The son-of-a-bitch—I beg your pardon ma'am—that snake I mean, the son-of-a-—well, dammit, that's what he was!"

"I don't mind," she said coolly. "The son-of-a-bitch was after you!" It was the first time she'd ever said the word but it slid out easily and she found she rather liked its taste.

"Just coiled on a rock. Spooked my mare."

"So then what did the son-of-a-bitch do?"

"I nailed him," he said. "And that's what I'm fixing to do to you if you use that word again."

"I'm not a child."

"Then don't act like one." He looked straight ahead and glowered and she thought he looked most marvelously, godly angry, that he probably killed that son-of-a-bitch rattlesnake just by glaring at it.

She stared through the window, wondered what she could say to rouse him to a perfect passion like her father in one of his glorious rages. She tried to think of something mature and fury-making to say but nothing came and she just sat and felt the rhythm of her own heart vibrating like a Segovia guitar.

He drew to the curb and leaned across her to open the door and his arm brushed against her breast. "I'll pick you up at five," he said stiffly.

She stepped out and she tingled where his arm had touched. She hoped he hadn't noticed, hadn't felt her heart beating its muted rhythm. "All right," she said. "And then you can tell me how you killed the son-of-a-bitch!"

He was waiting for her at five. He opened the door from the inside and pulled into traffic without saying anything. At the end of the block he turned off the usual route and when she turned to him he had a grim look.

"You're going the wrong way."

"No I'm not." He looked at her and his mouth smiled but his pale eyes were hard-probing. "I thought we'd take us a ride."

"What'll Daddy say?"

"Nothing. It's Friday." Nils Larsen would be at the beer hall having his usual for another hour or so.

Fergus drove past the edge of town and turned into a roadside park. He switched off the engine. "Now," he said, "we can talk."

"What about?" She supposed he was going to lecture her about her language.

"You ever think about getting married?"

"No," she said. "I'm going to be a concert pianist."

"Hell if that's any kind of life!"

"Hell if it isn't!" She tossed her head. "You got any better idea?"

"Yes," he said. "And ladies don't say hell."

"I just did."

"Then it's time you learned better."

"Who's going to teach me?"

"Me, maybe. And ladies also don't play pianos for a living. Not where I come from."

"What do ladies do, then?"

"Get married."

"And spend their lives just doing what their husbands say do?"

"That's right."

"And what if they don't? What if they tell their husbands to go to hell?"

"They get walloped!" He chuckled and looked at her with his eyes narrowed a little as if he'd like to do the same to her and she looked back and dared him but he just sat there.

She couldn't think of anything else to say so she got out of the car and said she wanted to take a walk and slammed the door behind her.

"Okay," he said, "if that suits your coporosity." They followed a path into a small grove. "You don't much know how to act," he said. "But I reckon you'd learn, with a husband."

"Since you're planning my life for me, Mr. Fergus White, just who do you propose I marry?"

"Me."

She stopped suddenly and sat on a rock. It felt cold through her skirt. "You?"

He stood looking down at her. "Why not? Ain't nobody else asked you, have they?"

Her heart pumped and she thought her throat would close shut but she swallowed hard. "What makes you think I want to be like your stupid ladies that just get bossed?"

"They also get protected," he said softly. "And loved."

"And—walloped?"

"Sometimes." He sat beside her on the damp stone.

"My bottom's cold," she said. She started to stand but he pulled her down again.

"What do you say?"

"I said my bottom's. . . ."

"About getting married?"

"To you?"

"Well, I ain't proposin' for Miles Standish!"

"Go live with Indians and rattlesnakes?"

"It's a heap more exciting than being an old maid music marm."

"I'll be a concert musician."

"Yeah, and I'm gonna scalp every Indian on the reservation and then go make movies about it. But in the meantime you better start making up your mind. We got to beat your daddy back."

"You don't just ask somebody to marry you, Fergus White! Not just out of the blue!"

"Why not? See a good filly, start to horse trade."

"Proposing to a lady isn't like buying a horse! You stretch it out, you say nice things. You tell a girl she's pretty and sweet and—you know."

"Hell's catoot!" he said. "You think I got that kind of time?"

"Then go marry yourself a squaw!" she cried.

"Are you saying no?"

"I am saying, hell no!" She jumped up. "And my bottom's cold!"

"Then I'll warm it up for you!" He grabbed her in sudden fury, threw her across his knees, and thrashed her roughly and thoroughly, and when he was through he pulled her upright and gave her a shake for good measure. "You little bitch!"

She'd angered him at last! He'd shown her who was boss! She threw her arms about his neck.

"Oh, Fergus!" she cried. "What I meant was yes! Oh, hell yes! You son-of-a-bitch!"

"So Fergus and Daddy had one son-of-a-bitching row and I went off with him thinking here was a real man. We got married in Amarillo, Texas. And then. . . ." Val shrugged and lit another cigarette.

"Then—what?"

"Then—nothing. The fuse fizzled. I haven't seen Fergus in a temper since. Nothing I do can make him mad. I used to try. I even screwed around a little, kind of hoping he'd find out, just to see if he was man enough to do anything about it. First it was Julián Romero. Then one or two others."

"Just whoever came along?"

"No. I was selective."

Yeah, thought Drake, *like a slot machine*. "He never suspected?"

"I think he was scared to!" She laughed. "I can't make him mad."

"From the female obsession with the macho image, good Lord deliver us," he intoned. "What in hell do women want?"

"What was your wife like?"

"She majored in psychology."

"What did she want, I mean?"

"A eunuch."

Val laughed her one-syllable laugh. "Maybe she'd like Fergus."

"Is that the trouble?"

"Oh, we sleep together. It's just not very exciting."

"What is exciting to you? What do you want?"

She made a vague wavy motion with her hands. "Out, I guess. Fergus— buys me things. Like that God-awful couch. And then grins like he's just shot the goddamned moon out of the sky."

That mouth was hard to draw. Restless. Down-pulling. "He's never denied you anything."

"Except the one thing I want."

"Which is. . . ?"

"To leave these goddamned mountains! Go where I could have a career."

"Oh balls!"

"To civilization."

"Strange," he said. "That's what I came here to find."

"Oh christ!"

"Maybe you should go back to Daddy."

"Why?"

"Because he'd do one of two things: he'd either spank you royally, which is not only what you deserve, but what you badly seem to want; or else he'd welcome home his darling daughter with open arms and gentle tears and you'd find he was just another ordinary human being. In either case you might appreciate Fergus more."

"You think I'd come crawling back to Fergus?"

"You think he'd let you?"

"With open arms."

"Don't be so everlasting sure."

"Well, I'm not here to discuss psychology. Will you let me have the money?"

"I asked you how much."

"Five hundred?"

"Are you going to Saint Louis?"

"No."

"Then you'll need more like five thou."

"I'll get a job."

He went to the bedroom, pulled a wad of bills from a small safe he'd had Fergus buy him. Val leaned against the doorframe as he counted out the money.

"I might pay you back some day," she said. "But don't hold your breath."

"Forget it."

"Or I could pay you now."

"How?"

"Christ, in the usual manner!"

Drake began to laugh. "Honey, this is not a two-dollar deal!"

"Bastard!"

"Sure." He handed her the wad.

"Okay. I offered."

Before she left she looked at the sketch. "You didn't finish it."

"No."

"Why do you run around with your goddamned sketch pad like an old lady with tatting? It isn't art."

"No. Some of us are born with taste, others with talent. Not many have both."

"What's that supposed to mean?"

"You don't like my Dasburg. *Chacun à son gout.* Just one question: have you thought what this'll do to Fergus?"

"I've got myself to think of." Her voice was flat and the flat planes of her cheeks went flatter as she sucked them in. "If it hurts Fergus, I'm sorry. I just can't look at that stinking couch any longer. With his stinking hair oil on the cushion!"

Drake didn't say anything.

"I really am," she said in a few moments. "Sorry, I mean. Only—oh, screw it! You'll go pick up the pieces, won't you? Put Humpty-Dumpty together again?"

"It's my guess he'll do that himself. Fergus is more of a man than you think," said Drake. "Or deserve."

▲

So Val was gone and the countryside knew it and less than twelve hours had passed. Drake added a few final shadings to the sketch while he gave Doña Rosalía time to get well away. He slashed a down-curving smile on the lips, and then—he wasn't sure why, but he didn't want that smirk following him around—he carried the face into the bedroom, put it in the safe and twirled shut the combination.

He set out for the trading post.

▲

Delfina Romero poured coffee for herself and Rosalía. Doña Felicia rested quietly now, though she'd had Delfina running all morning.

"And the picture," Rosalía told her, and her chins rippled, "you could see it plain as your nose!"

"What?"

"That mist. Like Carlos saw her through smoke. It's the way spirits always come, that fly out of their body. She was calling for help, that's plain."

"Why you suppose she didn't call to her own husband?"

"Maybe he didn't hear her. Anglos can't hear spirits. They're too lazy-fair." She took another *buñuelo*.

"Carlos is an Anglo."

"That's why he didn't understand. He didn't even know she came. He thought he just started that picture without no reason." She bit into the *buñuelo*, chewed hastily, and swallowed. "And wearing a funny thing around her neck that nobody ever seen before. How could he of just remembered what he ain't seen?"

Julián slouched into the kitchen and listened dull-eyed. Delfina poured him some coffee.

Doña Rosalía kept talking. "Carlos didn't believe Val was there! He didn't know he'd really seen her."

"Maybe he couldn't see her," Julián interrupted, "but he could hear her. He knew she was there all right!"

Both women looked at him. "How do you know?"

"'Cause he was talking to her, that's why."

"When?" The puffy folds around Rosalía's eyes didn't conceal a glisten.

"Las' night. I heard 'em, plain as day!"

The women glanced at each other. They both knew what state Julián had been in the night before.

"She said something about how damn good she was," Julián continued. "And he said 'Bullshit.'"

"*¡Tonto!*" said Delfina. "What you heard was in that bottle you had. Everybody knows Carlos don't talk that way to ladies!"

▲

"I'm a stupid damn son-of-a-bitch," said Fergus White. "Always was when it came to women." He paced his living room and his eyes were anguished. "My God—do you know I hadn't any more'n asked Val to marry me than I up and whupped her behind? Never have forgiven myself. How's that for smarts?"

"Should've kept it up," said Drake. "Wonder if it would've worked with Leona."

"I'm a peace-loving man," said Fergus. "Except for rattlers and politicians. But then I haul off and wallop Valentine Larsen because she cussed at me—scared me silly after I did it, too, I can tell you—and then danged if she didn't up and say she'd marry me anyhow! Never did figure it out."

"Never dive into the depths of a woman's mind," said Drake. "You might hit bottom."

"Then I had a row with the old man. 'I am asking to marry your daughter,' I said in a decent friendly manner, 'seeing as how nobody else has asked her,' and he starts exploding in all directions like those fireworks that went wild and burned Cipriano's barn. Well, when you're in a foxhole and surrounded, you got no choice but shoot your way out. First he said he was going to kill me, then he said he'd cut my balls off if I even touched his daughter.

"And then I made it worse. 'Beggin' your pardon, Sir,' I told him, 'but I already have!'

"Well, all hell broke loose and we took off. Val was scared of the old fart. And I was scared of Val. Guess ever' man's scared of something. With me it was women—the good kind anyhows. Plumb chicken. Didn't know how to court one, or even want to, till I saw Valentine Larsen."

Fergus began to pace. "I didn't have much time. Hung around Saint Louis long as I could pretendin' like I had business. I didn't even dare look at Val too straight. But I watched her plenty out of the corner of my eye. She walked straight and solid with hips like a boy's and big prideful breasts.

"In the army I went once to the opera, seen those big yellow-haired women with spears and horned helmets, and I could imagine her like that. Like something a man wouldn't dare come too close to.

"Except for one thing. Val Larsen had freckles—across her cheeks and on her arms and that made me know she was really human. I schemed how to get her alone but I didn't know how in seven shades of billy hell I was going to work it.

"Then that afternoon on the way to her goddamned music lesson I knew if ever I was going to lasso Val it better be soon. But I didn't know how to go about it. And then she shocked me—used some words she shouldn't even of known and I said so. But it came out gruffer'n I'd meant. And then when I reached acrost her to open the door, my clumsy arm knocked against her boob and I thought, 'Now you've screwed it up good; she'll think you're fresh.' All afternoon I tried to figure out what to say, and when I picked her up I still didn't know."

"You must've played it right."

"Well, when you're in quicksand you go under or get acrost."

"And you got across."

"Yeah. But I started out wrong—walloping her. Never did it again, I can tell you."

"Should have, maybe."

"Only one thing you ought to wallop a woman for and that's for screwing around. But that wasn't Val."

Fergus was still pacing. He stopped at Val's piano and plinked a high note. He'd bought it for her in Albuquerque. "I did everything for Val. Short of leaving here. Some things a man can't do."

"No," said Drake.

"She'd talk about how I'd ruined her career. And she got in the habit of cussing. I never did hold with a woman cussing. Seemed like she did it just to plague me. Sometimes I'd itch to wallop her again. But I didn't. You gave her plenty of money? I wouldn't want her to be in need."

"She won't be."

"I'll make it good."

"Forget it."

"Why didn't she just take some from the safe? It's hers too."

"I told her that. She wouldn't."

"That's Val," said Fergus. "She'd never do anything behind my back!" His voice broke. "But what in the name of seven shades of billy hell am I gonna do now?"

"I guess like you said," Drake said slowly, "once you're in quicksand you either go under or you get across." Then he said, "I guess you could find her if you wanted."

"No," said Fergus. He cracked his knuckles and paced. "Some things a man can't do."

▲

Doña Rosalía waylaid Drake in the *placita*. She had news, she puffed, and excitement swept through her like brush fire in the spring. Her little eyes glittered and her hands darted like pudgy birds. Tonito had talked to the kid that helped at the trading post.

"He saw poor little Val just before she disappeared!" Her quick tears brimmed. "She came in just when he was locking up. And—she didn't take no money from the safe! That proves she wasn't going shopping. Or nowhere!"

"Not necessarily."

"Wait till you hear the rest! That funny thing around her neck—in your picture. . . ." She took a deep breath. "She was wearing it! He noticed it because she never wore it before!"

"What funny thing?"

"You don't remember?" A thought coiled inside her small eyes and then it struck. "But it's in the picture! You drew it—and don't even remember it. Because you never seen it before! But she was wearing it—her spirit was—that's why you drew it! Carlos—I got to take that picture to Garcia. It's evidence!"

"You can't. It's disappeared."

She gasped. Her hands stopped gyrating and froze. "Disappeared?"

"Must have blown away."

"*¡Madre de Dios!*" She crossed herself. "Evil spirits took it! *Ay*, now I think of it I could feel them even when I was there this morning!" If there was anything Doña Rosalía knew about it was spirits.

So that's what gets in my shower, thought Drake, *and fouls up my water pressure and makes ghost noises in my pipes!*

"Oh, don't laugh, Carlos!" She crossed herself again. "You can't fight evil spirits. *Aaaayyyy!* We'll never see poor little Val again!"

14

*J*im thought they should handle things as quietly as possible and Drake said, "Sure."

"Because of the election," said Jim.

"Of course," said Drake. "I'm going to see Manby now. Thanks for the beer."

"I just don't understand it," said Jim. "Why you left—gave up everything . . ."

"I got tired of being the Tin Man."

". . . or why you came back."

"I was not biodegradable," said Drake. "I lay around like a tourist's beer can in the native sand."

"Oh," said Jim and they shook hands.

"Looks like snow. Good night for a fire," Drake said.

"We don't use the fireplace much. Too messy."

"Yes," said Drake. "I forgot."

It was nearing the stubbed-out end of day but Manby would still be in the office. A miserly sky emptied a few gray flakes that hit the pavement and gave up. Inside a house someone played the first shadowy notes of *Für Elise*. It sounded far away and sad. Drake stopped, stood in the sad gray air, and listened to the thin spare distant passion, waited for it to poise for the tumbling cascade where the notes plunge furiously over the cliff and then begin again, soft and deep in the still shadowy pool.

The unseen player hit a wrong note and the music stopped in space and suddenly wasn't anymore and he walked on toward Manby's new office.

The cool silk receptionist asked if he had an appointment and said Mr. Fremont was in conference and was really very busy and perhaps he would see one of the junior partners. "Or come back next week. It's nearly five anyhow, and. . . ."

"I'll wait," he said.

She said, "I really don't think. . . ."

"I know," said Drake. "Would you take Mr. Fremont a note?"

She pushed a note pad at him and he drew three emasculated rats on it like the sketch he'd left Joe and Manby a different life ago and under it he wrote, "Three Blind Mice, See how they ran: two ran back to the bank and the firm and the third ran into a Cat. Manby, pull out the Scotch. I must see you." He signed it "The Third Blind Rat."

Manby'd fixed himself quite a lair here, a plush windowless luxury suite with original de Grazias on the walls, piped-in soft music, and the expensive smell of leather, all thermostatically controlled, all hermetically sealed against the intrusions of the world and the weather and the wrong people—except for this one.

"Mr. Fremont will see you," said the cool slick voice. "Third door on the left."

His one-time partner, tweedy and well-jowled, stood behind his polished mahogany desk. His eyes looked mildly seasick.

"Hello, Manby," Drake said. "I have returned."

"Yes," said Manby, and his voice sounded a little seasick too. "Like MacArthur."

▲

It all came about when the big *políticos* came to see her. This peak of importance was neither sudden nor undeserved for by the time it happened Doña Rosalía had become a symbol. It was fitting and proper that the great men should come to her with their shining promises of progress.

Progress always came slowly to Descanso but it wasn't Doña Rosalía's fault. She knew the ways of the world and was happy to share her enlightenment. She went often to Española to shop and get permanent waves at the Bella Doña Beauty Shoppe and Style Salon. Sometimes Tonito drove her to Albuquerque or Santa Fé and once she went with Luis and Marta and the kids to Trinidad, Colorado, to see a *primo* of Luis on his father's side who was very sick and they all thought he was going to die. He didn't, though.

Doña Rosalía's house—or more correctly hers and Enrique's—had been the first in Descanso to ingest the electric wires the men strung up the mountain. Hers was the first butane water heater and (counting the latest one Carlos had installed) still only one of six. She had an electric refrigerator and range, too, though she mostly used her old wood stove because it cooked better. She boasted a septic tank into which her toilet emptied, though the pipes from her bathtub and kitchen sink channeled their overflow onto the garden; she planned to get a telephone.

"Who would you call?" Carlos once asked her.

"¡*Tonto!* She flipped her hands at him coquettishly. "You don't have to call anybody! There's a magic number you can call anytime, even in the middle of the night, or when the river floods—anytime—it goes all the way to Española and tells you what time it is!" Doña Rosalía was a woman of the world!

Before the *político* came, in another giant stride toward progress she bought a Sears-Roebuck fully automatic electric washing machine. On a deep-skied May morning—a Wednesday—Tonito hauled it up the mountainside and he and Segundo installed it in her kitchen in an excessive demonstration of faith, hope, and daring. Doña Rosalía closed the post office to supervise. Carlos, too, came to help, though with little hope and less faith.

The water tank, he observed, wasn't twenty feet above the town. There'd be no pressure unless they installed a pump as he had done.

His pump was for a shower she pointed out. A washing machine was another matter entirely and neither Tonito nor Segundo was inclined to engage in any discussion aesthetic, philosophic, or technical about the community water tank.

The first problem was where to put the thing. Doña Rosalía's old wringer model sat placidly on the back *portal* but the new machine would have to sit inside. That meant moving the electric refrigerator out beside the old washer and running the cord through the door and that, after thoughtful discussion over a six-pack, necessitated a trip to Colinas for a longer cord.

Drake enumerated other items they'd need. They listened patiently but didn't really hear. Carlos knew many things but like all gringos he was never content to do one thing at a time; and when Tonito got to Colinas he forgot what he was supposed to get. He even forgot there was anything he was supposed to remember.

Thursday they hooked up the refrigerator, pushed the washing machine into place, and discovered that the plug and outlet had no use for each other. A mountain lion might as well try to mate with a porcupine.

They traipsed again to Colinas on Friday.

On Saturday Segundo discovered the drain hose had nowhere to go.

"We need to run some pipe," said Drake. "I tried to tell you."

"You got to grow the beans before you pick 'em," said Segundo patiently. "Each thing in its time, Carlos."

They found pipe in Segundo's junk pile. Then they cut through the thick wall and ran the drainage to Doña Rosalía's three apple trees. By dark the shiny white wizard stood ready to perform and the men had enjoyed three days of beer and fraternity while rendering useful work. None but an Anglo would have accelerated the pace and destroyed the camaraderie.

During those three days a large portion of the population wandered in to watch, wonder, and advise. Doña Rosalía invited all to the unveiling. "You don't got to fill my machine with no hose," she said, "and you don't got to turn it through no wringer! Just push a button and the clothes get washed!"

Early Monday morning the ladies of Descanso and their young bore washing and nourishment to Doña Rosalía's. Some made several trips. It was a festive occasion.

Delfina Romero brought *bizcochitos*; Jesusita Salazar and Orlinda Baca bore *empanaditas*. Catalina Sifuentes, her newest at breast and three others in tow, had *buñuelos*. They chattered and exclaimed over the shiny machine and gossiped. Atiliana Villareál, morose as usual, said little but she came to witness and brought Pedro's new wife who already grew a baby and she sent dark looks at Soledad, who ripened too, this time with the seed of the Indian Cirilo.

Cirilo had appeared one day at Soledad's door, ill and homeless. He'd left the pueblo, joined the army, seen the larger world and, returning, found he belonged nowhere. When drunk and sick at the trader's he muttered that neither *médico* nor medicine man could cure him, Fergus suggested the *curandera* at Descanso. Soledad substituted well water for firewater and offered other consolations and he hadn't left since.

Those who could crowded into the kitchen and watched Doña Rosalía stuff clothes into the machine and carefully measure the soap the way the man at the store had instructed.

"¡Mira, mira!" Catalina called. "Sta listo!"

Doña Rosalía closed the lid.

She pushed the dial. The assembled ladies held their breaths. She turned the knob and those very close heard the magic click. Then—silence. Another click. Silence.

They waited for the magic.

A small frown creased between Doña Rosalía's brows then smoothed away. "I didn't turn it far enough." She nudged the dial.

They waited.

"I didn't turn it far enough yet," she said again. A dew of perspiration dampened her faint mustache.

She clicked the dial. The machine began to hum.

Ahhhhhh! Everyone exhaled.

The hum died.

First one and then another tried. They pushed the dial, they pulled it, they turned it to every point.

They sent for Tonito. They sent for Segundo.

They sent for Carlos. "I was afraid of this," he said.

A tear brimmed slightly in each of Doña Rosalía's eyes. "My beautiful machine ain't no good?"

"The machine's fine, only it needs pressure to fill."

"It won't work?"

"Not without water." He sighed. "We'll have to see about a pump, Doña Rosalía."

"That all it needs? Water?"

He nodded.

She laughed gaily. "*¡Tonto!*" she teased. "If that's all—we don't need no pump. We just be lazy-fair, Carlos! We wait!"

"For what?"

"For what, you ask me? For one these days the water to come!"

No day on our earth is lost; not if a sun ray warms or a raindrop falls or a bird wheels free on a freshening waft. Not if a cloud scuds or a kid goat bleats. *Ay,* and if the clothes don't get washed in the magic machine, they are no dirtier than before, *¿cómo no?* The *bizcochitos* and *buñuelos* and *empanaditas* were to enjoy and plenty of hot strong coffee for the day the automatic washer didn't wash. The children played in the sunshine and the women gossiped and everyone agreed that the man at the Sears-Roebuck store was full of words about what the machine would do but he forgot to tell what it wouldn't do. *Ay,* never trust a gringo selling automatic washing machines!

"But shall I tell you a thing of importance?" asked Doña Rosalía slowly. "I had this feeling. . . ."

"*¿Cómo?*" "*¿Qué pasa?*" "*¡Dime!*"

"*Bueno.*" She waited for everyone's attention and nodded wisely and the flesh beneath her chins shook. "The day before we went to buy the machine . . ." Her eyes darted about.

"*Sí, sí.*"

". . . I had a sign! Just before dark I carried water to my little plum tree and as I straightened up I looked up the hill, and saw . . . ." She looked about the room.

"*Sí,*—what is it?"

"Up by the water tank—I saw her plain—stood a *bruja!*"

"A *bruja!* A *bruja?*"

"Hunched over with a *rebozo* over her head."

"Are you sure?"

"Oh *sí.* Because . . . ." She looked around the room again.

"Yes, yes. *¿Por qué?*"

"I looked away a minute and when I looked back—she was gone!"

"*Ahhhhhhhh!*"

"And—just then I heard the cry of the owl and it flew into the sky—from the very place she stood!"

The ladies crossed themselves.

"It flew toward Pájaro!" Everyone knew of the witches of Pájaro.

There was no doubt, they agreed: a *bruja* had hexed the machine. No wonder the water couldn't flow in! *Ay,* one can't cross *brujas.* One just has to wait them out!

Her head nodded decisively. "And Carlos believes . . ." She laughed as one laughs at a child and shook her head and her chins quivered gently. "Our *pobre amigo* believes it is our tank not high enough in the sky!"

▲

Doña Rosalía's washing machine was a symbol, an outward and visible sign of an inward and energetic will: one day the water would flow.

Those who dwell in arid lands have learned to wait for the water.

The washer became a symbol of Doña Rosalía herself, who brought progress up their mountainside into their village; who led the way with septic tanks and electric wires and butane heaters; who, from her official office with the official sign in front of Luis and Marta's house that said "United States Post Office," dispensed the mail, such as it was, along with freshly fried *buñuelos* and the latest news of birth, death, and the tortuous journey between; who every morning with proper ceremony raised the Stars and Stripes—a bit tattered now by mountain weather—and who took it down every evening.

Doña Rosalía tempered worldliness with worship. She helped clean the church and mend the altar cloth.

Her energy propelled her about the village with her prognostications and news items and she was always where misfortune struck to help the ill or the bereaved whether or not they wished it. It was natural, then, that when the gods of history chose one to carry the banner of progress for Descanso, their eyes should fall on Doña Rosalía, with bigger things in mind than a fully automatic washing machine. That was only a symbol.

▲

Later she said there were omens. A low-flying golden eagle dropped two feathers in her path—a sign of change. Orlinda Baca dreamed that a stranger rode a burro across her bean field and trampled her plants and when she ran calling for him to stop he had no face. Cipriano Pacheco saw a fireball on the opposite mesa.

There were other signs, too, of a more corporeal nature. First came an increase in mail. In a sudden fit of efficiency, the postal service closed two small offices so Doña Rosalía had to handle the mail for Pájaro as well as for the hippy commune up the other branch of the Colinas road, locally dubbed Las Lucas—The Loonies—where some of the hippies still lived and several rich Anglos owned summer homes.

Tonito complained about the extra mail and Doña Rosalía had to sort it, which took extra time, and stash it, which took extra room. On the day the government checks came the traffic increased. Some grumbled that their peace was roiled like a swollen *rito* but Doña Rosalía pointed out that it brought profits to Antonio and Tomás and to Segundo as well. Her own importance expanded with her greater responsibilities.

Then came the *político*.

Políticos migrated seasonally like showy if predatory birds every two years, or four, or six, and they screeched or squawked (or twittered or tweed according to their species) but whatever the sound, the message was one of concern for the people of Descanso and the wonders they would work for them if these fine deserving people would vote them into office (or keep them there) for the next two years (or four or six). Then they'd fly to farther fields until the next season for promises wheeled around.

As a rule nobody paid much attention to the *político* birds because it was all just cock-a-doodle-do but this one was different. He was *un hombre muy importante* from Washington DC or Santa Fé (they couldn't remember which) and he pointed his big black car toward the frayed flag that marked the United States Post Office and asked for Rosalía Valdez.

She primped her hair, glad of her new permanent. He said he was charmed and wasn't it hot, even for July, which was always the way *políticos* began, but true enough. The sun sucked dry the *arroyos* and the *acequias* ran low. *Ay*, they surely needed rain, he said, and then he made a joke about not paying the Indians down in the pueblo enough for a good rain dance. Then he sobered and said yes, but it was her, Doña Rosalía, he wanted to talk to about a matter he could influence.

Her work load had increased, no?

Sí, she had Pájaro now, and Las Lucas. . . .

Then she must be paid more money. This should be designated a three- or even a four-hour post office and he personally would see to it. And maybe—he couldn't promise yet—but it was possible they might build a real post office in a building of its own.

¡Qué milagro!

Of course it depended on several factors.

Factories?

Factors. The country was beginning to attract people from Albuquerque and Santa Fé and back east—prominent people.

Sí, some *ricos* had built houses in Las Lucas.

A big real-estate company was interested in a development up the mountain and a guest ranch was in the offing, all of which would necessitate a better road if it came to anything. He for one was working for it because of his deep interest in Descanso and he knew what it could do for them—yes sir, he was all for progress!

He gave her a card and a large poster with his face on it. Maybe she could find some suitable place.

He turned his attention to a series of low growls that rolled from under a chair. "Here, puppy," he called, and he squatted down and held his hand toward Perdido. "What a pretty little dog," he said, which even for a *político* was straining the imagination. The growls rose to a sharp yelp as Perdido's privacy was threatened and then he snapped. The *político* jerked back his hand.

"He don't like strangers," said Doña Rosalía. But the gesture won her heart and she nailed the big poster on the wall so the life-sized face of the portly *político* smiled benevolently from amid *presidentes* and the other notables who glowered under wanted notices.

Doña Rosalía's mind began to balloon with dreams of a real post office in a building all its own.

▲

The clouds around the peak grew denser each day, sometimes with thunder and lightning, but no rain came. The *acequia* ran low. Dust clung to the leaves in the fields, it hung in the air and settled on the earthen walls and the *jacals* and the furry creatures inside them, and the children drove the sheep and goats to higher *ciénegas* to crop the dry grass. Man and beast and plant craved rain.

Strange men came to see Doña Rosalía.

First came the post office men. One was thin with sparse hair like a mangy coyote and steel-rimmed glasses. The other was fleshy like an overfed bear and tufts of rusty hair grew from his nostrils and furred the backs of his hands. Circles of sweat spread under his arms.

She thought they were *ricos* from Las Lucas—they didn't smile enough for *políticos*—and she pushed at her permanent wave and told them she hadn't sorted the mail yet. "You just sit in those chairs and have a nice *buñuelo* and I have it ready in a little. No, no, don't sit there."

Her warning came too late. Perdido emerged swiftly and bit the short rusty bear-man on his puffy ankle.

"It didn't make no blood," she said cheerfully. "Perdido don't like nobody in his chair!"

They hadn't come for mail the coyote said. Was she Rosalía Valdez?

"*Sí.*"

They were making a feasibility report, they said, on the possibility of a new post office. It had been brought to their attention that her present facilities might be inadequate as well as too far from the *placita*.

A grandchild wandered in, reached for a taste of *abuelita*'s sweet *café*, and upset the cup over a stack of letters. Coffee-splashed mail scattered onto the floor.

"*Ay, picarillo*," she chided. "What if these was guv-ment checks?" They were only *político* mail, however, to be dumped anyway. The men looked at each other.

Then they asked a lot of questions and wrote things on papers and left other papers for Doña Rosalía to fill out and said they'd be back.

"Meanwhile," snapped the Bear, "you need to get things in order."

"What things?"

"First, it is not up to you to decide which mail to deliver."

"Oh, the *político* mail? Don't nobody read it."

"How do you know?"

"*¡Adió!* The old ones, they mostly can't read. And the young ones, they don't care!"

"And we don't hang political posters in the post office," said Coyote gently.

"Or public benefactors among the wanted criminals!" said Bear, not so gently. "And that ragged flag's a disgrace." He was still rubbing his ankle.

A number of days passed, dry and dusty.

Then came the men about the building. They came in a red car and wore business suits and colored glasses to hide their eyes. One had a long face and a straw hat hung on the back of his head and the other had a round face and a nose like a circus clown. They were interested in locations to build the new post office on. Provided, of course—always provided—the project got approved and their bid was accepted. Perhaps she could help them?

She could. If they would please come with her she would show them several possible locations.

The first belonged to Cipriano Pacheco and his father. Of course, she agreed, it was no nearer the *placita* than the present post office.

The second belonged, she thought, to the Bacas. It was, she admitted, subject to spring flooding from the *arroyo*.

On the third stood Teresita's old hut which nobody would go near because of the malignant spirit it housed. She didn't know who owned it. *Sí*, it might be hard to get since there was nobody to get it from.

The fourth was quite suitable they all agreed. It was a rocky stretch; nothing grew on it but prickly desert things. To whom did it belong?

"Enrique Peralta."

Did she suppose he might sell it?

"I don't know," she said. "You go talk to him." She pointed to the house. But first they take her back to work, ¿no?

The men were soon back at the post office.

It hadn't suited Enrique to talk to strange gringos so he had covered his face with a stupid smile and spread his hands and said "*No comprendo*" to everything they said and directed them to Doña Rosalía.

She lived in the house with Señor Peralta?

Sí. He was her brother.

Why hadn't she told them in the first place?

¡A redo vaya! They hadn't asked!

She was joint owner?

¡Adió! Didn't she live there?

And the adjoining land?

Sí.

"How far?"

"To where Francisco's begins." It varied a little from year to year. She shrugged her plump shoulders.

Was there a deed?

Maybe so. She wasn't sure.

The one with the hat was beginning to frown but the round-nosed one combed his fingers through his hair and said he'd check it out. "Let's see what kind of money they may be talking first."

She didn't know. She spread her hands wide. Maybe they better talk to Enrique.

They'd tried that. Perhaps she should speak to him. Meanwhile just some sort of ball-park figure. . . .

What?

"What is land going for in Descanso?"

"Well. . . ." She smiled brightly. One best dealt with gringos by playing dumb. "Mostly it don't go at all."

"Can't be much. When did the last land change hands?"

"Well—Carlos, he moved in a house."

"When?"

She shrugged. "Long time."

"Do you know what he paid for the land?"

"Oh, he didn't buy no land." She couldn't remember anybody buying any land ever. "We don't much like to sell our land." Doña Rosalía began to feel a small discomfort like an itch between the shoulders. She hadn't really thought of selling the land—just of letting the guv-ment use it and pay rent, like they paid Luis, for as long as the post office was hers.

"Well, discuss it with your brother and we'll make some inquiries and be back in a week or so. We'll call ahead."

"I got no *telefón*."

"A neighbor, then."

"They got no *telefónes* either."

"Isn't there any phone in Descanso?"

"*Sí*, the *telefón* men they put up a little house—like a privy, but you could see inside—and it had a *telefón* you could talk in if you put money in the slot. Only. . . ."

"What?"

"It ain't worked for three, four years."

They flashed that gringo look at each other and said they'd be back soon.

Doña Rosalía told everyone in Descanso about her official negotiations for a new post office. They would have a grand new building with proper boxes for the mail and a counter, a new flag, and not only a new post office, but a new road with *ricos* coming up it. In short, progress was coming!

Most were impressed.

Orlinda Baca wasn't. She saw nothing wrong with what they had. Soledad was unenthusiastic which Doña Rosalía couldn't understand until she figured out that the new road might bring a gringo doctor who could make difficulties for Soledad as *curandera*.

The surprising doubter was Carlos.

She puffed over to tell him the news and found him in the pump house with a burst water pipe and a near-to-bursting temper. Water was everywhere.

"*Madre de Dios*, Carlos! You got you one good mess!"

"Yeah. Must have a *bruja* in my pump!"

She crossed herself.

250

He resumed his hacksaw attack on the burst member. "My own fault. Forgot to cut off the damn pressure switch."

She shook her head dolorously. "I always knew them pumps was no good!" Then she remembered the news she'd come to tell. Here was real progress, she declared, not tricky stuff like pumps.

He stopped sawing, sat back on his heels and wiped the sweat from his face. "Are you sure you want this kind of progress, Doña Rosalía? Will a new post office really mean much?"

"We like pretty buildings," she said. "We got our pride too!"

"You've always had pride. Without fancy government buildings."

"And a fine new road will come up the mountain and go someplace, not just stop here. Segundo will sell more gas. Antonio will have more business and Tomás too. There will be work for our people—building the new road, and later at the *rancho* where the *ricos* will pay to stay. And maybe we get a new water tank that the *bruja* can't hex and I'll have water for my fully automatic washing machine and you won't need that pump that blows up! And the school bus can come in and our children won't have to walk to the road in the cold."

"And they'll make them all go to the school in Colinas. Even the little ones. They'll close the school here you fought so hard to keep."

"Well," she said slowly, "maybe the school there is more better. They learn more things."

"Not all of it good. Look what Anglo ways did to Julián."

Julián had been back recently and Doña Rosalía had seen his flabby face and bloodshot eyes. Had she heard about the snake he tried to scare Father Andreas with? Drake told her the story as Andreas told it to him:

Pepito, resisting catechism classes, broke the blossoms off the roses the padre had planted in the church yard. The priest had first lectured him, then led him to tell his mama. They found Julián, impelled by old passion and new drink, glowering outside Soledad's door.

The *padre* recited Pepito's naughtiness.

"Why did you do it?" Soledad asked.

Pepito looked down at the gray dust and drew a circle with his foot.

"Wasn't it because you were angry?" prompted the priest. "Because I scolded you for being inattentive?"

"*Sí.*"

"You don't like catechism class? Look at me when you answer."

Pepito looked into the fiery blue stare and his chin quivered but he held it high. "No, Father," he said.

Julián, standing by, laughed. "Don't nobody like catechism class," he bleated. "Don't nobody believe that *chite!*"

Soledad came alive like a nest of bees, told him to go puke in the privy where he belonged, took Pepito and Andreas inside, and slammed the door.

Later Andreas found a large dead rattlesnake coiled on the altar. He sighed, threw it outside, and prayed for Julián's soul.

Rosalía shook her head dolefully at the story. "*Ay,* that Julián," she mourned. "But that got nothing to do with a new post office."

"Doña Rosalía, if Julián had stayed in Descanso he wouldn't have gone to ruin."

She shrugged. "Maybe *sí,* maybe no."

"He tried to be a gringo and he couldn't handle it but he can't come home again either. It's too late. And once your road brings the gringo ways up here. . . ."

"*Somos los pobres, Carlos,*" she said. "We are poor people. When the road comes . . . ."

"People will come. And maybe they'll spend some money but they'll be telling you how to live their way. It's always like that. Once you ran your sheep and goats in the *ciénegas* where the grass grew best. Now you have to petition *La Floresta* for a permit to hunt, to chop your wood, to graze your sheep, and nowhere any more, beyond your own few acres, can you herd your goats. Because the Anglos brought progress!"

Doña Rosalía laughed. "How you talk, Carlos! You don't understand no real progress—only just pumps that bust open! You wait. You just keep yourself lazy-fair and see!"

Doña Rosalía steamed off like a small bulldozer, determined, thought Drake, to destroy her own edifice. He picked up his hacksaw again.

Doña Rosalía prepared for whichever returned first—*político,* purchaser, or postal brass. Visions of the golden utopia about to open its shining doors stimulated a wave of energy. She journeyed to Española for a new permanent wave. She cleaned the office thoroughly and in doing so loosened chunks of plaster from the walls which made it seem shabbier—which, as she thought about it, wasn't a bad thing either.

She rehung the poster of the *político*'s face right between Lyndon Johnson and Franklin Roosevelt so now he was among *presidentes* instead of escaped criminals; she didn't see much difference except the *presidentes* were bigger and colored.

Unfortunately in the frenzy of cleaning she seemed to have lost the official papers the Coyote had left on her desk.

She didn't replace the frayed flag but she adorned it. Tonito helped himself to a string of plastic banners at a used-car lot in Española—bright red triangles that flapped in the slightest wind—and they hung them across the *portal* and around the door and angled them from the flagpole to the ground like a Christmas tree.

That same day she saw the letter for Alarico and sent Tonito to tell him. Alarico held it to the light, saw no check inside, tossed it in the trash, and returned to finish his pint of tokay on the bench in front of Romero's.

Doña Rosalía retrieved the missive, read it, and spread the news. The guv-ment was going to give Alarico a Bronze Star medal and make him a hero!

"What for?" he asked.

"For the war! For that big fight you had yourself on that Bataan place. You got to send some papers to this colonel."

"They gonna make me a hero?" A slow grin lit the old face and lifted the mustache. "After all these lots of years!"

"Well," said Doña Rosalía, "the guv-ment moves slow." She hoped it wouldn't take forty years to get her post office.

In mid-afternoon a week later the red car crawled up the mountain in a cloud of dust and rolled to a stop in front of the festooned flag. In the heavy air the dust hung then settled slowly on the car's bright skin. The long-faced man with the straw hat had a coughing spell.

Doña Rosalía puffed out to meet them under the clouds that massed on the mountain. "It rain pretty soon maybe," she said. "Ever' day the clouds come heavier. *Ay*, our *acequia* dries up, and our fields. . . ." She spread her hands in a wide arc.

Yes, it was certainly dry but they hadn't come to discuss the weather. Had she talked to her brother?

Sí, ever' night they talked.

About selling the land?

Well, mainly they talked about the beans and the corn and the chiles. He was very worried. "But I tell him, 'you just be lazy-fair, Enrique, the rain it come.'"

Already I feel the air change."

"But the land?"

"You look how I fix up the post office!" She swept her hands toward the pennants that hung languidly in the settling dust. The Clown-nose polished his colored glasses with a handkerchief and the hatted one frowned. She let her hands fall and led her guests inside. Clown-nose grinned a little at the *político* among the *presidentes* but Scarecrow still coughed into his handkerchief. Finally he blew his nose and cleared his throat.

"Well, what did he say?"

"Who?"

"Your brother. What did he say!"

"He say the crops will dry up if the rain she don't come soon."

"Does he want to sell the land?"

"Oh, he leave those kind of things to me."

"We're prepared to make a reasonable offer. Tentatively, of course." It was unirrigated, Scarecrow pointed out, useless as it stood. He named a figure.

Doña Rosalía froze. Had he said three thousand dollars? *¡Dios y María!* She would sell half of Descanso for such a sum! She stood and gaped.

"Provided, always, we get the go-ahead. You realize, of course, it must go through channels."

Still she stood. Were they serious? Did they mean it? Maybe she misunderstood. She frowned a little and tried to think of what to say.

"You can't expect city prices, you understand," said Scarecrow. "No market. Like you said, people don't buy land up here."

"We don't like to let go our land," she said. "Please, will you sit down?" She smiled. "But not in Perdido's chair!"

"Also, those old Spanish titles are confused as hell."

A small wind swept through and scattered some papers. She crossed to the open door and looked toward the mountain. *Ay*, up there the clouds boiled and from her flagpole the rows of bright little flags clicked like little motors in the sudden wind.

She closed the door. "You like some coffee?" She knew how to run a proper business meeting! "And *buñuelos*?"

"We'd like to discuss our offer."

"How much did you say?" They looked at one another quickly like two adults before a child. Before either could answer Diego Salazar came in. "Got me any mail, Doña Rosalía?" Of course Diego wouldn't have any mail—he never did. He was just curious to see the men, perhaps to catch a hint of how the negotiations proceeded. She pretended to hunt, introduced him to her guests, and poured him some coffee.

He nodded politely and stood with his cup. "We pray for the rain."

"Diego's our *mayordomo*," she explained. "The ditch boss."

"In spite of there ain't much ditch left to boss," he said. "The storm comes, maybe. *¡Ójala!*"

"We better get down the road before it hits," said Scarecrow nervously. "Bad enough when it's dry."

As Diego left Alarico came in and Doña Rosalía told them about the medal the guv-ment was going to give him. "And this *tonto* didn't even open that letter!"

"Wasn't no check inside," he said.

"*Ay, Dios*, if I didn't pull it from the trash this *burro* wouldn't be no hero!"

"You open your patrons' mail?"

"*¡A redo vaya!* Somebody got to!"

The men looked at each other again.

"My medal come yet?" asked Alarico.

"We didn't send them papers yet, *tonto*."

"Might's well be back in th' Army," he grumbled.

She poured Alarico coffee in Diego's cup and he drank it politely while she told the visitors about him fighting Japs in the 200th Coast Artillery. The men kept looking at their watches and out the window.

She was still talking about the war when Alarico left—about how the men starved all cut off without supplies, and about the Death March, and the Jap prison camp where they were penned like pigs and beaten worse, and. . . .

"Very interesting," said Clown-nose. "Mrs. Valdez, do you feel our offer's fair?"

She wished she knew if she'd heard right. "I don't know . . ." she hedged. A snarl of thunder rolled down the mountain, echoed against the cliff, and spilled to the desert below.

"This time it really come!" Tomás followed his words through the door and smiled widely. "*¿Cómo 'sta*, Doña Rosalía? You got me some letters?" Again she enacted the solemn ritual of looking, of introducing, of pouring coffee into the cup Alarico had drained.

"Your business does good, Tomás?"

"*Bien. Muy bien.* Last night. . . ."

A larger grumble thundered over them.

"We really must get down the road!" Scarecrow kept polishing his colored glasses.

"Your bus'ness goin' good too?" asked Tomás. Scarecrow fidgeted and Clown kept wiping his nose. Eventually Tomás said he better be going and, after several starts, left.

"You don't seem pleased with our offer, Mrs. Valdez."

"Well, you see. . . ."

They exchanged another glance. It darkened outside. From the door Doña Rosalía watched the clouds spill down the mountain.

"Let's quit playing games," said Clown-nose. "Would you settle for five thousand?"

"Five—thousand?"

"*Cinco mil dolares*—is that how you say it?"

¡Dios! Did they make fun of her? Did they tease her with such enormous sums? Did they laugh at her and call her a dumb Mexican?

The door opened and the wind swept in rain-scented. In bustled Delfina and Orlinda. "I think the rain come!" Orlinda cast sour eyes at the men.

"Do you know," said Delfina importantly, "Fernandita Villareál's pains have started?"

"*¡Gracias a Dios!* Atiliana will at last get a *nieto*!"

"May the Virgin grant he grow up better than José," mourned Orlinda.

"Antonio says do we got any mail?"

The ritual started again but before Doña Rosalía could pour coffee Scarecrow said somewhat testily that they were interrupting a business meeting and could they please have their gossip session later. As they left Orlinda shot back an I-told-you-so look.

Dark thunder churned. It rolled around the village, collided and echoed like the milling thoughts in Doña Rosalía's mind.

"Please lock the door, Mrs. Valdez." Scarecrow's voice was getting edgy. "Before you have to entertain all Descanso."

She hung out the sign and bolted the door.

He continued. "There's a little confusion over the title."

"There always is with these old grants," said Clown-nose.

"You and Enrique Peralta are joint owners?"

"*Sí.*"

"Who is . . ." Clown-nose consulted a paper from his briefcase. "Who is Agapito Peralta?"

"Luis is his papa. Not my Luis that lives in this house, my brother Luis— his boy. The *primo* of my Luis. He's dead now—may God rest his soul—a lot of years. Luis I mean. My brother."

"I see." It was obvious he didn't. "Is Agapito part owner?"

"No, no, he lives in Bernalillo."

"But he seems to be part owner of the property."

"Maybe so. Our papa left some rooms in our *casa* to me and some to Enrique. And Luis. So maybe Agapito got some."

"We don't care about the house, Mrs. Valdez. Just the little piece of land. Who owns that?"

"Well, I guess I don't know!" She spread her hands expansively. "You like some more coffee?"

"Would Agapito sign?"

"If I tell him."

A flash of lightning lit the room through the small window. Black clouds rolled. Doña Rosalía snapped on the electric light and the thunder cracked.

"We've got to get down that mountain," Scarecrow said and they looked at each other again. "Mrs. Valdez, you've got to quit stalling. Do you or don't you wish to sell us the land for the new post office?"

"You say—five thousan' dollars?"

"That's the offer." Again came the flash and crash from outside, almost simultaneously. "Provided it's approved."

Five thousand dollars! For Enrique and her and Luz! All that and a new post office too! Doña Rosalía was afraid she would cry; she couldn't speak because of a thickness in her throat. She tried to swallow and walked to the window to wait for it to pass, to say a silent Hail Mary for her great fortune.

The men looked at each other again. Clown-nose shrugged, and Scarecrow cleared his throat. "Very well, Mrs. Valdez," he said, and his voice was tired. "We'll make you one more offer and this is positively our top figure. We'll go to seventy-five."

She turned. "Seventy-five?"

"Seven thousand five hundred. Lump sum."

Another wave of incomprehension swept through her.

"Well? Yes or no?"

The thunder burst as if the whole top of the mountain had blown. Repeated flashes of lightning pierced the clouds. The electric light blinked and went dead—it was a sign, she later declared—and then the rushing rain fell. Sudden and blessed and wet it fell. It swept over Descanso and over the fields that stretched out from it.

"*Gracias a Dios*," whispered Doña Rosalía. They couldn't hear her words above the roar but they saw her nod.

"Good!" Clown-nose smiled. "Your hand on it?"

"*Sí*. My hand."

"Soon as we get the go-ahead I'll get a preliminary agreement drawn up. You only need to sign and get the others to."

"Let's get out of here," prodded Scarecrow, "while we can."

At the door Clown-nose turned. "You drive a hard bargain, Mrs. Valdez!" He was smiling and looked pleased with himself.

She primped her permanent wave.

The men bolted through sheets of rain and faintly above the rush of water she heard their engine catch and roar, heard the gravel scud behind the red car. The little flags danced like bright spirits.

Rosalía turned back inside; she lit the oil lamp. Its flow was comfortable. One could count on it. Always the life in the electric wires fled from the storm, ran back into the cage it came from, as the men of business ran down the mountain.

Ay, wait until she told Enrique about their wealth! Wait until she spread the news about her big deal. She drove a hard bargain, they'd said.

The rain pounded on the pitched roof of galvanized tin Luis had put over the flat earthen one, the lamplight glowed and Doña Rosalía smiled. She drove a hard bargain. *Ay*, she didn't do too bad. Not bad at all!

¿Por qué no? Wasn't she a woman of the world?

As July became August and August neared September, small doubts bored into her mind like the fat green worms in the corn.

They started soon after Coyote came to pick up the papers he'd left. She had trouble filling them out, she told him.

"What don't you understand?"

"Where they went to!" Her hands made parabolas.

"You lost them?"

"Not exactly. I think they got throwed out."

That seemed to put him in a bad temper which brought on a fit about the strings of bright little flags. He told her for God's sake to get them down and left with the dust all stirred up behind him.

She gave the pennants to Tomás who strung them across the front of the *cantina*. They didn't make his business grow but his patrons felt more festive.

Coyote mailed her more forms already filled out so all she had to do was sign and mail them back. She didn't like to put her name on things so important that would travel all the way to Washington but one must feed the burro if one wants him to carry wood so after the official papers lay on a table a week or so she sighed, signed, and sent them on their way.

Then she started to remember the omens.

She remembered the eagle who had dropped his feathers.

She remembered Orlinda's dream about the faceless man destroying the fields.

Three times she heard the hoot of the owl. It was the *bruja* from Pájaro, she told Enrique uneasily and she crossed herself.

Men came to see her from time to time about the new post office or the land. She never knew when they were coming, which was inconvenient, because it meant she had to keep regular hours and this was especially annoying now that hers was a four-hour office.

They made demands. She must process more mail. She must complete more reports and be more accurate and her many small decorations must go. So must her chairs. They frowned when her grandchildren came in to play. The post office grew less gracious.

Perdido bit several.

She began to wonder if the new post office without the chairs, without the children—without Perdido—might not be a lonely place to spend one's days.

More people began to appear. Some came from Las Lucas for mail and usually they slouched over to the *cantina* as well. Tomás at first wore a grin because his business increased; then a frown of worry began to cloud his face. It wasn't the same, he said. Used to be he served his friends; now the new people pushed his old customers—his neighbors, his *amigos*—aside. They insulted his Pilar and no longer could he order them out and throw beer cans the way he used to do at José.

"No longer am I master in my own *cantina*," he said sadly.

Antonio sold more soda pop and more candy bars and more cigarettes but he heard more loud complaints and he endured more abuse when he ran out of things. They made fun of him and his store and his village right in front of him and his friends didn't pass the time of day like they used to do.

"The new people," said Antonio. "They got no manners."

Segundo suffered too. The new people wanted to buy *gasolina* at all hours and when he irrigated his field or plastered his house or made 'dobe bricks they thought he should stop his work to come fill their tanks. They wanted him to wash their windshields and check their oil.

"*¡Chite!*" he complained. "Them gringos can't do nothing for theirselves!"

Nobody was sure just who these men were. Some came to make surveys, they said, for the road that might come through; others came about the development they might put in. Men with briefcases and frowns came through about the guest ranch they might build and others about the post office they might erect.

They all disliked Perdido.

No work began and no money came from the land the men had been in such a hurry to buy. "Rich men and *políticos*," she explained to her friends, "they got to make big words a long time first."

The worms in her mind spread and she remembered the words of Carlos. *They'll be telling you to live their way. It's always like that.*

Meanwhile Carlos told her not to sign anything until he looked it over—if it came at all.

He thought it might not?

He'd seen these things before. Chances were none of it would ever materialize. It was election year, remember. "Anyway, what will you do with all that money, Doña Rosalía?"

"First I buy me a TV."

"Good Lord! You won't have any reception up here. No picture."

"*Ay*, Carlos!" She laughed. "The pictures is inside the box! Just wait! Lazy-fair, Carlos! Lazy-fair!"

▲

The drought was broken. Summer showers continued, the corn grew tall, and the squash vines spread. The pods of the chiles swelled and those of the beans.

One day men walked through Pedro Villareál's chile field and trampled many plants. Pedro grabbed his gun and started for them. They saw he meant business and said they'd pay for the chiles but if the road went through this would be the best route.

Through his field?

He'd get more money for the right-of-way than he'd ever made from the crops.

He'd be damned if they could just come in like this! He'd kill the next one!

Words flew and villagers gathered.

"Hold on," the strangers said. "The road has to go somewhere. This field, and that orchard. . . ."

"Through my apricot trees?" quavered Francisco.

"Only those skirting the cemetery."

Along the *camposanto*? Those few . . . and Padre Lorenzo's. . . .

Their miracle tree!

Discontent grew to outrage. Those who had hailed progress held angry meetings at the schoolhouse about how to keep out the foreigners. They sent word to the *político* who started the whole thing. They wished to return to the old ways, the old dignity, the old peace. To be once more—Descanso. The resting place.

Some blamed Doña Rosalía.

Doña Rosalía blamed the *bruja* from Pájaro.

Padre Andreas feared trouble and told them to blame their own sinful hearts and superstitious ways.

Carlos said the whole thing was unnecessary, that it would all come to nothing. *Lazy-fair.*

Those who had prayed for progress now prayed for peace.

Whether it was prayer, prognostications, or the Pájaro *bruja*—¿*Quién sabe?*

One day when the first golden patches of autumn aspen blazed on the mountainside, Tonito brought in his pouch the letter to Doña Rosalía. There would be no money for the land. There would be no new post office. Due to unforeseen right-of-way difficulties an alternate route had been chosen through the commune popularly known as Las Lucas because of which, along with hardships imposed on residents there and at Pájaro, the branch offices in said communities would be reopened and that of Descanso would revert to a two-hour office . . . and a lot more words.

She huffed across the village to find Carlos. Perdido trailed morosely. "What does it mean?" she asked.

She drank a Coca-Cola in his patio while he read it through.

"It means your *político* friend needs votes from Pájaro and Las Lucas," he said. "Which squares with what Fergus has told me."

"No new post office?"

"Afraid not."

"That new road ain't coming through?"

"Guess not. Which means the guest ranch and the development have also fallen through. Too much static elsewhere."

"Up in Pájaro. . . ."

"Up in Pájaro—Fergus told me—they've been raising hell over losing their post office. Their postmistress. . . ."

"*Ay*, I knew it! That postmistress at Pájaro!" Doña Rosalía took a long meditative swig of Coke. "That's it! That postmistress—old Serafina Luna—they say. . . ." She set her glass down sharply, crossed herself, and looked around. "In Pájaro they say Serafina Luna is a *bruja*!" No more explanation was needed.

"*Vamonos*, Perdido." She stood. "We got to tell Antonio and Tomás and the others they got to worry no more. And Francisco—he ain't going to lose his trees! I told them I wouldn't let down my friends. Not Rosalía Valdez! I knew all along we didn't need that fancy building. I knew that building and that road and all them new people wasn't no good!"

"Did you really, Doña Rosalía?"

"*¡Ay, verdad!*" She pulled her *rebozo* about her shoulders. "You want I should tell you something, Carlos?" She perforated the air with a pudgy finger. "About roads—there's two kind of roads. The slow ones with bumps and holes and sometimes the trucks get stuck in them. Those kind of roads join people together. Our road—it ain't a very good road. Lot of times we can't get out. But I know the people along our road, all the way to Colinas, to stop and talk to.

"But the other kind—the big fast ones—they just take you along so quick that you ain't part of what's between. Them kind of roads don't hold people

262

together. Them kind chops us apart!" She nodded sharply and her chins jiggled.

"That's what they wanted to do to us. They wanted to cut through Francisco's trees! They wanted to cut us from our *camposanto*! Roads hadn't ought to do that, Carlos."

She pushed at her permanent wave and elevated her chins. "I knew all along it was a bad road they wanted. And I can read the signs. . . .

"That's why I called the whole deal off!"

15

"*A*nd that's your story?" Manby asked

"Some of it."

"I don't believe it."

"Neither did Joe," said Drake. "It doesn't matter."

"Just one question: why in hell didn't you shoot that lion when you had the chance?"

"I don't know. It would have been like shooting the Holy Ghost."

"Meaning you didn't really want a mountain lion at all," said Manby and he looked at Drake with one eyebrow higher than the other.

"Yes, I did," said Drake. "It was real. It doesn't count otherwise. I'll show you something," he said and he pulled the fetishes from his pocket.

"What are they?"

"Mountain lions. They're symbols."

"Of what?"

"I don't know," said Drake. "The thing I couldn't shoot maybe. I'll tell you a story. Once there was a young dog. . . ."

"Yeah. A shaggy one."

"Maybe," said Drake. "But he had a very long tail. His father was the canine king. One day his mother said, 'Son, you are the heir apparent. One day you will be top dog,' and his wife—who was a bitch—told him it was time he straightened up and started acting like a real prince.

"This made the puppy-prince nervous for he didn't want to rule the kingdom which he thought wasn't worth ruling anyhow. So he sat around and sulked and looked out the window at the purple haze on the horizon.

"One day he saw a movement in the distance; it was strange and shadowy and he said, 'I must go and find that faraway magic thing.'

"'Tell them not to wait dinner on me,' he told the maid. 'I have to go investigate strange movements on the border.' He tucked some dog biscuits and peanut butter and red licorice sticks into his overnight case and set out.

"He traveled far but always the mysterious moving thing stayed ahead of him. Sometimes it looked like a mounted horseman; other times it was more like a lion. Once he thought it might be a beautiful maiden in distress if he were lucky. But never could he catch up with it.

"Then one day the landscape seemed familiar and before he knew it he was back in his own kingdom.

"'Oh is that you?' asked his wife yawning. 'Where have you been?'

"'Around the wide world,' he said. 'I've been gone a year and a day.'

"'No you haven't,' she said. 'You always exaggerate.'

"'What did you accomplish?' asked his father sternly.

"'I sought truth,' he answered. 'But it always eluded me.'

"'You've frittered away your time,' said the king, 'chasing daydreams.'

"'No,' said the puppy-prince. 'What I sought was alive and real and I've learned much of the world though I have not found truth.'

"'Silly puppy,' said his mother fondly. 'You haven't been around the world! You could never have made such a journey!'

"'It's a small world,' said the puppy.

"'You've only been running around the palace walls!'

"'World or wall, what's the difference? I followed life and truth!'

"'No you didn't,' said the prime minister, who knew all about boundaries and security checks and enemy espionage. 'You don't even have a passport. It was only your own tail you were chasing!'

"'That too is alive and true,' said the puppy. 'Anyhow, what's wrong with chasing a little tail?'"

"Are you quite sane?" asked Manby.

"Is anyone?"

"I always thought I was."

"Pity," said Drake. "I read a newspaper last night," he said.

"Welcome home."

"Know what it said? Some bladder-brained legislator suffering from mental menopause is pushing a bill against blowing your nose in public. They bend their mashed-potato minds to momentous problems like that and expect me to follow the leader? No friend," he said, "I'll go chase my tail. As soon as you get me legally resurrected, I'll get out of everyone's hair."

"Where'll you go?"

"I don't know," said Drake. "Beyond."

"What are you looking for?"

"A civilized man. Camelot. Atlantis. The beginning of the trail. So I can follow Pan and find America again, maybe."

"For God's sake," said Manby. "And what is it you expect to find?"

"I don't know," said Drake. "My own tail, maybe, or a blue stone."

"I don't know what you're talking about."

"Never mind, just handle the details. I'll keep in touch," he said. "Right now there's someone I've got to see."

Manby's phone chimed soft musical notes and he said, "Yes?. . . . Yes, Leona, he is," and he motioned to Drake to sit down again.

"She's on her way," he said. "Might as well get it over with."

▲

They climbed again to the Rincón and there were four of them this time and a copper dog.

Single file they pushed through the piñon and juniper, past lemony chamizo clumps, through the bronze scrub oak and the yellowing aspen. The Indian Cirilo led, a tall bronze man, and his skin caught the sun's light and gave it back and when he spoke his voice was deep bronze too.

Behind him Pepito darted into the forest on either side like a wild fawn and Goso with him. The school would wait, Soledad said, and the Rincón would soon be winter-sealed. Pepito sucked the mountain into his small being, transformed it into the energy of joy, and released it again. He ducked through the white aspen logs of the *rico*'s into the pasture. The horses were gone down to winter grass. In the pines the boy and the dog bounded after butterfly or chipmunk and the wild things skittered beyond reach and stopped, more curious than afraid, and Pepito laughed.

Once they came on three white-tailed mule deer browsing. The buck watched the humans and Pepito smiled the dark wise smile of innocence; a life current flowed between the wild creature and the child creature and Drake

266

watched and the old ache rose. Seven years toward manhood, Pepito's legs stretched tough and weedy.

Walking behind Soledad, Drake watched her strong legs move with the same deep rhythm that pulsed from the earth's guts and she communed with the dark mother as Cirilo with the sun. From her broad hips her skirt swung softly, brushed her hard calves, and in front it rode high on her ripening belly.

Goso chased lizards and barked sharply when one slithered beneath a rock. "Can't you catch him, old boy?" Drake laughed. "*No importa*—it's only the chase that matters, you know."

At the place where old fire once swept, Pepito squatted, probed a sapling with a finger, examined a green seedling-child in this forest of burned-out passion. In this dead place life throbbed with nature's great energy of survival which is its own morality and Drake felt, from beneath the charred crust, the green push of life like that in Soledad's belly.

The old loneliness flooded through him, the emptiness of the mateless man, and a yearning filled him, a soul-hunger for some lost part of himself. Gradually it ebbed and left him trembling. Goso beside him licked his hand.

¡Mira, mira!" Pepito ran with a small object from near the sapling and passed it in cupped hands to Cirilo, to his Mama, to his Tío Carlos. It was a fragment of a bowl, once earth-red, darkened by ancient cooking fires. On its lip was incised the head of the Plumed Serpent from whose mouth, quick and sharp as thought, streaked the anguiform lightning that brings the sacred rain and the form and the rhythm were the powerful abstractions of the life force.

At a nod from Cirilo the child carried the ancient shard back to its bed of soil. As he carefully placed it where it had lain his small wristwatch flashed in the sun. His Tío Carlos had given him the watch when he started to school the year before, the only such extravagance among the children at school. Pepito delighted in reading it and for weeks plagued everyone. "It is ten minutes after seven," he piped. "It is six minutes until ten." No one listened but Pepito's joy demanded no response.

On they climbed through the tall conifers with needles blue-hued as if some sky stuff had rubbed off on their sharp high branches and then they came to the rock slide.

▲

Drake had described that last rise to Father Andreas the night before. "Rocks piled like breastworks guard the Rincón. Earth's treasures can't be gained too easily."

"What is it up there?" Andreas had asked.

"I don't know. Innocence I think."

"Oh, so now it's innocence you're seeking!" Andreas shot him the electric-blue look but the lines around his eyes were fine and worn and he was pale. He'd been in Albuquerque, lost three days there, and a dozen duties piled up and likely a burial on top of those, for Cipriano's father had passed beyond Soledad's help. Fernandita Villareál, learning the *curandera*'s arts, tended him while Soledad was gone. She would know when to call the priest.

"She called the *rezador*, too," Andreas said, and blackness shrouded his tones. "And you go up there hunting innocence!"

"The Rincón's like Eden before sin got invented."

"But it has been invented, friend. You're a big boy now and you're still digging in sandpiles looking for innocence!"

"Meaning?"

"Quit playing games. Go back to the world. You can't idle in neutral forever."

"Meaning get my ass in gear?"

"Something like that."

"And leave the only son I've ever sired?"

The electric blue arced from the priest's eyes to his own and held them but he didn't say anything. Drake broke the circuit with a short laugh. "Anyhow, do you? Accept the corruptions, I mean. The—sin, if you will?"

"I acknowledge its existence. And I believe in its forgiveness. And," he added slowly, "I'm learning to compromise." His full mouth twitched a little and the fine seams at its corners strained.

He referred to Domingo Pacheco, Drake knew. He had given him last rites but it was Amadeo Baca, the *rezador*, who intoned the prayers now over the dying brother.

Drake shrugged. "Might as well," he said. "You can't stop it. Why do you hate them so?"

"Because the superstition takes precedence over the faith!"

"It *is* their faith, Padre."

"Then perhaps theirs is greater than mine!" He strode to the window, looked through the night to the scattered panes of orange light that glowed from the squat houses, toward one where an old man lay dying. "Sometimes I think it is." His voice was low and ragged.

They hadn't talked much after that.

Drake focused on the gray rock breastworks that guarded the cirque. Cirilo's head and shoulders rose above the ridge and showed strong and bronze against the sky. Soledad's silhouette emerged beside him, first the flowing black mane, then the swelling thickness of growing life as she gained the ridge. She stretched her hand to the child to steady him on the slide and as he reached his small hand up to hers the little watch winked again in the sunlight. For the moment the child stood between them, then scurried over the lip, and the man and woman stood together. He, sun-growing, rose tall like the great Douglas fir by which his ancestors had climbed into the Sun Father's light. Beneath his tall strength she stood like the tamarisk, tough and tender, that shades the living and comforts the sad lost spirits that cry among her branches. The emptiness swept through Drake again, the mate-hunger, the soul-hunger, the terrible life-hunger, and he knew why he came to the Rincón.

It was the place of life.

He paused before he topped the last rise. He heard the vast silence of the Rincón a heartbeat before he stepped into the field of its compelling force.

He cleared the lip and felt the energy rise shimmering like waves of light, up from the lake, whose depths opened black into all the chthonic caverns of the earth, into the deep-flowing center of life.

Whence it all came.

Soledad's well connected too, through some arcane channels that led deep to the source. Three days earlier he had taken candy to the boys and bought goat cheese from her. He heard the creak of the pulley as she drew the bucket up the shaft, followed the sound into her garden, and drank from the lip of the pail. It still had the odd ghost taste, he commented.

"Cirilo says it's the taste of the snake. He says the serpent's what the ghost guards."

"Then it's a place of good," he said. "Even if it does taste funny."

"It heals. It healed you, Carlos. Cirilo says the snake wants something." She seemed to change the subject. "Cirilo and I—we get married soon. In the church, like Padre says." She patted her rounding belly. "Then we go live in the pueblo."

"Oh," he said, and there was a hollowness inside him and it grew greater at her words though it had nothing to do with Soledad. It had been a long time since he'd desired her. She hadn't come to him, nor he to her, since . . .

Not since Pepito.

The yellow autumn sun poured over them, into the bucket with the sparkling water. "Pepito," he said. "If you take him to the pueblo, I'll—I'll—miss him." His voice spread weakly, its force spent, as water diverted into the field sinks into the ground. "You'll all become Indians."

The Indian blood had always coursed strongly in Soledad's veins. "And Pepito too," he said, and his voice cracked.

"The Indian way is good."

"But Pepito's no Indian. Pepito's—damn it all Soledad, he's half Anglo!"

"Maybe-so half of him," she said. "Maybe no. I don't know. But the other part is mine!" She laughed and poured the water into the *olla*. He walked toward the wall, touched the tamarisk beside it whose scraping he had heard so many nights when the wind had keened darkly. What right had he to say anything about Pepito? What would he say if he could?

His voice lightened. "And what about the ghost? You're going off and leave her?"

She changed the subject again though he knew her mind, like the moccasined foot of the Indian, follows the game along a path the white man cannot see. "We go to the Rincón soon," she said. "You come too." Her husky voice still stirred him and her well-eyes were dark.

They wound down the path. The child darted ahead toward the lake, deep and autumn-dark and inward-pulling for the lonely sleep of winter, the time of renewing. Here was Earth Woman, mother of all the *ritos*, and the *acequias*, and of Soledad's well.

"Many spirits live here," said Cirilo.

Pepito raced up. "Can we stay all day?"

270

Cirilo pointed to a pine. "Until the sun is over that tree."

"What time will it be?" The child pointed to his watch.

"You can tell us." Cirilo grinned at something funny.

He made fire from the earth-grown wood with its sweet pitch inside and its energy rose in smoke to the sky. *Fire draws men into the god-circle*, Drake thought. *It carries their prayers to the high places.*

The men smoked squatting while Soledad and Pepito gathered brush for the fire, and autumn herbs. Cirilo sucked the smoke in slowly, exhaled the thin plumes to join the greater column rising, and it was rite-like.

"Smoke is a prayer," said Drake. "Or a spirit."

The dark man nodded. "The Indian has many gods. All living things have spirits inside. We are all part of the Great One." He grinned. "You make your God do all the work," he said. "You send your saints with messages and always you are asking for things. We don't expect so much. You ask gifts of your God but we work with ours to make the corn grow and the rain fall.

"Do you know the spider's web? Each thread fastens onto the next one. None pulls harder than the rest. The gods too must be careful not to tear the web for it is life that the spider spins carefully. She can hang from heaven on her one strong thread. But it takes the whole web to trap her dinner!" Cirilo let the mischief dart about his strong bronze face. He inhaled the blue smoke, let it flow through his breast, and expelled it in thin blue plumes.

"My people know the ways of the spider," he said. "We let the gods touch lightly."

"And the people?"

"They touch lightly too. The gods stretch from the center toward the sun. The people spin the threads between—to connect, but also to separate, or the balance is ruined and the web tears. We have learned to balance the gods."

The web is spun in beauty.

"I respect your way," said Drake. "But I don't understand it."

"No." Cirilo turned his obsidian eyes on the white man. "It is not your way."

"I envy you. Your way is so clear."

"We are like other men. We seek other ways too. I went off following yours."

"The other fellow's *ciénega* is greener? But then you found how shoddy our world really is."

"It is much larger than ours. Your ways are of science. You grow corn for all the world. We scarcely grow enough for our pueblo. I thought to keep some of your ways."

"It didn't work?"

Cirilo blew the smoke upward. "A man who follows two paths will fall into the canyon between. Soledad sent me back on my own mesa." His quick humor crinkled his eyes. "She mended my web."

Later Pepito threw sticks for Goso, sometimes into the water, and the dog swam after them and brought them back and shook water and everyone laughed.

They ate and the men smoked again and the boy and the dog lay quiet for a time. Soledad pulled the blue stone from the deep pocket of her skirt.

"Tell me about it, Mama."

"I've told you about it many times," she said, but in the way of children he would hear it again. "My *abuela* gave it to me," she said.

"Teresita? Who was a *bruja*?"

"They said she was. Her papa gave it to her. He told her to use it only for good."

"And did she?"

"I don't know."

"And you were afraid of it?"

"I didn't understand the power. Cirilo told me what it was."

"Like he told you about the ghost's treasure."

"*Sí*, he said the treasure was the snake."

"I don't like snakes," said Pepito.

"Snakes guard water," said Cirilo. "They bring the waters in the clouds and the rivers. So we don't kill the snakes."

"Does a serpent live in the lake?"

Cirilo nodded. "Deep inside it. Awanyu, with his mate."

Soledad was looking at the blue stone.

"Tell me about its magic, Mama."

"It's sky magic. The sun mated with the earth and left sky-seeds in her womb."

Even the gods must mate, Drake thought.

"The serpent gave the stone to my grandfather. It's a healing stone. It healed Cirilo and your Tío Carlos, too. Now the serpent wants it back. It must go back to the deep waters."

"Why?"

272

"Because it's time."

"Why don't you give it to our ghost in the well?"

"The lake's deeper. It connects with many wells and when he wishes the serpent will give it again in another well maybe."

"And our ghost will leave?"

"¿Quién sabe? But she will let us leave. We can go with Cirilo."

She pulled herself up, heavily now, walked to the edge of the lake and looked toward the dark center. Drake knew he was witnessing a rite, a high ceremony in which she and Cirilo were priest and priestess, the child acolyte to a mystery he only half understood, a drama to which he, Drake, the white man, was the only spectator. He rocked forward onto his knees, sat back on his heels, half-kneeling, his eyes on Soledad.

Cirilo walked to her, stood tall and still beside her and suddenly Drake felt as he had felt on the *potrero* the time when they came on the dead deer, that he had seen it all before, that it had happened in some deep pool of time wherein he swam suspended. He waited for the next step in the solemn dance. He knew what it must be and that it followed its own necessity.

Soledad looked once more at the blue stone, clutched her square brown hand around it, drew back her arm, and flung it hard. Over the lake it arced, a piece of sky seed, it sped in blue flight, plunged downward like a water bird diving into the black still center and it made a tiny splash and then the stillness sucked it deep. It had pierced the dark womb like blue sunlight and tiny ripples rolled, then smoothed into the broad surface, long before they reached the water's edge.

Cirilo and Soledad walked back toward the coals of the aging fire to the white man still kneeling, to the straight solemn child. Drake sensed the meaning of true mating. Father Andreas would read the church ceremony and they would touch his God lightly but the thread of the web was anchored tightly in the Rincón.

This was the place of joining.

"The sun is over the tree, Papa," cried Pepito, and Drake thought, *Papa: how easily it comes to his curly lips* and he knew another emptiness.

"Then we must go," said Cirilo.

"One more stick for Goso," begged the child and threw it into the lake. The dog bounded after it splashing. "He likes the lake too, Papa. Does he know the serpent lives inside?"

"I think so."

"He's afraid of snakes."

"Not this one." Goso scrambled from the water, stick in mouth, showered them with cold spray and pranced wriggling. "See, he's happy."

"How does he know this one's good?"

"How do you know?"

The child knelt at the water's edge, softly placed his palm flat on the surface, then cupped his hands into it, drew them up and standing let the drops fall in silver beads. He looked up at Cirilo, wiped the wet on his jeans, and nodded wisely.

"Because," he said, "I feel it in the water." They stood by the lake together and Drake watching felt a rightness flow between them.

Father, Son, and Holy Ghost.

Then it was time to leave.

"What does your clock say?" Cirilo asked.

"It says—it says two minutes after ten. But . . . ." A small frown rippled his face. "I forgot to wind it up," he said, and his voice grew small with shame.

"Well," said Cirilo, "I sure am glad something didn't forget to wind up the sun!"

At the lip of the cirque they looked back over the Rincón. They felt its power rise in waves and heard the rhythm of silence and as they looked a sudden flash of pure gold shot at them from a span of widespreading wing. The eagle circled the lake, arrogant and sure and noble. He circled his domain, untroubled by transient humankind, whole in his otherness, strong and male and sky-borne; but even he must be drawn by the female lake. Somewhere he too had a mate.

There shines the power and the glory, thought Drake. *There circles eternity*, and whether it was bird or spirit he didn't know. He only knew he would not see it again, that he would not come again to the Rincón. He sensed he would soon shed this pattern as the serpent sheds the old skin to grow into the new one and though he knew the necessity he felt a great sadness. Something close to prayer filled him and he thanked whatever forces pulsed at the top of the mountain for the gift of loneliness that sweeps the soul so bare that the beauty can steal in. He knew that only those who know the loneliness can perceive the beauty.

The eagle wheeled high.

"But he's a killer," said Drake. "For all the splendor."

"*Sí.* The eagle eats the rabbit, the man must shoot the dear. It is life's necessity."

"Troy dies so Rome can be born?"

"I don't know those gods," said Cirilo and he grinned. "But we let them in too. If they don't tear the web!"

In the aspen forest by the *rico*'s corral a quick rain fell, sharp and sudden, an autumn shower before the winter and the sharp smell of pine swept from the forest around. They ran for the aspens and crouched laughing in the golden light. Suspended in the rush of rain they watched the gray curtain sweep and the serpentine lightning thrust from the mouths of dark clouds, from the Plumed Serpent's mouth.

The shower became a mist. The westering sun struck the aspens and gold flame lit the forest. From the dark clouds beyond a rainbow arced and pale-breasted sparrows played in the wet branches and shook their wet feathers.

I will not come this way again.

They walked through rain-dripping pines and again he felt the yearning and it was as simple as mate-hunger and as subtle as the green seedling that pushed in the black-burnt place toward some next plane.

He wondered if it were akin to a religious experience. He didn't know. He only knew there was a mountain with storms and rainbows, with the deep lake and the sky-soaring eagle. He knew too that it was another mountain, not this one, that had the trail somewhere for his feet and he knew somewhere there was a mate who knew the loneliness.

Nobility still lived in eagle and serpent and lion and God—and, he knew, in Man. Places are yet left where Man and God can meet, in these strange centers where Earth Mother breathes and some god speaks the Word and some man who stands alone still listens and hears and makes it into language. Some rustic God still pipes and some Beethoven hears and because he is a man he makes a symphony.

They pushed on through the scrub oak that scratched at their arms with dripping branches. They pushed on to Descanso, toward the resting place, and Francisco's husky square voice sounded in his mind.

"'*Sta bueno*," it said.

▲

"'*Sta bueno*," said Francisco when Drake described the strange rite at the Rincón. "A time to mate, a time to die." He walked among his trees and he rested his hand on a branch.

Domingo was dead. "The bell tolled this morning. The women prepare the *velorio*." The smell of bread baking rose over Descanso. "*Ay*, we all have our time. A time to mate, a time to die."

"A time to leave," said Drake. They walked together in the glow of the low heavy sun.

"*Sí*." Francisco nodded. "You go to find your own mountain and your own woman. Back to your own people."

"Not yet. There's always *mañana*."

"Now you talk like a *mexicano*!" Francisco grinned and the fine-etched lines spread over his face. "It is like the bright days of autumn which seem to stretch into more bright days and always to bring another. Until the morning when you open your eyes to white frost and you know *mañana* is today."

"And—there's still Pepito."

"You cannot burden Pepito with your world."

"Haven't I done that already?" Drake asked harshly. "I can't prove it. But look at him! Julián hasn't that lightness to his skin! I've already burdened him. With my blood."

"Bloods mix, Carlos," the old man said quietly. "It's the paths of the heart that fight. Pepito must follow his mother's. You must leave him to do it and follow your own."

"The ways of the world are changing, Francisco! The world's coming in. Doña Rosalía's road will come, sooner or later the village will change. And the pueblo. I want to be here. I want to give him an education, damn it! It's an Anglo world he'll be living in!"

"He must change with his mother's people. You must change with yours."

"And—there's the thing I feel for him."

"*Ay*, there's always that."

"A while longer. . . ."

"*Mañana!*" Francisco broke a twig from a low branch. "The days still hold. For a little while."

▲

Drake sketched Alarico while the time held. The old soldier had dreamed of riding bravely astride to war and of performing heroic deeds. "But we didn't get no horses," he told Drake. "Just ack-ack guns."

"You fought in the biggest war in history." Drake's charcoal made

276

scratching noises as he shaded in Alarico's drooping mustache. "And in one of the greatest battles."

"They made us surrender," he said sadly. "We was ready to die. But that general surrendered us." He leaned against the sun-soaked wall and guzzled strawberry pop and let the heat run into his back. From the *camposanto* came the sounds of metal on rock as the young men dug Domingo's grave.

There was something in the old face that Drake couldn't catch. He started another sketch. "Tell me how it was."

Alarico talked of the war, of four starving months on Bataan, outnumbered and isolated, and of how they fought with outdated weapons and dwindling ammunition.

He talked of the Death March. "That's where they killed Ysidro." His eyes filled and for moments he couldn't talk. "Filthy Jap bastard bayoneted him when he stumbled and put his foot on him to pull out the blade. And we couldn't do nothing. We had to stand and watch."

He talked of the years in prison camp and Drake wondered how man could survive the horrors he told. The face under his charcoal began to quicken.

"How did you ever make it?" he asked.

"It was the Santo Niño," the old man said. "He brought me home."

He had come one night while Alarico slept and He looked like the wooden image on the altar at Descanso that Francisco carved and He smiled and gave him water from His little gourd and handed him a plate of tortillas and beans. Though Alarico awoke before he could eat or drink, he knew after that he'd get home.

He knew it in all the hell on the prison ship where men died in the airless holds and bodies rolled about them. He knew it slaving underground in the mine and freezing in the heatless barracks and through the countless beatings.

"And He brought me back to Descanso after," he said. "I couldn't talk to nobody. My Ana—she lies in the *camposanto* now—how do you tell Ana about a war? How do you tell Francisco how they killed his Ysidro who was too gentle? I ran away. I take Ana and go to Albuquerque."

There the dreams came. Ana was frightened when he woke up screaming. But he couldn't tell her.

They went to mass one morning and he looked around the big church and the saints were all plaster. They looked real, not like Francisco's *santos*. But *santos* shouldn't look like people. They should be different. They should have mystery in them. Francisco's saints had the Holy Ghost. That's why they were *santos*.

Suddenly he saw the Santo Niño again—not the plaster image but a living Santo Niño, the way He'd come back to him in the war. But now He was sad. *I brought you home*, the little *santo* said. *I gave you tortillas and water when you had none. I gave you hope when you had lost it. I brought you home. And then you went away.*

Home. He must go home. To Descanso.

"After that I came and the nightmares went away." Alarico finished his pop. "And now the guv-ment makes me a hero!" He dropped the bottle in the dirt, flexed his joint-swollen hands, and laughed. "They don't know how scared I got! Or about those dreams, like a sissy *niño*."

"You did the right thing? Coming back here?"

"A man needs his own kind, Carlos. A man's got to come home."

"Can you ever? Really I mean?"

"For me it was right. For another man—*¿quién sabe?*"

The charcoal scratched. A flight of sand-hill cranes called above and the sun slowly dulled behind the gauze of thin high clouds. "You're happy?"

Alarico shrugged. "Sometimes happy, sometimes sad. I eat good beans and tortillas and I know I'll lie in my own *camposanto*. Ain't that enough for a man?" He fixed his old eyes on something distant. He leaned his head back against the warm adobe wall, against the earthen wall darkening in the afternoon and he seemed to fade into it, earth into earth in the fading sunlight. He closed his eyes. Behind the curling mustache there was peace on his face.

You can go home again.

"But you know, Carlos—I'm proud to get that medal. Even if I wasn't no hero."

"My God, man, what do you call a hero?"

Alarico curled the end of his mustache. "A real hero?" His voice was a sigh and his eyes full of dreams. "Pancho Villa!" he said fervently. "*Ay*, there was a man!"

Drake blended the last bit of shading on his sketch, held it at arm's length, and squinted. Yes, this was right. The Holy Ghost was there. He'd add the medal later.

▲

Father Andreas didn't feel well that night. A touch of indigestion, he said.

"My cooking?" Drake grinned.

"Just tired." He'd helped dig the grave. It was hard going—they'd struck rock. He felt short of breath and had to sit down and his weakness made him angry.

"Not as young as you were, Padre."

"Who is?" he grumbled. "You sound like that Albuquerque doctor."

So that's why he went to the city. "Specialist?"

"Heart man. The doctor in Española insisted and I humored him. Entirely unnecessary."

"You overdo. And you let things bug you."

"Comes with the territory," said Andreas. "But I think I'll turn in."

In the night they heard it.

From the *morada* it came, a faint *alabado* like a high wind in reedy grass and the *pito* trilled. The procession neared and the sound swelled.

Drake got out of bed and crossed to the window to watch the strange fraternity pass. He knew in the other room Father Andreas would be watching too, clenching his fists in the dark silence.

Black-hooded figures, maybe a dozen, trudged slowly along the road, figures he knew in the *placita* by day. The wavering light of a smoky lantern flickered beams on a close-held *cuaderno* at the head of the dark band and from it the leaders sang words in high eerie notes to which the full chorus gave response. Through the voices the thin high notes of the *pito* twined snakelike.

In their own lone rhythm he heard the yucca whips striking heavily on flesh already pulpy from their weight. Against the pale moving sky the dark forms of the whips writhed, descended, and the dull *thwuck* of human pain beat as the flagellants atoned for the sins of their dead brother. Drake smelled the odor of blood as they passed by his window.

Another hooded lantern at the end of the ghostly parade lit a departing flagellant. Down his back coursed streams of dark blood.

These are my friends, Drake thought, *whom I joke with and drink with and clean the acequia with. But I don't know them. There's the Otherness. Always the Otherness.*

The dark procession passed. From the *morada* they wound to Cipriano's house where lay Domingo in a pool of candlelight. The voices passed and muted and the thud of the whips grew faint until only the piercing notes of the pipe threaded back through the night, that and the lingering odor of atonement.

A noise clicked from the living room.

"That you, Padre?" Drake switched on a lamp.

The priest leaned haggard against the *trastero*. He shook his head and managed a faint smile. It had happened before. Nothing to get alarmed at. He had some pills. Maybe a nip of brandy. . . .

Drake poured it quickly. "This'll steady you."

The priest's eyes burned blue and his hand trembled. "We've got to stop it. Somehow, God help me. These are my parishioners. . . ." He sat and bent his head on his hand.

"Shakes you up a bit, doesn't it?"

The priest swallowed a pill and gulped his brandy. He breathed more evenly. "How? How can I fight the superstition of centuries?" He was trembling.

"You can't. And when some of them are in stiff pain tomorrow at Domingo's funeral you must look away. Another shot?"

"I'm all right now. But I can't understand—I cannot comprehend."

"No," said Drake. "We never will."

▲

Drake liked to chop wood. There was something basic about storing fire against the icy *mañanas* to come, something clean and honest about doing what men have always done. He felt necessary, part of the web.

He leaned on his axe and patted Goso. He threw him a stick and watched his muscles work cleanly under his glistening coat.

A storm brewed. He looked toward the peak. The morning sun burned hot but the air that chased off the mountain chilled the sweat quickly. He smelled a sharp gray smell like distant rain. He'd learned to sense the changes during the years.

On the rise beyond the villagers clotted in the *camposanto*. The men in rusty black suits stood with bared heads and the women clutched dark *rebozos* over their heads. The keening notes of an *alabado* glided toward him on the yellow air. From the church the bell tolled in slow cadence.

The treble calls of a hundred high throats came from over Pájaro as a squadron of sand-hill cranes flew riverward and their voices like golden bubbles followed their southward flight. They didn't wait for some cold *mañana* to tell them it was time to go.

280

Drake watched until they skimmed beyond the far mesa and he thought *they too are becoming, all life is becoming, and the wonder comes in the swift-winging glimpses like the wings of the eagle at the Rincón, like the eyes of the lion on the ledge so long ago, like the bright explosions of civilization itself.*

Then the flight was gone and the deep sky empty like blue time through which the affairs of men streamed with treble calls like bubbles. Goso bounded back, immediate and panting. Drake grasped the axe again, attacked another log and perforated the air with the solid staccato rhythm of man-work. Beyond him from the weathered crosses the *alabado*'s shrill notes rose toward something beyond the mountain.

Neither the sounds of man's work nor of his faith carried far into the eternal stillness of the mountain and its valley.

Then came the cries.

A new sound and a new rhythm drove towards him like the debris that rides on a flash flood's crest. Drake dropped his axe and ran toward it.

They laid the shallow-breathing Father Andreas on Drake's couch. Drake gave him a swallow of brandy and threw a blanket over him. Soledad, chafing his wrists, said he needed a real *médico*.

Villagers chattered in clumps.

"*Ay*," moaned Doña Rosalía, "I knew something was about to happen." Rivulets coursed down her fat cheeks. "A crow swooped close—just when we walked outside our door! So close we could see his eyes!"

Drake leaned over the priest. "Pills?" Andreas gestured toward a pocket and Soledad administered them.

Drake ran to his bedroom. He knew what he'd do. He'd think about it later. He threw things into a canvas bag—toothbrush, razor, change of clothes, the sketch books, money. *How can I leave some for Pepito?* He lifted Francisco's *santo* from the mantel, wrapped it in underwear, and put it in the bag. He felt the tiny lions in his pocket.

Andreas was breathing better, but his face grayed.

"Plane gassed up?"

The priest nodded. "But I can't. . . ."

"I can."

Father Andreas made a weak motion.

"Padre, you're in no position to argue."

"It will pass." His voice rasped.

"We're not going to wait around and see."

"But that means. . . ."

"I know what it means." It meant there'd be questions that called for answers. It meant hell to pay when the dead returned from Cloud-Cuckoo-Land. It meant exit Carlos, enter Drake Cavanaugh. *Mañana* was here.

Andreas knew too. "Let's—let's leave it in God's hands."

"Too late, Padre." Drake grinned. "I have shifted my ass into gear!"

A sharp wind gusted from the mountain. Enrique and Francisco carried the priest and Drake went ahead with Segundo to the plane. "What happened?"

"He already look kinda sick. Then when he seen the blood. . . ."

"What blood?"

"On the *mortaja*. You know."

He knew. He'd seen blood-spattered corpses of dead *hermanos* before and blood-spattered walls after the flagellants left the *velorio*. It was morbid. But hell, Father Andreas had seen it before, too.

"Well," Segundo continued, "he kept looking at it, and he get madder. He can't understand—so he kept getting redder like a stove with too hot fire. Then the *rezador* started the last *alabado*. . . ."

"Okay, I get the picture." They were at the plane. "Let's get that damned back seat out." It wasn't the first time—Andreas had carried patients before—and it didn't take long.

Behind them the villagers stood about in anxious black patches. "Get him in, make him comfortable." Not much lying-down room in a Super Cub but it wouldn't be for long.

The priest was still grumbling. "Wind coming up. . . ."

"This isn't booked as a pleasure cruise, Padre." He started to untie the ropes.

"I can help, Tío Carlos!" Pepito ran toward him and laughing back at Mario, he fell. No one paid attention; he wasn't hurt. But his shiny watch had broken!

He pulled to his feet, stood looking at the smashed face, and his dark eyes swelled with tears. Then like some stoic ancestor he blinked them back and walked toward Drake with his back straight. "I broke the watch you gave me, Tío Carlos," he said, and his voice quivered. "I have broked the watch!"

"Couldn't be helped, old man. I'll bring you—I'll send you another."

"No," said the child. "You don't need to. I can tell Indian time now!" He said it proudly and his mouth curved into a very small smile. "It's better anyhow. Nobody won't never smash the sun!"

Drake looked into the young-old eyes and felt the power of alien genes behind them, of long race memories not his, and they were like the lion's eyes that long ago day as if something of the great Mind behind all life looked out and he remembered how he couldn't shoot her, he couldn't betray the. . . .

The Otherness.

Drake's throat clogged. He blinked quickly, leaned over the last mooring and reached down to fondle Goso's downy ears. "Take care of him for me." He straightened and rested his hand on the child's small square shoulder. "And— don't forget your Tío Carlos too soon."

Francisco put a stained hand on his shoulder. "*Vaya con Dios,*" he said.

Then he was in the plane, pushing the starter button, feeling the old response of the motor, and checking the panel. He raised his hand to salute the old *santero,* saw Francisco return the gesture, saw his lips make the words.

"'*Sta bueno!*"

The wind gusted. He looked behind him. "All set, Padre?" Andreas tried to smile.

He taxied to the end of the *prado,* hoped it didn't bump too much, and turned the plane. "Hang on, Padre!" *And goodbye Carlos.* He looked across the *prado,* saw Francisco's trees and his own house and the gaunt crosses that rose from the *camposanto* beyond. He saw on its hill the dark low *morada* and the *calvario;* and above, perched like a great gray vulture, Pájaro.

The cross-slashed mountain gleamed above.

His friends clustered on the edges of the *prado*—Doña Rosalía and Tomás and Diego. He saw Cipriano who had just buried a father and Alarico, the old soldier straight and lean with his mustache blowing. He saw Soledad who had given him back to life.

He saw Pepito, waving, with a large copper dog. Pepito would go to the pueblo, he would learn the ancient tongue, and perhaps the ancient wisdom; Drake knew it was right. *I sought a gene memory,* he thought, *and it was only a memory. Now Pepito carries my genes back to the center I sought as Soledad threw the blue stone into the lake.*

He swallowed the thick hurt in his throat and opened the throttle.

The stick felt good in his hands. A surge of the old feeling swept through him as he felt himself airborne, held a full-throttle climb, and pointed south, away from the mountain, toward. . . .

What? Toward a jet lag of three centuries and a lot of heartbeats for one thing. How many time zones does one cross from the New Stone Age to the Spanish Inquisition to the age of fuckup? A goddamned minefield of international date lines in one hour by a clock that didn't even exist where he was coming from. Hell, he was entitled to a baker's dozen jet lags, jet sags, jet drags. He fingered the fetishes in his pocket.

He glanced back at Father Andreas again and smiled. "Welcome aboard, ladies and gentlemen, we are now departing Paradise for Albuquerque." Santa Fé was closer, but not much, and the padre seemed to be breathing okay so he'd opt for the doctor he'd been seeing. "Thank you for flying Holy Ghost Line and we hope you enjoy our champagne flight!"

He glanced at the chart beside him. VOR frequency 113.2. "On our way, Padre," he said. "Back to the vale of gears!" He switched on the radio.

Behind them lifted the peak and as it receded they gained perspective and, banking, Drake saw the wholeness of its shape come clear and as the canyon floor moved beneath he began to perceive a shape to the years at Descanso too; in time there'd be a pattern to it all, maybe. Couldn't think of that now. They had to get the hell to Albuquerque.

"Still okay?"

Andreas didn't answer. His lips moved. "Lord, I believe. Help thou my unbelief." Over and again he repeated the litany.

Drake framed his own sort of plea though he hadn't been on speaking terms with the old boy much. To something out there he said, *Let me get him there in time, keep the old ticker pumping a little longer, don't let this be for nothing!*

They hit turbulence in patches, pitched in the currents.

Andreas kept muttering, "Lord, I believe. . . ."

He saw familiar formations. The Jemez towered blue off his right wing and somewhere down there two stone lions guarded their silent sacred forces and above them rose the Hill where other forces had been loosened like the wild winds from the bag of the sleeping Odysseus. Los Alamos, ugly and artificial, spread on the mountain like acne.

Beyond the valleys and *potreros* were Albuquerque, Leona, and hell to pay.

Leona. There'd been a woman inside once before he'd driven her away with his sharp humor and his quest for something she'd never understood. Hell to pay for her too. *Don't think about it now. Just keep Andreas breathing. . . .*

"Padre—what doctor?"

The priest's voice was ragged. "Flexner. Junius Flexner."

Pojoaque. He gained altitude, heard the signal, trimmed for level flight, and centered the needle on the radial. He picked up the mike. "Albuquerque radio this is Super Cub eight-six-four-one-delta. This is an emergency. Over."

"Four-one-delta go ahead."

Hell to pay.

"This is four-one-delta. Father Andreas Herzog with me. Heart attack I think. Get me an ambulance. Alert Saint Joseph's and Doctor Junius Flexner. I'm on your twenty-two-degrees radial about six five miles out. Estimating arrival in four zero minutes. Over."

Four zero stinking minutes to the American dream.

"Roger four-one-delta. . . ." Four zero minutes to home again. "Wind twenty knots gusting to thirty from one nine zero degrees." *Can you go home again, Tom Wolfe?* "Altimeter two niner point eight five. . . ." *Not a fair question. Tom didn't have Leona.* "Call Albuquerque tower on one eighteen point three when ten miles out. Over."

River valley and *potrero* flowed below. And behind: a blue stone deep in a lake. Its ripples hadn't reached shore but the lake was different now. A golden eagle perched on his cliff with his mate and glided over crag and *ciénega*, though no human saw. In the *camposanto* Domingo rested and the earth was a little different. Molecules whirled in space and each tiny pull against the largest suns did its own part to keep the web intact.

In Descanso life closed behind the winging plane as the lake closed on the stone. Doña Rosalía read her signs and Alarico sat against the sun-warmed walls with strawberry soda and memories. Francisco worked squint-eyed on a *santo* until his lips cracked into a smile. "*'Sta bueno!*" The wedding hadn't come off but Soledad and Cirilo weren't concerned; they'd had their ceremony.

Pepito ran with Goso and grew toward a manhood Drake would not see. Bells tolled that he would not hear but he'd left his own small ripple.

Below, the river snaked black between yellow cottonwoods and dark mesas. Southward stretched the desert, a plane of endless coral in morning light and it changed and shimmered in mauve dust. Always the colors of the land changed. They seemed to grow, to move, to breathe, as infinite as the woman inside, and he thought, *This is the Word before it is spoken, this is the uncreated world, the unspoken Word. This land of desert and mesa and mountain and quick sun and shadow never is, but is always becoming, like the flight of the cranes.* In the southwest distance he watched a storm move, watched the gray curtain of rain blow toward the southern deserts.

The strata of canyon walls told their geologic tale and it occurred to Drake that men had their strata too, that civilization deposited its own layers over the fire-rock core, and each man in himself. *Body, soul, and mind, these three, and the greatest of these is mind. The Holy Trinity,* he thought, and his mouth quirked.

The waves of the past closed behind him and he was no longer flying *from,* but *to.*

Bernalillo. Coronado Airport. Switch to tower frequency. Brown smog below. Request clearance.

"Still okay, Padre?"

The city lay like a frayed rug beneath the brown. "Four one delta cleared for straight-in approach to runway one eight. . . . Wind. . . . Altimeter. . . . You are cleared to land."

Then the runway and his own reality rose to meet him. *Make the landings smooth,* he thought. *Both of them.* The plane's he could manage.

Men ran from the ambulance with a few terse words and a two-fingered salute to the still-breathing priest.

Check back into the world. Plane. Priest. Prodigal. In that order. "I'll follow in a cab," he told the paramedics and then the claxon blared shrill and hoarse like an old southside prostitute and they bore Father Andreas to whatever *mañana* he had.

Drake taxied the plane to the tie-down spot. *Just go through the motions. Cut the engine. Clear your mind. Concentrate on Andreas, not Drake. Cab to Saint Joseph's. One motion at a time and allow for jet lag.*

He cut through the ragged gray wind.

16

*M*anby offered to leave them alone but Drake said no. It would be more civilized with a third party.

Leona looked as if a centipede had just crawled down her cleavage but being civilized she smiled a marblesmile. "Hello, Drake."

"You always did have guts," he said.

She held out her gloved hand. "It's quite a shock." She pulled off her gloves finger by finger. They were dark brown kid.

"You don't have to endure Banquo at the feast," he said. "I've already eaten and I'm just passing through."

"Is that supposed to be funny?" she asked and then she said she really did think he owed her an explanation. She sat and crossed one leg over the other.

"*Nil nisi divinum stabile est,*" he said. "I like to chase my tail." Leona's legs had kept their shape, he saw.

"Would you like a drink?" Manby asked and she said not unless he had some hemlock handy.

"Have a Scotch, Leona," said Drake.

She looked away from him to the wall and then she waded through the moss-green carpet to straighten a picture. It was a Ben Turner with yellow aspens and green pines. "It's wrong," she said, and Manby asked didn't she like it.

"Oh, the picture?" she said. "I was looking at the angle. Meanwhile," she said to Drake, "would it be asking too much for you to keep a low profile? Until after the election at least?"

"Fear not, lady M," he said, "your constituents won't see Banquo."

"I do wish you'd quit changing the subject." She looked at the wall again.

Drake agreed it was all very bad taste. "And you won't believe me," he said, "but I really am sorry. I'm a flaky bastard—always was."

"Not always," she said.

"No," he said. "There was something good between us back in the beginning. But somewhere we took a path to a swamp instead of a mountain."

She let a softness touch her face and he glimpsed a girl he'd once loved briefly before the path grew boggy. But then the softness was gone and the smile was just a stale leftover.

"Manby will tell you the story," he said, "if you're interested." He drained his glass and stood and said he was sorry for the whole rotten mess and that he really meant it.

"You're still impossible," she said, "but you've gotten nicer," and he said in his next life he'd grow a tail so he could wag it and meanwhile should he lick her hand and he grinned the grin that always infuriated her.

"You'll have to excuse me now," he said. "I've got to find a cab."

Manby offered to drop him at his motel but he said, "No, thanks anyway. I've got to sit up with a sick father."

Outside it was dark and the wind blew.

▲

Drake threw a leather portfolio on a chair. "They had you in intensive care, so I split." Father Andreas was harnessed to an I-V contraption and had the vulnerable look hospital gadgets give a man. He was in a double room but the other bed wasn't occupied. It was whiter than Manby's deep-piled office but no more sterile and it was honest sterility. He pulled up a straight-backed chair, turned its back to the bed, and straddled it.

A skinny nurse glided in on rubber soles and checked the I-V. She had frizzy hair and wore her smile like a badge. "How are we feeling?" She nodded to Drake the way Manby's silk secretary had done, with the mild suspicion of a well-mannered guardian dragon. She thrust the thermometer under the tongue, counted the pulse, wound the blood-pressure gadget around the arm. No blue stone or snake water cluttered her tool box.

"Vital signs good, Father." Her voice was like starched cotton. She marked her chart and squished out.

"I guess we've come back to the world," Drake said. "Both of us."

Andreas turned toward Drake. The eyes burned blue again and the gray look had gone. "You reported in?"

"I have returned from the dead, confirmed my identity, and reconfirmed my insanity. I dropped by last night but you were asleep."

"So now. . . ?"

"You can take off your hair shirt and I can nurse jet lag."

"What about your wife?"

"Not as bad as I expected. Leona's gone into politics and found herself a proper husband."

"Oh, may the Good Lord help us!"

"He feeds the roses while she's on crusade."

"But—that leaves you . . . ."

"Neatly sprung! Actually it simplifies things. A little red tape. . . ."

The beak-nosed face moved restlessly against the white pillow. "If it hadn't been for me . . . ."

"I'd have come back anyhow. Listen, Padre. Take off your goddamned guilt complex and listen. You only hurried up the process a little. The resting time was over: it was time to pick up my little bow and arrow and go on with the hunt."

"For what, Drake? What is it you're hunting?" The eyes burned into him and Andreas seemed feverish.

"This is exciting you too much."

"It only excites the nurse. *What is it you're hunting?*"

"I told you. Life. The Word. Listen, Padre. I didn't come back for you. You just lit the fuse, got my ass in gear. It was time—I knew it, only I didn't have the guts—I kept wanting to do something for Pepito—for my son, Father."

"Do you know that?"

Drake looked down at his hands that clutched the chair back. "No," he said, "I don't even know that." He didn't say anything for a long moment then finally lifted his head. "So. So this got me in action before I could think, maybe back out. Like diving into cold water suddenly. It's better that way. It was time to go on with the hunt."

"*For what?*"

Drake laughed. "That's what I found at Descanso: what the hunt was for." He leaned over the chair back and began to talk, slowly at first.

"I blathered a lot about civilization—remember? I yelled like an Irishman at a wake and chased its remains. So I took a pulse in Descanso and checked for vital signs—like your nurse—and charted my findings. And hunted for the magic ingredient.

"Well, I found it. You know, courage says it all. Without courage the rest doesn't mean anything. Anyhow—sometimes it happens that—a people of courage. . . ." He chose the words precisely and willed them to convey an importance. "Sometimes a people of courage find themselves in a place of spirit. Or spirits. Or maybe the courage calls the spirit out of the place, I don't know. But there it is and they aren't afraid to listen to it. And to stand up to the spirits. To say, 'I'm a Man, and the Holy Ghost is in me, too.'

"It's hubris to have dared be Man and invent civilization. Man did it. Not the beasts and not the gods. Man! But first we had to know the beasts and the gods. Because they have the otherness.

"Well, I've known the otherness and the oneness. I've felt the great mysterious life. And finding them I've found Man.

"I know now what Prometheus said when he was chained on the rock. 'Zeus, old padre,' he said, 'the sacred things are also of men, for whom the gods made the world.' And civilization is worth saving because a Beethoven can rise among the Sweeneys."

"Sweeney too is a man," said the priest softly.

"No he isn't. He won't dare to be. It was a man who heard the Word in the center and went beyond it and invented the wheel. And then put his shoulder to it because he had courage. And he invented the alphabet so he could do something with the word.

"Homer heard it by his wine-dark sea and wove it into poetry. And Pan piped—but it was Man who heard the pipes and said 'I can do better' and made a symphony! That's what the great high crests were all about—the Greeks and the Renaissance and the Elizabethans. And America—they dared 'in the course of human events' to be men. *Human* events. They heard the Word and rewrote it. They heard the song and improved it.

"And then the Sweeneys follow—and wallow—and we sink to mindless mud again. Every era has its nerds."

A cart with rattling dishes clattered down the hall and the smell of overdone food invaded.

"I went back to the medieval world in Descanso and beyond that I journeyed to the New Stone Age where lions still guard Shipapolima. I saw the marriage of the Indian way to that of the Spaniards when a blue sky-stone shot into a lake of the earth. I learned to listen to spirits in spirit places. I saw true faith for the first time. I saw what was good of medievalism still left."

He strode to the window, turned back to the man on the bed. "But I'm not a medieval man. I'm not man the receiver. I'm not a groveler to the god. I want to climb a mountain. I'm going to other mystic places on the earth and listen to these gods and breathe their courage if my lungs can take it. I'm going to the groves of Delphi. I'll hunt the spirits at Stonehenge and in the abbey at Glastonbury. I'm going to the heathered hills of Scotland and hear the voices of my own ancestors and find the memories of my own past lives.

"And maybe I'll add a small ripple in the lake with my own blue stone. I'll try. In these sacred places I'll look as straight as I can. I'll try to see the rough magic and transform it into lines on paper, because that's what being a man is all about.

"And I'll find my mate. She'll hear the same pipes playing the same song."

He turned again to the window and looked down on the swirls of dust that rode low on the gray wind. He turned back, walked to the foot of the bed, looked on the intent face with its listening eyes. "Father," he said slowly, "I left my son in Descanso. It was the hardest thing I've ever done."

The priest lifted his hand. "It was best," he said quietly and let it fall again.

"Yes. And Soledad. She made me well again. I'd have stayed with her. Claimed Pepito if she'd let me. She knew better."

"Tell me—I don't know about such things—did you beget him in love?"

Drake pulled a cigarette from his pocket then thought he probably shouldn't smoke it here and broke it in two. "Love? Define it. It was—instinctual, like a child at the breast. A need to survive. But there's got to be more. A—a sacramental quality. An outward and visible sign of an inward and—intellectual communion. Which couldn't be."

His voice broke. He knelt by the bed, his head against it. "Still," he said, "it engendered life. Forgive me, Father, for I have sinned." He stood again and limped to the window. "But I don't regret that life. I love that small life. That's why I gave it back to him.

"So I've come back. And—coming—I've found some pulse still beats. Some vital signs. Do you know what I did this morning before I came here? I went to a bookstore. People still read books and not all of them were trash. And

I did something else. I bought a ticket. Baryshnikov is coming. That is, I tried to buy a ticket—they were all sold out." He laughed. "People want to see him, for whatever reason. And one or two in that audience will understand and some fire from Olympos will pass to them.

"And I'll find my mountain, and its own blue stone, and I'll picnic on the trail."

The mobile mouth smiled faintly. "Not rush to the top?"

"It's enough to know something's up there. The answer. The otherness. Because it isn't the answer we seek. It's the question. The right mountain. The trail up. The Navajos call it Beauty Way. 'In beauty I walk,' they chant and at the end, 'In beauty it is finished.'

"It wasn't a lion I sought when I went poling off from the world nine years ago. And if I'd killed her, I'd have killed the dream. I'd have caught the 'winged joy' and destroyed it. And myself."

Father Andreas stared at the crucifix on the wall. When he spoke his voice was sad but it wasn't strained any longer. "'In the Beginning was the Word,'" he intoned, "'and the Word was of God. . . .'"

Drake, staring through the window, didn't turn. "But Man transformed it into language."

"You admit the Word was of God," said the priest. "You've found some sort of faith, however strange."

"No, but I know it exists."

"And I, who've prayed for it so long—Drake, when we were flying—was it yesterday?—I thought I was dying. And I was afraid. I was afraid of death."

"I doubt if you're the first."

"I tried to make an act of contrition but my faith was weak."

Drake turned from the window. "Have you ever tried to make friends with a cat?" His smile carved one side of his face. "You try to coax it and it just sits and mocks you and twitches its tail. But when you ignore it you find it rubbing against your ankles. You have to let it come to you."

"And recognize it when it comes."

"In any form. Tiger-striped or tabby. Or tawny-eyed, living in a cave."

"You asked me once what I was running from," said the priest. "It made me angry because I was running. I guess we both know why."

"Go and run no more."

"We can't, can we? Run from our sins?"

"Why should we want to? Why fight them? Because sin couldn't exist, Father, if there was no God to sin against. And if there's no sin there's no virtue either. And if there's no choice to make, there's no soul—nor any need of one. That's why the nihilists are so dreary."

"You do acknowledge a God?"

"I think there's something out there. So there's also sin. Don't knock it. So you got scared and ran. But it was only a lion on the ledge. So your faith was weak. Is that so awful? I think the sin of knowing is a ton more deadly than not knowing. I guess even your leader had doubts sometimes. Without doubt you wouldn't need faith, would you? The mystery encompasses the doubt. Otherwise it would just be science."

"So we both went to Descanso. If we didn't dream it. You were chasing a God you weren't too sure of catching and I chased a lion ditto. I guess they were the same."

"My lamb and your lion?"

"And you wore a hair shirt. I preferred a mail of irony. But I've heard the pipes and so have you if you'd listen. You believe in your Father, Father, believe also in you. In Man."

"Do you?"

"The ones who count."

"They all count."

"Okay. But take off your hair shirt and let the sweet mountain air come in. And the song with it."

"The *alabado*?" An edge of mockery honed the thin voice.

"It's there too."

The priest didn't reply. His eyes were closed. Then he spoke softly. "Descanso seems unreal from here."

"Yes. Did it happen? Was it all a dream, Padre?" He felt the fetishes in his pocket. They were smooth and solid.

"And you'll keep on hunting?"

"And learning. Perfecting my own small craft, to carry my own small ember from the fire."

"What will you do when the money runs out?"

"Go to work, I suppose."

"Practice law again?"

Drake grinned. "No. Tend an orchard maybe. Maybe they'd let me water the tree at Glastonbury. Or maybe I'll draw caricatures of tourists at Covent Garden for half a pound. Then someday I'll come back to my own country. That's where Pan waits, I think, for the noise to pass by so he can pipe his song again, and he guards a small blue stone. In this vast unfinished Southwest along the Beauty Way.

"But first I've got to earn it. We all do."

The frizzy-haired nurse came in like the tide. I-V, temp, pulse, charts. "The blood pressure's up a weensie," she chided.

"We were climbing a mountain," said Father Andreas.

"Chasing mountain lions," said Drake. "Increases the heartbeat."

The dragon's eye grew frosty. "The Father needs to rest." The white uniform glided out.

"Okay." Drake gestured to the portfolio. "My drawings. Thought they might amuse you."

"What will you do with them?"

"They're yours. When Descanso's gone—the Descanso we knew—they'll remind you how it was. It's worth the preserving."

"I may die."

"Yes," said Drake. "Or you may not. There's always a catch."

"If I should—just out of curiosity—would you pray for me?"

"Probably not. Hell, Padre, you wouldn't be comfortable unless you served your full discipline in Purgatory. That's another fascinating topic we can discuss. Anyway, I'll be around a while. Legalities, you know. My purgatory."

"And then?"

"Then I'll be off to find my own blue stone. And if I should miss you—well—see you at the top of the mountain!"

Outside the gray wind blew the first flakes of winter against his face and Drake felt the loneliness and the freedom. He breathed the cold, he deep-filled his lungs with the smell of *mañana* and it was good.

Somewhere beyond the wind a mountain loomed, cross-gashed, Pan-haunted, lake-wombed, and the living Mother breathed inside and waited and smiled a womansmile and listened for the Word.

Glossary of Spanish Terms

abuelo, -a a grandfather, grandmother. Also bogeyman
acabo anyhow
acequia irrigation ditch
acequia madre the mother ditch, from which the smaller ones branch
aguardiente whiskey
agüelos, los the grandfathers; the bogeyman
alabado hymn of praise
álamo cottonwood tree
amador lover, sweetheart
amigo, amiguito friend
arbol, arbolito tree, little tree
arroyo a watercourse, usually dry in New Mexico
Ave María llena de gracia Hail Mary full of grace

baile a dance
barbasco an evergreen bush
bizcochito sugar cookie
bobo fool
borracho drunk
broma a bad joke
bruja witch
bueno, -a good
buenos días good morning
bulto carved statue of a saint
buñuelo a fritter

cabrito kid goat

cabrón billy goat; cuckold

Calvario a high place near a morada representing the hill of Calvary

calzones trousers

campana bell

camposanto cemetery

cantina bar, tavern, saloon

capitán captain

carreta de la Muerte cart of death, wherein a carved skeleton carrying a bow and arrow is seated, to be pulled in the Good Friday procession by the Penitent Brothers

carita a term of endearment

casa house

casa grande large or great house

cerdo cerdoso hairy pig

cerveza beer

chamizo a plant whose yellow flowers are often used in making dyes

chango clown

chilorio a midnight chile feast served at a velorio

chinches bedbugs

ciénega meadow

cienegoso muddy

¿Cómo no? Isn't that so?

compañero companion

copita a drink

cuarto de adorno a parlor or best room

curandera a folk-medicine healer

dime show me

Dios God

empanaditas fried fruit pies

En el nombre del Padre, del Hijo, y el Espiritu Santo in the name of the Father, the Son, and the Holy Ghost

¡Eschucha! Listen!

estufa stove

farolitos candles placed in paper sacks, lit along a path on Christmas Eve to light the way for the Christ child; often called luminarias

Floresta, La The Forest Service

fogón fireplace

frijoles pinto beans

fuego fire

¡Fuera! Go away! Scat!

gallo a strutting cock

gato,-a, gatito,-a cat, kitten

gavilán sparrow hawk; a term of opprobium

genízaro an Indian captive rescued from Apache, Comanche, Ute, or Navajo marauders by Spanish settlers, with whom he subsequently lived, and usually intermarried, or a descendant, usually of mixed blood

gordo, gordito a fat one; little fat man

gozo, gozoso joy, joyful

gracias a Dios thanks to God

gringo term Mexican soldiers applied to American troops during the Mexican War, now applied (often in an uncomplimentary context) to all Anglo Americans

guitarrista guitarist

hermandad brotherhood

Hermanos Penitentes Penitent Brothers, comprising the Brothers of Light and the Brothers of Blood; see separate entry following this glossary

hidalgo nobleman; highborn gentleman

hijo son

¡Hijo! Damn!

hombre man

horno outdoor beehive-shaped ovens widely used by Hispanics and Pueblo Indians in the Southwest

jacal small hut, or shed of mud-chinked poles

kiva sacred chamber in the pueblos

koshare clown in Keres pueblos

ladrón thief, best thief, or leader of thieves

león lion

Los Pastores *The Shepherds*, a Christmas play performed in New Mexico villages, wherein the shepherds travel to Bethlehem with gifts for the Christ child

Llorona, La ghost of a crying woman seeking something, often one whose children have died at birth; a ghost seeking atonement; subject of many folk tales, with many variations

¡Madre de Dios! Mother of God!

¡Mal ajo! Confound it!

mal ojo evil eye

mañana tomorrow

masa finely ground cornmeal used in tortillas

matraca rattle used by Penitent Brothers in ceremonies

mayordomo a foreman; the ditch boss, who oversees irrigation, and hence highly respected in the small communities of dry New Mexico

médica a general folk healer, herbalist, and midwife

milagro miracle

¡Mira! Look!

¡Mis Crismes! Merry Christmas!

morada chapel and meeting house for the Penitent Brothers

mortaja shroud, grave clothes

mujer woman

muy very

nicho a niche, or recess in a wall, in which statues of saints are placed

nieto, -a grandson, granddaughter

niño, -a little boy or girl

¿No es verdad? Isn't that so?

No comprendo inglés I don't understand English

nombre name

novio fiancé

¡Ójala! a common exclamation meaning I wish! or God grant!

olla a clay pot

Oremos Let us pray; Christmas candies given to children; the children who go door-to-door asking for Christmas treats and threatening to smash windows and doors if refused—a Christmas "trick-or-treat" custom

oshá wild celery, the root of which is believed to protect against snakes

otro que tal another such

padre father; priest

pájaro, pajarito little bird

panocha a sweet mixture of sprouted grains, which traditionally the women carry to the morada to sustain the fasting Penitent Brothers during their Holy Week Vigil

panzón fat-bellied man

partera midwife

pendejos fools

picarillo rascal

pito shrill flutelike instrument used in Penitent services

placita plaza of a small village

poco tiempo pretty soon; later; in a little while

policía police

político politician

¿por qué no? why not?

portal porch, entry way, or portico

potrero large fingers of lava projecting onto lower land and creating enormous abysses between projections. These huge tongues and the gorges between spread along the Río Grande and taper into the valley. Cliffs rise from 1,000 to 2,500 feet. Cf. Charles F. Lummis, *The Land of Poco Tiempo* (New York: Charles Scribner's Sons, 1913).

prado meadow

presa conduit, dam

primo, -a cousin

¡Pues! Well! Well then!

puta prostitute

¿Quién es? Who is it?

¿Quién sabe? Who knows?

¿Qué es eso? What is it?

¡Qué importa! Who cares? Big deal!

quelites wild greens
¡Qué milagroso! What a miracle! How marvelous!
¿Qué pasa? What's going on? What's happening?
querida term of endearment
¿Qué tal? How goes it?

ranchero rancher
ranchito small ranch
rebozo dark shawl worn by women, especially older ones, draped over the head
    and partially muffling the face
reredos altar screen
retablo painting of a saint, on a wooden board
rezador Penitent prayer leader
rico rich man
rincón cove, or corner
río river
rito small river, creek

sacristán sexton
sala hall or large room
santo saint, or statue of saint
santero wood carver who makes *santos*
Santo Niño the Christ child
simpático, -a pleasant, attractive; sympathetic
simplón, -a simpleton
sinvergüenzo rogue
sobrino, -a nephew, niece
soldado soldier
sombra ghost, shadow, shade
soquete mud, plaster
'sta bueno it is good

tápalo shawl
tío, tía uncle, aunt
toloache Jimson weed, used when boiled as a hallucinogen
tonto silly one, fool

traguillo small drink of liquor
trastero wooden cupboard
turista tourist
¡Uta! Damn!

¡Válgame! Help me! Give me strength!
vamonos let's go
¡Vamos! Go on! Go away!
vaquero cowboy
vaya go; leave
velorio wake, vigil
viejo, -a old man, old woman
viga roof beam
vino wine

yerbas herbs; medicinal plants
yeso gypsum

¡Zape! Scat! Get away!
zopo stupid
zorra strumpet

Los Hermanos Penitentes
The Penitent Brothers

The Penitent Brotherhood, or Penitentes, is a Roman Catholic lay society found in Hispanic villages throughout northern New Mexico and in southern Colorado. Its practices, brought from Spain by the conquistadors, were formalized soon after the reconquest of de Vargas in 1692. Throughout the eighteenth and nineteenth centuries the order grew in necessity and importance as the Franciscan friars, too few from the beginning, were largely recalled after the Crown withdrew its support.

In the absence of priests, and fifteen hundred miles from the Bishopric of Durango, the *Hermanos Penitentes* grew increasingly influential, especially in the more isolated rural communities, and were largely responsible for keeping alive the Roman Catholic faith in New Mexico and ensuring the very survival of their small communities. After Mexican independence in 1821, most of the few remaining priests were driven out, and the *Hermandad* tightened its organization and drew into close secrecy.

Ceremonial rites included flagellation, cross-bearing, and a symbolic Good Friday crucifixion, practices which, as communication increased during the nineteenth century, the church fathers condemned. When the *Hermandad* refused to abandon these practices, the order was outlawed. Even this failed to eradicate the Brotherhood or its customs, and in 1947 Archbishop Edwin V. Byrne officially reinstated the order, extending welcome to all chapters who agreed to moderate their practices.

To what extent the more isolated *moradas* have complied is known only to those within. It has been more or less left to individual priests to deal with the matter as each believes best in his community—a situation reflected in this story by the disparate viewpoints of Padre Lorenzo and Father Andreas.

The low windowless structures that dot the hills of northern New Mexico are *moradas*, each marked by a large wooden cross that towers above. These are generally closed to all but members, for herein are held their meetings and ceremonies.

Although conducted routinely for such events as wakes, funerals, burials, and other observances, the rites center around the Passion of Christ. The Lenten season is observed with fasting, prayer, flagellation, and the singing of *alabados*, beginning with the ceremony of the Last Supper and climaxing on Good Friday with a symbolic reenactment of the Crucifixion.

To be chosen the *Cristo* is the highest honor. Following a service in the *morada*, during which the chosen brother is condemned to death, he drags a heavy wooden cross to a nearby hill designated the *Calvario*, accompanied by penitents in white cotton trousers and black hoods, barefoot on the rocky, cactus-bristled ground, who flagellate their own bare backs with yucca whips. Traditionally the *Cristo* is lashed to his cross, where he remains until he faints, after which he is taken down and cared for until he regains consciousness.

Should he die (which rarely happens) he is buried with highest honor. His family is said to learn of his death when they find his empty shoes on their doorstep the next morning.

The high point in the drama follows with the *Tieneblas*. The altar candles are extinguished one by one as the *rezador* reads Psalms, until the *morada* is in complete darkness, whereupon wild shrieking, whirring of *matracas*, wailing of *pitos*, rattling of chains, and thunder of drums and sticks erupt to signify the earth's convulsions on Christ's death. Prayer and cacophony alternate until, one by one, the candles are relit.

The brotherhood still wraps itself in secrecy, even more intensely in recent times as a result of Anglo Protestant curiosity and written sensationalism, which intrudes on—and often mocks—the serious religiosity of their services. Although the rites of the *Penitentes* and often considered bizarre by outsiders, the character of Hispanic life in New Mexico has been deeply incised by the dedicated faith of the *Hermanos Penitentes*.